YBP 1|2021 27-

D0848317

Lineberger Memorial Library
LTSS, Lenoir-Rhyne University
4201 North Main Street
Columbia, SC 29203

LOEB CLASSICAL LIBRARY

FOUNDED BY JAMES LOEB 1911

EDITED BY
JEFFREY HENDERSON

PETRONIUS

SENECA

LCL 15

PETRONIUS

SATYRICON

SENECA

APOCOLOCYNTOSIS

EDITED AND TRANSLATED BY
GARETH SCHMELING

HARVARD UNIVERSITY PRESS
CAMBRIDGE, MASSACHUSETTS
LONDON, ENGLAND
2020

Copyright © 2020 by the President and Fellows
of Harvard College
All rights reserved

First published 2020

LOEB CLASSICAL LIBRARY® is a registered trademark
of the President and Fellows of Harvard College

Library of Congress Control Number 2020935306
CIP data available from the Library of Congress

ISBN 978-0-674-99737-0

Composed in ZephGreek and ZephText by
Technologies 'N Typography, Merrimac, Massachusetts.
Printed on acid-free paper and bound by
Maple Press, York, Pennsylvania

CONTENTS

ACKNOWLEDGMENTS   vii

PETRONIUS

    INTRODUCTION   3

    GENERAL BIBLIOGRAPHY   51

    SATYRICON   68

SENECA

    INTRODUCTION   455

    GENERAL BIBLIOGRAPHY   471

    APOCOLOCYNTOSIS   476

APPENDIX: SEATING CHART   519

INDEXES

    OF CHARACTERS IN PETRONIUS   521

    OF OTHER NAMES IN PETRONIUS   527

ACKNOWLEDGMENTS

My interest in preparing an edition of the *Satyrica* (more commonly known as the *Satyricon*) has evolved over many years. It began as a joint project with J. P. Sullivan, but was voided by his untimely death. As I later prepared materials for my *Commentary on the Satyrica of Petronius* (OUP 2011), it became clear that I would have to establish a Latin text with apparatus and translation. Over time it became a useful tool and then the backbone of my *Commentary*. My first Latin text was the one Sullivan and I had prepared some years earlier; over time it was greatly modified, but I could no longer benefit from Sullivan's advice. Sullivan died in 1993 and thus could not appreciate Müller's radical changes from his 1983 Petronius text to those of his 1995 and 2003 editions.

Over the last many years I have been helped and guided by communications and discussions with various colleagues, who have taken the time to alert me to special items regarding Petronius and his *Satyrica*: J. N. Adams, John Bodel, Stephen Harrison, and Giulio Vannini. Aldo Setaioli was a valuable aid in dealing with the text of the *Apocolocyntosis*. Special thanks are given here to Leofranc Holford-Strevens, who tutored me in many areas of Latin and the ancient world. To those connected to the Loeb Classical Library (LCL) with whom I have cor-

ACKNOWLEDGMENTS

responded, I would like to thank Jeffrey Henderson, General Editor of the LCL; Richard Thomas, Executive Trustee of the LCL; and then in particular Michael B. Sullivan, Managing Editor of the LCL, whose vast learning in Latin and the classical world he was happy to share with me, and thus keep me on the straight and narrow. This volume is dedicated to Silvia Montiglio, wife, friend, scholar, and *sine qua non*.

PETRONIUS

SATYRICON

INTRODUCTION

AUTHOR AND DATE

Petronius and the *Satyrica* (also known as the *Satyricon liber*, hence the popular title *Satyricon*), author and work, are both surrounded by mysteries. Almost everything that we know about Petronius is found in Tacitus, *Annals* 16.17–19. By the force of his rhetoric he has made Petronius memorable, appealing, eccentric (*Ann.* 16.18): *nam illi dies per somnum, nox officiis et oblectamentis vitae transigebatur; utque alios industria, ita hunc ignavia ad famam protulerat* . . . ("he spent his days sleeping and his nights working and enjoying himself. Diligence is the usual basis of success, but with him it was idleness . . ."), but he writes not one word about the *Satyrica* or something similar, though he makes the effort to include 104 words (*Ann.* 16.19) about Petronius' suicide, forced on him by Nero in AD 66: *neque tamen praeceps vitam expulit, sed incisas venas, ut libitum, obligatas aperire rursum et alloqui amicos, non per seria aut quibus gloriam constantiae peteret* . . . *ut quamquam coacta mors fortuitae similis esset* ("Not that he was hasty in taking leave of his life. On the contrary he opened his veins and then, as the fancy took him, he bound them up or reopened them, and all the while talked with friends, but not on serious topics

3

or something calculated to win admiration for his courage
. . . so that his death, though forced on him, should appear
natural"). Much of our understanding of Petronius the
person rests on Tacitus' depiction of his character and
suicide, one of the most famous in history owing to the
power of Tacitus' rhetoric, whose mastery of which we
must always treat with caution, lest we take all that he says
for fact and nothing for fiction. He notes that in Nero's
court Petronius held some sort of nonofficial post of *ele-
gantiae arbiter*, and this title *Arbiter* sticks to Petronius as
if it were a cognomen, whereas it is surely a sobriquet.

The *tria nomina* of Petronius are in doubt: Tacitus refers to him as Gaius Petronius, Pliny the Elder (*NH* 37.20)
and Plutarch (*Quomodo adulator, Mor.* 60e) as Titus. If we
grant that the Petronius of Tacitus wrote, but did not nec-
essarily finish, the *Satyrica* by 66, and that he was proconsul in Bithynia (*Ann.* 16.18) in 60–61 (or 61–62) and then
consul suffectus in Rome in 62 (*mox consul*), scholars have
found a likely candidate in Titus Petronius Niger: so Sullivan[1] (32), Walsh[1] (244), Bodel[1], Rose[5] (47–55), the last
of whom also notes that a Publius Petronius listed in the
Fasti Consulares was condemned under Nero. Recent
evidence from Ephesus (Eck, 227) dating to July 62 spells
out a name in Greek, Publius Petronius Niger; for an agnostic view of the praenomen and the date of the *Satyrica*,
see Völker–Rohmann. Both Pliny the Elder and Plutarch
comment on the strained relationship between Nero and
his *Arbiter*.

The dating of Titus Petronius Niger to *consul suffectus*
in 62 and of his suicide about 66 is almost universally accepted. What is not so readily accepted and cannot be
proved beyond a shadow of doubt is that this Neronian

Petronius can be identified as the author of the *Satyrica*. Back in 1856 Beck[1] had argued for an Augustan date for the *Satyrica*; in his earlier days Marmorale[1] held the traditional view, but then Marmorale[2] posited a date of composition in the late second century; Smith believed that the *Satyrica* belonged to the principate of Tiberius or Caligula; Martin held to a date in the Flavian period; Roth has now argued strongly for a date of 115, in the reign of Trajan.

Among the remaining ancient testimonia regarding Petronius, Marius Mercator, who died after 431 (*Liber subnotationum in verba Juliani* 4.1 [Migne 48, p. 126], and 5.1 [p. 133]) links Petronius to Martial in the use of obscene language. The sixth-century Byzantine writer Johannes Lydus (*de Magistratibus* 1.41) links Petronius to Juvenal and accuses both of lowering the standards of satire. But it is with Macrobius (Macrobius Ambrosius Theodosius), writing after 431, that we obtain our first connection of the name Petronius (Arbiter, actually) to a work of fiction (*In Somn.* 1.2.8): *argumenta fictis casibus amatorum referta, quibus vel multum se Arbiter exercuit vel Apuleium nonnumquam lusisse miramur* ("plots packed with the fictitious adventures of people in love, a genre to which the Arbiter applied himself a good deal and with which to our surprise Apuleius sometimes trifled"). Of Macrobius' precise knowledge of the contents of these *argumenta* we can be fairly certain, because he groups Petronius with Apuleius, the same comparison we make today. We assume that Macrobius is referring to the *Satyrica* and to the *Metamorphoses*, and that only by knowing Tacitus' description of Petronius as *arbiter* and having read his fiction could he make these observations.

5

A WORK OF FICTION

The Latin *Satyrica* is often referred to as a satire of early imperial manners, especially of freedmen, slaves, and marginal characters from the Greek-speaking Near East. Most of the names of the characters are Greek, and the action of the extant *Satyrica* takes place in predominantly Greek southern Italy, first in the area around the Bay of Naples and later in Croton. If the *Satyrica* is satire, it is of a most gentle and general kind. The characters created by Petronius are both ill-mannered and sympathetic, and they are creations in fiction: the central actor in the *Cena Trimalchionis* (26.7–78, a section that comprises one-third of the work) is not a parody of Nero, but a humorous portrayal of a wealthy freedman. Like Eumolpus, poet, scoundrel, marvelous storyteller, and chief actor of the last third of the *Satyrica* (83–141), Trimalchio is one of the most memorable characters in Latin literature. The first-person narrator of the *Satyrica* is Encolpius, and everything that readers learn about the characters and actions in the *Satyrica*, they learn from Encolpius. The narrator is an older Encolpius looking back at episodes in his earlier life, and in that sense the *Satyrica* can be read as the confessions of a very literate narrator who describes himself almost without exception as a failure, but in settings that regularly characterize him as a bad example of a mythical hero (Schmeling[6]). The main characters of the outer structure of the story appear in triads, first Encolpius–Ascyltos–Giton, then Encolpius–Eumolpus–Giton, all of whom live on the margins of society, stealing what they need and engineering elaborate hoaxes to get more than they need:

the glue that holds the triad together is sex, and this triadic structure also gives the story its inherent instability of rivalry.

The reader of the *Satyrica* recognizes from the first words that the work is extant only in fragments, and that much that had been narrated by Encolpius has been lost. In addition, attached to the Latin text of the *Satyrica* is a collection of fifty-one fragments from disparate sources, which with varying degrees of certitude have been attributed to the Arbiter, Petronius, or the *Satyrica* (but no one knows where, or even if, these fragments actually belong in the work). From meager medieval evidence (Schmeling[4], xxii), the extant *Satyrica* can be said to come from Books 14, 15, 16, and since the work has numerous affinities to the *Odyssey* in twenty-four books, scholars have suggested that the complete *Satyrica* must also have consisted of twenty-four books. If that is so, then we possess little of the original work. Even though the *Satyrica* apparently was a long narrative work, the extant text (except for the *Cena*) is not at all a narrative but rather a collection of disjointed pieces and mutilated excerpts, totaling about 35,000 words.

The reader of the *Satyrica* also notices from almost the beginning that the work is a mixture of prose and poetry. Many of the characters in the *Satyrica* are poets, and thus the reader should not be surprised that the work contains so much poetry: not only thirty poems (not counting the *Fragmenta*), ranging from 2 verses to 295, but in nine different meters; see Ernout (211–13) for a list. This mixture is often described as a *prosimetrum*. The mixed form has led some critics such as Northrop Frye to see a specific genre behind it and to categorize this novel as Menippean Satire, with Varro's *Saturae Menippeae* as the reference point. The moralizing of Menippean Satire, once found in so many places in the *Satyrica*, turns out on closer inspection not to be there: see Schmeling[2]. The most recent Teubner editor of Varro's *Saturae Menippeae*, Raymond Astbury, finds no connections between that work and the *Satyrica*, save the use of *prosimetrum*. A search for satire in Petronius should probably be replaced by a search for parody of contemporary writers such as Seneca and Lucan. The present editor would set aside any label of satire and read the work as a resourceful clash of understanding and misunderstanding reality.

GENRE: NOVELS ROMAN AND GREEK

Because the *Satyrica* owes so much to the *Odyssey* (see list in Schmeling[4], 639), it had once been classified as a *Reiseroman* (Travel Novel), Homer being credited as the inventor of the form. But that designation was not long-lived. For some time now the genre-term novel has been applied to the *Satyrica*, as it is to the other two extant Latin novels and the five Greek. Though the *Satyrica* can be easily included under Henry James' definition of novels as "large, loose, baggy monsters," it is the definition of the novel by E. M. Forster in *Aspects of the Novel* (p. 2) that seems best to resonate with the *Satyrica*: "The novel is a formidable mass, and it is so amorphous—no mountain to climb . . . It is most distinctly one of the moister areas of literature—irrigated by a hundred rills and occasionally degenerating into a swamp . . . Perhaps we ought to define what a novel is . . . This will not take a second . . . [it is]

8

a fiction in prose of a certain extent." This definition is oversimplified so as to set aside difficulties.

Attaching the name of a specific genre to the *Satyrica* is in fact an interpretation of it, and in today's academic climate interpretation is a bad word. Petronius has been described as writing an original work, but with the discovery of the *Iolaus* novel, Peter Parsons claimed that "Natural reason long ago revealed that Petronius had a Greek model"—never mind that *Iolaus* dated to the second century. As long ago as 1899, Heinze had reasoned that the *Satyrica* was a parody of the Greek novels, but most Greek novels we now know were written after the *Satyrica*. And in 2004 Jensson concluded that the whole "*Satyrica* is a Roman remake of a lost Greek text of the same title and belongs . . . to the oldest type of Greco-Roman novel, known in antiquity as Milesian fiction" (329). Most scholars agree that there are at least two short Milesian Tales inserted into the extant *Satyrica*, both narrated by the poet Eumolpus, who is a better storyteller than he is a poet: "The Pergamene Boy" (*Sat.* 85–87) and the famous "Widow of Ephesus" (*Sat.* 111–12). Harrison[1] comments on the nature of Milesian Tales and how these short episodes fit into the structure of the novels of both Apuleius and Petronius; such inserted episodes are not biographical in the Roman novels but are in the Greek. And this difference separates Milesian Tales from the *Satyrica*; there is perhaps a connection with Apuleius, who in his *Metamorphoses* mentions Milesian Tales several times. It is just possible, however, that Petronius wrote an original work in Latin, is owed much credit for both form and content of the emerging ancient novel, and is the writer being copied, not the writer copying. Here I will proceed on the

9

assumption that Petronius wrote an original Latin novel, and borrowed much from earlier canonical Greek sources, as we would expect from an educated Roman writer.

In the classical scheme of ancient novels, there are five extant Greek (by Chariton, Xenophon of Ephesus, Achilles Tatius, Longus, and Heliodorus) plus numerous fringe novels and fragments (see Stephens—Winkler on the Greek fragments), and three Latin (by Petronius, Apuleius, and the anonymous *History of Apollonius King of Tyre*). What these eight works have in common is their genre: we now refer to all of them as novels. Scholars in the nineteenth century and most of the twentieth denounced the Greco-Roman novel as fit only for the poor in spirit, and at best called them romances. But in the literary post-modern climate, the ancient novels have been re-examined and found worthy of academic attention.

The rise in importance of the ancient novel in university curricula has not escaped the notice of the scholars in English and French literature, who had always considered the birth and rise of the novel to fall into the confines of their departments (for a discussion see Hawthorne, 16–52) and defined the novel so that it excluded the ancient ones. These scholars of insular approaches have been countered by Margaret Doody so successfully that while they still hold to their opinions, they are reticent to speak too loudly.

The five extant Greek novels share the same generic designation as the *Satyrica*. But the novel spectrum is very broad, and the ideal Greek novels with their pair of heterosexual protagonists falling in love, being separated, and then seeking legitimate marriage, are far away in sentiment from the *Satyrica*, with its triad of homosexual protagonists, wealthy freedmen, unsuccessful poets, and a narrator who relates in detail the specifics of his impotence. If the Petronius of Tacitus is the author of the *Satyrica*, then the extant Greek novels appear after his death in 66. It is just possible that Chariton is a contemporary of this Petronius, but the former writing in Aphrodiasias in Asia Minor was almost certainly unknown to the latter in Rome. It is possible that there were early works similar to the *Iolaus* and its low-life characters, and that Petronius knew of them. The actors in the Quartilla episode (*Sat.* 16–26) clearly fit the definition of low- or lower-life characters. Henderson would like to see Petronian scholars step back from assumptions about dating and genre and consider the literary history with a focus on all imperial novels, Latin and Greek.

Petronius looks back to the great Greek historians, tragedians, and philosophers, and to the Roman poets Virgil and Horace (and he clearly knows Ovid and uses him), and the overall structure of the novel finds a kind of pattern in Homer's *Odyssey*. The *Cena Trimalchionis*, which constitutes one-third of the *Satyrica*, looks back to the *Symposium* of Plato and the *Cena Nasidieni* of Horace (*Sat.* 2.8). The homosexual affairs of Encolpius call to mind close parallels in the *Phaedrus* and the *Symposiuim*; Encolpius invokes in his poetry the memory and words of Dido and Aeneas. Panayotakis[2] notes that Petronius borrows from, alludes to, and uses the most famous writers of the classical world, established names from the canon. The great epics, tragedies, histories, myths, and poems of the past are the grist for Petronius' mill. The five extant Greek novels are full of adventure and great fun, but except in episodes like that of Quartilla (16–26) Petronius wants to walk in the garden with Virgil and Horace and bring back the best the Greeks and Romans had written. The structure of his plot, the various registers of his Latin, the cadences of his sentences, all speak of an educated establishment writer. For discussions of genre as it relates to the *Satyrica*, see Schmeling[1], Christensen–Torlone, Jensson, Vannini[1] (70–72, 192–215), and Schmeling[4] (xxv–xlviii).

SHORT OVERVIEW

The extant novel begins well past the middle of the plot, and the narrator of everything is Encolpius, one of the triad of main characters, along with Ascyltos and Giton. The situation of the *Satyrica*, except for the central part occupied by the *Cena Trimalchionis*, is unstable and for the most part overly emotional, owing in great part to the basic instability of the triadic structure of main characters. The homosexual relationship among the three is marked by jealousy and physical violence. When Ascyltos leaves the narrative, he is immediately replaced by Eumolpus, and a new but continuing unstable triad is formed.

The nature of the plot of the *Satyrica* is episodic, and because the extant work is constructed of fragments of various lengths, the episodes are not always organically connected. The prose is punctuated by many short poems, and by longer ones after Eumolpus enters the story. The novel seems to divide itself into seven episodes; the episode called the Banquet of Trimalchio is by far the longest. The first episode (chs. 1–11) has many gaps, but we do learn immediately that the relationship among the three central figures is so toxic that Ascyltos agrees to leave the group and strike out on his own, after they have partaken of a free meal promised to them. Encolpius discusses the sad state of education and the arts with the rhetorician Agamemnon, who invites the triad to the Banquet of Trimalchio. It is clear that the triad has no steady source of income and that they live on the margin of society, cadging free meals, stealing, and robbing. All the action seems to take place in the Naples area, probably around Puteoli. The first episode ends with a gap in the text and has no real connection to the second.

The second episode (chs. 12–15) is a brief narrative about an evening in the forum in which the triad recovers some gold coins that they had stolen and then lost. The position of the second episode also has no connection with the third, and is thus isolated. But internal references to the gold coins make it clear that several or many scenes, which would explain how the gold coins were stolen and then lost, are no longer extant.

The third episode (chs. 16–26.5) is devoted to the visit of Quartilla, a priestess of the somewhat comic deity Priapus, her maids, and various *cinaedi* ("catamites") to the lodgings of our triad. Quartilla accuses the triad of having interrupted and observed the secret rites performed in a ceremony dedicated to Priapus: all rites and religious rituals performed in the name of Priapus involve various forms of sex, both hetero- and homosexual. Quartilla stage-manages the whole episode, which ends with her seven-year-old attendant being deflowered by Giton, as Quartilla watches everything through a slit she has made in the door. The reputation for obscenity that always hangs over the *Satyrica* surely arises from the details of this section. The third episode ends with a gap, and does not lead to the next episode.

The fourth episode (chs. 26.7–78) is the most famous part of the *Satyrica* and is called the *Cena Trimalchionis*, or Banquet of Trimalchio, and constitutes one-third of the extant novel. The *Cena* is dominated by Trimalchio, a wealthy freedman (ex-slave) from Asia who holds nightly feasts for guests, some of whom he knows and others he does not. His Latin is low-grade, his dress is in bad taste, his conversations are all about himself, the various courses of his dinner are presented with much fanfare but (though plentiful) are made up of common foods, the serving dishes all bear his name and their weight in silver. But in the final result Petronius makes a sympathetic and warm human being out of Trimalchio, who offers not so much a dinner as a dinner theater. The freedmen sitting at his table have riveting stories to tell about how they became wealthy, and they do so in levels of Latin that give scholars a great mine of nonliterary or substandard Latin (*sermo plebeius*) to go with the great number of graffiti surviving from the walls of Pompeii. Trimalchio is extremely superstitious about names of people, cocks crowing, and astrological signs, and is obsessed with dying. His wife, Fortunata, manages his large household, but objects fiercely to his fondling little boys at the banquet in her presence. Trimalchio rehearses his life story, commissions a large and ornate funeral monument for himself, has his will read out loud to the assembled banquet guests, stretches out on his couch with all his funeral clothes about him, and instructs the guests to imagine that they have been invited to the commemoration of his death. The funeral trumpets are blown so loudly that the nearby fire brigade believes it is a fire alarm, breaks into the house, and brings the *Cena* to an end. The *Cena* is almost a self-contained unit, and there are many editions and translations of just this part of the *Satyrica*—also this section of the *Satyrica* contains no obscene or offensive actions or words, and so can be read in schools.

The fifth episode (chs. 79–90) begins with the triad escaping the labyrinth of Trimalchio's house, and the continuing sexual animosity between them. In a dramatic fight, Giton chooses Ascyltos for an older partner, and they run off. Encolpius is crushed, but somewhat heartened by meeting Eumolpus, an aging poet, who recites his verses everywhere, and replaces Ascyltos in the triad of lovers when Encolpius recovers Giton in chapter 91. In chapters 85 to 87 Eumolpus relates in prose the so-called "Pergamene Youth," one of the gems of Latin literature. Eumolpus might be the most interesting character drawn by Petronius, because he displays so many aspects of his personality, only a few of which are sexual.

The sixth episode (chs. 91–115) opens with Encolpius recovering Giton, and Eumolpus showing himself to be a lover of young boys but not as vicious a person as Ascyltos; though a poet, he can engage in bloody brawls with the best of them. Giton makes various attempts at suicide throughout the plot, none of which are serious, and generally involve razors meant for the stage. At 99.6, for no apparent reason, the new triad boards a ship, departs the Naples area, and heads south along the Italian coast. Unbeknownst to Encolpius and Giton, the owner and captain of the ship on which Eumolpus has booked passage is a man called Lichas, who has with him the beautiful Tryphaena. In one or more lost episodes, Encolpius and Giton had robbed and outraged the pair to the point that they want the young boys dead. Eumolpus, who came late into the plot, knows nothing of the bad blood among the people on the ship. The modern reader of ancient novels in-

15

volving those who sail on ships suspects that all will end in shipwreck. Having read the novels of Saint Paul, which seem to involve him in shipwrecks, no sane person would remain on a ship once the fiery-tongued rabble-rouser was spotted among the passengers. When told about the history of the affairs with Lichas, Eumolpus disguises Encolpius and Giton as runaway slaves, but their identity is discovered, and the two lads endure just a few of the forty lashes ordered for them, before the old love of Tryphaena for the boys is revived. To entertain the people on the ship and divert the anger over past deeds, Eumolpus tells the story of the "Widow of Ephesus," another of the most memorable pieces of Latin prose. The ship is becalmed just before it is hit by a terrible storm in which Lichas, the only casualty, drowns; Eumolpus survives, even as he writes out his poetry on parchment.

The seventh and final episode (chs. 116–141) takes place on the road to Croton and in the city of Croton in southern Italy. To while away the time during the long walk to Croton after the shipwreck, Eumolpus recites a 295-line poem on the civil war between Caesar and Pompey. Eumolpus then devises a scheme to defraud the legacy hunters, of which Croton has many: he pretends to be a very rich man who has been shipwrecked and is awaiting new ships that are bringing some of his money and slaves. In the meantime, he needs help and promises to include those who assist him in his will. He is given vast amounts of money, which he shares with Encolpius and Giton, who are acting as his slaves. Eumolpus deceives the legacy hunters of Croton until the very end of the extant novel. Much of the last episode is taken up with the erotic pursuits of Encolpius, who has found the beautiful Circe, but who is impotent just at those crucial times when he is about to have sex with her. While at two different times two priestesses of Priapus try with various incantations and aphrodisiacs to cure Encolpius, their failures are spectacular, and Encolpius blames his impotence on Priapus himself. The elderly Eumolpus succeeds in extracting money from the legacy hunters, and also succeeds in all of his sexual adventures. Encolpius finds beauty in several women in Croton: the fact that he cannot succeed sexually with any of them provides much humor for the reader and much humiliation for Encolpius.

SECONDARY LITERATURE: SCHOLARLY WORK

The wealth of secondary material on Petronius and his *Satyrica* is impressive, and even a cursory search will reward the researcher with vast riches. In this section I try to bring some structure to the secondary material in arranging it by subject matter that all Petronians use. All items listed here have discrete entries in the General Bibliography that follows this Introduction; unless otherwise stated, all items are arranged chronologically.

1. *Bibliographies*

Gaselee[1], from the earliest Latin editions in 1482 to 1909, plus secondary materials.

Schmeling–Stuckey, expansion of material in Gaselee[1], description of manuscripts, editions, translations, and scholarship published up to 1975.

Bowie–Harrison, listing of recent scholarship on all the ancient novels.

Holzberg[1], listing of materials on the *Satyrica* from 1965 to 1995.

Vannini[1], extensive, detailed, and indexed bibliography from 1975 to 2005.

Petronian Society Newsletter (*PSN*), vol. 1 (1970)–today. All issues can be accessed on the *Ancient Narrative* website, www.ancientnarrative.com, then to Archives.

2. *Studies on the Manuscripts*

Tornaesius (Jean de Tournes); Pithoeus (Pierre Pithou); Burman; Jacobs; Bücheler[1] (introduction); Beck[2]; Gaselee[2]; Sage; Ernout (introduction); Müller[1] (introduction); de la Mare; Richardson.

3. *Latin Editions*

There are several hundred printed editions beginning in 1482 (*med.*): see Schmeling–Stuckey (#1–197), Vannini[1] (#28–52); the first editor to show a complete extant *Satyrica* is Hadrianides in 1669. The early (before the discovery of the *Cena* manuscript, *H*) critical editions of Sambucus (*s*, 1565), de Tournes (*t*, 1575), Pierre Pithou (p^1, 1577; p^2, 1587), and the *editio princeps* by Frambotti of the *Cena* manuscript (*patav.*, 1664) all draw comments below in the section on The Text.

The modern Latin editions of quality that contain everything we have of the extant *Satyrica* begin, I would argue, with Burman[1–2] (1709, 1743), and then follow through Bücheler[1–6] (1862–1922) and Konrad Müller[1–6] (1961–2003). Though there are other usable editions, for example, Ernout and Giardina–Cuccioli Melloni, they are clearly ancillary to Burman, Bücheler, and Müller, whose grasp of the text's tradition and the quality of their readings set them apart.

The *Cena Trimalchionis* is often read as if it were a text just barely connected to the *Satyrica*. As a text it is short enough to be used in secondary schools, and unlike much of the rest of the *Satyrica*, need not be bowdlerized to meet with Judaeo-Christian sensitivities. Thus the *Cena* has taken on a life of its own and is available in Latin with explanatory remarks suited to young students. There are several good editions of the *Cena* (1905–1999) that deal with Petronian Latin and its relationship to the graffiti at Pompeii: Lowe, Friedländer[2], Maiuri, Marmorale[1], Sedgwick, Perrochat, Smith, Öberg.

4. *Translations*

For all translations of Latin from Bulgarian to Welsh, see Schmeling–Stuckey (198–742), Vannini[1] (53–107). Since this present edition addresses primarily an English-reading audience, I single out only recent and potentially useful translations with notes: Sullivan[2], Walsh[2], Branham–Kinney, Ruden, and Raphael.

5. *Commentaries and Major Works with Essays on the* Satyrica

Collignon, a large work in French showing from which writers Petronius borrows, and which ancient writers use him.

Sullivan[1], essays on dating, identification, reconstruction, genre, and reception.

Walsh[1], emphasis on historical material, and comparison with Apuleius' *Metamorphoses*.

Panayotakis[1], running commentary on the *Satyrica* as a parody of mime.

Harrison[2], long introductory essay with anthology of past articles on Roman novelists.

Hofmann, collection of essays on all Latin novels, Latin hagiography, and reception.

Courtney[3], companion on the whole of the *Satyrica*.

Rimell, essays on corporealities, eating substances and excreting them as literature.

Herman, wide-ranging and influential essays on Petroniana.

Jensson, discussion of large parts of the *Satyrica* in relation to Milesian Tales.

Habermehl, running commentary in German on chapters 79 to 110.

Vannini[2], running commentary in Italian with text on chapters 100 to 115.

Schmeling[4], running commentary in English on the whole of the *Satyrica*.

Prag–Repath, essays on the *Satyrica* only, ranging from Neronian culture to the reception of the *Satyrica* in literature, the performing arts, and film.

6. Works with a Specific Focus

Poetry in the *Satyrica*: Stubbe, Courtney[2], Connors.

Date of and identification of Petronius: Rose[5], Martin, D'Arms, Bodel[1], Henderson, Völker–Rohmann, Roth.

Examination of the position of freedmen in the *Satyrica*: D'Arms, Bodel[1].

Search for Petronius' personal voice in the narrative of
Encolpius: Conte.

Study of laughter in the *Satyrica*, one of the novel's dom-
inant emotions: Plaza.

Studies on the nature and levels of Latin in the *Satyrica*: Stefenelli, Petersmann, Boyce, Adams[2], Schmeling[4]
(xxv–xxx).

The place of the *Satyrica* among the ancient novels: Perry,
Hägg, Holzberg[2], Schmeling[3], Whitmarsh, Prag–Repath, Cueva–Byrne.

7. *Reception and Intertextuality*

Bibliographies: Schmeling–Stuckey (2045–2074), Vannini
(540–607, 1201–1331).

Reception of the *Satyrica* in the late nineteenth and early
twentieth centuries, especially T. S. Eliot: Schmeling–
Rebman.

Lists of modern novels that look back to Petronius: Gagliardi, Doody.

Self-referentiality and recycling: Rimell.

Essays on reception in literature: Panayotakis–Zimmerman–Keulen, Pinheiro–Harrison.

Essays on reception in the *Fellini-Satyricon* and English
novels: Prag–Repath.

8. *Works Dealing with the* Fragmenta, *the Fifty-
One Pieces Attached to Modern Latin Editions*

At the conclusion of the *Satyrica* proper in this Loeb edition, the reader will find all fifty-one *Fragmenta* in Latin
plus translation and notes. The best introduction to the

21

Fragmenta of the *Satyrica* is that by Courtney[2], who discusses many poems in the *Satyrica* proper and then goes on to review a number of poems in the *Fragmenta*. In addition to a section on the manuscripts of the *Fragmenta*, he also looks at their authenticity, an issue which is not yet settled for these items; some Latin texts of the *Satyrica* print very few of the *Fragmenta*. Sommariva works almost exclusively on the texts attributed to Petronius in the *Anthologia Latina* (*Fragmenta* 26–51), while Ciaffi has written on many aspects of Petronius and his connection to Fulgentius, a medieval writer who died in 532. In his works Fulgentius cites Petronius thirteen times, and he is the author of references in *Fragmenta* 6–13, 25.

THE TEXT

The post-classical *Testimonia* are conveniently gathered by Müller[6] (xxxii–xli), and I will use some of them to tell an important part of the story of the tradition of the survival of the *Satyrica* in the Middle Ages. Twenty-five of the fifty-one (26–51) *Fragmenta* of the *Satyrica*, always printed at the conclusion of the modern Latin texts, are cross-referenced with the appropriate poems in the *Anthologia Latina*. The earliest recorded words of Petronius/ Arbiter (we assume from the *Satyrica*) are from the pen (*Fragmenta* 19, 20) of a certain Terentianus Maurus—the name might indicate a North African connection—who lived in the late second to early third centuries. Thus there is an apparent gap of something like 150 years between the death of Petronius and the earliest extant quotation from his work. This early reference, however, was not an indication of things to come: ancient plus medieval

Testimonia take up barely twelve pages in Müller[6]. Even though the original *Satyrica* apparently was a long narrative work, the extant text (except for the *Cena*) is not at all a narrative but rather a collection of disjointed pieces, mutilated excerpts, totaling about 35,000 words. By comparison Apuleius' *Metamorphoses* has 51,000 words. The *Satyrica* was surely subject to normal wear and tear inflicted over millennia, but the extant pieces seem to be in many places the end-product of methodical attempts to shorten it or remove sections. And once excerpts had been made, originals were not properly preserved, or, worse, were abandoned. But perhaps the harshness of all aspects of life from late antiquity to the early modern period was particularly detrimental to Petronius. Jumping ahead for a moment to the fifteenth century and much more luxurious conditions for collectors and copyists, we must be both amazed at how many copies of manuscripts *A* and *H* were found and copied by and for Poggio Bracciolini (1380–1459), besides those sent to Niccolò Niccoli for further copies to be made, and shocked that all copies that we know once existed in England, Cologne, Rome, and Florence have been lost.

With a modicum of confidence it might be said that in the Middle Ages the *Satyrica* consisted of at least sixteen books: *Fragmenta* 7 citing 20.7 mentions Book 14; manuscript *A* at its beginning and end mentions Books 15 and 16 (de la Mare, 241). Poggio's *Epistle* 2.3 to Niccoli mentions Book 15. Except for the continuity at 26.7–78, the rest of the text of the *Satyrica* can be described as a collection of excerpts. Some years ago I offered a reconstruction of the *Satyrica* (Schmeling[3], 460–61); the reconstruction given by Vannini[2] (5–7) is better. We both agree,

23

however, that what survives of the *Satyrica* is from the second half of the work; Vannini[2] (7) thinks that he can show some deductive evidence that allows him to conjecture Books 13 to 21.

If Terentianus Maurus was from North Africa, it would add significance to the appearance there later under the Kingdom of the Vandals (destroyed by Belisarius in 533–34) of the first meaningful traces of the text of the *Satyrica* since the death of its author. Fulgentius (†532), bishop of Ruspe, mentions Petronius by name thirteen times and cites him in three of his secular treatises (*Mythologiae, Expositio Virgilianae Continentiae, Expositio Sermonum Antiquorum*), where he hands down to us 82.5 vv. 1–4, and *Fragmenta* 6–13, 25, 28, 38, 44. For the *Fragmenta* of Petronius, I follow the numbering system of Müller[5-6].

Because the poems that make up *Fragmenta* 26 to 51 are included in the *Anthologia Latina*, it has been suggested that at least some of the poems (or fragments) were excerpted from the *Satyrica* for the *Anthologia Latina* in the learned world of Vandal North Africa just before or around the time Fulgentius died. The poems attributed to Petronius and found in the *Anthologia Latina* come from three manuscripts: Z = Leidensis Vossianus lat. Q. 86, ca. 850; Y = Leidensis Vossianus lat. F. 111, ca. 810; X = Bellovacensis deperditus. The large amount of Petronian material noted by Fulgentius encourages scholars to conclude that Fulgentius and the compilers of the *Anthologia Latina*, both working in the same area and at the same time, had access to a text of the *Satyrica* more complete than we have. While Fulgentius and the compilers of the *Anthologia Latina* were active in North Africa circa 530, the best and most extensive extant collection in the *Antho-*

logia Latina, Salmasianus (Parisinus lat. 10381), was made far to the north in or near Rome circa 800; so Spallone, who adds that Salmasianus is a faithful copy of a sixth-century manuscript. If that manuscript was made in North Africa circa 530, how it came to be copied in Rome cannot be determined, but it could certainly have contained poems by Petronius; although the Salmasianus contains only one *Petronianum*, and that spurious (*Anth. Lat.* 218 R), its first eleven quires, which are missing, could have held material from the original collection, possibly including poems from the *Satyrica*, made in North Africa. Tarrant is agnostic: "It must also remain for the moment an open question whether this anthology or another is the source for the poems preserved only in Leidensis Voss. Lat. Q. 86 . . ." (12), that is, *Fragmenta* 26 to 41 in manuscript Z.

Almost a century after Fulgentius, Isidore, bishop of Seville circa 600–630, from a Roman family influential in the Spain of the Visigoths and who had close ties to Vandal North Africa, is able to include in his *Etymologiae* seven references to the *Satyrica*, once mentioning the name Petronius (*Fragmenta* 14, 44). Isidore had access either to a fairly complete text or to a rich secondary source. Also in Spain, but fifty years later in the reign of the Visigoth Ervigius (680–687), Julian, bishop of Toledo (680–690), in his *Ars Grammatica* 2.12.19, quotes without attribution the verse from 14.2 v. 5. About 810 the poem at 14.2, together with one at 83.10 and *Fragmenta* 42–43, was included in Leidensis Vossianus lat. F. 111 (= *Y*), a codex that comprises texts that seem to have connections to Toledo (Reynolds, xviii f.; Reeve[2], 26–27); Vannini[2] (39[1]) reports that Ernesto Stagni has suggested to him that Theodulf, born in Spain of Visigothic descent, bishop of Orléans circa 798–818 and abbot of Fleury, who helped to prepare manuscripts, could have been instrumental in importing the *Satyrica* to France from Spain. Finally, in a list of books belonging to Wulfhad, bishop of Bourges (866–876), the name *Petronii* appears with Christian writers (*Testimonia* 8); might this be a Petronius of Bologna? After the quotation by Julian (†690), the *Satyrica* is not cited again in extant sources until the middle of the ninth century.

In that century at least one exemplar (archetype = ω; cf. Stemmata below) of the *Satyrica* survived (unfortunately there is no description of it), most likely in France, and then most likely in Fleury (Reynolds–Wilson, 101; Reeve[1], 299); Ullman intimates that the special *liber* of Pithoeus 1565 was probably the *vetus Benedictinum exemplar*, later cited in *p*, so called after the Benedictine Abbey at Fleury. Müller[6] (iv f.), and Vannini[2] (39) opt for Auxerre as the French home of ω. It is agreed that the oldest (ninth-century) MS of the *excerpta brevia* is *B*, and belonged to Saint-Germain-d'Auxerre; Pithoeus (Pierre Pithou, 1539–1596) named it Autissiodurensis after the place of origin, as he thought. Heiricus (†846), a well-known excerptor, was a monk at Saint-Germain, and *B* displays a careful surgery of excerpts with incisions carefully resewn (*Testimonia* 9). Heiricus knew a source larger than that of the *O* class, to which *B* belongs, cf. 119 v. 5 *fulvum quae* Heiricus *L*: *quae fulvum O*; Heiricus knew the word *septifluus* from 133.3 v. 4. Autissiodurensis (Auxerre), written in the ninth century, is *B*. Heiricus was known as an enthusiastic and careful preparer of excerpts: in his *Collectanea* he added the excerpts he had made to those selected by Lupus of Ferrières from Suetonius and

Valerius Maximus. The work of Valerius Maximus was widespread, and there exists a manuscript personally corrected by Lupus (†862), of which his student Heiricus made excerpts (von Albrecht, 1081), thus the argument for *B* and Auxerre. The argument about the home of the archetype is another matter, however: in the ninth century it is probable that a sizable part of the last half of the *Satyrica* was extant. Since Fleury had a productive scriptorium, a case can be made for it as the home of the archetype; since Auxerre seems not to have had a scriptorium, it is unlikely to have been the home of a large, rare manuscript (von Büren). The archetype, later known at Orléans or in the larger area of North-Central France (see below on John of Salisbury and ϕ) where the *Florilegium Gallicum* was put together, would have consisted of the last half of the *Satyrica* (see above on sixteen books of the *Satyrica*).

From the archetype preserved at Fleury descend all the manuscripts and edition prototypes we now have: four manuscript classes, *O*, *H*, ϕ, *L*, and the first printed editions (*med.*, *ven.*, *par.*, *s*). Reeve[1] (299) speculates that that the archetype "survived long enough to be used in s. XII–XIII by John of Salisbury" [†1180] . . . and "if John took a copy from France to Canterbury, that would account for the echoes in the Canterbury Tales. . . ." In the narrative that follows, it can be conjectured from the evidence that the archetype remained at Fleury and that John took a copy to Canterbury; he perhaps also took a copy of the *excerpta brevia* (cf. Poggio in London, *Ep. 1*.7). The teacher of John either at Paris or Chartres was Thierry of Chartres (fl. 1140), who himself reports a passage from *O*, *L* (*Testimonia* 15). John apparently had access to as much

27

of the *Satyrica* as is extant today, and in his *Policraticus* cites material from *O*, *H*, and *L*: at 8.7 he mentions the exceedingly rare title *Cena Trimalchionis*, and at 8.11 reports the Milesian Tale of the *Matrona Ephesi*. *Testimonia* 16 records all the quotations from the *Satyrica* in the *Policraticus*; Vannini[2] (56–58). Stirnemann–Poirel suggest (1) that the *Florilegium Gallicum*, believed by Rouse and others to have been compiled in Orléans, originated in a wider area of North-Central France, and (2) that John had some responsibility in its assembly. Poirel had earlier suggested that "l'école de Jean de Salisbury" also had some responsibility for the inclusion of the Petronian quotation (1.3) in the anonymous *De patientia* (ca. 1170) r. 39 s. *melitos verborum globulos* (Paris., BNF n. acq. lat. 1791, fols. 109r–21r). Though John is important for the tradition of the *Satyrica* in the years between placing the archetype in Fleury and Poggio's discovery of δ in England circa 1420, he seems to paraphrase the *Satyrica* rather than to copy it. Nothing in John's text determines a reading in the *Satyrica*. For this reason he is not used in my apparatus as a primary source. Still in England and still near or just after John, the work of one Helias Rubeus Tripolanensis = Elias of Thriplow (a village near Cambridge) has been shown by Marvin Colker to be full of allusions to, but not quotations from, the *Satyrica*. In 1975 Colker[1] published the *Analecta Dubliensia*, three anonymous medieval Latin texts including "Petronius Redivivus" (Dublin, Trinity College MS 602, fols. 132r–49v, a codex in English hands of the first half of the thirteenth century, which had belonged to the Benedictine Abbey of St. Catherine's, Canterbury). In 1992 Colker[2] showed that the Petronian content of the Dublin MS and the Petronian allusions in the *Serum Senectutis* (London, British Library, MS Sloane 441, s. xv, fols. 1r–62r) were both gathered by Elias from passages in *O*, *H*, and *L*. All the material is now conveniently presented in Colker[3]; Vannini[1] (439–40); Vannini[2] (58). The coincidence of two sets of writing (by John and by Elias) connected to Canterbury, appearing within a short time, each with numerous references to the rare text of Petronius, perhaps indicates the presence there of a substantial amount of the *Satyrica*.

About two and a half centuries after the death of John of Salisbury, when Poggio lived in London (1418–1423), he discovered a manuscript, δ, of the *excerpta brevia* (Vannini[2], 42) and sent it to Niccoli in Florence (*Ep.* 2.3). Perhaps John had taken a copy of these excerpts as well as a copy of ω to England. Though Poggio did not seem to know *H* and *L*, classes of manuscripts known to John and Elias, his dispatch of δ to Niccoli marks the return of Petronius to Italy (de la Mare; Rini). Three classes of manuscripts (*O*, *H*, *L*) are thus probably to be found in England during the last years of John and into the fifteenth century.

At this point in the review of the manuscript tradition of the *Satyrica*, it is appropriate to look back to France once more, and to review the significant material in Bern 276 (early s. xiii, central France), that is, the work of an annotator. Bern 276 is a manuscript of the *Vocabularium* of Papias and of Huguccio. In 1978 Reeve–Rouse found three citations (from *Fragmenta* 15, 16) of the *Satyrica* written in the margins by someone who had access to rare works (Reynolds, p. xxxviii, and his Index of Manuscripts) and lived near Orléans in the second half of the thirteenth century; the manuscript was owned by Jean de Guignecourt (on whom see Stagni[2], 219[1]) at the end of the fourteenth century, and then by Pierre Daniel in the second half of the sixteenth, who for the first time mentioned the Fragments of Petronius (Vannini[1], 440); at Daniel's death his library and Bern 276 went to Jacques Bongars. Reeve[1] (298), who records that the annotator "cites Petronius at least eight times," adds several observations about the significance of the marginalia: because of the way the annotator misspells *Satiricon*, he was dealing with a manuscript close to *P*; and especially, in the late thirteenth century near Orléans, the annotator could consult "passages of the *Satyrica* absent from *L*." *Fragmenta* 15–16 in Bern 276 were later (after 1565) excerpted by Pierre Daniel "ex glossario S. Dionysii." Vannini[1] (441) suggests that Bern 276 is the glossarium named by Daniel. Richardson (64) notes that Bern 276 now tallies eleven citations from Petronius, and Stagni[2] has added a twelfth from 111.2. And then Stagni[2] (221) identified the annotator as Guido de Grana (†1284), "che intorno al 1270–75 commentò un poema duecentesco pubblicato . . ." (Richardson, 63–82; Stagni[2–3]; Vannini[1], 440–41; Vannini[2], 58).

1. *O* in the apparatus = consensus of *BRP*. *O* also employed in superscript in the text is identified with the so-called *excerpta brevia* class, δ, and *O*δ is a frequent combination.

Everything in the *O* class is also recorded in the *L* class, so-called *excerpta longa*.

The symbol *O* = consensus of MSS *B* from the ninth century, and *R* and *P* from the twelfth. *O*δ (plus variants) is employed in the apparatus to indicate the expanded class of the *excerpta brevia*, which includes *BRP*, plus the fifteen manuscripts copied in Italy in the Quattrocento, all descended from δ, plus the printed editions, *med.*, *ven.*, *par.*, *s* (= *editio Sambuci*). The class *O* or *Oδ* transmits less than one-third of the extant text in severely excerpted fragments, which delicately avoid scenes of homosexuality; preserve sections of poetic content, dialogue, and literary criticism; and retain the whole of the *Matrona Ephesi*. The excerptor chose sections for preservation and then carefully resewed them so that no one should recognize that they were pieces from a much larger whole—except for the readers who much later would have access to the other classes of manuscripts, *H*, *φ*, and *L*.

Müller[6] (v–vii) and Vannini[2] (40) relate what is almost an amusing story of the great lengths gone to in order to hide the excerptions. I give one example illustrating the deletion of a passage of homosexual content. At 8.4 the excerptor deletes everything after Ascyltos' *dedissem poenas*, until he arrives at 9.4 and begins again with *cum ego proclamarem . . . invenisti*. Ascyltos had been speaking inside a narrative by Giton, and by resuming it with Giton's *cum ego proclamarem*, the excerptor indeed deletes a homosexual scene and still makes good sense of the narrative except for the inexplicable change in speakers.

O (*B*)	like Λ and *H*, but unlike *φ* and *L*, is not a composite; cf. the Stemmata.
B	Bernensis 357, fols. 34v–41, and Leidensis Vossianus Q. 30, fols. 57–58, s. ix[2], Saint-Germain-d'Auxerre, derived from *O* without intermediaries. The dissolution of the codex and the loss of four folia probably occurred after the death of its owner Pierre Daniel

(1530–1603), who had lent it to Pithoeus, and whose library was divided between Jacques Bongars (1534–1612), who got the Bern folia, and Paul Petau (1568–1614) the Leiden folia (Richardson, 132–36). The first two folia (3.3–80.9) of the four lost were recovered in Leiden, the last two (81–109.10) are still lost. Pithoeus refers to *B* as "Autis." (Autissiodurensis), so identified by Bücheler[1], xviii f.; Reeve[1], 295; Müller[4], 383.

R Parisinus lat. 6842 D, fols. 74–91, s. xii[ex], complete, derived from *O* through one or more intermediaries. Employed more widely by Müller than by Bücheler.

P Parisinus lat. 8049, fols. 17v–25r, s. xii[ex], complete, derived from *O* through one or more intermediaries, more remote than *R*.

R and *P* are much more likely to show errors than *B* is, and both use many abbreviations. *P* is vital especially when *B* is not extant, and *RP* represent the class *O*. A number of readings of *P* agree with those cited in p^v and t^{mg} and attributed to a *codex Bituricus* ("Bit.," "Brit."), with which *P* should be identified, so called by Pithoeus, who in his fancy named it after Jean duc de Berry (1340–1415), who had owned it (Reeve[1], 295; Richardson, 48–52). The parent of *P*, which in the stemma is indicated by π, probably of French origin, is used also by ϕ, δ, *L*. For doubts about the identification of Bituricus, cf. Vannini[2], 41.

Of the consensus *O*, it is clear that *P* or its parent *π* is the most closely related to the manuscripts and editions subsumed under *δ*.

δ   the now lost codex discovered by Poggio in England circa 1420 and sent from England to Niccoli in Florence; it is the *particula Petronii* mentioned by Poggio *Ep.* 2.3, who now (1423) is back in Rome and asks Niccoli to return it to him. It is related to the *O* class in that it too preserves the same *excerpta brevia* of the *Satyrica*. While also related to the *O* consensus, *δ* and *δs* (*Ms*) numerous times deviate from it, and these are often apparent because they contaminate *L*, as in 122 v. 149 *mansuescit BR, rp: mansuescunt Pδs, lct. Oδ* and *Pδ* occur with great frequency in a detailed apparatus and indicate the close relationship of *O* and *δ*. The reliability of *δ* is less than that of *P* (Müller[6], viii f.). The stemma indicates that *P* and *δ* both descend from *π*, and from *δ* come two offshoots, *α* and *ξ*, both also lost, and from these descend all fifteen codices related to the *O* class, written in the fifteenth century in Italy, plus the printed editions *med.*, *ven.*, *par.*, *s*. On the history of *δ* and its descendants, cf. de la Mare. Bücheler and Ernout at intervals adduce readings from these descendants. Müller demonstrated that they belong in two groups, which he called *α* and *ξ*; some of the *α* set showing similar gaps at 16–25.6; further on the split in *α* and *ξ*, see Vannini[2] (42–43);

on the manuscripts of α and ξ sets, de la Mare (223–36) holds that the α set was written in northern Italy and the ξ in Florence.

α	codex deperditus.
A	Parisinus lat. 7989, pp. 185–205 = *excerpta brevia* (pp. 206–29 = *H*, *Cena Trimalchionis*).
Barb	Vaticanus Barberinianus lat. 4, fols. 1–28; fol. 4v is left blank, probably indicating a lacuna in the exemplar, which is made real here by a lacuna at 16–25.6 quae vite-; the lacuna continues in its descendants *med.*, *ven.*, *par.*; cf. de la Mare (225², 222²), who gave the MS the name *Barb*.
M	Müller[1] (xi f.) hypothesized that the source of *med.*, *ven.*, and *par.* was a manuscript related to *Barb*, which he named *M*, which symbol he then used to indicate a consensus of the three. From *Barb* (*M*) pass down:
med.	*editio Mediolanensis* (ca. 1482), *editio princeps* of the *excerpta brevia*, by Puteolanus (Francesco dal Pozzo, †1490); unknown to sixteenth-century French scholars; cf. Rini, 19–33. From this descend:
ven.	*editio Veneta* (1499), by Bernardinus de Vitalibus; reprinting of *med.* with changes; unknown to sixteenth-century French scholars; cf. Rini, 19–33.

par. *editio Parisiensis/Chalderiana* (1520), by
Reginaldus Chalderius (Regnault
Chaudière, d. 1554?), reprinting of *med.*
with changes; used by many scholars on
first reading the *Satyrica*. From *par.* but
corrected with a better manuscript,
identified with *W* (Müller[1], p. xii; Richardson, 11), descends *s*, which was influential on *L*.

s *editio Sambuci* (János Zsámboky, 1531–
1584; Antwerp, 1565). Influential final
edition of the *O* class, recognized as special because Sambucus produced a
printed edition (corrected with *W*) superior to *par.*; influences *m* but not *r*; used
by Scaliger.

E Messanensis, destroyed in a fire 1848.
I Indianensis, Notre Dame 58, fols. 1–61;
Richardson, *Scriptorium*, 38 (1984), 89–
100.
F Leidensis Vossianus lat. O. 81, fols. 27–54r.
K Vaticanus lat. 1671, fols. 1–38r.
S Bellunensis Lollinianus 25, fols. 52–84r.
ξ codex deperditus. In the 1500 Catalogue of
the Convent of San Marco, there might
be a trace of this MS at no. 903, cf. de la
Mare, 231–33.
J Florentinus Laurentianus pl. 37.25, fols.
1–18.

V	Vindobonensis 179 (Endlicher 218), fols. 1–29.
W	Vindobonensis 3198 (Endlicher 108), fols. 42v–63, owned by Sambucus and used by him in his 1565 edition.
C	Vaticanus Urbinas lat. 670, fols. 38–66r.
D	Florentinus Laurentianus pl. 47.31, fols. 128–47.
G	Guelferbytanus extravag. 299, fols. 17–58.
o	Vindobonensis ser. n. 4755, fols. 1–28.
Q	Vaticanus lat. 3403, fols. 31v–61.

2. *H* = Cena Trimalchionis class

H   Parisinus lat. 7989 (olim Traguriensis); pp. 206–29 contain the *Cena Trimalchionis*. (For pp. 185–205, which contain *A*, *excerpta brevia* of the *O* class, and a descendant of δ, see above.) *H*, *O* (*B*), and Λ, unlike φ and *L*, are not composites. Gaselee[2] offers a photographic reproduction and de la Mare 240–47 a detailed description. Paris. lat 7989, found in ca. 1653 in the Cippico library at Traù in Dalmatia (now Trogir in Croatia) by Marino Statileo (Marin Statilić), consists of 250 pages of various Latin authors. The Catullus section ends on p. 179 with an important date for this codex, written by scribe, November 20, 1423. Below follows de la Mare's analysis of the copying of *H* and *A* through the letters of Poggio, and finally to its appearance in Traù.
(1) Poggio in England to Niccoli in Florence, June 13, 1420, *Ep. 1*.7: "De Petronio (sc. *ex-*

cerptis brevibus) quod scire cupis, quid tractet, lege Macrobii principium super somnio Scipionis . . . Est autem homo gravis versu, et prosa constans." Poggio had discovered δ.

(2) Poggio in Rome to Niccoli in Florence, May 28, 1423, *Ep.* 2.3: "Allatus est mihi ex Colonia xv liber (sc. *Cena*) Petronii Arbitri, quem curavi transcribendum modo, cum illac iter feci. Mittas ad me oro Bucolicam Calpurnii et particulam Petronii (sc. δ) quas misi tibi ex Britannia." Poggio had found the *Cena* manuscript.

(3) Poggio in Rome to Niccoli in Florence, September 11, 1423, *Ep.* 2.4: "Petronium (sc. *Cenam*) ad te non misi sperans ipsemet afferre ad te liberum." Poggio will send the MS of the *Cena* to Niccoli, if they cannot arrange a meeting.

(4) Poggio in Rome to Niccoli in Florence, November 6, 1423, *Ep.* 2.7: "Si ibimus ad vos, me conferam subito; et nunc Petronium (sc. *Cena*) habebitis." Poggio then invites Niccoli to Rome to stay with him. On p. 179 of the codex there is a date, November 20, 1423. Manuscripts *A* and *H* are copied later in the codex and so some time has elapsed.

(5) Poggio in Rome to Niccoli in Florence, September 13, 1429, *Ep.* 4.2: "Tenuisti Lucretium duodecim annis, et item Asconium Pedianum et septem annis aut amplius Petronium Arbitrum (sc. *Cena*)." On his visit to Rome in

1424 Niccoli had secured the *Cena* and taken it back to Florence, apparently never to return it to Poggio.

As we have seen, from δ, sent by Poggio to Niccoli (*Ep.* 2.3), two copies were made (α and ξ): from α was made MS *A*, probably in late 1423 or early 1424, in Florence. Since the *Cena* was also in Florence at that time, it too was copied into the Traguriensis right after *A*, in the period 1424–25. Further, de la Mare noted that Giorgio Begna from Dalmatia was in Florence in August 1425, where he had finished copying Caesar's *Civil War*. Begna was not the scribe of the Traguriensis, but he was an avid collector of classical manuscripts, and was a friend of Pietro Cippico of Traù. It is suggested that the Traguriensis passed from Begna on his death in 1438 to Cippico, in whose library the codex resided until rediscovered by Statileo. Lučin (233–37) in a section on Claudian's *Phoenix* has recognized the hand of Marcus Marullus (Marko Marulić, 1450–1524), a humanist working in Split and Traù, as the sixteenth-century annotator of the codex. He has also identified Marulić as annotator "c" in de la Mare's scheme, who added notes to manuscript *A* but not to *H*. The presence of the Traguriensis at Traù in the late fifteenth or early sixteenth century, is thus assured; Vannini[1], 100–101.

patav.   editio princeps of the *Cena*, ed., P. Frambotti (Padua, 1664).

3. φ = *Florilegium Gallicum* class

Φ   archetype of the *Florilegium Gallicum*, compiled about the end of the twelfth century in Orléans (Rouse, 135–38), or before 1165, perhaps with help from John of Salisbury, from exemplars of libraries far beyond Orléans (Stirnemann-Poirel 178–80), preserved in manuscripts of the twelfth to fourteenth centuries. It deals with a variety of proverbs and *sententiae*, shows a fondness for passages of poetry, and contains the *Matrona Ephesi*. It is likely that readings of the *florilegia* are present in many marginalia, hidden perhaps as "al.," "v.c.," and add to the general composite nature of *L*. The Petronian excerpts from the *Florilegium Gallicum* are edited by Brandis–Ehlers, and by Hamacher, 121–38, of whose collations of the *florilegia* I make use; the latter's sigla are set out here:

ϕ^p Parisinus lat. 7647 (olim Thuaneus), fols. 110v–12, s. xii^{ex}.

ϕ^c Escorialensis lat. Q. I. 14, fols. 92v–95r, s. xiv^{in}.

ϕ^a Atrebaticus 64, fols. 64–5, s. xiv.

ϕ^v Hamburgensis 53c in scrin., fols. 1–2, s. xiii^{in}.

ϕ^n Parisinus lat. 17903 (olim Nostradamensis 188), fols. 70v–72, s. xiii. Ullman notes that this MS was a source used by Vincentius for his *Speculum Historiale*.

ϕ^b Berolinensis Diez B Sant. 60, fols. 28v–29r, s. xiv^{med}.

4. *L* = *Excerpta Longa* class

L   consensus of *ldmrtp*. The *excerpta longa* are preserved only in manuscripts and editions of the second half of the sixteenth century: none is a true medieval MS. Two are printed editions, the others are secondary sources, collations of manuscripts, edition prototypes; written between 1565 and 1587, but for reasons of necessity assigned the status of manuscripts (Richardson, 3). According to van Thiel (1–24), with credit to Merkelbach (cf. also Müller[6], xii), all the constituent parts of L are composite, they contain everything in O and ϕ, and thus they hold larger portions of the text than the other classes. Unlike O and ϕ, which are selections of a text, L is a compilation or conflation, and it reunites the shorter fragments of O via π, ϕ, and the larger fragments of Λ from which ϕ too descends (cf. Stemmata): where L agrees with ϕ against O (π), it can be deduced that the readings go back to Λ (Vannini[2], 48), which is dated to the twelfth century at the latest. Only in L are found the indications <***> of lacunae. The compilation of L, dated by van Thiel to the twelfth century, is dated by Müller[4] (428) to the end of the thirteenth.

From L descend two codices now lost: one of these called Cuiacianus belonged to Cuiacius (Jacques Cujas, 1522–1590), born in Toulouse, a professor, jurist, collector (Richardson, 137), who cites passages from Petronius as early as 1562, and lent it to Joseph Scaliger (1540–1609), to Denis Labey de Batilly (1551–1607), collaborator with Tornaesius (Jean II de Tournes, 1539–1615) on t, and to Pithoeus; the second is Benedictinus (*vetus Benedictinum exemplar*), owned by Pithoeus and prob-

ably originating at the Benedictine abbey at
Fleury (Ullman, 141).

A third codex, Memmianus, lost, copied from β (a
descendant of Benedictinus) in the sixteenth century, owned by Memmius (Henri de Mesmes,
1532–1596) and lent to Turnebus (Adrien de Turnebus, 1512–1573) for his *Adversaria* of 1564–
1573; from it descend *m*, *Da* (Dalecampianus),
owned by Dalecampius (Jacques Dalechamps,
1513–1588; lost, s. xvi; transcribed from *Memm.*,
used only by *t*, identified by Goldast), *d*, *r*. Manuscripts *dmr* are first used in texts by Müller.

l   Leidensis Scaligerianus 61, fols. 4–45r (1571), copied from the Cuiacianus by Scaliger, who chose
variant readings (not regularly noted, cf. 95.3, 121
v. 120, 130.2) also from Bituricus = *P*, from *s*
(some of the readings in *s* are probably conjectures of Sambucus; cf. Müller[1], xvi–xviii), and from
ϕ (Ullman, 147–50). Scaliger also had available
material for his *Catalecta* (*c*), which sets forth a
large number of the poems of Petronius or attributed. From the Cuiacianus arise also citations in
the texts of Tornaesius (*t*) and Pithoeus (p^2), and
in their appendices of variants (t^v, p^{2v}). Vannini[2]
(49), is convinced that for the Cuiacianus there
are additional readings, often unreported by editors in the inventory of notes in *r*, fols. 51–52, and
in the editions of Melchior Goldast and Joh. Pet.
Lotichius, which should be credited to Pithoeus,
to whom Cuiacius had lent his manuscript in 1587
for the publication of p^2, but also eighteen years
earlier, in 1569, Pithoeus apparently had the Cuia-

41

cianus before Scaliger did. Ullman (142) seem-
ingly was the first to note this: in the *Scaligeriana
sive excerpta ex ore I. Scaligeri*, ed. Jacques and
Pierre Dupuy (The Hague, 1669²), 83, Scaliger
mentions the loan to Pithoeus and its date. In a
letter to me, Leofranc Holford-Strevens comments that this edition is piratical, that the title
page lies about the editorship, and that in the first
edition (The Hague, 1666), the citation is on
page 85.

c   *Scaligeri Catalecta* (Leiden, 1573²). Important for
the poems in the *Satyrica*.

d   Bern, Burgerbibliothek, Bong. IV. 665 (10), fols.
11v–13r (also known as Petri Danielis schedae
Bernenses), ca. 1565, contains 1–15.4 frontis.
Transcription by Richardson (88–92, pls. 5–8). It
was copied, not directly from *Memm.* but from an
incomplete apograph (*fr.* in the stemma), by
Pierre Daniel (1530–1603) on the last four pages
of an edition by Muretus (Marc-Antoine Muret,
1526–1585) of Cicero's *Philippics* (Paris, 1562),
that he had acquired in Paris on October 27, 1563;
Vannini² (53).

m   Vaticanus lat. 11428 (olim Mureti), fols. 1r–14v, contains the text until 80.9 v. 1 quate-. Derived from
Memm., conflated with *s*, and so copied in or after
1565, belonged to Muretus (Richardson, 9–23, pl.
9). Vannini² (204¹) notes that Muretus made cor-
rections and conjectures to a copy of *par.*, now
held in the Biblioteca Nazionale Centrale di
Roma, 69.1. F. 4.

r   Londiniensis Lambethanus 693, fols. 7r–41v, 51r–52v, before 1572, also called Rogertianus because it belonged to Daniel Rogers (1538–1591), copied by an unknown hand, the only complete descendant of *Memm.*; it also makes use of *fr.* (see above under *d*), since in the margin of f. 9v (near 15.4 frontis) it notes *non plura habebat* [sic] *exemplaria*, but probably not of *d* itself; not conflated with *s*; Richardson (119–31, pls. 11–13). It was annotated by Rogers and lent in 1572 to Janus Dousa (Jan van der Does, 1545–1604), who used it for his *Praecidanea* (1583). After the text there is copied a manuscript version of *Notae*, fols. 51r–52v, published by Goldast, who assigns them to François Daniel, and by Lotichius, who assigns them to Puteanus (Claude Dupuy, 1545–1594; Richardson, 99–118, pl. 13). Stagni[1] (206[4]) is certain that Pithoeus is the author of the *Notae*. For the marginal notes, cf. Richardson (119–31), Vannini[2] (50–53). The oddest spelling mistakes seem to occur most often in *r* (e.g., *ptrocasiati* 82.3).

t   *editio Tornaesiana* (Lyon, 1575), first printed edition of *L*, edited by Denis Lebey de Batilly and Tornaesius, who used *Da*. The editors also used other sources: Cuiacianus beginning at 112; *par.*; *s*; very likely ϕ^p; *c* for the poems; the *Adversaria* of Turnebus; variants of Bituricus ("Brit.") = *P*, relayed by Pithoeus; readings marked "v. c. Pit.," which might indicate Benedictinus; readings from Pithoeus marked "Pith."

t^v "Variae lectiones ex collatione v. c." At the end of the
text, pp. 109–10, t adds an inventory of variants
from Cuiacianus.

p consensus of the two *editiones Pithoeanae*, which are
carefully edited and make the most of the witnesses available to Pithoeus. Vannini[2] (55) cautions
that the asterisks in p are not used exclusively to
announce lacunae; they can also indicate a corruption or a note in the margins.

p^v consensus of the two *varietates lectionum*; *vetus
Pithoei* indicates the readings of Benedictinus
copied out by Pithoeus in p^v.

p^1 editio Pithoeana (Paris, 1577), established on: *vetus
codex* identified as Benedictinus; Autiss(ioduren-
sis) identified as B; Bit(uricus) identified as P; t
with its readings from Cuiacianus; readings from a
MS of ϕ. At the end of the text in a supplement
are collected many variants marked by source.

p^{1v} "Varietas lectionum."

p^2 editio Pithoeana altera (Paris, 1587). For the revised
edition Pithoeus had also the use of Thol(osanus),
to be identified with the Cuiacianus (Ullman).
Readings from the Tholosanus are collected in p^{2v}.
There are a few instances where the readings in p^1
are preferred to those in p^2 (e.g., *cliensve* 5 v. 5;
accerse 121 v. 117; *solerent* 132.12).

p^{2v} "Varietas lectionum in Satyrico Petronii." Readings
of Tholosanus are also copied here by Pithoeus.
After the Varietas there is an inventory of *Notae*,
probably assembled by Pithoeus; after the *Notae* is
found the *Collectanea* said to be by F. Pithoeus
(François Pithou, 1543–1617).

44

STEMMATA

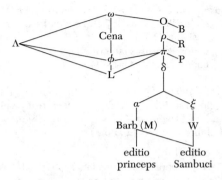

Figure 1. Stemma from archetype to Sambucus, modified from van Thiel, p. 20; Müller[4], pp. 448, 390.

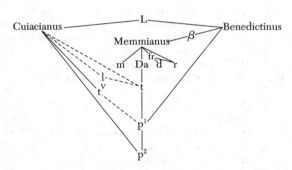

Figure 2. Stemma for L, modified Richardson, Fig. 2a; modified from Müller[4], p. 404.

SIGLA

O consensus of codices *BRP*; *excerpta brevia* Oδ
  B   codex Bernensis 357 and codex Leidensis Vossianus Q. 30, s. ix
  R   codex Parisinus lat. 6842 D, s. xii
  P   codex Parisinus lat. 8049, s. xii

δ   codex = *particula Petronii* (Testimonia 21), found by Poggio Bracciolini in 1420, now lost, from which descend all fifteen codices written in Italy in s. xv, divided into two sets (α and ξ)

  α   codex lost
    A   codex Parisinus lat. 7989, pp. 185–205; *excerpta brevia*
    Barb codex Vaticanus Barberinianus 4
    med. *editio princeps Mediolanensis* (ca. 1482)
  M *ven.* *editio Veneta* (1499)
    par. *editio Parisiensis* (1520)
    s   *editio Sambuci* (1565)
    E   codex Messanensis (destroyed in a fire in 1848)
    I   codex Indianensis Notre Dame 58
    F   codex Leidensis Vossianus O. 81
    K   codex Vaticanus lat. 1671
    S   codex Bellunensis Lollinianus 25
  ξ   codex lost
    J   codex Florentinus Laurentianus pl. 37.25
    V   codex Vindobonensis 179
    W   codex Vindobonensis 3198
    C   codex Vaticanus Urbinas lat. 670

D	codex Florentinus Laurentianus pl. 47.31
G	codex Guelferbytanus extravag. 299
o	codex Vindobonensis ser. n. 4755
Q	codex Vaticanus lat. 3403

H   That part of codex Parisinus lat. 7989, pp. 206–29, that contains the *Cena Trimalchionis*, s. xv (Testimonia 21)

patav. *editio princeps* of the *Cena* (Padua, 1664)

Φ   archetype of the *Florilegium Gallicum*, s. xii

L   consensus of *ldmrtp, excerpta longa*

    l   codex Leidensis Scaligerianus 61 (written in 1571)

    c   *Catalecta* of Scaliger (Leiden, 1573^2)

    d   codex Bong. IV. 665. (10), Bern (ca. 1565) (Petri Danielis schedae Bernenses)

    m   codex Vaticanus lat. 11428 (written after *annum* 1565)

    r   codex Londiniensis Lambethanus 693 (written before 1572)

    t   de Tourne edition (Lyon, 1575)

    t^v "Variae lectiones ex collatione v.c.," that is, from the codex Cuiacianus

    p   consensus of the two editions by Pithou, p^1 and p^2

    p^v consensus of the two "Varietates lectionum"; *vetus* of Pithou indicates the readings of the codex Benedictinus

    p^1 Pithou first edition (Paris, 1577)

    p^{1v} "Varietas lectionum"

p^2 Pithou second edition (Paris, 1587)
p^{2v} "Varietas lectionum in Satyrico Petronii";
         readings of the codex Tholosanus, surely
         the codex Cuiacianus

SIGLA OF THE BELLUM CIVILE
(chs. 119–24)

M_1 codex Monacensis 23713, s. xvi
V_2 codex Vindobonensis 3198 (W), s. xv
Dr codex Dresdensis 141, s. xv

SIGLA OF THE FRAGMENTA

Z   codex Leidensis Vossianus lat. Q. 86, s. ix, from
     which Scaliger in 1573 edited fragmenta 26–41
     (*Anth. Lat.* 464–79 R; 462–77 ShB)

Y   codex Leidensis Vossianus lat. F. 111, s. ix, from
     which Scaliger in 1573 edited fragmenta 42–43
     (*Anth. Lat.* 650–51 R), which also contain verses
     in 14.2 and 83.10

X   codex Bellovacensis, today deperditus, from which
     Claudius Binetus claims that in 1579 he edited
     fragmenta 44–45 (*Anth. Lat.* 690–97 R)

SYMBOLS AND ABBREVIATIONS USED
IN THE LATIN TEXT

⟨ ⟩   letters enclosed in angle brackets must be
         added to the text
{ }   letters enclosed in braces must be deleted

†	corruptions that defy correction
<***>	lacunae based on the authority of the manuscripts
<. . .>	lacunae suggested by editors of the Latin text
l^c	corrector of the codex l
l^{ac}	the reading of the codex l before correction
l^{mg}	notes made in the margin of codex l

excerpta brevia	the short excerpts of the Latin text, i.e., manuscripts of the O or $O\delta$ class
excerpta longa	the long excerpts of the Latin text, i.e., manuscripts of the L class
s. ix	saeculo ix = ninth century; s. = saeculo (century) plus the Roman numeral for the century

NOTES TO THE FORMAT OF THE LATIN TEXT

The *Satyrica* is traditionally divided into 141 sections, which are indicated here by Arabic numbers followed by a period; subsections, which are now required in all scholarly literature, are indicated by marginal numbers with the corresponding breaks indicated by vertical lines within the text; manuscripts that support the readings in the text are set in superscript at the beginning of the supported passage; small numerals in superscript set after a word refer to the notes in the apparatus criticus at the bottom of the Latin page.

Thus the *Satyrica* in Latin for section 2 appears as follows:

[OφL]2. qui inter haec nutriuntur non magis sapere possunt
quam bene olere qui in culina habitant. | [OL]pace vestra   2
liceat dixisse, primi omnium[3] eloquentiam perdidistis. le-
vibus enim atque inanibus sonis ludibria quaedam exci-
tando effecistis ut corpus orationis enervaretur et caderet.

[OφL] indicates the three groups of manuscripts that support the sentence that follows.
2. indicates section number 2 of 141 sections.
[OL] indicates a change and that only two groups of manuscripts now support what follows.
Marginal 2 indicates subsection number 2 in section
   number 2.
omnium[3] indicates that note number 3 in the textual
   notes at the bottom of the page refers to *omnium*.

   Poems are set in block format with line numbers to the
left of the verse.

GENERAL BIBLIOGRAPHY

Adams[1], J. N. Exchange of letters with G. Schmeling.

Adams[2], J. N. "Petronius and the New Non-Literary Latin." In Herman, 11–23.

Albrecht, M. von. *A History of Roman Literature.* 2 vols. Rev. G. Schmeling. Leiden, 1997.

Anton, C. G. *Petronii Arbitri Satyricon ex recensione Petri Burmanni passim reficta cum Supplementis Nodotianis, notas criticas . . . addidit C. G. Antonius.* Leipzig, 1781.

Astbury, R. "Petronius, *P. Oxy.* 3010, and Menippean Satire." *CP* 72 (1977): 22–31.

Baehrens, E. *Poetae Latini Minores.* 4 vols. Leipzig, 1882.

Bailey[1], D. R. Shackleton. *Anthologia Latina.* Stuttgart, 1982.

Bailey[2], D. R. Shackleton. "On Petronius." *AJP* 108 (1987): 458–64.

Barthius (K. von Barth, 1587–1658). "Racemationes." In Goldast, 487–521, cited as in Bücheler.

Beck[1], C. *The Age of Petronius.* Cambridge, MA, 1856.

Beck[2], C. *The Manuscripts of the Satyricon of Petronius Arbiter Described and Collated.* Cambridge, MA, 1863.

Binetus, C. *C. Petronii Arbitri itemque aliorum quorundam veterum epigrammata hactenus non edita.* Poitiers, 1579.

Blommendaal, E. *Animadversiones Petronianae*. PhD diss., Leiden, 1908.

Bodel[1], J. *The Freedmen in the Satyricon of Petronius*. PhD diss., Michigan, 1984.

Bodel[2], J. "Missing Links: *thymatulum* or *tomaculum*." *HSCP* 92 (1989): 349–66.

Bodel[3], J. "Trimalchio's Underworld." In *The Search for the Ancient Novel*, edited by J. Tatum, 237–59. Baltimore, 1994.

Bongars, J. (1534–1612). In Burman[2].

Boschius, J. *Titi Petronii Arbitri Equitis Romani Satyricon. Johannes Boschius ad scriptorum exemplarium fidem castigavit & notas adjecit*. Amsterdam, 1677. Enlarged edition with the addition of the Trogir Fragment = *H*. Amsterdam, 1690.

Bouhier, J. *Poème de Pétrone sur la Guerre Civile entre César et Pompée . . . avec des Remarques . . .* Amsterdam, 1737.

Bowie, E. L., and S. J. Harrison. "The Romance of the Novel." *JRS* 89 (1993): 159–78.

Boyce, B. *The Language of the Freedmen in Petronius' Cena Trimalchionis*. Leiden, 1991.

Brandis, T., and W. Ehlers. "Zu den Petronexzerpten des *Florilegium Gallicum*." *Philologus* 118 (1974): 85–112.

Branham, R. B., and D. Kinney, trans. *Satyricon: Petronius*. Berkeley, 1996.

Brassicanus, J. A. (1500–39). In Burman[2].

Braswell, B. "Zu Petron 34,4." *Philologus* 125 (1981): 152–55.

Broukhusius, J. (1649–1710). In Burman[2].

Bücheler, F. *Petronii Arbitri Satirarum reliquiae . . . (editio maior* and *editio minor*). Berlin, 1862[1]. Other editions: 1871^2, 1882^3, 1904^4, 1912^5, 1922^6. *Editio maior* repr. Berlin, 1958, 1963; 1912^5 and 1922^6 revised by W. Heraeus.

Büren, V. von. "Auxerre, lieu de production de manuscrits?" In *Études d'exégèse carolingienne: autour d'Haymon d'Auxerre*, 167–86. Turnhout, 2007.

Burman (P., 1664–1741). *Titi Petronii Arbitri Satyricôn quae supersunt* . . . Utrecht, 1709^1. 2nd ed. revised by J. J. Reiske and C. Burman. 2 vols. Amsterdam, 1743^2; repr. Hildesheim, 1974. Gaselee, *Transactions of the Bibliographical Society*, 10 (1909): 186, notes that the second edition is inferior from every point of view.

Bursian, C. In Bücheler.

Busche, K. "Zu Petronius." RhM^2 66 (1911): 452–57.

Campanile, E. "Letture petroniane." *SIFC* 46 (1974): 41–50.

Canterus, G. (1542–1575). *Novarum lectionum libri octo.* Antwerp, 1571; 3.14 = note on 132.15 v. 7.

Christ, J. F. (1700–1756). *Villaticum.* Leipzig, 1746. In Bücheler.

Christesen, P., and Z. Torlone. "*Ex omnibus in unum, nec hoc nec illud*: Genre in Petronius." *MD* 49 (2002): 137–72.

Ciaffi, V. *Fulgenzio e Petronio.* Turin, 1963.

Colker[1], M. *Analecta Dublinensia: Three Medieval Latin Texts in the Library of Trinity College Dublin.* Cambridge, MA, 1975.

Colker[2], M. "New Light on the Use and Transmission of Petronius." *Manuscripta* 36 (1992): 200–209.

Colker[3], M. *Petronius Redivivus et Helias Tripolanensis.* Leiden, 2007.

Colladonius, G. (1508–1594). In Bücheler.

53

Collignon, A. *Étude sur Pétrone.* Paris 1892.

Connors, C. *Petronius the Poet: Verse and Literary Tradition in the Satyricon.* Cambridge, 1998.

Conte, G. B. *The Hidden Author: An Interpretation of Petronius's Satyricon.* Berkeley, 1996.

Corbett, P. "More Petroniana." *CP* 64 (1969): 111–13.

Cornelissen, J. J. "Ad Petronium." *Mnemosyne*[2] 10 (1882): 295–300.

Courtney[1], E. "Some Passages of Petronius." *BICS* 17 (1970): 65–69.

Courtney[2], E. *The Poems of Petronius.* Atlanta, 1991.

Courtney[3], E. *A Companion to Petronius.* Oxford, 2001.

Crusius, C. (1715–1775). In Bücheler.

Cueva, E., and S. Byrne, eds. *A Companion to the Ancient Novel.* Chichester, 2014.

Cuiacius (Iacobus; Jacques Cujas, 1522–1590). *Ad Tres Postremos Lib. Cod. Dn. Iustiniani Commentarii.* Lyon, 1562. Cuiacius, who owned the codex Cuiacianus, now lost, which was used by Scaliger (= codex *l*) and others, and together with codex Benedictinus also lost, proves *L* = *excerpta longa*.

Cuperus (Gijsbert Kuiper, 1644–1716). In Burman[2].

Daniel (Pierre, 1530–1603). "Notae." In Goldast, 75–98.

Daniel, Fr. (François, 1559–1617). "Notae." In Goldast 57–67; a manuscript version, less complete but more correct, is found in *r*, fols. 51–52; work should probably be credited to P. Pithou, Vannini[2] (49[38]). In these notes there are readings of an old codex (sc. Cuiacianus.

D'Arms, J. *Commerce and Social Standing in Ancient Rome.* Cambridge, MA, 1981.

Delz, J. Review of Müller[1] in *Gnomon* 34 (1962): 676–84.

Deroux, C. "L'établissement du texte de Pétrone, *Sat.* 29.9." *Latomus* 62 (2003): 680–82.

Deufert, M. "Das Traumgedicht des Petron: Überlegungen zu Text und Kontext von *A.L.* 651 (Petron frg. 30 Müller)." *Hermes* 124 (1996): 76–87.

Doody, M. *The True Story of the Novel.* New Brunswick, NJ, 1996.

Dousa (J. van der Does, 1545–1604). *Iani Dousae Nordovicis, Pro Satyrico Petronii Arbitri, viri consularis, Praecidaneorum libri tres* (Leiden, 1583). In Goldast, 185–359; Burman[2], 1–64. It is always bound with: Dousa, I., *Petronii Arbitri Viri Consularis Satyricon.* Leiden, 1585; Paris, 1585, 1587.

Dousa fil. (J. van der Does, 1571–1597). In Goldast.

Eck, W. "Miscellanea prosopographica." *ZPE* 42 (1981): 227 [227–56].

Ehlers, W. Letters to Müller.

Ernout, A. *Pétrone, Le Satiricon, texte établi et traduit.* Paris, 1958[4].

Forster, E. M. *Aspects of the Novel.* London, 1927.

Fraenkel, Ed. Letters to Müller.

Francius (Pieter de Frans, 1645–1704). In Bücheler.

Friedländer, L. *Petronii Cena Trimanlchionis, mit deutscher Übersetzung und erklärenden Anmerkungen.* Leipzig, 1906[2].

Frye, N. *Anatomy of Fiction.* Princeton, 1957.

Fuchs, H. "Verderbnisse im Petrontext." In *Studien zur Textgeschichte und Textkritik*, edited by H. Dahlmann and R. Merkelbach, 57–82. Köln, 1959).

Gagliardi, D. *Petronio e il Romanzo Moderno.* Florence, 1993.

Gaselle[1], S. "The Bibliography of Petronius." *Transactions of the Bibliographical Society* 10 (1910): 141–233.

Gaselee[2], S. *A Collotype Reproduction of that Portion of the Codex Paris. 7189, Commonly Called the Codex Traguriensis.* Cambridge, 1915.

Gaselee[3], S. "Petroniana." *CQ* 38 (1944): 76–77.

George, P. "Petroniana." *CQ*[2] 17 (1967): 130–32.

Gevaerts, Jean-Gaspard (1593–1666). In Burman[2].

Giardina, G., and R. Cuccioli Melloni. *Petronii Arbitri Satyricon.* Turin, 1995.

Gifanius, O. *Titi Lucretii Cari De Rerum Natura libri sex.* Leiden, 1595. (See esp. p. 313.)

Goesius (W. van der Goes, 1611–1686). In Burman[2].

Goldast, Melchior (1578–1635). *T. Petronii Arbitri, Equitis Romani Satiricon, cum Petroniorum fragmentis, noviter recensitum, interpolatum et auctum. Accesserunt seorsim notae et observationes variorum.* Frankfurt, 1610[1], Lyon, 1615[2], Lyon, 1618[3], Frankfurt, 1621[4].

Goldbach, Ch. (1690–1764). In *Thesauri Epistolici Lacroziani*, Tomus I, edited by Johann Uhl, 143. Leipzig, 1742. Conjecture made in 1718; reference from Holford-Strevens.

Graevius (J. G., 1632–1703). In Burman[2].

Gronovius (J. F., 1611–1671). In Burman[2].

Gronovius, Jac. (1645–1716). In Bücheler.

Gurlitt, L., trans. *Petronius, Satiren.* Berlin, 1923.

Habermehl, P. *Petronius, Satyrica 79–141: ein philologisch-literarischer Kommentar, Band 1, Sat. 79–110.* Berlin, 2006.

Hadrianides, M. *Titi Petronii Arbitri Equitis Romani Satyricon, cum fragmento nuper Tragurii reperto.* Amsterdam, 1669.

Hägg, T. *The Novel in Antiquity.* Oxford, 1983.

Hamacher, J. *Florilegium Gallicum: Prolegomena und Edition der Exzerpte von Petron bis Cicero, De Oratore.* Bern, 1975. (See esp. pp. 121–38.)

Harrison[1], S. J. "The Milesian Tales and the Roman Novel." *GCN* 9 (1998): 61–73.

Harrison[2], S. J., ed. *Oxford Reading in the Roman Novel.* Oxford, 1999.

Harrison[3], S. J. "Some Problems in the Text of Petronius." In Herman, 127–37.

Haupt, M. *Opuscula III.* Leipzig, 1876. (See esp. pp. 377, 583.)

Hawthorne, J. *Studying the Novel.* London, 1997[3].

Heinsius, N. (1620–81). In Burman[2].

Helm, R. "Nachaugusteische nichtchristliche Dichter." *Lustrum* 1 (1956): 229–36.

Henderson, J. "The *Satyrica* and the Greek Novel: Revisions and Some Open Questions." *IJCT* 17.4 (2010): 483–96.

Heraeus, W. "Supplementa adnotationum." In Bücheler[5–6] and *Kleine Schriften*, edited by J. B. Hofmann Heidelberg, 1937.

Herman, J., ed. *Petroniana: Gendenkschrift für Hubert Petersmann.* Heidelberg, 2003.

Hofmann, H., ed. *Latin Fiction: The Latin Novel in Context.* London, 1999.

Holford-Strevens, L. Exchange of letters with G. Schmeling.

Holzberg[1], N. "Petron 1965–1995." In K. Müller, *Petronius Satyrica*, 544–60. Zurich, 1995.

Holzberg[2], N. *Der antike Roman.* Düsseldorf, 2001.

Housman, A. E. *M. Manilii Astronomicon.* Cambridge, 1937[2].

Humphreys, S., and J. P. Sullivan. "Petronius 114.3." *Latomus* 21 (1962): 372–73.

Jacobs, F. *Integer Commentarius Frid. Jacobsii in Petron. Arbitr. Satir. ineditus.* Handwritten copy in Cambridge University Library, dated April 1793; shelf mark Add.3556.

Jahn, O. In Bücheler.

James, H. Preface to the Revised Version of *The Tragic Muse.* In *The Art of the Novel: Critical Prefaces*, 84. New York, 1934.

Jensson, G. *The Recollections of Encolpius: The Satyricon of Petronius as Milesian Fiction.* Groningen, 2004.

Jungermann, G. In Goldast and Burman[2].

Junius (A. de Jonghe, 1511–1575). Junius' notes are recorded by Goldast (28–35), who dates them to 1562, and transcribes them from a copy of *par.*; cf. Vannini[1], 180[65].

Kaibel, G. Notes in his copy of Petronius passed on to Müller by Ed. Fraenkel.

Klotz, C. (1738–1771). *Antiburmannus.* Jena, 1761. Also in Bücheler.

Krohn, C. *Quaestiones ad Anthologiam Latinam spectantes.* PhD diss., Halle, 1887.

Lachmann, K. *Karl Lachmanns Briefe an Moritz Haupt.* Edited by J. Vahlen. Berlin, 1892.

La Penna, A. "L'ariete di Polifemo in Petronio." *Maia* 35 (1983): 123–24.

Leo, F. Notes in Georg Kaibel's copy of Petronius passed on to Müller by Ed. Fraenkel.

Lindenbrog, F. (1573–1648). In Bücheler.

Lipsius (J. Lips, 1547–1606). In Goldast and Burman[2].

Lowe, W. *Petronii Cena Trimalchionis.* Cambridge, 1905.

Lučin, B. "Marulićeva ruka na trogirskom kodeksu Petronija (codex Parisiensis Lat. 7989 olim Traguriensis)." *Colloquia Maruliana* 14 (2005): 315–22; Vannini[1], 100–101.

Magnelli, E. "Petr. *Sat.* 119 (*Bell. civ.* 9)." *Eikasmos* 12 (2001): 259–62.

Maiuri, A. *La Cena Trimalchionis di Petronio Arbitro.* Naples, 1945.

Mare, A. C. de la. "The Return of Petronius to Italy." In *Medieval Learning and Literature: Essays presented to R. W. Hunt,* edited by J. Alexander and M. Gibson, 220–54, pls. 20–28. Oxford, 1976.

Marmorale[1], E. *Petronii Arbitri Cena Trimalchionis.* Florence, 1947.

Marmorale[2], E. *La Questione Petroniana.* Bari, 1948.

Martin, R. E. "Quelques remarques concernant la date du *Satiricon.*" *REL* 53 (1975): 182–224.

Mentelius (J. Mentel, 1597–1671), writing under the pseudonym Caius Tilebomenus. In Burman[2].

Mommsen, Th. In Bücheler.

Mössler, I. *Quaestionum Petronianarum specimen, quo Poema de Bello Civili cum Pharsalia Lucani comparatur.* Hirschberg, 1857.

Müller, K. *Petronii Arbitri Satyricon.* Munich, 1961[1]; *Petronius Satyrica* (Munich, 1965[2], 1978[3], 1983[4]); *Petronius Satyricon Reliquiae* (Stuttgart and Leipzig, 1995[5], Munich and Leipzig, 2003[6]).

Müller, L. "Sammelsurien." *Jahrbücher für classische Philologie* 93 (1866): 385–400, at 395 (on fr. 34.3); 861–68, at 863–64 (on 23. 3); 95 (1867), 483–512, at 512 (on fr. 51. 1).

Muncker, Th. (1640–1681). In Boschius and Burman[2].

Muretus, M.-A. (1526–1585). Cf. codices *m* and *d*.

Neumann, G. "*Lupatria* in Petron c. 37.6 und das Problem der hybriden Bildungen." *WJA*, ns 6a (1980): 173–80.

Nisbet, R. G. M. Review of Müller[1] in *JRS* 52 (1962): 227–32.

Novák, R. In Bücheler[5-6] and Heraeus.

Öberg, J. *Petronius, Cena Trimalchionis*. Stockholm, 1999.

Oevering, M. In Boschius and Burman[2].

Orelli, J. K. von. *Lectiones Petronianae*. Zurich, 1836.

Oudendorp, F. van (1696–1761). In Bücheler.

Palmerius, J. M. *Spicilegiorum commentarius primus*. Frankfurt, 1580. Also in Burman[2].

Panayotakis[1], C. *Theatrum Mundi: Theatrical Elements in the Satyrica of Petronius*. Leiden, 1995.

Panayotakis[2], C. "Petronius and the Roman Literary Tradition." In Prag–Repath, 48–64.

Panayotakis, S., M. Zimmerman, and W. Keulen, eds. *The Ancient Novel and Beyond*. Leiden, 2003.

Parsons, P. "A Greek *Satyricon*?" *BICS* 18 (1971): 53–68.

Passerat (J., 1534–1602). In Burman[2].

Peerlkamp (P. H., 1786–1865). In Bücheler.

Perrochat, P. *Le Festin de Trimalcion*. Paris, 1952.

Perry, B. E. *The Ancient Romances*. Berkeley, 1967.

Petersmann, H. *Petrons urbane Prosa*. Vienna, 1977.

Petschenig, M. "Bemerkungen zu den *poetae Latini minores*." *Philologus* 48 (1889): 562–64. On fr. 34. 4 *inter tam crassas*: Petschenig proposed this reading before Walter, to whom Muller[6] gives the credit.

Pinheiro, M. F., and S. J. Harrison, eds. *Fictional Traces: Reception of the Ancient Novel*. Ancient Narrative Supplements 14.2. Groningen, 2011.

Pithoeus, Fr. (François Pithou, 1543–1617). "Ad idem Petronii Arbitri *Satyricon, Collectanea.*" In p^2, 25–78 = Goldast, 145–85, and Burman[2].

Pithoeus 1565 (Pierre Pithou, 1539–1596). *Adversariorum Subsecivorum libri II.* Paris, 1565.

Pithoeus, P. *Petronii Arbitri Satyricon Ex veteribus Libris emendatius & amplius.* Paris, 1577 = p^1 (in Sigla). 2nd ed. *Petronii Arbitri Satyricon. Adiecta sunt veterum quorundam poetarum carmina non dissimilis argumenti.* Paris, 1587 = p^2 (in Sigla).

Pius[1] (Ioannes Baptista Pius, Giovanni Battista Pio, †ca. 1540). In Bücheler; everything except Pius[2].

Pius[2], I. B. *Enarrationes allegoricae fabularum Fulgentii Placiadis.* Milan, 1498; sig. [fv]^r, et *Plautus integer cum interpretatione* (Milan, 1500), sigs. [s viii]^v–t i ^{r} on 135.8 vv. 16–17.

Plaza, M. *Laughter and Derision in Petronius' Satyrica.* Stockholm, 2000.

Poirel, D. "La patience, l'un et la Trinité. Un traité inédit de l'école de Jean de Salisbury." *ALMA* 61 (2003): 65–109.

Prag, J, and I. Repath, eds. *Petronius: A Handbook.* Chichester 2013[2].

Puteanus (Claude Dupuy, 1545–1594). In Burman[2].

Puteolanus (Francesco dal Pozzo, †1490). *Petronii Arbitri Satyrica Fragmenta Quae Extant.* Milan, 1482 = *med.* (in Sigla).

Putschius, H. (Elias van Putschen, 1580–1606). In Goldast.

Raphael, F., trans. *Satyrica.* London, 2003.

Reeve[1], M. D. "Petronius." In Reynolds, 295–300.

Reeve[2], M. D. "Ausonius." In Reynolds, 26–28.

Reeve, M. D., and R. H. Rouse. "New Light on the Transmission of Donatus's *Commentum Terentii*." *Viator* 9 (1968): 235–49.

Reinesius, Th. (1587–1667). In Burman[2].

Reiske, J. J. (1716–1774). In Burman[2], Anton, and Bücheler. He was proofreader of the manuscript of Burman[2] and added more than 140 of his own conjectures, for which Caspar Burman bitterly attacked him; he defended himself in "Libellus animadversionum ad alteram editionem Burmannianam Petronii." *Miscellanea Lipsiensia Nova* 6 (1748): 93–114, 272–307, 488–523, 650–85.

Reynolds, L. D., ed. *Texts and Transmission: A Survey of the Latin Classics*. Oxford, 1983.

Reynolds, L. D., and N. G. Wilson. *Scribes and Scholars*. Oxford, 2012[4].

Ribbeck, O. *Geschichte der römischen Dichtung*. 3 vols. Stuttgart, 1887–1892, iii. 150–59, and in Bücheler.

Richardson, T. Wade. *Reading and Variant in Petronius: Studies in the French Humanists and their Manuscript Sources*. Toronto, 1993.

Riese, A. *Anthologia Latina*. Leipzig, 1894–1906.

Rimell, V. *Petronius and the Anatomy of Fiction*. Cambridge, 2002.

Rini, A. *Petronius in Italy*. New York, 1937.

Rittershusius (C. Rittershausen, 1560–1613). "Notae." In Goldast, 359–65, and Burman[2].

Rose[1], K. Letters exchanged between K. Rose and J. P. Sullivan, some in the hands of G. Schmeling.

Rose[2], K. "Petroniana." *C&M* 26 (1965): 222–32.

Rose[3], K. "Petroniana." *Latomus* 26 (1967): 130–38.

Rose[4], K. "Petroniana." *RhM*[2] 111 (1968): 253–60.

Rose[5], K. *The Date and Author of the Satyricon.* Leiden, 1971.

Rose, K., and J. P. Sullivan. "Trimalchio's Zodiac Dish (Petronius, *Sat.* 35.1–5)." *CQ*[2] 18 (1968): 180–84.

Roth, U. "Liberating the *Cena.*" *CQ* 66.2 (2016): 614–34.

Rouse, R. H. "Florilegia and Latin Classical Authors in Twelfth- and Thirteenth-Century Orléans." *Viator* 10 (1979): 131–60, at 135–38.

Ruden, S., trans. *Satyricon.* Indianapolis, 2000.

Sage, E. T. *The Manuscripts of Petronius.* Unpublished manuscript, typewritten. In the Regenstein Library, Special Collections, Bib. Number 4366973, University of Chicago. 1936.

Salmasius (Claude Saumaise, 1588–1653). *De Usuris Liber.* Leiden, 1638. (See esp. p. 344, on 14.7, 15.4, 8.)

Salmasius. In Burman[2] except for above.

Sambucus (János Zsámboky, 1531–1584). *Petronii Arbitri Massiliensis Satyrici Fragmenta, Restituta et Aucta.* Antwerp, 1565 = *s* (in Sigla).

Scaliger (I. I., 1540–1609). Codex Leidensis Scaligeranus 61 (1571) = *l* (in Sigla); *Scaligeri Catalecta* (*Publii Virgilii Maronis Appendix . . . Iosephi Scaligeri in eandem Appendicem* (Lyon, 1573[2]) = *c* (in Sigla).

Scheffer (J., 1621–1679). "Notarum in Petronii fragm. Tragur. Specilegium [*sic*]." In *Lectionum Academicarum liber*, 227–79. Hamburg, 1675. Also in Burman[2].

Schmeling[1], G. "The *Satyricon*: Forms in Search of a Genre." *CB* 47 (1971): 49–53.

Schmeling[2], G. "Genre and the *Satyrica*: Menippean Satire and the Novel." In *Satura Lanx*, edited by C. Klodt, 105–117. Hildesheim, 1996.

Schmeling[3], G., ed. *The Novel in the Ancient World.* Leiden, 2003[2].

Schmeling[4], G. *A Commentary on the Satyrica of Petronius.* Oxford, 2011.

Schmeling[5], G. Letters, notes, files, scribblings in texts exchanged between G. Schmeling and J. P. Sullivan plus K. F. C. Rose. "Schmeling[5]" is used as a matter of convenient reference, and he does not take all the credit for them; J. P. Sullivan and K. F. C. Rose are deceased and cannot defend themselves.

Schmeling[6], G. "The Autobiography of Encolpius: Reading the *Satyrica* as the Confessions of the First-Person Narrator." In *Dynamics of Ancient Prose: Biographic, Novelistic, Apologetic*, edited by T. Thorsen and S. Harrison, 73–87. Berlin, 2018.

Schmeling, G., and D. Rebman. "T. S. Eliot and Petronius." *CLS* (1975): 393–410.

Schmeling, G., and J. Stuckey. *A Bibliography of Petronius.* Leiden, 1977.

Schoppius (G., 1576–1649). "Symbola Critica in T. Petroni Arbitri Satyricon" (1604). In I. Gonsález de Salas, *T. Petroni Arbitri E. R. Satiricon*, 449–62. Frankfurt, 1629.

Scriverius (P. Schrijver, 1576–1660). In Burman[2].

Sedgwick, W. *The Cena Trimalchionis of Petronius.* Oxford, 1950[2].

Segebade, J. *Observationes grammaticae et criticae in Petronium.* PhD diss., Halle, 1880.

Smith, M. *Petronii Cena Trimalchionis.* Oxford, 1975.

Sommariva, G. *Petronio nell' Anthologia Latina.* Sarzana, 2004.

Spallone, M. "Il Par. Lat. 10328 (Salmasiano) dal manoscritto alto-medievale ad una raccolta enciclopedica tardo-antica." *IMU* 25 (1982): 1–71.

Stagni[1], E. "Ricerche sulla tradizione manoscritta di Petronio: l'*editio princeps* dei 'longa' e i codici di Tornesio." *MD* 30 (1993): 205–30.

Stagni[2], E. "Medioevo francese e classici latini: un nome ritrovato." *MD* 34 (1995): 219–24.

Stagni[3], E. "Testi latini e biblioteche tra Parigi e la valle della Loira (secoli XII–XIII): il manoscritto di Guido de Grana." In *Boccaccio e le letterature romanze tra medioevo e rinascimento*, edited by S. Mazzoni Peruzzi, 221–87, at 260–80. Florence, 2006.

Stefenelli, A. *Die Volksprache im Werk des Petrons in Hinblick auf die romanischen Sprachen.* Vienna, 1962.

Stephens, S. A., and J. J. Winkler. *Ancient Greek Novels. The Fragments: Introduction, Text, Translation and Commentary.* Princeton, 1995.

Stirnemann, P., and D. Poirel. "Nicolas de Montiéramey, Jean de Salisbury et deux florilèges d'auteurs antiques." *RHT*, ns 1 (2006): 173–88, at 178–80 .

Stöcker, C. *Humor bei Petron.* PhD diss., Erlangen, 1969.

Strelitz, A. "Emendationes Petronii Satirarum." *NJPhP* 119 (1879): 629–34, 833–45.

Stubbe, H. *Die Verseinlagen im Petron.* Leipzig, 1933.

Studer, T. *Observationes criticae in Petronii Coenam Trimalchionis.* Bern, 1839.

Sullivan[1], J. P. *The Satyricon of Petronius: A Literary Study.* London, 1968.

Sullivan[2], J. P., trans. *Petronius: The Satyricon.* Harmondsworth, 1986[5].

Suringar, E. *Spicilegia critica ad Petronium de Bello Civili.* Lingen, 1812.

Tarrant, R. "Anthologia Latina." In Reynolds, 9–13.

Thiel, H. van. *Petron: Überlieferung und Rekonstruktion.* Leiden, 1971.

Thielmann, P. "Zu Petronius." *Philologus* 43 (1884): 356–58.

Thomas, P. "Ad Petronium *Sat.* 129." *Mnemosyne*[2] 21 (1893): 179.

Tornaesius (Jean II de Tournes, 1539–1615). *Petronii Arbitri Satyricon.* Lyon, 1575 = *t* (in Sigla).

Triller, D. *Observationum criticarum in varios Graecos et Latinos auctores libri quattuor.* Frankfurt, 1742.

Turnebus (Adrien de Tournèbe, 1512–1565). *Adversariorum libri XXX* (Paris, 1564). In Burman[2]; cf. *Memm.* (in Stemma) lent to Turnebus.

Ullman, B. L. "The Text of Petronius in the Sixteenth Century." *CP* 25 (1930): 128–54.

Vannini[1], G. *Petronius, 1975–2005: Bilancio critico e nuove proposte = Lustrum,* 49 (2007).

Vannini[2], G. *Petronii Arbitri Satyricon 100–115: Edizione critica e commento.* Berlin, 2010.

Vincentius Bellovacensis (Vincent of Beauvais, ca. 1190–1264). *Speculum Maius* (*Hist.* 21.25; *Doctr.* 4.94, 168) on 137.9; cf *Testimonia* 14a. Ullman notes that Vincentius used ϕ^n.

Völker, T., and D. Rohmann. "*Praenomen Petronii*: The Date and Author of the *Satyricon* Reconsidered." *CQ* 61.2 (2011): 660–76.

Vossius, I. *Gaius Valerius Catullus et in eum Isaaci Vossii Observationes.* Leiden, 1684. (See esp. p. 92, on 22.1).

Walsh[1], P. G. *The Roman Novel.* Cambridge, 1970.

Walsh[2], P. G., trans. *The Satyricon.* Oxford, 1996.

Watt, W. S. "Notes on Petronius." *C&M* 37 (1986): 173–84.

Wehle, W. *Observationes Criticae in Petronium.* PhD diss., Bonn, 1861.

Whitmarsh, T., ed. *The Cambridge Companion to the Greek and Roman Novel.* Cambridge, 2008.

Winterbottom, M. "Six Conjectures." *CR* 22 (1976): 11–12.

Winterfeld, P. von. "Ad Scriptores Latinos Coniectanea." *Philologus* 55 (1896): 190.

Wouweren, J. à (Johann von Wowern, 1574–1612). *Petronii Satyricon.* Leiden, 1604. In Goldast.

PETRONII SATYRICA

O (= *BRP*), L (= *ldmrtp*)

PETRONII ARBITRI SATYRICON (SATIRICON *B*, *d*)
B, *drtp*: Arbiter Satyricon *GL* 6.153.33 (*Aelius Festus
Asmonius sive Apthonius*): INCIPIUNT EXCERTA PE-
TRONII SATYRICI *R*: Petronii arbitri satirarum liber
INCIPIT (*in marg. eadem manu* Petronii arbitri affranii
Satirici liber incipit) *P*: Petronii Arbitri Satyri fragmenta
ex libro quinto decimo et sexto decimo *A*: C. PETRONII
ARBITRI AFRANII SATYRICI LIBER DESUNT
MULTA *l*

⟨ * * * ⟩

[OL]1. "num alio genere furiarum declamatores inquietan-
tur, qui clamant: 'haec vulnera pro libertate publica ex-
cepi, hunc oculum pro vobis impendi; date mihi {ducem}[1]
qui me ducat ad liberos meos, nam succisi poplites mem-
2 bra non sustinent'? | haec ipsa tolerabilia essent, si ad
eloquentiam ituris viam facerent. nunc et rerum tumore

---

[1] *deleted Jacobs*

---

[1] Encolpius is the narrator of the whole novel; Agamemnon is
a teacher of rhetoric and a character in the *Satyrica* until ch. 78.

SATYRICON

1. [Encolpius[1] is near the end of his part of a dialogue with Agamemnon] . . . "Are our teachers of rhetoric tormented by another pack of Furies when they shout out: 'These wounds I got fighting for our country's liberty, this eye I sacrificed for you. Give me someone to guide me to my children, for my knees have been hamstrung[2] and cannot bear the weight of my body.' Even such statements might have been tolerable, if they had cleared a path for those seeking eloquence. In reality the only achievement of the

[2] Prisoners of war were often hamstrung to prevent escape.

et sententiarum vanissimo strepitu hoc tantum proficiunt, ut cum in forum venerint, putent se in alium orbem terrarum delatos. | et ideo $^{O\phi L}$ego adulescentulos existimo in scholis stultissimos fieri, quia nihil ex his quae in usu habemus aut audiunt aut vident, ^{OL}sed piratas cum catenis in litore stantes, sed[2] tyrannos edicta scribentes quibus imperent filiis ut patrum suorum capita praecidant, sed responsa in pestilentiam data ut virgines tres aut plures immolentur, sed mellitos verborum globulos et omnia dicta factaque quasi papavere et sesamo sparsa. $^{O\phi L}$2. qui inter haec nutriuntur non magis sapere possunt quam bene olere qui in culina habitant. | ^{OL}pace vestra liceat dixisse, primi omnium[3] eloquentiam perdidistis. levibus enim atque inanibus sonis ludibria quaedam excitando effecistis ut corpus orationis enervaretur et caderet. | nondum iuvenes declamationibus continebantur, cum Sophocles aut Euripides invenerunt verba quibus deberent loqui. | nondum umbraticus doctor ingenia deleverat, cum Pindarus novemque lyrici Homericis versibus canere timuerunt. | et ne poetas {quidem}[4] ad testimonium citem, certe neque Platona neque Demosthenen ad hoc genus exercitationis accessisse video.[5] | grandis et ut ita dicam

---

2 sed *s, l*: et
3 omnium $\delta s, l$: omnem
4 *deleted Bücheler*
5 video *Turnebus, p^2*: et ideo

---

3 Encolpius' criticism of rhetoricians probably does not represent the opinions of Petronius, and lamenting the decline of oratory is a parody (of current opinions and fads), which itself is hackneyed.

inflated subject matter and of the absolutely empty sounds of the maxims is that when the young speakers enter court, they think they have been conveyed into another world. This is why I believe that our young boys are converted into total fools in schools of rhetoric, because they hear and see nothing used in everyday life but only topics like pirates with chains standing on the beach, like tyrants writing edicts ordering sons to decapitate their own fathers, like oracular responses in time of plague recommending that three or more virgins be sacrificed, like honeyed clusters of expressions, and all words and actions, as it were, sprinkled with poppy seed and sesame.[3] 2. Youngsters who are fed on this fare can no more gain good sense than those who live in the kitchen can smell clean. Forgive my bluntness, but I have to tell you that you above all others have impoverished eloquence. Your feeble and empty sounds have brought about only a certain frivolousness, with the result that oratory has lost its vigor and fallen flat. Young men were not yet restricted to declamations, when Sophocles and Euripides found the language they needed.[4] No sequestered pedant in his ivory tower had as yet ruined all the genius in students, when Pindar and the nine lyric poets[5] carefully shied away from Homeric lines in composing their own. Not that I need to have recourse to the poets for evidence; I certainly do not see that Plato or Demosthenes took up this kind of train-

[4] These two along with Aeschylus were the great tragedians of fifth-century Athens.

[5] Pindar is usually included in the canon of the nine lyric poets, along with Alcaeus, Sappho, Anacreon, Alcman, Stesichorus, Ibycus, Simonides, and Bacchylides.

pudica oratio non est maculosa nec turgida, sed naturali
7 pulchritudine exsurgit. | nuper ventosa istaec et enormis
loquacitas Athenas ex Asia commigravit animosque iuve-
num ad magna surgentes veluti pestilenti quodam sidere
afflavit, semelque corrupta eloquentia e⟨repta⟩ regula[6]
8 stetit et obmutuit. | ad summam, quis postea[7] Thucydidis,
quis Hyperidis ad famam processit? ac ne carmen quidem
sani coloris enituit, sed omnia quasi eodem cibo pasta non
9 potuerunt usque ad senectutem canescere. | pictura quo-
que non alium exitum fecit, postquam Aegyptiorum audacia tam magnae artis compendiariam invenit."

3. non est passus Agamemnon me diutius declamare in
porticu quam ipse in schola sudaverat, sed "adulescens"
inquit "quoniam sermonem habes non publici saporis et,
quod rarissimum est, amas bonam mentem, non fraudabo
2 te arte secreta. | nil mirum ⟨si⟩[8] in his exercitationibus
doctores peccant, qui necesse habent cum insanientibus
furere. nam $^{O\phi L}$nisi dixerint quae adulescentuli probent,
3 ut ait Cicero, 'soli in scholis relinquentur.' | ^{OL}sicut $^{O\phi L}$ficti
adulatores cum cenas divitum captant nihil prius meditan-

---

[6] corrupta eloquentia e⟨repta⟩ regula stetit *Courtney*[1]
[7] ad summam quis postea *Scriverius*: quis postea ad summam
[8] nil mirum ⟨si⟩ *Leo*: nimirum

---

[6] Ridicule of the florid Asianic style and praise of the plain
Attic are commonplace in comments on oratory and education.

[7] Thucydides was a penetrating historian of the Peloponnesian War, but unlike the renowned fourth-century Hyperides,
he was not a good model for orators.

[8] Comments on the decline of contemporary art are a trite
subject (cf. Vitr. *De arch.* 7.5.4; Plin. *NH* 35.2, 28).

ing. Elevated and what I would call a pure style is not full of highly colored and bombastic phrases. It rises sublime because of its intrinsic beauty. Just lately this breezy and formless verbosity has migrated from Asia to Athens.[6] Its breath as from some malignant star fell upon the eager spirits of our youth, as they sought to rise to greatness, and once the norms were removed the eloquence in speech ceased and grew dumb. So, who now has gained the renown of Thucydides[7] or Hyperides? Even poetry has not preserved its healthy glow, but all art has been fed, as it were, on the same diet and thus not able to survive long enough to reach gray-haired old age. Painting also suffered a similar consequence,[8] once the unscrupulous Egyptians found shortcuts[9] to such high art."

3. Agamemnon could not allow me to declaim in the colonnade longer than he had sweated over delivering a speech in the school: "Young man," he said, "since your speech shows extraordinary taste, and what is special about you is that you appreciate intellectual qualities, I shall not try to deceive you by withholding secrets of my art. It is not at all surprising if teachers make shameful concessions in these school exercises. They have to act like madmen and play their part with lunatics. For unless their speeches win the approval of their pupils, the teachers will, as Cicero[10] says, be left all alone in the schools. Teachers are like mock flatterers on the stage cadging dinners

---

[9] Shortcuts in painting might refer to impressionism, first employed by Antiphanes of Alexandria in the fourth century (cf. Plin. *NH* 35.110 on Philoxenus and similar shortcuts).

[10] Cic. *Cael.* 17.41.

73

tur quam id quod putant gratissimum auditoribus fore |
(nec enim aliter impetrabunt quod petunt nisi quasdam
4   insidias auribus fecerint), | ^{OL}sic eloquentiae magister, nisi
tamquam ^{OφL}piscator eam imposuerit hamis escam, quam
scierit appetituros esse pisciculos, sine praedae spe moritur[9] in scopulo. ^{OL}4. quid ergo est? parentes obiurgatione
digni sunt, qui nolunt liberos suos severa lege proficere. |
2   primum enim sic ut omnia, spes quoque suas ambitioni
donant. deinde cum ad vota properant, cruda adhuc studia
in forum propellunt[10] et eloquentiam, qua nihil esse maius
3   confitentur, pueris induunt adhuc nascentibus. | quod si
paterentur laborum gradus fieri, ut studiosi iuvenes lec-
tione severa irrigarentur, ut sapientiae praeceptis animos
componerent, ut verba artifici[11] stilo effoderent, ut quod
vellent imitari diu audirent, ‹si persuaderent›[12] sibi nihil
esse magnificum quod pueris placeret, iam illa grandis
4   oratio haberet maiestatis suae pondus. | nunc pueri in
scholis ludunt, iuvenes ridentur in foro, et quod utroque
turpius est, quod quisque perperam didicit, in senectute
5   infitiari[13] non vult. | sed ne me putes improbasse sche-
dium[14] Lucilianae humilitatis, quod sentio et ipse carmine
effingam:

     [9] moritur *B*: moratur
     [10] propellunt *L*: impellunt
     [11] artifici *Sullivan*[2]: atroci *O, L*: Attico *Müller*
     [12] *added Winterbottom*
     [13] infitiari *Bailey*[2]: confiteri
     [14] schedium *Pithoeus, l*^{mg}*t*^{mg}: schadium *or* studium

from the rich, who calculate first what they think the audience would especially like to hear. For in no other way will they get what they are after, unless they lay traps for their listeners. Likewise, unless the teacher of rhetoric becomes like a fisherman and baits his hook with what he knows the little fish will bite on, he languishes all alone on his rock without any hope of a catch. 4. So, what is the answer? It is the parents who deserve reproach for refusing to allow their children to make progress through stern discipline. In the first place, they sacrifice their young hopefuls, like everything else, to ambition. Then in overeagerness to fulfill their objectives, they push the immature schoolboys into public life, and as they claim that nothing is mightier than eloquence, they dress their boys up in it, while they are still very young. Whereas if they would allow a step-by-step approach so that the young boys would work hard, steep themselves in serious reading, train their minds in philosophical wisdom, dig out the right expressions with a stylish pen, listen carefully to the models they wish to imitate, and convince themselves that their adolescent taste has no real worth, then the great oratory of the past could maintain its influence and splendor. But as things stand, boys in school follow frivolous pursuits, young men are laughed at in court, and what is more shameful than both, these same people in old age are unwilling to admit that their education was largely defective. I would not, however, want you to think I disapprove of the improvisational, low-level, utterances of Lucilius,[11] therefore like him I shall express my views in verse:

[11] The father of Roman satire, died in 101 BC.

^{OφL}5. artis severae si quis ambit[15] effectus
mentemque magnis applicat, prius mores
frugalitatis lege poliat[16] exactae.[17]
nec curet alto regiam trucem vultu
5   cliensque[18] cenas impotentium captet,
nec perditis addictus obruat vino
mentis calorem, neve plausor in scaenam[19]
sedeat redemptus histrionis[20] ad rictus.[21]
sed sive armigerae rident Tritonidis arces
10   seu Lacedaemonio tellus habitata colono
Sirenumque[22] domus, det primos versibus annos
Maeoniumque bibat felici pectore fontem.
mox et Socratico plenus grege mittat habenas
liber et ingentis quatiat Demosthenis arma.
15   hinc Romana manus circumfluat et modo Graio
vox operata[23] sono mutet suffusa saporem.
interdum subducta foro det pagina cursum
et fortuna sonet celeri distincta meatu;
dent epulas et bella truci memorata canore,
20   grandiaque indomiti Ciceronis verba minentur.
his animum succinge bonis: sic flumine largo
plenus Pierio defundes[24] pectore verba."

15 ambit *t*^{mg}: amat   16 poliat *Heinsius*: polleat
17 exactae *Müller*: exacta
18 cliensque *O, L*: cliensve *cp*², *editors*
19 scenam *Heinsius*: scena
20 histrionis *Turnebus*: *various readings*
21 ad rictus *Ribbeck*: addictus
22 Sirenumque *O, L*: Sirenumve *Bücheler*
23 vox operata *Müller*: exonerata
24 defundes *l*^{mg}: diffundes

76

5. If anyone seeks success in the harsh demands of art and sets his mind to great deeds, he must first put his behavior in good order, adhering to the laws of disciplined living. Let him disdain the haughty palace's insolent look of disapproval. Let him not, like a dependent, cadge for dinners from drunken hosts, or attach himself to the damned and drown the brilliant flame of his mind in wine, or sit as part of a hired claque in the theater and applaud the actor's silly faces. ‹What does he need to do?› Whether the citadel of armed Tritonis[12] smiles on him, (10) or the land inhabited by the Spartan immigrant, or the home of the Sirens,[13] let him give his earliest years to poetry, and let him drink at the Maeonian[14] fount with a happy heart. When he is replete with the learning of Socrates' school, let him loose the reins as a free spirit and wield the heavy armor of great Demosthenes. After this, let the company of Roman writers pour round him, and let his voice, just now occupied with Greek sounds with which it was mixed and fused, transform his style. Meanwhile, let his writings cast off the court's constraints and run free, and let Fortune resound, varied by the swiftness of her course. Let his phrases give meaning to the feasts and wars recorded in fierce epic songs, (20) and let them project the mighty words of undaunted Cicero. Clothe your soul in such virtues: thus inspired from a heart beloved of the Muses[15] you will pour out words in a great torrent."

[12] Athena.

[13] References to southern Italy.

[14] Maeonia was Homer's birthplace according to one tradition.

[15] Mount Pierus, sacred to the Muses.

^{OL}6. dum hunc diligentius audio, non notavi mihi Ascylti fugam et dum in hoc dictorum aestu mutus[25] incedo, ingens scholasticorum turba in porticum venit, ut apparebat, ab extemporali declamatione nesciocuius, qui

2 Agamemnonis suasoriam exceperat. | dum ergo iuvenes sententias rident ordinemque totius dictionis infamant, opportune subduxi me et cursim Ascylton persequi coepi.

3 | sed nec viam diligenter tenebam {quia}[26] nec quo[27]

4 <loco>[28] stabulam esset sciebam. | itaque quocumque ieram, eodem revertebar, donec et cursu fatigatus et sudore iam madens accedo aniculam quandam, quae agreste holus vendebat, et 7. "rogo" inquam "mater, numquid scis ubi ego habitem?" delectata est[29] illa urbanitate tam stulta et "quidni sciam?" inquit consurrexitque et coepit me

2 praecedere. | divinam ego putabam et <subsequi coepi>.[30] subinde ut in locum secretiorem venimus, centonem anus

3 urbana reiecit et "hic" inquit "debes habitare." | cum ego negarem me agnoscere domum,video quosdam inter titu-

4 los nudasque meretrices furtim spatiantes. | tarde, immo iam sero intellexi me in fornicem esse deductum. execratus itaque aniculae insidias operui caput et per medium lupanar fugere coepi in alteram partem, cum ecce in ipso aditu occurrit mihi aeque lassus ac moriens Ascyltos; pu-

---

[25] mutus *Delz*: motus   [26] *deleted Goldast*
[27] quo *O, L*: quod *editors*
[28] *added Dousa,* p^2
[29] est *B*: *omitted others*
[30] *added Schmeling*^{5}

---

[16] The second member of the first triad of central actors: Encolpius, Ascyltos, Giton.

6. Since I was listening to Agamemnon too intently, I failed to notice that Ascyltos[16] had slipped away. In this surge of words I was silent, just walking along, when a large crowd of students flowed into the colonnade, apparently from some improvised declamation delivered by someone who had followed Agamemnon's rhetorical discourse of persuasion. So while the young men were laughing at his epigrams and poking fun at the arrangement of his whole speech, I seized the opportunity to slip away and hurried off to hunt for Ascyltos. But I was not paying enough attention to the route, nor was I sure of the way to our lodgings, so in whatever direction I went, I kept coming back to the same place, until worn out by walking and dripping with sweat I went up to an old woman selling farm vegetables, 7. and said: "Please, mother, do you happen to know where I live?" She was amused by my fools' wit and said: "Why shouldn't I know?" She stood up and began to lead the way. I thought that she was some kind of clairvoyant and began to follow her. Then when we came to an out of the way place, the witty old creature drew back a patchwork curtain and said: "This is where you should be staying." I was just saying that I did not recognize the place, when I noticed some men furtively working their way among the price tags and unclothed prostitutes. Slowly and indeed a bit too late I realized that I had been led into a brothel.[17] Cursing the old woman's tricks, I covered my head and began to run through the middle of the brothel to the far end, when right at the entrance Ascyltos met me, as exhausted and half-dead as

[17] Though brief, this section offers the most detailed description of a Roman brothel.

5 tares ab eadem anicula esse deductum. | itaque ut ridens
eum consalutavi, quid in loco tam deformi faceret quaesivi. 8. sudorem ille manibus detersit et "si scires" inquit
2 "quae mihi acciderunt." "quid novi?" inquam ego. | at ille
deficiens "cum errarem" inquit "per totam civitatem nec
invenirem quo loco stabulum reliquissem, accessit ad me
pater familiae et ducem se itineris humanissime promisit.
3 | per anfractus deinde obscurissimos egressus in hunc lo-
cum me perduxit prolatoque peculio coepit rogare stu-
4 prum. | ^{L}iam pro cella meretrix assem exegerat, ^{OL}iam ille
mihi iniecerat manum, et nisi valentior fuissem, dedissem
poenas." <. . .> ^{L}adeo ubique omnes mihi videbantur satyrion bibisse.

⟨ * * * ⟩

iunctis viribus molestum contempsimus

⟨ * * * ⟩

9. quasi per caliginem vidi Gitona in crepidine semitae
2 stantem et in eundem locum me conieci. <. . .> | cum quae-
rerem numquid nobis in prandium frater parasset, consedit puer super lectum et manantes lacrimas pollice ex-
3 tersit.[31] | perturbatus ego habitu fratris quid accidisset
quaesivi. at ille tarde quidem et invitus, sed postquam
4 precibus etiam iracundiam miscui, | "tuus" inquit "iste
frater seu comes paulo ante in conductum accucurrit
5 coepitque mihi velle pudorem extorquere. | ^{OL}cum ego

---

[31] extersit *Fr. Pithoeus*: expressit

---

[18] The coin is an *as* (plural *asses*), a basic monetary unit used
in the *Satyrica*: 1 *aureus* (gold) = 25 *denarii* (silver) = 100 *sester-
tii* (bronze) = 400 *asses* (copper).

myself. You would have thought the same old woman had escorted him there. And so I greeted him with a smile and asked him what he was doing in such a disgusting place. 8. He wiped away the sweat with his hands and said: "If you only knew what happened to me!" I said: "What happened?" He was used up: "Though I was wandering all over town," he said, "I did not find where I had left our lodgings, when a respectable gentleman approached me and very kindly offered to be my guide. He led me through the darkest alleys and brought me to this place, and then proceeded to take out his wallet and proposition me for sex. By this time the madam had already got an *as*[18] for the use of a room, and the fellow had put his hands on me. If I had not been the stronger one, I would have paid the penalty." . . . Everyone in the whole place seemed to be high on aphrodisiacs. . . . By joining forces we kept the bothersome fellow away from us. . . .

9. As if through a fog I saw Giton standing on the curb of an alley and hurried toward him. . . . When I questioned my boy-partner[19] whether he had prepared something for our lunch, the lad sat on the bed and wiped off a trickle of tears with his thumb. I was upset by his appearance and asked what had happened. He was slow and reluctant to answer, but when I mixed angry words with my requests, he said: "That partner or companion of yours a short while ago rushed into our lodgings and wanted to rape me.

[19] Boy-partner is my rendering of *frater*. By this I indicate the younger-boy homosexual lover of the pair. The word *frater* is also used to mean "partner, homosexual lover of the same age."

proclamarem, gladium strinxit et 'si Lucretia es' inquit
6 'Tarquinium invenisti.'" | ^Lquibus ego auditis intentavi in
oculos Ascylti manus et "quid dicis" inquam "muliebris
patientiae scortum, cuius ne spiritus ⟨quidem⟩³² purus
7 est?" | inhorrescere se finxit Ascyltos, mox sublatis fortius
8 manibus longe maiore nisu clamavit: | "non taces" inquit
9 "gladiator obscene, quem de ruina³³ harena dimisit? | non
taces, nocturne percussor, qui ne tum quidem, cum forti-
10 ter faceres, cum pura muliere pugnasti, | cuius eadem
ratione in viridario frater fui qua nunc in deversorio puer
est?" "subduxisti te" inquam "a praeceptoris colloquio."
10. "quid ego,³⁴ homo stultissimus, facere debui, cum
fame morerer? an videlicet audirem sententias, id est
2 vitrea fracta et somniorum interpretamenta? | multo,
mehercules, turpior es tu,³⁵ qui ut foris cenares poetam
3 laudasti." | itaque ex turpissima lite in risum diffusi paca-
tius ad reliqua secessimus. |

⟨ * * * ⟩

4 rursus in memoriam revocatus iniuriae "Ascylte" inquam
"intellego nobis convenire non posse. itaque communes
sarcinulas partiamur ac paupertatem nostram privatis
5 quaestibus temptemus expellere. | et tu litteras scis et ego.

---

³² added Bücheler
³³ de ruina defended Schmeling⁴: others obelize
³⁴ ego lrp: ergo   ³⁵ multo mehercules turpior es tu
Bücheler: multo me turpior es tu hercule

---

²⁰ Latin gladius (sword) here should probably be understood
as penis; such a usage appears elsewhere in Petronius (cf. Plaut.
Cas. 909).
²¹ Sextus Tarquinius (son of Tarquin the Proud, the last king

When I screamed, he drew his sword[20] and said: 'If you are Lucretia, you have met your Tarquin.'"[21] On hearing this I shook my fist in Ascyltos' face and said: "What do you say about this, you easy-to-lay female whore, even your breath smells like dirty sex?" Ascyltos pretended to bristle but then became more aggressive, raised his fists, and with greater effort than I had shown, screamed: "Shut up, you filthy gladiator, even that brothel expelled your impotent self.[22] Shut up, you midnight assassin. Even on your good days when you were not impotent, you never had it off with a clean girl. Was I not your passive partner that time in the garden, just as the lad here is your boy-partner in our lodgings?" I said: "You slipped away from the declamation of the professor." 10. He replied: "You big fool, what did you expect me to do, since I was dying of hunger, listen to his platitudes, all of them, I suppose, really broken glass and interpretations of dreams? By god, you are worse than I am, flattering a poet to cadge an invitation to dinner." And so our sordid dispute dissolved into laughter, and we turned peacefully to remaining tasks. . . . But then the memory of his insult came back to me, and I said: "Ascyltos, I realize that we cannot get along together. Let us divide our small belongings and try to keep poverty from our door by making a living each by himself. You have an education just like me.

of Rome) in the mythical tradition of the city raped Lucretia, the wife of a nobleman, the act that brought about the replacement of the Monarchy with the Republic.

[22] I interpret *de ruina harena dimisit* to mean that the brothel sent him away (with kicks and a warning not to waste the girls' time) after charging him with impotence.

ne quaestibus tuis obstem, aliquid aliud promittam; alio-
qui mille causae quotidie nos collident et per totam urbem
6 rumoribus different." | non recusavit Ascyltos et "hodie"
inquit "quia tamquam scholastici ad cenam promisimus,
non perdamus noctem. cras autem, quia hoc libet, et habi-
7 tationem mihi prospiciam et aliquem fratrem." | $^{\phi L}$"tardum
est" inquam "differre quod placet."

⟨ * * * ⟩

^{L}hanc tam praecipitem divisionem libido faciebat; iam
dudum enim amoliri cupiebam custodem molestum, ut
veterem cum Gitone meo rationem reducerem.[36]

⟨ * * * ⟩

11. postquam lustravi oculis totam urbem, in cellulam
redii osculisque tandem bona fide exactis alligo artissimis
complexibus puerum fruorque votis usque ad invidiam
2 felicibus. | nec adhuc quidem omnia erant facta, cum As-
cyltos furtim se foribus admovit discussisque fortissime
claustris invenit me cum fratre ludentem. risu itaque plau-
suque cellulam implevit, opertum me amiculo evolvit et |
3 "quid agebas" inquit "frater sanctissime? quid? vesticontu-
4 bernium[37] facis?" | nec se solum intra verba continuit, sed
lorum de pera solvit et me coepit non perfunctorie verbe-
rare, adiectis etiam petulantibus dictis: "sic dividere cum
fratre nolito."

⟨ * * * ⟩

12. veniebamus in forum deficiente iam die, in quo
notavimus frequentiam rerum venalium, non quidem
pretiosarum sed tamen quarum fidem male ambulantem
2 obscuritas temporis facillime tegeret. | cum ergo et ipsi

[36] reducerem *Bücheler*: deducerem *or* diducerem
[37] vesticontubernium *Turnebus*, $l^{mg}mtp$: verti contubernium

I do not want to interfere with your success, so I will do something different from you. Otherwise every day a thousand issues will cause conflicts between us and get us talked about all over the town." Ascyltos had no objection and added: "As regards today, since we have accepted an invitation to dinner on the basis of being scholars, let us not waste the evening. But tomorrow, since this is the way you want it, I will look for new lodgings and another partner." I said: "It is just wasting time to put off what is decided." . . . My sexual urges were the cause of the abruptness of this split-up; for some time now I wanted to be rid of my irritating attendant, so that I might take up again my old relationship with Giton. . . .

11. I went sightseeing everywhere in town before going back to our small room, and at last claimed real kisses. I held the boy tightly in my arms and enjoyed what I had prayed for, indeed something to be envied. The affair had not yet reached its climax, when Ascyltos sneaked up to the door, forcefully shattered the bolts, and found me playing with my boy-partner. He filled the little room with laughter and clapping, rolled me out of the bed clothes that covered me, and said: "What are you up to, my most pious partner? What is it? Are you setting up house under the blanket?" Not limiting himself to insults, he took the strap from his bag and began seriously to whip me, adding offensive remarks: "Do not share in this way with your partner." . . .

12. We walked into the market just as it was getting dark and noted a quantity of things for sale, none of them of any great value, just the kind of products whose dubious quality the dim light of evening could most easily conceal.

raptum latrocinio pallium detulissemus, uti occasione op-
portunissima coepimus atque in quodam angulo laciniam
extremam concutere, si quem forte emptorem splendor[38]
3 vestis posset adducere. | nec diu moratus rusticus quidam
familiaris oculis meis cum muliercula comite propius ac-
4 cessit ac diligentius considerare pallium coepit. | invicem
Ascyltos iniecit contemplationem <in tunicam imposi-
tam>[39] super umeros rustici {emptoris}[40] ac subito exani-
5 matus conticuit. | ac ne ipse quidem sine aliquo motu[41]
hominem conspexi, nam videbatur ille mihi esse qui tuni-
6 culam in solitudine invenerat. plane is ipse erat. | sed cum
Ascyltos timeret fidem oculorum, ne quid temere faceret,
prius tamquam emptor propius accessit detraxitque umeris laciniam et diligentius tenuit.[42] 13. o lusum fortunae
mirabilem! nam adhuc nec suturae quidem attulerat
rusticus curiosas manus, sed tamquam mendici spolium
2 etiam fastidiose venditabat. | Ascyltos postquam deposi-
tum esse inviolatum vidit et personam vendentis contemp-
tam, seduxit me paululum a turba et "scis" inquit "frater,
3 rediisse ad nos thesaurum de quo querebar? | illa est tuni-
cula adhuc, ut apparet, intactis aureis plena. quid ergo
4 facimus aut quo iure rem nostram vindicamus?" | exhila-
ratus ego non tantum quia praedam videbam, sed etiam
quod fortuna me a turpissima suspicione dimiserat, negavi
circuitu agendum, sed plane iure civili dimicandum, ut si

38 splendor *l*: splendida
39 *added Müller*
40 *deleted Fraenkel*
41 motu *t*: metu
42 tenuit *L*: temptavit *Burman*

86

As for ourselves, we had brought along the stolen cloak,[23] and proceeded to take advantage of the favorable opportunity to shake out just the very edge of the garment in a corner of the market, hoping that its bright color would attract a chance buyer. Without delay a peasant, who looked familiar to me, and a female companion approached closely and began to examine the cloak carefully. Ascyltos in turn cast a glance at the tunic hanging on the shoulders of the peasant and suddenly stood breathless and quiet. I myself lost some composure at the sight of the man, for he seemed to me to be the very person who had found the tunic out in the country: this was clearly the same man. Ascyltos, afraid to trust his eyes for fear of doing something rash, first drew closer as if he were a customer, then pulled the edge of the tunic from the peasant's shoulders and carefully felt it. 13. What a wonderful stroke of luck: the peasant had not as yet put his prying hands along the seam, and he was advertising the thing for sale in a disdainful manner, as though it were the property of a beggar. Once Ascyltos realized our cache was still untouched and the seller was a nobody, he took me off a little from the crowd and said: "Do you know, partner, the treasure whose loss I was complaining about has come back to us? That is our tunic, and it appears still to be stuffed with our gold coins—they are intact. So what are we going to do about asserting our legal rights over our own property?" I was thrilled not only because I could see the prize, but also because Fortune had cleared me of a loathsome suspicion. I opposed any devious methods and held that civil action should be pursued openly, so that if

23 From a lost episode of the *Satyrica*.

nollet alienam rem domino reddere, ad interdictum veniret. 14. contra Ascyltos leges timebat et "quis" aiebat "hoc
loco nos novit aut quis habebit dicentibus fidem? mihi
plane placet emere, quamvis nostrum sit, quod agnosci-
mus, et ᵠᴸparvo aere recuperare potius thesaurum quam
in ambiguam litem descendere:⁴³ |

2   ᴼᵠᴸquid faciunt leges, ubi sola pecunia regnat
         aut ubi paupertas vincere nulla potest?
       ᴼᴸipsi qui Cynica traducunt tempora pera⁴⁴
         non numquam nummis vendere verba solent.⁴⁵
   5   ᴼᵠᴸergo iudicium nihil est nisi publica merces,
       ᴼᴸatque eques in causa qui sedet empta probat." |

3 ᴸsed praeter unum dipondium {sicel}⁴⁶ lupinosque qui-
4 bus⁴⁷ destinaveramus mercari, nihil ad manum erat. | ita-
que ne interim praeda discederet, vel minoris pallium
addicere placuit et⁴⁸ pretium maioris compendii leviorem
5 facere⁴⁹ iacturam. | cum primum ergo explicuimus mer-
cem, mulier aperto capite, quae cum rustico steterat, in-
spectis diligentius signis iniecit utramque laciniae manum
magnaque vociferatione "latrones tenete"⁵⁰ clamavit. |
6 contra nos perturbati, ne videremur nihil agere, et ipsi
scissam et sordidam tenere coepimus tunicam atque eadem invidia proclamare nostra esse spolia quae illi possi-

---

⁴³ descendere. *L places the next six verses after 13.4* veniret;
Anton transferred them here.   ⁴⁴ pera *Heinsius:* cera
⁴⁵ vendere verba ⟨vera *Y*⟩ solent *Y, L:* verba solent emere
⁴⁶ *deleted Gaselee*³
⁴⁷ ⟨quo⟩ lupinos{que quibus} *Fraenkel*
⁴⁸ et *Bücheler:* ut   ⁴⁹ facere *Bücheler:* faceret
⁵⁰ latrones tenete *r*ᵐᵍ: latrones tenere

the peasant should refuse to hand over property that was not his own, to its rightful owners, then he would be subject to a court order. 14. But Ascyltos objected to my approach because he feared the laws: "Who knows us in this place, or who will believe what we say? Though we have identified the thing as belonging to us, it seems best to me to buy it and recover our valuable property by laying out a few coins rather than to file a lawsuit where the result is uncertain: What can laws do where money alone rules, and where poverty cannot win a thing? Even Cynics[24] who sneer at modern ways are at times not averse to selling their scruples to fatten their purses. So lawsuits turn on nothing more than ordinary bribes, and the knight who sits as juror fixes the amounts at which he can be bought." But we had no ready cash except for a *dupondius*[25] and some stage money with which we intended to engage in trade. So in the meantime to ensure that our stash would not disappear, we decided to knock down the price of our cloak and take a small loss for the sake of a greater gain. As soon as we unrolled our merchandise, the woman standing by the peasant with her head uncovered examined carefully the marks on the cloak, seized the edge with both hands and screamed at the top of her voice: "Grab hold of those thieves!" We were in a panic, but rather than to appear to do nothing, we began to grab at the torn and shabby tunic and to shout back with the same rancor that the goods they held had been plundered from us. But the

[24] The philosophical sect called Cynics, founded by Diogenes in the fourth century, preached that happiness could be achieved only by renouncing all material goods.

[25] *dupondius* = 2 *asses*; stage money = counterfeit.

7 derent. | sed nullo genere par erat causa nostra,[51] et co-
ciones, qui[52] ad clamorem confluxerant, nostram scilicet
de more ridebant invidiam, quod pro illa parte vindica⟨ri-
vide⟩bant[53] pretiossimam vestem, pro hac pannuciam ne
8 centonibus quidem bonis dignam. | hinc Ascyltos repente[54]
risum discussit, qui silentio facto: 15. "videmus"[55] inquit
"suam cuique rem esse carissimam; reddant nobis tunicam
2 nostram et pallium suum recipiant." | etsi rustico mulie-
rique placebat permutatio, advocati tamen importune[56]
nocturni, qui volebant pallium lucri facere, flagitabant uti
apud se utraque deponerentur ac postero die iudex que-
3 relam inspiceret. | neque enim res tantum quae viderentur
in controversiam esse, sed longe aliud quaeri ⟨debere⟩,[57]
quod[58] in utraque parte scilicet latrocinii suspicio habere-
4 tur. | iam sequestri placebant, et nescioquis ex cocionibus,
calvus, tuberosissimae frontis, qui solebat aliquando etiam
causas agere, invaserat pallium exhibiturumque crastino
5 die affirmabat. | ceterum apparebat nihil aliud quaeri nisi
ut semel deposita veste ⟨l⟩is[59] inter praedones strangula-
retur et nos metu criminis non veniremus ad constitutum.
6 | idem plane et nos volebamus. itaque utriusque partis
7 votum casus adiuvit. | indignatus enim rusticus, quod nos
centonem exhibendum postularemus, misit in faciem Ascylti tunicam et liberatos querela iussit pallium deponere,

[51] nostra L: nam l   [52] cociones qui Salmasius: conciones
quae L; the same at 15.4, 8   [53] added Strelitz
[54] repente Müller: p(a)ene
[55] videmus Jungermann: videamus
[56] importune Nisbet: iam pene
[57] added Bailey[2]   [58] quod t[mg]: omit others
[59] veste ⟨l⟩is added Fuchs: veste is l[mg]: vestis

dispute was in no way even, and the dealers who had flocked round because of the noise laughed to be sure, as is there custom, at our madness. For they saw one side demanding the return of an extremely valuable cloak, and the other a ragged tunic not worth patching with good material. At this point Ascyltos suddenly broke up their laughter, and silence ensued: 15. "We see," he said, "that everyone likes his own things best. Let them return the tunic to us and take back their cloak." Even if the peasant and the woman were agreeable to the exchange, nevertheless those serving as night witnesses,[26] who wanted to make a profit out of the cloak, demanded in a bullying fashion that both items be deposited with them and that a judge should look into the dispute the next day. They contended that it was not only a matter of the counterclaims to the garments, but a far greater issue arose, since of course a suspicion of theft fell on both parties. It was agreed that trustees should be appointed, and one of the dealers, a bald man with warts all over his face, who sometimes used to plead cases in court, had made a move to seize the cloak and asserted that he would produce it the next day. But clearly the intent was that once the cloak was deposited with him, the dispute would be choked off by the thieves, and out of fear of being charged with a crime we would not appear for the appointed case. We also wished for the same thing ⟨as the peasant⟩, and as it turned out, both sides got what they hoped for. The peasant, outraged because we demanded that the patched garment would have to be produced in court, threw it in Ascyltos' face, demanding of us, now that we had no grievance, to hand over

[26] The technical status of *nocturni* is unclear.

91

8 quod solum litem faciebat. ‹. . .› | et recuperato, ut puta-
bamus, thesauro in deversorium praecipites abimus prae-
clusisque foribus ridere acumen non minus cocionum
quam calumniantium coepimus, quod nobis ingenti calli-
ditate pecuniam reddidissent. |

9   *ᵩᴸ*nolo quod cupio statim tenere,
        nec victoria mi placet parata.

                        ‹ * * * ›

*ᴼᴸ*16. sed ut primum beneficio Gitonis praeparata nos
implevimus cena, ostium {non}[60] satis audaci strepitu ex-
2 sonuit impulsum. | cum et ipsi ergo pallidi rogaremus quis
esset, "aperi" inquit "iam scies." dumque loquimur, sera
sua sponte delapsa cecidit reclusaeque subito fores admi-
3 serunt intrantem. | mulier autem erat operto capite, illa
scilicet quae paulo ante cum rustico steterat,[61] et "me
derisisse" inquit "vos putabis? ego sum ancilla Quartil-
4 lae, cuius vos sacra[62] ante cryptam turbastis. | ecce ipsa
venit ad stabulum petitque ut vobiscum loqui liceat. nolite
perturbari. nec accusat errorem vestrum nec punit, immo
potius miratur quis deus iuvenes tam urbanos in suam
regionem detulerit." 17. tacentibus adhuc nobis et ad neu-
tram partem assentationem flectentibus intravit ipsa, una
comitata virgine, sedensque super torum meum diu flevit.
2 | ac ne tunc quidem nos ullum adiecimus verbum, sed
attoniti expectavimus lacrimas ad ostentationem doloris

---

[60] *deleted l*ᶜ
[61] illa scilicet . . . steterat *O, L: deleted Jacobs*
[62] sacra *Salmasius:* sacram *or* sacrum

the cloak, the only item now in dispute. . . . After we had, as we thought, regained the treasure, we hurried back to our lodgings. Once the doors were shut, we began to laugh at the shrewdness of the dealers and our accusers alike, because by being hugely cunning they had returned our money to us. "I never want to grasp quickly what I desire; a ready-made victory does not appeal to me." . . .

16. But as soon as we had satisfied our hunger with the dinner kindly prepared for us by Giton, an emphatic knock resounded at the door. We turned pale and asked who was there. "Open the door," a voice said, "and you will soon know who." During the course of this exchange the door bolt fell off of its own accord, and the door, suddenly thrown open, admitted our visitor.[27] It was a woman with a covered head, the same one, to be sure, who a little earlier had accompanied the peasant, and she said: "Were you thinking you'd fooled me? I'm the maid of Quartilla, and it was the performance of her religious rituals in front of the grotto that you interrupted. She's coming in person to your lodgings and asks for the favor of speaking with you. Don't get upset; she's not here to reproach you for your mistake or to punish you. On the contrary, she wonders what deity brought such refined young men to her neighborhood." 17. We had still not uttered a sound, nor had we indicated approval or disapproval of her words, when the lady herself entered with one girl attending, sat down on my bed and burst into a long bout of tears. Even then we did not say a word but waited in amazement for this tearful exhibition of grief to end. Once the ostenta-

---

[27] Epiphany as a literary motif; a priestess of Priapus is about to appear.

3 paratas. | ut ergo tam ambitiosus detumuit[63] imber, retexit
superbum pallio caput et manibus inter se usque ad ar-
4 ticulorum strepitum constrictis | "quaenam est" inquit
"haec audacia, aut ubi fabulas etiam antecessura latrocinia
didicistis? misereor mediusfidius vestri; neque enim im-
5 pune quisquam quod non licuit adspexit. | utique nostra
regio tam praesentibus plena est numinibus ut facilius
6 possis deum quam hominem invenire. | ac ne me putetis
ultionis causa huc venisse, aetate magis vestra commoveor
quam iniuria mea. imprudentes enim, ut adhuc puto, ad-
7 misistis inexpiabile scelus. | ipsa quidem illa nocte vexata
tam periculoso inhorrui frigore ut tertianae etiam impetum timeam. et ideo medicinam somnio[64] petii iussaque
sum vos perquirere atque impetum morbi monstrata sub-
8 tilitate lenire. | sed de remedio non tam valde laboro;
maior enim in praecordiis dolor saevit, qui me usque ad
necessitatem mortis deducit, ne scilicet iuvenili impulsi
licentia quod in sacello Priapi vidistis vulgetis deorumque
9 consilia proferatis in populum. | protendo igitur ad genua
vestra supinas manus petoque et oro ne nocturnas reli-
giones iocum risumque faciatis neve traducere velitis tot
annorum secreta, quae vix mille[65] homines noverunt."

18. secundum hanc deprecationem lacrimas rursus
effudit gemitibusque largis concussa tota facie ac pectore
2 torum meum pressit. | ego eodem tempore et misericordia
turbatus et metu bonum animum habere eam iussi et de
3 utroque esse securam: | nam neque sacra quemquam

[63] detumuit *Gruterus*: detonuit
[64] somnio *r*: somno
[65] mille *O, L*: tres *Nisbet* (iii *for* M)

94

tious show of tears subsided, she uncovered her proud head from her cloak, wringing her hands together until the joints cracked. "Why've you acted so impulsively?" she said. "Where'd you learn about the kind of robberies surpassing even those told about in old stories? The gods know that I'm sorry for you. For no one lives unpunished after having seen forbidden things, especially as our district's so full of bodily-present divinities that it's easier to find a god here than a man. Please don't think I've come here to avenge myself. I'm more concerned about your tender years than the wrongs done to me, for I still believe that it was in thoughtlessness that you committed this unforgivable crime. On that night I was restless, and I shivered from such a dangerous chill that I feared an attack of tertian fever. So I sought a remedy in my dreams and was instructed to seek you out and to alleviate the onslaught of the illness by a clever method that was revealed to me. But it is not the cure that concerns me most. There is a greater grief raging in my heart that has brought me right down to certain death: I fear that in your youthful recklessness you will make public what you saw in the shrine of Priapus, and reveal the workings of the gods' designs to the world outside. So I stretch out my suppliant hands to your knees, begging and pleading with you not to turn our nocturnal rituals into a laughingstock, and not to betray our age-old secrets which are known to barely a thousand people."

18. After this plea she again poured out her tears, and shaking with deep sobs pressed her whole face and breast into my bed. Torn at the same time between sympathy and fear, I encouraged her to take heart and to be comforted about both her concerns: none of us would betray her

vulgaturum, et si quod praeterea aliud remedium ad
tertianam deus illi monstrasset, adiuvaturos nos divinam
4 prudentiam[66] vel periculo nostro. | hilarior post hanc pol-
licitationem facta mulier basiavit me spissius et ex lacrimis
in risum mota descendentes ab aure capillos meos lenta[67]
5 manu duxit | ᴸet "facio" inquit "indutias vobiscum et a
constituta lite dimitto. quod ᴼᴸsi non adnuissetis de hac
medicina quam peto, iam parata erat in crastinum turba
quae et iniuriam meam vindicaret et dignitatem: |

6   ᴼᵠᴸcontemni turpe est, legem donare superbum:
          hoc amo, quod possum qua libet ire via.
       nam sane et sapiens contemptus iurgia nectit,[68]
          et qui non iugulat, victor abire solet." |

〈 * * * 〉

7 ᴼᴸcomplosis deinde manibus in tantum repente risum effusa est ut timeremus. idem ex altera parte et ancilla fecit
quae prior venerat, idem virguncula quae una intraverat.
19. omnia mimico risu exsonuerant, cum interim nos,
quare[69] tam repentina esset mutatio animorum facta,
ignoraremus ac modo nosmet ipsos modo mulieres intue-
remur. |

〈 * * * 〉

2 ᴸ"ideo vetui hodie in hoc deversorio quemquam mortalium admitti, ut remedium tertianae sine ulla interpella-
3 tione a vobis acciperem." | ut haec dixit Quartilla, Ascyltos
quidem paulisper obstupuit, ego autem frigidior hieme
4 Gallica factus nullum potui verbum emittere. | sed ne quid

---

[66] prudentiam *O, lm*: providentiam
[67] lenta *Bongars*: tentata *or* temptata
[68] nectit *s*ᵐᵍ, *t*ᵐᵍ: flectit   [69] quare *Gaselee*³: quae

rituals, and if the god had revealed to her any other additional cure for her fever, we would be ready to assist divine providence, no matter the dangers to us. The woman became more cheerful after this promise, kissed me again and again, and changing tears into laughter, gently stroked the hair falling over my ears. "I'm making a truce with you," she said, "and discharge you from the suit brought against you. But if you hadn't agreed to the remedy I'm after, there's a crowd of men ready for tomorrow to avenge my injuries and vindicate my honor: It's disgraceful to be demeaned, it's insolent to impose the law on me; but I like the fact that I'm able to take any road I choose. Even the wise man weaves combative words intended to harm, if he is offended, and the fighter who is merciful often goes away the victor." . . . Then she clapped her hands and suddenly burst into such a peal of laughter that we were frightened. The maid who had entered first behaved in the same way on the other side of us, and so did the little girl who came in with Quartilla. 19. The whole place rang with the laughter of low mime,[28] and while we were in the dark as to the reason for this sudden change of mood, we kept looking now at each other, now at the women. . . . "Therefore I have given orders that no mortal man be admitted to this lodging today, so that I can get from you the cure for my tertian fever without any interruptions." When Quartilla said this, Ascyltos was struck dumb for a moment, while I had become more frigid than a Gallic winter and could not speak. The com-

[28] A few sections of the *Satyrica* are best read as vulgar mimes.

tristius expectarem, comitatus faciebat. tres enim erant
mulierculae, si quid vellent conari {infirmissimae scili-
cet}[70] contra nos, ⟨quibus⟩[71] si nihil aliud, virilis sexus
5 esset, et[72] praecincti certe altius eramus. | immo ego sic
iam paria composueram, ut si depugnandum foret, ipse
cum Quartilla consisterem, Ascyltos cum ancilla, Giton
cum virgine. |

⟨ * * * ⟩

6 tunc vero excidit omnis constantia attonitis, et mors non
dubia miserorum oculos coepit obducere.

⟨ * * * ⟩

20. "rogo" inquam "domina, si quid tristius paras, celerius confice; neque enim tam magnum facinus admisimus
ut debeamus torti perire." |

⟨ * * * ⟩

2 ancilla quae Psyche vocabatur lodiculam in pavimento
diligenter extendit.

⟨ * * * ⟩

sollicitavit inguina mea mille iam mortibus frigida. |

⟨ * * * ⟩

3 operuerat Ascyltos pallio caput, admonitus scilicet
ᵠᴸpericulosum esse alienis intervenire secretis. |

⟨ * * * ⟩

4 ᴸduas institas ancilla protulit de sinu alteraque pedes nos-
tros alligavit, altera manus. |

⟨ * * * ⟩

5 Ascyltos iam deficiente fabularum contextu "quid ergo?"[73]
6 inquit "non sum dignus qui bibam?" | ancilla risu meo
prodita complosit manus et "apposui quidem ⟨***⟩ adu-
7 lescens, solus tantum medicamentum ebibisti?" | "itane
est?" inquit Quartilla "quicquid satyrii fuit, Encolpius
ebibit?"

⟨ * * * ⟩

position of the company, however, removed any fear from me about expecting worse to come. After all, they were three mere women: if they tried anything against us, whatever else was said about us, at least we were of the male sex, and our clothes were certainly hitched higher than theirs. In fact, I had already worked it out how we would be paired up, so that if we had to fight, I would face Quartilla myself, Ascyltos the maid, and Giton the girl. . . . But then all our courage dissolved in our bewilderment, and certain death began to cover our unhappy eyes. . . .

20. "I ask you, madam," I said, "if you have anything worse in store, do it quickly. Surely we have not committed such a heinous crime that we deserve to be tortured before we die." . . . The maid whose name was Psyche carefully spread a blanket over the hard floor. . . . She molested my genitalia, already cold from a thousand deaths. . . . Ascyltos had pulled his cloak over his head, clearly having been warned that it was dangerous to interfere with other people's secrets. . . . The maid produced two flounces from her dress and tied our feet together with one and our hands with the other. . . . As the thread of our conversation was unraveling, Ascyltos asked: "What about me? Do I not deserve a drink?" The maid, encouraged by my laughter, clapped her hands and said: "But I did set one down next to you . . . Young Encolpius, have you drunk the entire potion by yourself?" Quartilla said: "Did he really? Has Encolpius drunk all the aphrodisiac there was?" . . .

---

70 *deleted Rose*[4]   71 *added Dousa*
72 sexus esset, et *mrtp*: sexus esset, at *l*: sexus. sed et p^{2v}
73 ergo *L*: ego *Goldast*

non indecenti risu latera commovit. |

⟨ * * * ⟩

8 *OL*ac ne Giton quidem ultimo risum tenuit, utique postquam virguncula cervicem eius invasit et non repugnanti
puero innumerabilia oscula dedit.

⟨ * * * * ⟩

*L*21. volebamus miseri exclamare, sed nec in auxilio
erat quisquam, et hinc Psyche acu comatoria cupienti mihi
invocare Quiritum fidem malas pungebat, illinc puella
penicillo, quod et ipsum satyrio tinxerat, Ascylton oppri-
mebat. |

⟨ * * * * ⟩

2 ultimo cinaedus supervenit myrtea subornatus gausapa[74]
cinguloque succinctus ⟨cerasino, qui⟩[75] modo extortis nos
clunibus cecidit, modo basiis olidissimis inquinavit, donec
Quartilla ballaenaceum tenens virgam alteque succincta
iussit infelicibus dari missionem. |

⟨ * * * * ⟩

3 uterque nostrum religiosissimis iuravit verbis inter duos
periturum esse tam horrible secretum. |

⟨ * * * * ⟩

4 intraverunt palaestritae complures[76] et nos legitimo per-
5 fusos oleo refecerunt. | utcumque igitur[77] lassitudine
abiecta cenatoria repetimus et in proximam cellam ducti
sumus, in qua tres lecti strati erant et reliquus lautitiarum
6 apparatus splendidissime expositus. | iussi ergo discubui-
mus, et gustatione mirifica initiati vino etiam Falerno
7 inundamur. | excepti etiam pluribus ferculis cum labere-
mur in somnum, "itane est?" inquit Quartilla "etiam dor-

---

[74] gausapa *Putschius*: gausapia   [75] *added Schmeling*[5]

Her sides shook in a rather captivating way. . . . In the end even Giton did not hold back his laughter, especially after the little girl threw her arms around his neck and gave the compliant boy countless kisses. . . .

21. In our distress we wanted to scream for help, but there was no one to come to our aid. On the one side Psyche was sticking a hairpin into my cheek, whenever I tried to call for help, and on the other the young girl was harassing Ascyltos with a cosmetic brush she had soaked in aphrodisiac. . . . At the end a catamite appeared on the scene, dressed in a myrtle green cloak and hitched up with a cherry colored belt, who first pulled our buttocks apart and beat his way in, then befouled us with the stinkiest kisses, until Quartilla appeared carrying a whalebone staff and, hitching her skirts up high, ordered our release from unhappy service. . . . We both took a solemn oath that such a terrifying secret would die with the two of us. . . . Several gym attendants came in and having rubbed us down with the usual oil, refreshed us. Somehow or other we threw off our fatigue, resumed dressing for dinner and were led into an adjoining room, where three couches had been laid and every other refinement of gracious living had been arranged. So we reclined on the couches as instructed, and beginning with a wonderful hors d'oeuvre, we were also supplied with a stream of wine, even some Falernian. After having been served several main courses, we began to fall asleep, at which Quartilla said: "What's all this? Are you actually thinking about going to sleep, when you know

---

76 complures *Bücheler*: quamplures
77 igitur *L*: ergo *l*

mire vobis in mente est, cum sciatis Priapi genio pervigi-
lium deberi?"

⟨ * * * ⟩

22. cum Ascyltos gravatus tot malis in somnum labere-
tur, illa quae iniuria depulsa fuerat ancilla totam faciem
eius fuligine larga[78] perfricuit et non sentientis latera[79]

2 umerosque sopi{ti}onibus[80] pinxit. | iam ego etiam tot
malis fatigatus minimum veluti gustum hauseram somni;
idem et tota intra forisque familia fecerat, atque alii circa
pedes discumbentium sparsi iacebant, alii parietibus
appliciti, quidam in ipso limine coniunctis marcebant[81]

3 capitibus; | lucernae quoque umore defectae tenue et
extremum lumen spargebant: cum duo Syri expilaturi
{lagoenam}[82] triclinium intraverunt, dumque inter argen-

4 tum avidius rixantur, diductam fregerunt lagoenam. | ce-
cidit etiam mensa cum argento, et ancillae super torum
marcentis excussum forte altius poculum caput fregit. ad
quem ictum exclamavit illa pariterque et fures prodidit et

5 partem ebriorum excitavit. | Syri illi qui venerant ad prae-
dam postquam se deprehensos intellexerunt, pariter secundum lectum conciderunt, ut putares hoc convenisse,
et stertere tamquam olim dormientes coeperunt. |

6 iam et tricliniarches experrectus lucernis occidentibus
oleum infuderat, et pueri detersis paulisper oculis redierant ad ministerium, cum intrans cymbalistra et crepitans
aera omnes excitavit. 23. refectum igitur est convivium et

---

[78] larga *Jungermann*: longa
[79] latera *Delz*: labra
[80] *deleted Vossius*
[81] marcebant *L*: manebant *l*
[82] *deleted Jahn*

that a whole night's vigil is obligatory for the guardian spirit of Priapus?" . . .

22. When Ascyltos, exhausted by so many troubles, was falling asleep, the maid who had been so rudely rejected, rubbed a lot of soot over his face and painted his torso and shoulders with graffiti-like penises without his feeling anything. I too by now was worn out by these evil ordeals and had taken a tiny taste of sleep, as had the whole household of slaves, both those in the room and those outside. Some slaves were lying spread around the feet of the reclining diners, others were propped up against the walls, and still others stayed in the doorway where their heads supported each other. Then too the lamps were running out of oil and spreading a thin dying light, when two Syrians bent on robbing the place entered the dining room. They became overly greedy while quarreling about the silver, and pulled apart a large jug and broke it. The table holding the silver fell over, and a drinking cup, accidently knocked off from a very high shelf, cracked the head of a maid, as she lay drooping over a couch. The blow made her scream, and this both gave away the thieves and woke up some of the drunken company. Once the Syrian thieves who had come for booty understood they were trapped, they dropped together next to a couch, as though this had been their plan all along, and began to snore as if they were asleep for a good while.

By this time the dining-room steward had been awakened and poured oil into the flickering lamps. The slave boys had rubbed their eyes a bit and returned to their duties, when a female cymbal player entered and woke up everyone with her clash of brass. 23. Then the party re-

103

rursus Quartilla ad bibendum revocavit. adiuvit hilarita-
tem comissantis cymbalistria⟨e cantus⟩.[83] |

⟨ * * * ⟩

2 intrat cinaedus, homo omnium insulsissimus et plane illa
domo dignus, qui ut infractis manibus congemuit, eius-
modi carmina effudit: |

3   "huc huc ⟨cito⟩[84] convenite nunc, spatalocinaedi,
       pede tendite, cursum addite, convolate planta,
       femore ⟨o⟩[85] facili, clune agili, {et}[86] manu
              procaces,
       molles, veteres, Deliaci manu recisi." |

4 consumptis versibus suis immundissimo me basio conspuit. mox et super lectum venit atque omni vi detexit
5 recusantem. | super inguina mea diu multumque frustra
moluit. {per}fluebant[87] per frontem sudantis acaciae rivi,
et inter rugas malarum tantum erat cretae, ut putares
detectum parietem nimbo laborare. 24. non tenui ego diutius lacrimas, sed ad ultimam perductus tristitiam "quaeso"
inquam "domina, certe embasicoetan iusseras dari." |
2 complosit illa tenerius manus et "o" inquit "hominem acu-
tum atque urbanitatis vern⟨ac⟩ulae[88] fontem. quid? tu
3 non intellexeras cinaedum embasicoetan vocari?" | deinde
{ut}[89] contubernali meo ⟨ne⟩[90] melius succederet, "per
fidem" inquam "num[91] Ascyltos in hoc triclinio solus ferias
4 agit?" | "ita" inquit Quartilla "et Ascylto embasicoetas
detur." ab hac voce equum cinaedus mutavit transituque

---

[83] *added Bücheler*   [84] *added Luc. Müller*
[85] *added Fraenkel*   [86] *omitted l*   [87] *deleted Müller*
[88] *added Schoppius*   [89] *deleted Fraenkel*
[90] *added Fraenkel*   [91] num *Rose*[4]: nostrum

sumed with Quartilla calling us back to our drinking, and the song of the cymbal player added to the merriment of the reveling priestess. . . . A catamite entered, a most repulsive person and clearly worthy of that house, who snapped his fingers, huffed a bit and then blurted out lines something like these: "This way, here quickly assemble you sodomites, stretch a leg, add some speed, fly here with winged feet and supple thighs, insolent with foppish buttocks and hands, soft youths, old rakes, and those castrated by the hand of Delian Apollo." Once he had delivered his lines, he spit all over me with the most loathsome kisses. He then climbed on to my couch and using all his strength pulled off my coverings in spite of my resistance. Over my genitalia he ground away long and hard to no avail. Streams of cosmetic acacia gum ran down his sweating forehead: there was so much face powder in the wrinkles of his cheeks that you would have thought him an uncovered wall flaking in a rainstorm. 24. I did not hold back my tears any longer, but having been brought to extreme misery said: "Please, lady, surely what you had ordered to be given to me was a lewd mug."[29] At this she clapped her hands daintily and said: "What a clever fellow you are and a fount of natural wit. Hadn't you realized that a catamite is also called a lewd mug?" Then, so that events might not turn out better for my partner than for me, I said: "Be fair. Is Ascyltos the only one in this dining room who gets to enjoy a holiday?" Quartilla said: "Just so. Ascyltos too must be given a lewd mug." After these words the catamite changed

[29] *embasicoetas* is both a drinking vessel in the shape of a phallus, through which revelers could drink wine, thus creating a joke about *fellatio*, and a term for a catamite.

ad comitem meum facto clunibus eum basiisque distrivit.
5 | *OL*stabat inter haec Giton et risu dissolvebat ilia sua. ita-
que conspicata eum Quartilla, cuius esset puer diligentis-
6   sima sciscitatione quaesivit. | cum ego fratrem meum esse
dixissem, "quare ergo" inquit "me non basiavit?" voca-
7   tumque ad se in osculum applicuit. | mox manum etiam
demisit in sinum et pertractato vasculo tam rudi "haec"
inquit "belle cras in promulside libidinis nostrae militabit;
hodie enim post asellum diaria non sumo."

25. cum haec diceret, ad aurem eius Psyche ridens
accessit, et cum dixisset nescioquid, "ita, ita" inquit Quartilla "bene admonuisti. cur non, quia bellissima occasio
2   est, devirginatur Pannychis nostra?" | continuoque pro-
ducta est puella satis bella et quae non plus quam septem
annos habere videbatur, {et}[92] ea ipsa quae primum cum
3   Quartilla in cellam venerat nostram. | plaudentibus ergo
universis et postulantibus nuptias {fecerunt},[93] obstupui
ego et nec Gitona, verecundissimum puerum, sufficere
huic petulantiae affirmavi, nec puellam eius aetatis esse,
4   ut muliebris patientiae legem posset accipere. | "ita" inquit
Quartilla "minor est ista quam ego fui, cum primum virum
passa sum? Iunonem meam iratam habeam, si umquam
5   me meminerim virginem fuisse. | nam et infans cum pari-
bus inquinata sum, et subinde procedentibus[94] annis
maioribus me pueris applicui, donec ad {hanc}[95] aetatem
6   perveni. | hinc etiam puto proverbium natum illud, {ut
dicatur}[96] posse taurum tollere, qui[97] vitulum sustulerit."

---

[92] *deleted Ernout*   [93] *deleted Mommsen*
[94] procedentibus *Brassicanus*: prodeuntibus
[95] *deleted Fraenkel*   [96] *omitted lr, deleted Bücheler*
[97] qui *B*: quae

horses and mounted my partner and ground him down with his buttocks and kisses. While all this was going on, Giton was standing there, splitting his sides in laughter. So Quartilla looked over at him, and with the greatest interest asked whose boy he was. When I replied that he was my boy-partner, she said: "Why then hasn't he kissed me?" She called him to her, kissed him, and then slipped her hand into his underwear and fondled his very immature implement and said: "Tomorrow this'll serve nicely as an hors d'oeuvre to whet my appetite. As I've already taken in a large piece today, I don't want common rations."

25. As she said this, a smiling Psyche approached and whispered something in her ear. "Yes, yes," Quartilla said, "you did well to remind me. This is the perfect moment for it, so why shouldn't our Pannychis surrender her virginity?" Without delay a pretty, young girl was brought in, who seemed no more than seven years old,[30] the same one that earlier had come into the room with Quartilla. While all applauded and demanded a wedding, I was astonished and assured them that Giton, a most modest boy, was not up to such wantonness, nor was the girl old enough to take on the heavy duty of becoming a woman. "Really?" said Quartilla. "Is she any younger than I was when I took on my first man? May Juno strike me down, if ever I remember being a virgin. Already as a child I was made dirty with boys my own age, and as I grew up I turned to older boys until I reached maturity. I think that's how the proverb, 'The one who can carry a calf, can carry a bull,' arose."

[30] Marriage for a seven-year-old girl was unusual but not illegal.

7 | igitur ne maiorem iniuriam in secreto frater acciperet,
consurrexi ad officium nuptiale. 26. iam Psyche puellae
caput involverat flammeo, iam embasicoetas praeferebat
facem, iam ebriae mulieres longum agmen plaudentes
2 fecerant thalamumque incesta exornaverant veste, | cum[98]
Quartilla quoque iocantium libidine accensa et ipsa sur-
3 rexit correptumque Gitona in cubiculum traxit. | sine du-
bio non repugnaverat puer, ac ne puella quidem triste[99]
4 expaverat nuptiarum nomen. | itaque cum inclusi iacerent,
consedimus ante limen thalami, et in primis Quartilla per
rimam improbe diductam[100] applicuerat oculum curiosum
lusumque puerilem libidinosa speculabatur diligentia. |
5 me quoque ad idem spectaculum lenta manu traxit, et quia
considerantium haeserant vultus, quicquid a spectaculo
vacabat, commovebat obiter labra et me tamquam furtivis
subinde osculis verberabat. |

⟨ * * * ⟩

6 [L]abiecti in lectis sine metu reliquam exegimus noctem. |

⟨ * * * ⟩

7 [H]venerat iam tertius dies, id est expectatio liberae cenae, sed tot vulneribus confossis fuga magis placebat
8 quam quies. | itaque cum maesti deliberaremus quonam
genere praesentem evitaremus procellam, unus servus
9 Agamemnonis interpellavit trepidantes et | "quid? vos"

98 cum *Bücheler*: tum
99 triste *Fraenkel*: tristis
100 diductam $l^{mg}t^{mg}$: deductam

---

31 Many of the trappings of this travesty of a wedding are
documented for actual Roman weddings.

Fearing that my boy-partner would suffer greater harm if he went alone, I rose to celebrate the wedding ceremony. 26. By now Psyche had draped a flame colored marriage[31] veil over the girl's head, and the lewd-mug catamite was leading the way with a torch. Clapping their hands, the drunken women had formed a long reception line and adorned the bridal chamber with indecent tapestry. Quartilla herself, aroused by the show of lust of those playing about, rose to her feet, grabbed Giton and dragged him into the bedroom. The boy had obviously offered no resistance, and even the girl was not sad nor had she been frightened at the name of marriage. And so when they were shut in and lying down, we sat at the threshold of the wedding chamber. Quartilla quickly attached her wanton eye to a chink in the door she had wickedly slit and spied with prurient interest on their childish play. With a gentle hand she dragged me down to watch the same spectacle, and since our faces were close together as we watched, whenever there was a moment she could spare from the show, she moved her lips on to mine and beat me as it were with stolen kisses. . . . We threw ourselves into bed and spent the rest of the night without fear. . . .

The third day had come, and that meant a free dinner[32] was in prospect, but we were stabbed by so many wounds and preferred flight to relaxation. While in our sad state we were planning how we might avoid the coming storm, one of Agamemnon's servants intruded into our unsettled affairs and asked: "What's going on? Don't you know at

[32] *liberae cenae*. This does not refer to the upcoming banquet of Trimalchio, but to the meal served to men the night before they were to face wild beasts in the arena, that is, their last meal.

inquit "nescitis, hodie apud quem fiat? Trimalchio, lautissimus homo, ⟨qui⟩[101] horologium in triclinio et bucinatorem habet subornatum, ut subinde sciat quantum de vita

10 perdiderit." | amicimur ergo dilgenter obliti omnium malorum, et Gitona libentissime servile officium tuentem {usque hoc}[102] iubemus in balneum[103] sequi.

27. nos interim vestiti errare coepimus, immo iocari magis et circulis ludentium[104] accedere, cum subito *HL*videmus senem calvum, tunica vestitum russea, inter pueros

2 capillatos ludentem pila. | nec tam pueri nos, quamquam erat operae pretium, ad spectaculum duxerant, quam ipse pater familiae, qui soleatus pila prasina exercebatur. nec amplius eam repetebat quae terram contigerat, sed follem

3 plenum habebat servus sufficiebatque ludentibus. | notavimus enim res novas. nam duo spadones in diversa parte circuli stabant, quorum alter matellam tenebat argenteam, alter numerabat pilas, non quidem eas quae inter manus nisu[105] expellente vibrabant, sed eas quae in terram

4 decidebant. | cum has ergo miraremur lautitias, *H*accurrit Menelaus et "hic est" inquit "apud quem cubitum poni-

5 tis, et quidem[106] iam principium cenae videtis." | et iam

---

101 *added Schmeling*[5]   102 *deleted Heraeus*
103 balneum *Bücheler*: balneo
104 ludentium *Heinsius*: ludentem
105 nisu *Jahn*: lusu *H*: luxu *L*
106 quidem *Bücheler*: quid

---

33 The host of the *Cena* and the chief actor of chapters 26 to 78. His name means thrice-king. Encolpius does not know the host because he and his partners are attending the banquet as *umbrae* (ghosts), that is, guests not invited by the host but by

whose house you're dining today? Trimalchio[33] is your host. He's a most refined man: he has a water clock in his dining room, and a trumpeter who's always in uniform, so that he constantly knows how much of his life he's lost." We forgot about all our troubles and dressed carefully. We told Giton, who had very willingly assumed the role of servant, to follow us to the baths.

27. Already dressed in our dinner clothes, we began meanwhile to stroll about, or rather to joke to one another, as we came upon a group doing exercises. All of a sudden we noticed an old bald man, dressed in a red shirt and playing ball with some long-haired boys. Although these deserved closer inspection, it was the head of the house who got our attention: he was wearing house slippers and throwing around green balls.[34] If a ball hit the ground, he did not pick it up, but a slave with a bagful of balls supplied them to the players.[35] We observed some new features in the game: two eunuchs stood at different points of the circle of players, one held a silver chamber pot, and the other counted the balls, not those flying from hand to hand and vigorously thrown, but those which fell to the ground. While we stood and marveled at the display of luxury, Menelaus[36] hurried toward us and said: "This is your host, and it is his table where you will put your elbows. In fact you are witnessing the beginning of the banquet." Mene-

someone like Agamemnon, a frequent diner at Trimalchio's table and permitted to invite guests.

[34] The use of colors in the *Cena* of Trimalchio is notable.

[35] This game might be *lusus trigo*, in which players form a triangle and throw a ball.

[36] An assistant of Agamemnon.

non loquebatur Menelaus, cum ^{HL'}Trimalchio digitis[107]
concrepuit, ad quod signum matellam spado ludenti sub-
6 iecit. | exonerata ille vescia aquam poposcit ad manus,
digitosque paululum adspersos in capite pueri tersit.
28. longum erat singula excipere. itaque intravimus
balneum, et sudore calfacti momento temporis ad frigi-
2 dam eximus. | iam Trimalchio unguento perfusus tergeba-
3 tur, non linteis, sed palliis ex lana mollissima factis. | tres
interim iatraliptae in conspectu eius Falernum potabant,
^Het cum plurimum rixantes effunderent, Trimalchio hoc
4 suum propin esse[108] dicebat. | ^{HL}hinc involutus coccina
gausapa lecticae impositus est praecedentibus phaleratis
cursoribus quattuor et chiramaxio, in quo deliciae eius
vehebantur, puer vetulus, lippus, domino Trimalchione
5 deformior. | cum ergo auferretur, ad caput eius cum mini-
mis symphoniacus tibiis accessit et tamquam in aurem
aliquid secreto diceret, toto itinere cantavit. |
6 sequimur nos admiratione iam saturi et cum Agamem-
none ad ianuam pervenimus, ^Hin cuius poste libellus erat
7 cum hac inscriptione fixus: | "quisquis servus sine domi-
8 nico iussu foras exierit, accipiet plagas centum." | ^{HL}in
aditu autem ipso stabat ostiarius prasinatus, cerasino suc-
cinctus cingulo, atque in lance argentea pisum purgabat. |

---

[107] digitis *Schmeling*[5]: digitos
[108] propin esse *Heraeus*: propinasse

---

[37] According to Suetonius (*Ner.* 30), among the escorts
around the emperor were men dressed in such a fashion. Trimalchio imitates imperial customs, but Petronius does not parody
Nero, an unhealthy thing to do.
[38] His name is Croesus; cf. ch. 64.5.

laus was just finishing speaking, when Trimalchio snapped his fingers, at which signal a eunuch held the chamber pot for him, as he proceeded to play. Once his bladder had been emptied, he called for some water to clean his hands, put a little on his fingers and then wiped them on the boy's head.

28. It would be tiresome to go through everything that happened. Anyway we entered the baths proper, and once we had begun to sweat, we moved on quickly to the cold water. Trimalchio, already doused with perfumed oil, was now being rubbed down, not with linen but with the softest woolen towels. Meanwhile his three physiotherapists were drinking Falernian wine right before his eyes, and as they were quarreling, they spilled a lot, but Trimalchio announced that they were really pouring an aperitif to his health. He was then wrapped in a scarlet gown and placed in a litter. Four couriers decked out in medals[37] preceded him, as did his little darling,[38] who was conveyed in a handcart, a shriveled-looking bleary-eyed youngster, uglier than his master. As Trimalchio was carried off, a musician holding tiny pipes played close to his head and accompanied him the whole way, as if he were whispering secrets in his ear.

Awestruck we followed him and with Agamemnon approached the dining-room door, on the post of which a notice had been attached:

ANY SLAVE LEAVING THE HOUSE
WITHOUT HIS MASTER'S PERMISSION
WILL RECEIVE ONE HUNDRED LASHES

Right at the entrance stood a porter dressed in green, girded up with a cherry-colored belt, shelling peas in a

9 super limen autem cavea pendebat aurea, in qua pica varia
intrantes salutabat. 29. ceterum ego dum omnia stupeo,
paene resupinatus crura mea fregi. ad sinistram enim in-
trantibus non longe ab ostiarii cella canis ingens, catena
vinctus, in pariete erat pictus superque quadrata littera
2 scriptum "cave canem." | et collegae quidem mei riserunt,
ego autem collecto spiritu non destiti totum parietem per-
3 sequi. | erat autem venalicium <cum>[109] titulis pictum, et
ipse Trimalchio capillatus caduceum tenebat Minervaque
4 ducente Romam intrabat. | hinc quemadmodum ratioci-
nari didicisset dein<de>que[110] dispensator factus esset,
omnia diligenter curiosus pictor cum inscriptione reddi-
5 derat. | in deficiente vero iam porticu levatum mento in
6 tribunal excelsum Mercurius rapiebat. | praesto erat For-
tuna <cum>[111] cornu abundanti {copiosa}[112] et tres Parcae
7 aurea pensa torquentes. | notavi etiam in porticu gregem
8 cursorum cum magistro se exercentem. | praeterea grande
armarium in angulo vidi, in cuius aedicula erant Lares
argentei positi Venerisque signum marmoreum et pyxis
aurea non pusilla, in qua barbam ipsius conditam esse
9 dicebant. | interrogare ergo atriensem coepi, quas in me-
dio picturas haberet.[113] "Iliada et Odyssian" inquit *H*"ac
Laenatis gladiatorium munus." 30. non licebat ultimas
etiam[114] considerare. <. . .> nos *HL*iam ad triclinium per-

---

[109] *added Burman*   [110] *added Schmeling*   [111] *added Wehle*
[112] *deleted Goesius*   [113] haberet *Deroux*: haberent
[114] ultimas etiam *Rose*[1]: multaciam *H*: multa etiam *Scheffer*

---

[39] Several chained large dogs are painted on walls or set in
floor mosaics at Pompeii with the words *cave canem*.
[40] The deity who watches over businessmen like Trimalchio.

114

silver dish. Over the doorway hung a golden cage, inside which was a dappled magpie that greeted all those entering. 29. As I stood gaping at all of this, I almost fell flat on my back and broke my legs. To our left as we went in and not far from the porter's room was a wall painting of a huge dog[39] tied with a chain, and over it in big capitals was written: BEWARE OF THE DOG. My companions laughed at me, but when I got my breath back, I proceeded to inspect the entire wall. There was a mural of a slave market with an inscription of prices and names. Trimalchio himself was portrayed with long hair and holding a caduceus of Mercury,[40] escorted by Minerva, and entering Rome. After this the painstaking and careful painter had depicted with commentary below the pictures, all the details of how Trimalchio had learned accounting and then been made steward. Just where the colonnade ended Mercury hauled him up by the chin and was taking him to a high dais; Fortune with her horn of plenty and the three Fates spinning out their golden threads stood nearby. Also in the colonnade I noticed a group of runners practicing with their trainer, and in a corner I saw a large cabinet that contained a small shrine, in which were the silver household gods, a marble figure of Venus, and a large golden box holding, they said, the master's beard.[41] So I proceeded to ask the porter about the subjects of the other pictures on exhibit. He replied: "The *Iliad*, the *Odyssey*, and the gladiatorial show put on by Laenas." 30. It was impossible actually to inspect those at the end. . . . We now

[41] Suetonius (*Ner.* 12) notes that Nero preserved his own beard. Romans had such a custom but not Asians like Trimalchio, who here apes his local betters.

veneramus, in cuius parte prima procurator rationes acci-
piebat. et quod praecipue miratus sum, in postibus triclinii
fasces erant cum securibus fixi, quorum imam[115] partem
quasi embolum navis aeneum finiebat, in quo erat scrip-
2 tum: | "C.[116] Pompeio Trimalchioni, seviro Augustali,
3 Cinnamus dispensator." | sub eodem titulo et lucerna bi-
lychnis de camera pendebat, et duae tabulae ‹erant›[117] in
utroque poste defixae, quarum altera, si bene memini, hoc
habebat inscriptum: "III et pridie Kalendas Ianuarias C.
4 noster foras cenat," | altera lunae cursum stellarumque
septem imagines pictas; et qui dies boni quique incom-
modi essent, distinguente bulla notabantur. |
5 [H]his repleti voluptatibus cum conaremur {in}[118] triclinium intrare, exclamavit unus ex pueris, qui supra hoc
6 officium erat positus: "dextro pede." | sine dubio paulisper
trepidavimus, ne contra praeceptum aliquis nostrum li-
7 men transiret. | [HL]ceterum ut pariter movimus dextros
gressus, servus nobis despoliatus procubuit ad pedes ac
rogare coepit ut se poenae eriperemus: nec magnum esse

---

115 imam $m^{mg}p^2$: unam   116 C. *Burman*: CH. *H, l*
117 *added Schmeling*[5]
118 *deleted Schmeling*[5]

---

42 Bundles of rods and axes are consular insignia to which
Trimalchio is not entitled, but he displays them anyway; the beak
of a ship would belong to a victorious admiral; the rank of *sevir*
was low but the highest hope of a former slave such as Trimalchio.
A *sevir Augustalis* (*sevir* = one of six men) was a local official
responsible for seeing to the worship of the emperor.

43 Sun, Earth, Mercury, Venus, Mars, Jupiter, Saturn. Trimalchio is portrayed as someone obsessed with astrology, supersti-

had gone through to the dining room, at the entrance of which sat the steward, approving accounts. I was especially astonished to see a bundle of rods and axes attached to the doorposts of the dining room, held up from below by something like a bronze beak of a ship,[42] and showing this inscription:

> TO GAIUS POMPEIUS TRIMALCHIO
> SEVIR OF THE COLLEGE OF AUGUSTUS
> PRESENTED BY HIS STEWARD CINNAMUS

A two-armed lamp also bearing the same inscription hung from the ceiling, and on each doorpost there was attached a notice. If I remember right, one of them had this inscription:

> OUR GAIUS DINES OUT ON THE
> 30TH AND 31ST OF DECEMBER

The other displayed the phases of the moon and representation of the seven stars.[43] Lucky and unlucky days were marked with distinctive indicators.

When we had enough of these delights, we attempted to enter the dining room, but one of the slaves, who was assigned this job at the entrance, shouted out: "Right foot first." For a moment, of course, we hesitated, in case someone of us should break the house rule about crossing the threshold. But just as all of us together were stepping forward with our right feet, a slave who had been stripped for flogging fell at our feet and began pleading with us to rescue him from punishment. What he had done to get in

tions (e.g., entering rooms right foot first), and premonitions of death.

117

8   peccatum suum, propter quod periclitaretur; | subducta
    enim sibi vestimenta dispensatoris in balneo, quae vix
9   fuissent $\bar{X}$ [119] sestertiorum. | rettulimus ergo dextros pedes
    dispensatoremque in atrio[120] aureos numerantem depre-
10 cati sumus, ut servo remitteret poenam. | superbus ille
    sustulit vultum et "non tam iactura me movet" inquit
11 "quam neglegentia nequissimi servi. | vestimenta mea
    cubitoria perdidit, quae mihi natali meo cliens quidam
    donaverat, Tyria sine dubio, sed iam semel lota. quid ergo
    est? dono vobis eum." 31. obligati tam grandi beneficio
    cum intrassemus triclinium, occurrit nobis ille idem ser-
    vus, pro quo rogaveramus, et stupentibus spississima basia
2   impegit gratias agens humanitati nostrae. | "ad summam,
    statim scietis" ait "cui dederitis beneficium. vinum domi-
    nicum ministratoris gratia est." |
3   tandem ergo discubuimus pueris Alexandrinis aquam
    in manus nivatam infundentibus aliisque insequentibus ad
    pedes ac paronychia cum ingenti subtilitate tollentibus. |
4   ac ne in hoc quidem tam molesto tacebant officio, sed
5   obiter cantabant. | ego experiri volui an tota familia can-
6   taret, itaque potionem poposci. | paratissimus puer non
    minus me acido cantico excepit, et quisquis aliquid roga-
7   tus erat ut daret: | pantomimorum chorum,[121] non patris

---

[119] $\bar{X}$ (= dena sestertia) *l*: decem
[120] atrio *Heinsius*: precario *H*, *L*: oecario *Heraeus*
[121] pantomimorum chorum *Schmeling*: pantomimi chorum

---

[44] An exorbitant amount, but the use of monetary figures by
Trimalchio, his staff, and his friends goes past exaggeration into
the realm of fantasy.

trouble, he said, was just a trifling offense: the steward's clothes had been stolen from him in the baths, but the garments were worth less than ten thousand sesterces.[44] So we stepped back with our right feet and appealed to the steward, who meanwhile was counting out gold coins in his office, to grant the slave remission. The arrogant man raised his head: "It's not so much the actual loss that bothers me," he said, "as that worthless slave's carelessness. He lost the dinner clothes that had been given to me for my birthday by one of my dependents. Of course they were genuine Tyrian purple, but had already been cleaned once. What's the big deal? I forgive him for your sake."[45] 31. Because of such great kindness we were in his debt, and when we entered the dining room, the same slave for whom we had pleaded ran up to us and to our amazement forced a rain of kisses on us and thanked us for our good deed. "In short," he said, "you'll soon know the kind of man to whom you gave your favor: 'The master's wine is in the butler's gift.'"

At last we reclined on the couches. Some young Alexandrian slaves poured snow-cooled water over our hands, while others went for our feet and with great skill pared our hangnails. Even in this unpleasant duty they were not silent but sang while they worked. I wanted to find out if the whole household could sing, so I asked for a drink. A slave was immediately ready and repeated my order in a shrill voice, as did any slave who was asked to do something: you would have thought it was a troupe of mimes

[45] This scene has been preplanned, and the reader will witness throughout the *Cena* not so much a dinner as a dinner theater.

8 familiae triclinium crederes. | allata est tamen gustatio
valde lauta; nam iam omnes discubuerant praeter unum
Trimalchionem, cui locus novo more primus servabatur. |
9 ceterum in promulsidari asellus erat Corinthius cum bi-
saccio positus, qui habebat olivas in altera parte albas, in
10 altera nigras. | tegebant asellum duae lances, in quarum
marginibus nomen Trimalchionis inscriptum erat et argenti pondus. ponticuli etiam ferruminati sustinebant
11 glires melle ac papavere sparsos. | fuerunt et thumatula[122]
ferventia[123] supra craticulam argenteam posita, et infra
craticulam Syriaca pruna cum granis Punici mali.

32. in his eramus lautitiis, cum ipse Trimalchio ad symphoniam allatus est positusque inter cervicalia minutis-
2 sima expressit imprudentibus risum. | pallio enim cocci-
neo adrasum exeruerat[124] caput circaque oneratas veste
cervices laticlaviam immiserat mappam fimbriis hinc at-
3 que illinc pendentibus. | habebat etiam in minimo digito
sinistrae manus anulum grandem subauratum, extremo
vero articulo digiti sequentis minorem, ut mihi videbatur,
totum aureum, sed plane ferreis veluti stellis ferrumina-
4 tum. | et ne has tantum ostenderet divitias, dextrum nuda-

122 thumatula *H, Bodel*[2]: tomacula
123 ferventia *placed here* t[mg]: *placed before* argenteam *H, L*
124 exeruerat *Stöcker*: excluserat *H*: incluserat *L*

46 This place at the three tables of the triclinium is called
summus in summo; normally the host sat at *summus in imo*; cf.
Luke 14:10: "But when you are invited, go and sit in the lowest
place, so that when your host comes he may say to you, 'Friend,
go up higher.'" See Appendix.

and not the attractions of a gentleman's dining room. All the same an exquisite hors d'oeuvre was brought out, for all the guests had taken their places on the couches except for Trimalchio himself, for whom in the new fashion the highest place[46] was being reserved. In the tray for serving hors d'oeuvres had been placed a Corinthian bronze donkey with panniers, one holding white olives on one side and black on the other. Set above the donkey were two dishes, on the rims of which were engraved the name of Trimalchio and the weight of the silver. Little bridges were soldered between the dishes, which held dormice dipped in honey and sprinkled with poppy seed. There were also hot sausages sprinkled with thyme lying on a silver grill, and beneath the grill damsons with pomegranate seeds.

32. We were in the midst of these delicacies, when Trimalchio himself was carried in to the sound of music. The spectacle of him propped up among a bunch of the tiniest pillows elicited laughter from the unwary, for he had poked his shaven head out from his scarlet cloak, and around his neck overloaded with clothes, had thrown a napkin with a broad purple stripe[47] and fringes hanging from it all round. On the little finger of his left hand he wore an enormous gilt ring and a smaller one on the top joint of the next finger, which seemed to me to be solid gold, but was clearly studded with iron star-shapes.[48] Not content with this display of wealth, he bared his right arm

[47] The broad purple stripe indicated senatorial rank, but Trimalchio gets around the restrictions of the custom by putting the stripe on his napkin and not on his tunic.

[48] Gold rings are worn by members of the order of *equites* = knights, and Trimalchio apes them but not too closely.

vit lacertum armilla aurea cultum et eboreo circulo lamina
splendente conexo.[125] 33. ut deinde pinna argentea dentes
perfodit, "amici," inquit "nondum mihi suave erat in triclinium venire, sed ne diutius absens morae vobis essem,[126]

2 omnem voluptatem mihi negavi. | permittitis tamen finiri
lusum." sequebatur puer cum tabula terebinthina et crys-
tallinis tesseris, notavique rem omnium delicatissimam.
pro calculis enim albis ac nigris aureos argenteosque
habebat denarios. |

3 interim dum ille omnium textorum dicta inter lusum
consumit, gustantibus adhuc nobis repositorium allatum
est cum corbe, in quo gallina erat lignea patentibus in

4 orbem alis, quales esse solent quae incubant ova. | acces-
sere continuo duo servi et symphonia strepente scrutari
paleam coeperunt erutaque subinde pavonina ova divisere

5 convivis. | convertit ad hanc scaenam Trimalchio vultum
et "amici," ait "pavonis ova gallinae iussi supponi. et
mehercules timeo ne iam concepti[127] sint; temptemus ta-

6 men, si adhuc sorbilia sunt." | accipimus nos cochlearia
non minus selibras pendentia ovaque ex farina pingui figu-

7 rata pertundimus. | ego quidem paene proieci partem

8 meam, nam videbatur mihi iam in pullum coisse. | deinde
ut audivi veterem convivam: "hic nescioquid boni debet
esse," persecutus putamen manu pinguissimam ficedulam
inveni piperato vitello circumdatam.

[125] conexo *Bücheler*: connexum

[126] triclinium . . . absens *H* . . . essem *Heinsius*: triclinium
absens more vobis venire sed ne diutius absenti vos essem *H*

[127] concepti *H*: concepta

adorned with a golden bracelet and an ivory bangle clasped with a plate of bright metal. 33. Then as he dug round his teeth with a silver toothpick, he said: "My friends, it was not yet convenient for me to come to the dining room, but I didn't wish my absence to delay you any longer, and so I've denied myself all pleasure. Permit me, however, to finish the game." A slave boy with a terebinth board and crystal dice followed him, and I noticed a most fastidious element: in the place of white and black counters he used *aurei* and silver *denarii*.[49]

During the course of the game he used up all the common swearwords. While we were eating the hors d'oeuvres, a large platter was brought in holding a basket, in which there was a wooden hen with its wings spread in a circle, just as hens are accustomed to do when brooding over eggs. Two slaves at once came up and to the roaring sound of music began to hunt in the straw. They immediately drew out peahens' eggs and distributed them to the guests. Trimalchio turned his face to this staged scene and said: "My friends, I ordered a peahen's eggs to be placed under the hen. And by god I'm afraid that now they're ready to hatch. Let's test, however, whether they're still fresh enough to suck." We grabbed spoons weighing not less than half a pound and perforated the eggs which were made of fine flour. I almost threw away my portion, for it seemed to me that it had formed into a chick, but then I heard an experienced guest say: "I don't know what, but there's something good in this." I poked through the shell with my finger and found a very fat fig pecker, coated in peppered egg yolk.

[49] 1 *aureus* (gold) coin = 25 *denarii* (silver).

34. iam Trimalchio eadem omnia lusu intermisso po-
poscerat feceratque potestatem clara voce, si quis nostrum
iterum vellet mulsum sumere, cum subito signum symphonia datur et gustatoria pariter a choro cantante rapiun-
2 tur. | ceterum inter tumultum cum forte paropsis excidis-
set et puer iacentem sustulisset, animadvertit Trimalchio
colaphisque obiurgari puerum ac proicere rursus paropsi-
3 dem iussit. | insecutus est lecticarius[128] argentumque inter
4 reliqua purgamenta scopis coepit everrere.[129] | [H]subinde
intraverunt duo Aethiopes capillati cum pusillis utribus,
quales solent habere[130] qui harenam in amphitheatro spar-
gunt, vinumque dedere in manus; aquam enim nemo por-
5 rexit. | [HL]laudatus propter elegantias dominus "aequum"
inquit "Mars amat. itaque iussi[131] suam cuique mensam
assignari. obiter et putidissimi[132] servi minorem nobis aes-
6 tum frequentia sua facient." | statim allatae sunt amphorae
vitreae diligenter gypsatae, quarum in cervicibus pittacia
erant affixa cum hoc titulo: "Falernum Opimianum anno-
7 rum centum." | dum titulos perlegimus, complosit Trimal-
chio manus et "eheu"[133] inquit "ergo diutius vivit [H]vinum
quam homuncio. quare tangomenas faciamus. [HL]vita vinum est.[134] verum Opimianum praesto. heri non tam bo-
8 num posui, et multo honestiores cenabant." | potantibus
ergo <nobis> et accuratissime {nobis}[135] lautitias miranti-

---

[128] <supel>lecticarius *conjectured Dousa*
[129] everrere *Goesius*: verrere   [130] habere *Braswell*: esse
[131] iussi *Burman*: iussit
[132] putidissimi *Heinsius*: pudissimi
[133] eheu *Heinsius*: heheu
[134] vinum vita est *Goesius, editors*
[135] nobis *transposed Bücheler*

34. Trimalchio had by now broken off the game, asked for all the same dishes, and in a loud voice had given an opportunity to any of us who wished, to take a second glass of sweetened wine. Suddenly a signal was given by the music, and all the hors d'oeuvres were taken away simultaneously by a singing troupe of servants. But in all the confusion, when a serving dish happened to fall and a servant boy had picked it up from the floor, Trimalchio noticed him and ordered that his ears be boxed and that he should throw the dish down again. A litter bearer followed and with a broom began to sweep out the silver dish with the rest of the rubbish. Then two long-haired Ethiopians moved in with little wineskins, just like the men who moisten the sand in the amphitheater, and gave us wine for our hands, for no one offered us water. After our host was praised for the elegant arrangements, he said: "Mars loves a fair playing field, and so I gave orders for each guest to be assigned his own table. In that way really stinking slaves will make us less hot by crowding round." Just then some glass wine jars carefully sealed with gypsum were brought in, with labels fastened to their necks, inscribed: "Falernian wine of Opimius' vintage,[50] one hundred years old." As we were reading through the labels, Trimalchio clapped his hands and said: "It's sad, but wine lives longer than miserable man. So let's drink our fill. Life goes best with wine. I'm serving genuine Opimian wine. Yesterday I offered not such good wine, and the guests at dinner were of a better class." As we drank the wine and commented in detail on the luxurious appointments, a

[50] Opimius was consul in 121 BC.

bus larvam argenteam attulit servus sic aptatam, ut articuli
eius vertebraeque luxatae[136] in omnem partem flecteren-
9 tur. | hanc cum super mensam semel iterumque abiecisset
et catenatio mobilis aliquot figuras exprimeret, Trimalchio
adiecit: |

10   *HφL*"eheu nos miseros, quam totus homuncio nil est!
   sic erimus cuncti, postquam nos auferet Orcus.
   ergo vivamus, dum licet esse bene."

*HL*35. laudationem ferculum est insecutum plane non
pro expectatione magnum; novitas tamen omnium conver-
2 tit oculos. | rotundum enim repositorium duodecim habe-
bat signa in orbe disposita, super quae[137] proprium conve-
3 nientemque materiae structor imposuerat cibum: | super
Arietem cicer arietinum, super Taurum bubulae frustum,
super Geminos testiculos ac rienes, super Cancrum coro-
nam, super Leonem ficum Africanam, super Virginem
4 steriliculam, | super Libram stateram in cuius altera parte
scriblita erat, in altera placenta, *H*super Scorpionem {pis-
ciculum marinum}[138] ‹locustam marinam›,[139] *HL*super
Sagittarium oclopectam,[140] super Capricornum {locustam
marinam} ‹caprum et cornutam›,[141] super Aquarium an-
5 serem, super Pisces duos mullos. | in medio autem caespes
6 cum herbis excisus favum sustinebat. | circumferebat
Aegyptius puer clibano argenteo panem, atque ipse etiam
taeterrima voce de Laserpiciario mimo canticum extorsit.

136 luxatae *Heinsius; cf. Plin. NH* 30.79: laxatae
137 super quae *Casaubonus:* superque   138 *deleted Gaselee*[2]
139 locustam marinam *transposed Gaselee*[2]
140 oclopectam *Heraeus:* oclopetam *H:* odopetam *L*
141 *added Rose–Sullivan*

slave brought in a silver skeleton,[51] so constructed that its joints and spine, being loosely fitted, could be turned in all directions. When he had thrown it down on the table several times, and the supple sections showed various postures, Trimalchio commented: "Alas, we're sad creatures, poor man's all nothing. Thus we'll all be, after Orcus takes us away. Therefore let's enjoy life, while we can live well."

35. A dish, certainly not as large as expected, followed after our praise of Trimalchio's verses. Its novelty, however, turned the eyes of all toward it. The circular tray had the twelve signs of the Zodiac in sequence round it, and over each of them the chef had laid appropriate food matching the sign.[52] Over Aries he had set chickpeas fashioned into rams' heads; over Taurus a piece of beef; over Gemini testicles and kidneys; over Cancer a crown; over Leo an African fig; over Virgo a barren sow's womb; over Libra a scale on one arm of which was a cheese cake and on the other a honey cheese cake; over Scorpio a lobster; over Sagittarius a bird that aims at the eye; over Capricorn a boar fish and horned fish; over Aquarius a goose; over Pisces two mullets. In the middle of the tray a piece of turf, hewn out with its blades of grass, supported a honeycomb. An Egyptian slave boy carried round bread in a silver portable oven, and the master himself in a most hideous voice mangled a song out of the mime *Laserpi-*

[51] Skeletons were brought to banquets to remind the guests that death awaits everyone, and therefore they should enjoy the moment. Skeletons appear in paintings of banquet scenes.

[52] The dish with the astrological signs reinforces the impression of Trimalchio's superstitious nature.

7 | nos ut tristiores ad tam viles accessimus cibos, "suadeo" inquit Trimalchio "cenemus; hoc est ius cenae." 36. haec ut dixit, ad symphoniam quattuor tripudiantes procurre-

2 runt superioremque partem repositorii abstulerunt. | quo facto videmus infra scilicet in altero ferculo altilia et sumina leporemque in medio pinnis subornatum, ut Pega-

3 sus videretur. | notavimus etiam circa angulos repositorii Marsyas quattuor, ex quorum utriculis garum piperatum

4 currebat super pisces, qui quasi in euripo natabant. | da-mus omnes plausum a familia inceptum et res electissimas

5 ridentes aggredimur. | non minus et Trimalchio eiusmodi

6 methodio laetus "Carpe" inquit. | processit statim scissor et ad symphoniam gesticulatus ita laceravit obsonium, ut

7 putares essedarium hydraule cantante pugnare. | ingere-bat nihilo minus Trimalchio lentissima voce: "Carpe, Carpe." ego suspicatus ad aliquam urbanitatem totiens iteratam vocem pertinere, non erubui eum qui supra me

8 accumbebat hoc ipsum interrogare. | at ille, qui saepius eiusmodi ludos spectaverat, "vides illum" inquit "qui obso-nium carpit: Carpus vocatur. itaque quotienscumque dicit 'Carpe,' eodem verbo et vocat et imperat."

    37. non potui amplius quicquam gustare, sed conversus ad eum, ut quam plurima exciperem, longe accersere fa-bulas coepi, sciscitarique quae esset mulier illa, quae huc

2 atque illuc discurreret. | "uxor" inquit "Trimalchionis, For-

3 tunata appellatur, quae nummos modio metitur. | et modo

---

[53] *Carpe* is the vocative of the slave's name as well as the im-perative of the verb *carpere* (to carve).

[54] Hermeros sits at *imus in summo*.

128

ciarius. With rather sour faces we approached such cheap fare, and Trimalchio said: "I encourage you to eat up. This is the sauce of the dinner." 36. As he spoke, four three-step dancers ran up in time with the music and removed the top part of the tray. Once this had been done, we saw below in another dish fat fowls, sows' udders, and in the middle a hare decked out with wings to look like Pegasus. We noticed also four representations of Marsyas at the corners of the dish, from whose wineskins a peppery fish sauce ran over the fish that were swimming as if in a channel. We all joined in the clapping which the slaves had begun, and with big smiles attacked the choice delicacies. No less was Trimalchio pleased with the trick and said: "Carver!" The carver at once came forward, and making wild motions in time to the music, cut up the meat in such a way that you would have thought he was a chariot-gladiator fighting to the accompaniment of a water-organist. In a very slow voice Trimalchio all the same continued to duplicate the word: "Carve 'er, Carver!" I suspected that so much repetition belonged to a sophisticated joke, so I did not blush to question the man who reclined just above me. He had often seen performances of this kind and said: "You see the fellow carving the meat? His name's Carver, so whenever Trimalchio says 'Carver,'[53] with the same word he both names the man and gives instructions."

37. I was not able to eat anything more but turned to my neighbor[54] to learn as much as possible. I began to ask about all the gossip and to inquire who that woman was who kept running to and fro. "That's Trimalchio's wife, Fortunata," he said, "and she measures her money by the bushel. Yet just a little while ago, what was she? You'll

modo quid fuit? ignoscet mihi genius tuus, noluisses de
4 manu illius panem accipere. | nunc, nec quid nec quare,
5 in caelum abiit et Trimalchionis topanta[142] est. | ad sum-
mam, mero meridie si dixerit illi tenebras esse, credet. |
6 [H]ipse nescit quid habeat, adeo saplutus est; sed haec lupa-
7 tris[143] providet omnia, est ubi[144] non putes. | est sicca,
sobria, bonorum consiliorum—vides tantum auri[145]—est
tamen malae linguae, pica pulvinaris. quem amat, amat;
8 quem non amat, non amat. | ipse Trimalchio fundos habet,
quantum[146] milvi volant, nummorum nummos. argenti[147]
in ostiarii illius cella plus iacet quam quisquam in fortunis
9 habet. | familia vero babae babae, non mehercules puto
10 decumam partem esse quae dominum suum noverit. | ad
summam, quemvis ex istis babaecalis in rutae folium con-
iciet. 38. nec est quod putes illum quicquam emere. omnia
domi nascuntur: lana, citrea,[148] piper; lacte gallinaceum si
2 quaesieris, invenies. | ad summam, parum illi bona lana
nascebatur: arietes a Tarento emit et eos ‹testi›culavit[149]
3 in gregem. | mel Atticum ut domi nasceretur, apes ab
Athenis iussit afferri; obiter et vernaculae quae sunt, me-
4 liusculae a Graeculis fient. | ecce intra hos dies scripsit, ut
illi ex India semen boletorum mitteretur. nam mulam qui-
5 dem nullam habet quae non ex onagro nata sit. | vides tot
culcit{r}as: nulla non aut conchyliatum aut coccineum to-
6 mentum habet. tanta est animi beatitudo. | reliquos autem

142 τὰ πάντα *l*[mg]   143 lupatris *Neumann*: lupatria
144 est ubi *Müller*: et ubi
145 vides tantum auri *Sullivan*[2]: tantum auri vides
146 quantum *Scheffer*: qua
147 argenti *Giardina–Cuccioli Melloni*: argentum
148 citrea *Jacobs*: credae   149 *added Bücheler*

pardon me, good sir, but you wouldn't have taken a piece of bread from her hand. Now without any what or why she's gone up to the heavens and is Trimalchio's everything. In short, if she tells him at high noon that it's dark, he'll believe it. He's so rich that he himself doesn't know how much he's got. But this lynx looks after everything, even where you wouldn't think to find her. She is thrifty and sound and full of good advice—you see all this gold that she watches over—she has a rough tongue, a veritable magpie on the couch. She likes whom she likes; dislikes whom she dislikes. Trimalchio himself has estates of the size that only kites can fly over, and bags of money. There's more silver lying in his porter's room than any of us has in his whole fortune. As for the size of his household, my god, I don't think that one out of ten of them knows his master by sight. In short, he can throw any of these lightweights into a cooking pot. 38. You must not suppose that there's anything that he buys. Everything's homegrown: wool, citrus fruit, pepper; poultry milk if you ask for it, you'll find. For example, the wool he was raising wasn't any too good, so he bought rams from Tarentum and banged them into his ewes. He ordered bees brought from Athens so that Attic honey would be homegrown; and incidentally the native bees will be improved by the little Greek ones. And note that within the last few days he wrote for a cargo of mushroom spawn[55] to be sent from India. Also, he doesn't have one mule which isn't the offspring of a wild ass. You see all these cushions: every one has purple or scarlet stuffing. Such a happy and rich spirit he has. As for his

[55] The speaker does not know that mushrooms do not have seeds.

7 collibertos eius cave contemnas. | valde sucos{s}i sunt.
vides illum qui in imo imus recumbit: hodie sua octingenta
possidet. de nihilo crevit. modo solebat collo[150] suo ligna
8 portare. | sed quomodo dicunt—ego nihil scio, sed au-
divi—quom[151] Inciboni pilleum rapuisset, {et}[152] thesau-
9 rum invenit. | ego nemini invideo, si quoi[153] deus dedit.
10 est tamen sub alapa et non vult sibi male. | itaque proxime
cenaculum[154] hoc titulo proscripsit: 'C. Pompeius Diogenes ex Kalendis Iuliis cenaculum locat; ipse enim do-
11 mum emit.' | quid ille qui libertini loco iacet, quam bene
12 se habuit. non impropero illi. | sestertium suum vidit de-
cies, sed male vacillavit. non puto illum capillos liberos
habere, nec mehercules sua culpa; ipso enim homo melior
non est; sed liberti scelerati, qui omnia ad se fecerunt. |
13 scito autem: sociorum olla male fervet, et ubi semel res
14 inclinata est, amici de medio. | et quam honestam ne-
15 gotiationem exercuit, quod illum sic vides. | libitinarius
fuit. solebat sic cenare quomodo rex: apros gausapatos,
opera pis‹ca›toria,[155] avis,[156] ‹. . .› cocos, pistores. plus
vini sub mensa effundebatur, quam aliquis in cella habet.
16 | phantasia, non homo. inclinatis quoque rebus suis, cum
timeret ne creditores illum conturbare existimarent, hoc

---

[150] modo solebat collo *Wehle*: solebat collo modo
[151] quom *Bücheler*: quomodô *H*: cum *Müller*
[152] *deleted Scheffer*   [153] quoi *Goesius*: quo
[154] cenaculum *Bücheler*: cum
[155] *added Holford-Strevens*   [156] avis *Scheffer*: vis

---

[56] C. Pompeius Diogenes sits at *imus in imo*.
[57] Twice the amount of money needed for a man to enter the equestrian class.

fellow freedmen, be careful not to look down on them.
They have plenty of money. The man you see who's reclining at the end of the bottom couch[56] is today worth 800,000
sesterces.[57] He's grown from nothing. Just the other day
he was carrying logs on his back. People say—I know nothing, but I've heard—that when he grabbed a goblin's cap,
he found a treasure.[58] I envy no one, if a god favors him.
Still, he has just been freed, and he doesn't wish himself
harm. And so he just recently put up this notice near his
garret: 'Gaius Pompeius Diogenes is renting out this upper room from July 1st; he is buying a house.' What about
that person who's reclining in the freedman's place,[59] how
well off he was. I'm not blaming him. He saw a million
sesterces, and then he began to stumble. I think that even
his hair's mortgaged, but surely it's not his fault; there's no
better fellow alive; but his freedmen are crooks who've
done everything to suit their own interests. You know how
it is: a pot belonging to partners goes off the boil, and once
affairs take a turn for the worse, friends quickly desert the
scene. What a respectable business he had, but as for seeing him like this, it just goes to show. He was an undertaker. He used to dine like a king: boars in blankets, fish
dishes, birds . . . he had cooks, bakers. More wine was
poured out under his table than any of us has in his cellar.
He was a bigger than life image, not a man. As his affairs
failed, he was concerned that his creditors shouldn't think
that he was bankrupt, and so he advertised a sale with this

---

[58] An *incubo*, something like a gnome, guards a treasure that
could be seized only by stealing its cap.

[59] Proculus sits at *medius in imo*.

titulo auctionem[157] proscripsit: '<C.>[158] Iulius Proculus auctionem faciet rerum supervacuarum.'"

39. interpellavit tam dulces fabulas Trimalchio; nam iam sublatum erat ferculum, hilaresque convivae vino ser-
2 monibusque publicatis operam coeperunt dare. | is ergo reclinatus in cubitum "hoc vinum" inquit "vos oportet
3 suave faciatis. pisces natare oportet. | rogo, me putatis illa cena esse contentum, quam in theca repositorii videratis?
4 'sic notus Ulixes?' quid ergo est? | oportet enim inter cenandum philologiam nosse. patrono meo ossa bene quiescant, qui me hominem inter homines voluit esse. nam mihi nihil novi potest afferri, sicut ille fericulus talem[159] habuit
5 praxim. | caelus hic, in quo duodecim dii habitant, in totidem se figuras convertit, et modo fit Aries. itaque quisquis nascitur illo signo, multa pecora habet, multum lanae, caput praeterea durum, frontem expudoratam, cornum acutum. plurimi hoc signo scholastici nascuntur et ari-
6 etilli."[160] | laudamus urbanitatem mathematici; itaque adiecit: "deinde totus caelus Taurulus fit. itaque tunc calci-
7 trosi nascuntur et bubulci et qui se ipsi pascunt. | in Geminis autem nascuntur bigae et boves et colei et qui
8 utrosque parietes linunt. | in Cancro ego natus sum. ideo multis pedibus sto, et in mari et in terra multa possideo; nam Cancer et hoc et illoc quadrat. et ideo iam dudum
9 nihil supra illum posui, ne genesim meam premerem. | in
10 Leone cataphagae nascuntur et imperiosi; | in Virgine

157 auctionem *Scheffer*: caucionem
158 *added Bücheler*   159 talem *Studer*: ta mel
160 arietilli *Reinesius*: arieti illi

60 Verg. *Aen*. 2.44.

poster: 'Gaius Julius Proculus will hold a sale of his surplus store of goods.'"

39. Trimalchio interrupted these very delightful pieces of small talk. For by now the course had been removed, and the spirited guests had begun to turn their attention to the wine and general conversation. He leaned back on his elbow and said: "You ought to show your appreciation of the wine. Fish must swim. I ask you, did you think that I'd be satisfied with the dinner which you'd seen on the cover of the tray? 'Is this the familiar Ulysses?'[60] So, what was all that? Even when at dinner we must pursue learning. May the gods let the bones of my patron rest in peace, who wanted me to be a man among men. For nothing new can be brought to me, as this dish already showed. This is the sky where the twelve gods live, and it transforms itself into as many figures. First it becomes Aries, the Ram, and anyone born under the sign has many flocks, a lot of wool, and moreover a hard head, a shameless forehead, a sharp horn. Very many declamation buffs and their little rams are born under this sign." We praised the quick understanding of our astrologer, and so he went on: "Then the whole sky changes into a young bull, Taurus, when obstinate people are born and plowmen and those who provide food for themselves. Under Gemini, the Twins, are born chariot pairs, pairs of oxen, men with balls, and those who smear both sides of the walls. I was born under Cancer, the Crab, and so I stand on many feet, and I possess many things on sea and land, for the Crab fits both here and there. And therefore I earlier placed nothing over the Crab for fear of weighing down my natal star. Under Leo, the Lion, are born gluttons and potentates; under Virgo are born those addicted to women, and runaways and

135

mulierosi[161] et fugitivi et compediti; in Libra laniones et
11 unguentarii et quicumque aliquid expendunt;[162] | in Scor-
pione venerarii et percussores; in Sagittario strabones, qui
12 holera spectant, lardum tollunt; | in Capricorno aerum-
nosi, quibus prae mala sua cornua nascuntur; in Aquario
copones et cucurbitae; in Piscibus obsonatores et rhe-
13 tores. | sic orbis vertitur, tamquam mola, et semper aliquid
⟨boni aut⟩[163] mali facit, ut homines aut nascantur aut
14 pereant. | quod autem in medio caespitem videtis et super
15 caespitem favum, nihil sine ratione facio. | terra mater est
in medio quasi ovum corrotundata, et omnia bona in se
habet tamquam favus."

40. "sophos" universi clamamus et sublatis manibus ad
cameram iuramus Hipparchum Aratumque comparandos
illi {homines}[164] non fuisse, donec advenerunt ministri ac
toralia praeposuerunt[165] toris, in quibus retia erant picta
subsessoresque cum venabulis et totus venationis appara-
2 tus. | necdum sciebamus, ⟨quo⟩[166] mitteremus suspiciones
nostras, cum extra triclinium clamor sublatus est ingens,
et ecce canes Laconici etiam circa mensam discurrere
3 coeperunt. | secutum est hos repositorium, in quo positus
erat primae magnitudinis aper, et quidem pilleatus, e
cuius dentibus sportellae dependebant duae palmulis tex-
4 tae, altera caryotis altera thebaicis repleta. | circa autem

161 mulierosi *Jac. Gronovius*: mulieres
162 expendunt *Burman*: expediunt
163 *added Bailey*[2]
164 *deleted Müller*
165 toralia praeposuerant *Mentelius*: tolaria proposuerunt
166 *added Mentelius*

chained slaves; under Libra, the Scales, are born butchers and perfume sellers and those who weigh things; under Scorpio are born poisoners and assassins; under Sagittarius, the archer, are born cross-eyed men who take the bacon while looking at the vegetables; under Capricorn, the Goat, are born those who suffer and for their troubles horns sprout; under Aquarius, the water carrier, are born innkeepers and those with water on the brain; under Pisces, the Fish, are born chefs and teachers of rhetoric who fish for pupils. So the world turns round like a millstone, and always does something good or bad, so that men are either born or die. As for the turf you see in the center and the honeycomb on the turf, I do nothing without a reason. Mother earth's in the middle, rounded like an egg, and holds within herself all good things as if a honeycomb."

40. "Bravo," we all cried and with our hands raised toward the ceiling swore that Hipparchus and Aratus[61] could not be compared with him, until the servants came in and spread coverlets over the couches. On these were embroidered nets and hunters lying in wait with hunting spears and all the equipment of this sport. Not yet did we know where to turn our expectations, when a large disturbance was raised outside the dining room, and Spartan dogs began to run about, even around the table. A tray followed them, on which had been placed a huge boar, wearing a cap of freedom, and from his tusks hung two little baskets woven from palm leaves, one filled with sweet Syrian dates and the other with dry Egyptian. The

[61] Famous astronomers: Aratus (ca. 315–240), Hipparchus (ca. 190–120).

minores porcelli ex coptoplacentis facti, quasi uberibus
imminerent, ‹qui›[167] scrofam esse positam significabant.
5 et hi quidem apophoreti fuerunt. | ceterum ad scinden-
dum aprum non ille Carpus accessit, qui altilia laceraverat,
sed barbatus ingens, fasciis cruralibus alligatus et alicula
subornatus polymita, strictoque venatorio cultro latus apri
vehementer percussit, ex cuius plaga turdi evolaverunt. |
6 parati aucupes cum harundinibus fuerunt et eos circa tri-
7 clinium volitantes momento exceperunt. | inde cum suum
cuique iussisset referri Trimalchio, adiecit: "etiam videte,
quam porcus ille silvaticus lotam[168] comederit glandem."
8 | statim pueri ad sportellas accesserunt, quae pendebant
e dentibus, thebaicasque et caryotas ad numerum divisere
cenantibus.

41. interim ego, qui privatum habebam secessum, in
multas cogitationes diductus sum, quare aper pilleatus
2 intrasset. | postquam itaque omnis bacalusias consumpsi,
duravi interrogare illum interpretem meum, quid me tor-
3 queret. | at ille: "plane etiam hoc servus tuus indicare
4 potest; non enim aenigma est, sed res aperta. | hic aper,
cum heri summa cena ‹eu›m[169] vindicasset, a convivis
dismissus ‹est›;[170] itaque hodie tamquam libertus in con-
5 vivium revertitur." | damnavi ego stuporem meum et nihil
amplius interrogavi, ne viderer numquam inter honestos
6 cenasse. | dum haec loquimur, puer speciosus, vitibus

---

[167] *added Bücheler*   [168] lotam *Muncker*: totam
[169] *added Bücheler*   [170] *added Heinsius*

---

[62] This boar is an example of the so-called *porcus Troianus*, or
Trojan pig: the *aper* is first stuffed with other animals and foods

boar was surrounded by rather small piglets made of hard cake, hovering, as it were, over the teats, which indicated that it was a sow. These piglets were meant as gifts to be taken away. But that Carpus who had mangled the fowls did not come in to cut up the boar, instead a huge bearded man with cloth bands wrapped round his legs and dressed in a multicolored hunting coat. He drew a hunting knife and drove it vigorously into the boar's side. From this gash thrushes flew out;[62] fowlers were ready with limed reeds and quickly caught the birds as they flew around the dining room. After Trimalchio had ordered that each guest be given his own portion, he added: "And have a look at what fine acorns this woodland boar's been eating." At once slave boys came to the baskets which hung from the boar's tusks and in time to the music distributed the dry and fresh dates to the diners.

41. In the meantime I was retreating into private thoughts, and been taken off into much speculation about why the boar had entered wearing a cap of freedom. After having ticked off even remote possibilities, I screwed up my courage to put the question which was troubling me to that informant of mine. He said: "Certainly your humble servant can explain that too. It's no riddle, the thing's quite obvious. Although yesterday the main course had laid claim to this boar, the diners let him go; so today he comes back to the feast as a freedman." I cursed my lack of wit and asked no more questions, for fear of seeming never to have dined among respectable people. As we were speaking, a handsome slave boy wreathed with vine leaves and

(e.g., birds, sausages), and then its belly is slashed open and the foods roll out—just as the Greek soldiers exited the Trojan Horse.

hederisque redimitus, modo Bromium, interdum Lyaeum
Euhiumque confessus, calathisco uvas circumtulit et poe-
7   mata domini sui acutissima voce traduxit. | ad quem so-
num conversus Trimalchio "Dionyse" inquit "liber esto."
8   puer detraxit pilleum apro capitique suo imposuit. | tum
Trimalchio rursus adiecit: "non negabitis me" inquit "habere Liberum patrem." laudavimus dictum {Trimalchio-
nis}[171] et circumeuntem[172] puerum sane perbasiamus. |

9   ab hoc ferculo Trimalchio ad lasanum[173] surrexit. nos
libertatem sine tyranno nacti coepimus invitare conviva-
10   rum sermones. | Dama[174] itaque primus cum pataracina
poposcisset, "dies" inquit "nihil est. dum versas te, nox fit.
itaque nihil est melius quam de cubiculo recta in tricli-
11   nium ire. | et mundum frigus habuimus. vix me balneus
12   calfecit. tamen calda potio vestiarius est. | staminatas duxi,
et plane matus sum. vinus mihi in cerebrum abiit."

    42. excepit Seleucus fabulae partem et "ego" inquit
"non cotidie lavor; baliscus enim fullo est, aqua dentes
2   habet, et cor nostrum cotidie liquescit. | sed cum mulsi
pultarium obduxi, frigori laecasin dico. nec sane lavare
3   potui; fui enim hodie in funus. | homo bellus, tam bonus
Chrysanthus animam ebulliit. modo modo me appellavit.
4   videor mihi cum illo loqui. | heu, eheu, utres inflati ambu-

---

[171] *deleted Fraenkel*
[172] circumeuntem *Scheffer*: circumeuntes
[173] lasanum *Scheffer*: lasammum
[174] Dama *Heinsius*: clamat

---

[63] *liber* = free, and is also the name (*Liber*) of the Italian deity
associated with Dionysus (as god of wine). Trimalchio is obsessed
to associate himself with the word *liber* and hopes that his audi-

ivy, impersonating Bacchus, now as the Thunderer, now as the Deliverer, now as the Inspirer, carried round grapes in a small basket, and paraded his master's verses in very shrill voice. Trimalchio turned toward this sound and said: "Dionysius, now be Liber." The slave boy snatched the cap of freedom from the boar and put it on his own head. Then Trimalchio again commented: "You'll not deny that my father's Liber." We applauded his use of words and kissed the boy heartily, as he went round.[63]

After this course Trimalchio rose to go to the lavatory. Without the tyrant we acquired our freedom and began to draw out the conversation of the guests. Dama spoke first after demanding larger wine cups: "Day's nothing; as you turn round it becomes night. So there's nothing better than to go from the bedroom straight into the dining room. We've had a nifty cold spell. The bath hardly warmed me up. But a hot drink's as good as an overcoat. I had some drinks the size of jugs, and I'm clearly drunk. The wine's gone to my head."

42. Seleucus took up his part of the small talk and said: "I don't bathe every day; in fact a bath's like getting dry-cleaned, the water's got teeth, and my insides melt away daily. But when I've swallowed a jug of mead, I say fuck off to the cold. Of course I wasn't able to bathe, since I was at a funeral today. A fine fellow, a very good man, Chrysanthus gave up the ghost. It was just the other day that he greeted me. I seem to be talking to him now. Damn, we're nothing but ambulatory bladders of wind.

ence will come to associate *liber* with him, so that slowly but surely they will think of *Trimalchio liber* (freeborn Trimalchio) and not *Trimalchio libertus* (Trimalchio the ex-slave).

141

lamus. minoris[175] quam muscae sumus, ⟨illae⟩[176] tamen
aliquam virtutem habent, nos non pluris sumus quam bul-
5 lae. | et quid si non abstinax fuisset! quinque dies aquam
in os suum non coniecit, non micam panis. tamen abiit ad
plures. medici illum perdiderunt, immo magis malus fa-
tus; medicus enim nihil aliud est quam animi consolatio. |
6 tamen bene elatus est, vitali lecto, stragulis bonis. planctus
est optime—manu misit aliquot—etiam si maligne illum
7 ploravit uxor. | quid si non illam optime accepisset! sed
mulier quae mulier milvinum genus. neminem nihil boni
facere oportet; aeque est enim ac si in puteum conicias.
sed antiquus amor cancer est."

43. molestus fuit, Philerosque[177] proclamavit: "vivo-
rum meminerimus. ille habet quod sibi debebatur: honeste vixit, honeste obiit. quid habet quod queratur? ab
asse crevit[178] et paratus fuit quadrantem de stercore mor-
dicus tollere. itaque crevit, quicquid tetigit,[179] tamquam
2 favus. | puto mehercules illum reliquisse solida centum, et
3 omnia in nummis habuit. | de re tamen ego verum dicam,
{qui} linguam caninam comedi⟨t⟩:[180] durae buccae fuit,
4 linguosus, discordia, non homo. | frater eius fortis fuit,
amicus amico, manu plena, uncta[181] mensa. et inter initia
malam parram pilavit, sed recorrexit costas illius prima
vindemia: vendidit enim vinum, quantum ipse voluit. et

[175] minoris *Scheffer*: minores
[176] *added Ernout*
[177] Philerosque *Bücheler*: Phileros qui
[178] ab asse crevit *Scheffer*: abbas secrevit
[179] tetigit *Delz*: crevit
[180] {qui} . . . comedi⟨t⟩ *Jacobs*
[181] plena uncta *Reinesius*: uncta plena

We're worth less than flies, for they at least have some significance, while we're worth no more than bubbles. And what if he had not gone on a fasting cure? For five days he didn't throw any water or a crumb of bread into his mouth. Yet he joined the dead. The doctors killed him—much more likely it was his bad luck, since a doctor's nothing other than a comfort for the mind. Still, he was carried out decently, on a bier, with a good pall. The mourning ceremony over him was very good—for he freed some slaves— even if his wife was very grudging with her tears. And how would it have been, if he'd not treated her extremely well! But women as a sex are really only a race of kites. None of us should do no good to any of them; it's just the same as if you threw it all into a well. But a long-lived love affair's a festering sore."

43. He was annoying us, and Phileros shouted out: "Let's think about the living. He got what he deserved: he lived decently and died decently. What's he have to complain about? He started out with an *as* and was ready to pick up a *quadrans*[64] with his teeth out of the shit. And then whatever he touched grew like a honeycomb. By god, I think that he left a nice round hundred thousand sesterces, and all of it in liquid assets. But I have to tell the truth about this, he was a Cynic: he used rough speech, was quarrelsome, and was disagreement personified, not a man. His brother was a decent fellow, a friend to his friends, openhanded, and kept a good table. Chrysanthus had some bad luck, when he initially went into business, but his first vintage put his accounts back into the black: for he sold his wine at whatever price he wanted. But what

[64] *quadrans* is a coin worth one-quarter of an *as*.

quod illius mentum sustulit, hereditatem accepit, ex qua
5 plus involavit quam illi relictum est. | et ille stips, dum
fratri suo irascitur, nesciocui terrae filio patrimonium ele-
6 gavit. longe fugit, quisquis suos fugit. | habuit autem ora-
cularios servos, qui illum pessum dederunt. *Hφλ*numquam
autem recte faciet, qui cito credit, *H*utique homo nego-
7 tians. tamen verum quod frunitus est, quam diu vixit. | cui
datum <inter>est,[182] non cui destinatum. plane Fortunae
filius, in manu illius plumbum aurum fiebat. facile est autem, ubi omnia quadrata currunt. et quot putas illum annos secum tulisse? septuaginta et supra. sed corneolus
8 fuit, aetatem bene ferebat, niger tamquam corvus. | nove-
ram hominem olim oliorum, et adhuc salax erat. non
mehercules illum puto in domo canem reliquisse. immo
etiam pullarius[183] erat, omnis Minervae homo. nec im-
probo, hoc solum enim secum tulit."

44. haec Phileros dixit, illa Ganymedes: "narratis quod
nec ad caelum nec ad terram pertinet, cum interim nemo
2 curat, quid annona mordet. | non mehercules hodie buc-
cam panis invenire potui. et quomodo siccitas perseverat.
3 | iam annum esur<it>io[184] fuit. aedilibus[185] male eveniat,
qui cum pistoribus colludunt 'serva me, servabo te.' itaque
populus minutus laborat; nam isti maiores maxillae sem-
4 per Saturnalia agunt. | o si haberemus illos leones, quos

---

[182] *added Harrison*[3]
[183] pullarius *Burman*: puellarius
[184] *added Goldbach*
[185] aedilibus *patav.*: aediles

really raised his chin was that he received an legacy, from which he appropriated more than had been given to him as his share. And that blockhead, just because he was angry with his brother, left the family fortune to some nobody. Whoever flees from his family, flees a long way. He listened to the bad advice of his servants as though they were oracles, and they ruined him. The man who gives credit quickly will never do well, especially a business man. But it's true that he enjoyed himself as long as he lived. What matters is the person to whom it's given, not the person for whom it's intended. He was clearly Fortune's favorite, in whose hands lead turned into gold. It's easy when everything's running smoothly. And how many years do you think he carried? More than seventy. But he was tough-skinned, and bore his years well, his hair was still black as a crow. I had known him for a very long time, and up to the last he was lecherous. By god, I think that in his house he did not leave the dog unmolested. He was fond of boys also, and open to all kinds of sex. I don't blame him for his debauchery; it was the only thing he took with him."

44. After Phileros' comments, Ganymede said: "You all are talking about things that have nothing to do with heaven or earth, and at the same time not one of you cares how much the price of wheat grinds us down. I swear I couldn't afford a mouthful of bread today. And look how the drought still continues. For a year now there's been starvation. I hope the aediles go to hell, for they're in league with the bakers: 'You look after me and I'll look after you.' So the little people suffer hardships, because those with the big jaws grind them down and never stop celebrating Saturnalia. If only we had those lionhearted

145

5 ego hic inveni, cum primum ex Asia veni. | illud erat vi-
vere. simila ⟨si⟩ siligine inferior es⟨s⟩et,[186] larvas sic istos
6 percolopabant, ut illis Iuppiter iratus esset. | sed memini
Safinium: tunc habitabat ad arcem veterem, me puero,
7 piper, non homo. | is quacumque ibat, terram adurebat.
sed rectus, sed certus, amicus amico, cum quo audacter
8 posses in tenebris micare. | in curia autem quomodo sin-
gulos {vel} pilabat {tractabat},[187] nec schemas loquebatur
9 sed derectum.[188] | cum ageret porro in foro, sic illius vox
crescebat tamquam tuba. nec sudavit umquam nec expuit,
10 puto eum[189] nescioquid as⟨s⟩i{a dis}[190] habuisse. | et quam
benignus resalutare, nomina omnium reddere, tamquam
11 unus de nobis. | itaque illo tempore annona pro luto erat.
asse panem quem emisses, non potuisses cum altero de-
12 vorare. | nunc oculum bublum vidi maiorem. heu, heu,
quotidie peius. haec colonia retroversus crescit tamquam
13 coda vituli. | sed quare {non}[191] habemus aedilem ⟨non⟩
trium cauniarum, qui sibi mavult assem quam vitam nostram? itaque domi gaudet, plus in die nummorum accipit,
14 quam alter patrimonium habet. | iam scio unde acceperit
denarios mille aureos. sed si nos coleos haberemus, non

[186] simila ⟨si⟩ siligine inferior es⟨s⟩et *Bücheler*: similia sicilia
interiores et   [187] {vel} *and* {tractabat} *deleted Scheffer*
[188] derectum *Reiske*: dilectum
[189] eum *Mentelius*: enim
[190] as⟨s⟩i {a dis} *Schmeling*[5]: assi a dis *Burman*: asia dis
[191] {non} . . . ⟨non⟩ *transposed Bücheler*

[65] A game between two players: the first flashes a number of
fingers, and the second tries to guess the number of fingers. It is
still played in parts of Italy.

real men I found here, when first I arrived from Asia. Then life was good. If daily flour were found inferior to the finest, they punched out those devils in such a way that they thought god almighty was angry with them. Safinius stands out in my memory: at that time when I was a boy, he was living by the old arch, not so much a man as a pot of hot sauce. He scorched the ground wherever he went. But he was straight, trustworthy, a reliable friend, with whom you could confidently play morra[65] in the dark. How he used to dress them down, one by one, in the local council house, not using fancy phrases but straight talk. And then when he pleaded in court, his voice swelled to sound like a trumpet. He never sweated or spat, for I think that he possessed some kind of internal dryness. And how kindly he returned your greetings and addressed everyone by his name, as if he were one of us. So at that time wheat was dirt cheap. The bread you would've bought for one *as*, you and a friend couldn't devour. But now I've seen bull's eyes bigger than bread loaves. It's really sad how things get worse daily. This colony grows backward like a calf's tail. But why do we put up with an aedile not worth three Caunian figs, who sets more value on an *as* for himself than on our lives? He sits at home laughing and takes in more money in a day than another man has for his fortune. For you see, I know where he got the hundred thousand sesterces[66] from. If we'd any balls, he would not be so pleased

---

[66] 1,000 *aurei* = 100,00 sesterces, the amount needed to qualify for the aedileship; Ganymede implies that this aedileship was bought with bribes. The food supply was regulated by aediles, who would conspire with growers, wholesalers, and bakers to keep the prices high.

tantum sibi placeret. nunc populus est domi leones, foras
15 vulpes. | quod ad me attinet, iam pannos meos comedi, et
16 si perseverat haec annona, casulas meas vendam. | quid
enim futurum est, si nec dii nec homines huius[192] coloniae
miserentur? ita meos fruniscar, ut ego puto omnia illa
17 ⟨ab⟩[193] aedilibus[194] fieri.[195] | [HφL]nemo enim caelum cae-
lum putat, nemo ieiunium servat, nemo Iovem pili facit,
18 sed omnes opertis oculis bona sua computant. | [H]antea
stolatae ibant nudis pedibus in clivum, passis capillis,
mentibus puris, et Iovem aquam exorabant. itaque statim
urceatim plovebat: aut tunc aut numquam: et omnes redibant[196] tamquam udi[197] mures. itaque dii pedes lanatos
habent, quia nos religiosi non sumus. agri iacent—"

45. "oro te" inquit Echion centonarius "melius loquere.
2 | 'modo sic, modo sic' inquit rusticus; varium porcum per-
diderat. [HφL]quod hodie non est, cras erit: sic vita trudi-
3 tur.[198] | [H]non mehercules patria melior dici potest, si ho-
mines haberet. sed laborat hoc tempore, nec haec sola.[199]
4 non debemus delicati esse, ubique medius caelus est. | tu
si aliubi[200] fueris, dices hic porcos coctos ambulare. et ecce
habituri sumus munus excellente in triduo[201] die festa;
5 familia non lanisticia, sed plurimi liberti. | et Titus noster

192 huius *Scheffer*: eius   193 *added Schmeling*
194 aedilibus *H*: a diibus *Bücheler*
195 fieri *Mentelius*: fleri
196 redibant *Jacobs*: ridebant
197 tamquam udi *Schmeling after Holford-Strevens*: udi tamquam *Triller*: ut dii tamquam *H*
198 truditur φ: tiditur   199 sola *Reiske*: sua
200 aliubi *Scheffer*: alicubi
201 in triduo *Heinsius*: inter duo

with himself. Today people are lions at home, but foxes outdoors. As for me, I've already borrowed against the rags on my back, and if the high price of wheat holds, I'll have to sell my cottage. What'll happen in the future to this colony, if neither the gods nor men take pity on it? As I hope to have the joy of my children, I think that all these things going wrong are caused by the aediles. Of course no one believes that heaven's heaven, no one observes the fast, no one thinks that Jupiter's worth a damn, but all of them with their eyes piously closed, are really tallying up their net worth. In the good old days the women in long robes used to walk barefoot up the hill with lose hair, pure in spirit, and pray to Jupiter to send rain. It immediately rained in buckets; it was either then or never, and all of them returned home as if they were wet mice. And so the gods wrap their feet in wool, because we are not devout. The fields lie barren—"

45. "I ask you," said Echion, the rag merchant, "to speak about cheerful things. 'Win some, lose some,' said the peasant; he'd lost his checkered pig. What's not here today, will be here tomorrow: in that way life pushes on. I swear that a better town can't be named, if only it had real men. It's in distress at this time, but it's not alone. We ought not to be so spoiled, everywhere the sky above's the same. If you're anywhere else, you'll say that in the streets here the pigs walk round roasted. Just think, we're about to have a splendid spectacle in three days during the holiday. Not simply a troupe of gladiators from the local training school, but a bunch of experienced gladiators who'd been freed after valuable service.[67] And our friend Titus

[67] My interpretation here of *liberti*.

magnum animum habet et est caldicerebrius: aut hoc aut illud, erit quid[202] utique. nam illi domesticus sum, non est
6 mixcix. | ferrum optimum daturus est, sine fuga,[203] carnarium in medio, ut amphitheater videat. et habet unde: relictum est illi sestertium trecenties, decessit illius pater male. ut quadringenta impendat, non sentiet patrimonium
7 illius, et sempiterno nominabitur. | iam Manios aliquot habet et mulierem essedariam et dispensatorem Glyconis, qui deprehensus est, cum dominam suam delectaretur. videbis populi rixam inter zelotypos et amasiunculos. |
8 Glyco autem, sestertiarius homo, dispensatorem ad bestias dedit. hoc est se ipsum traducere. quid servus peccavit, qui coactus est facere? magis illa matella digna fuit quam taurus iactaret. sed qui asinum non potest, stratum
9 caedit. | quid autem Glyco putabat Hermogenis filicem umquam bonum exitum facturam? ille milvo volanti poterat ungues resecare; colubra restem non parit. Glyco, Glyco[204] dedit suas; itaque quamdiu vixerit, habebit stig-
10 mam, nec illam nisi Orcus delebit. | sed sibi quisque peccat. sed subolfacio, quia nobis epulum daturus est Mammea, binos denarios mihi et meis. quod si hoc fecerit,
11 eripiet[205] Norbano totum favorem. | scias oportet plenis velis hunc vincitturum. et revera, quid ille nobis boni fecit? dedit gladiatores sestertiarios iam decrepitos, quos si suf-

---

202 quid *Muncker*: quod
203 fuga *Scheffer*: fuca
204 Glico Glico *H*
205 eripiet *Scheffer*: erripiat

---

68 The two unknown men are rivals for some local office.

thinks big and is hotheaded; it'll be either this or that, but
at least something. I'm on familiar terms with him, and
he's not given to half-measures. He'll provide really good
gladiatorial sword fighting, no running off to fight another
day, but a butcher's shop in front of our eyes, so that the
whole amphitheater can see it. And he has the wherewithal: thirty million sesterces were bequeathed to him on
the sad death of his father. He can spend four hundred
thousand sesterces without his estate feeling it, and his
name will live for ever. He's already assembled some creatures capable of entertaining the crowd, and a woman
gladiator on a chariot, and the steward of Glyco caught in
the act of satisfying his wife. You'll see brawls in the common crowds between jealous husbands and ladies' men. A
man like Glyco is almost worthless, and then to throw his
steward to the beasts! This act only gives him away in
public. What crime did the slave commit? He was forced
to have sex with his mistress. That piss-pot of a mistress is
the one who better deserves to be tossed by the bull. But
the man who can't beat his ass, beats the saddle. How'd
Glyco imagine that a stinkweed woman from the seed of
Hermogenes would ever come to a good end? That fellow
could cut back the claws of a kite in flight. Snakes like him
don't give birth to ropes. Glyco, Glyco, he's paid the price.
And so as long as he lives, he'll have this mark on him, and
only death will wipe it out. But each man has his faults.
Now I smell a banquet Mammaea will give us worth two
denarii each for me and my guild members. If he brings
this off, he will strip Norbanus[68] of his status as favorite.
You should know that he will win, and win with full sails.
To be honest, what good has Norbanus ever done for us?
He provided some low-cost gladiators, already way past

flasses cecidissent; iam meliores bestiarios vidi. occidit de
lucerna equites, putares eos gallos gallinaceos; alter bur-
dubasta, alter loripes, tertiarius mortuus pro mortuo, qui
12 habuit[206] nervia praecisa. | unus alicuius flaturae fuit
Thraex, qui et ipse ad dictata pugnavit. ad summam, omnes postea secti sunt; adeo de magna turba 'adhibete' ac-
13 ceperant, plane fugae merae. | 'munus tamen' inquit 'tibi
dedi': et ego tibi plodo. computa, et tibi plus do quam
accepi. manus manum lavat. 46. videris mihi, Agamemnon, dicere: 'quid iste argutat molestus?' quia tu, qui potes
loquere, non loquis.[207] non es nostrae fasciae, et ideo pau-
perorum verba derides. scimus te prae litteras fatuum
2 esse. | quid ergo est? aliqua die te persuadeam, ut ad vil-
lam venias et videas casulas nostras? inveniemus quod
manducemus, pullum, ova: belle erit, etiam si omnia hoc
anno tempestas depravavit:[208] inveniemus ergo unde sa-
3 turi fiamus. | et iam tibi discipulus crescit cicaro meus. iam
quattuor partis[209] dicit; si vixerit, habebis ad latus servu-
lum. nam quicquid illi vacat, caput de tabula non tollit.
ingeniosus est et bono filo, etiam si in aves[210] morbosus
4 est. | ego illi iam tres cardeles occidi, et dixi quia mustella
comedit. invenit tamen alias nenias, et libentissime pingit.
5 | ceterum iam Graeculis calcem impingit et Latinas coepit

[206] habuit *Scheffer*: habet
[207] loquis *Burman*: loqui
[208] depravavit *Müller*: dispare pallavit
[209] partis *Scheffer*: parti
[210] aves *Triller*: naves

[69] The type of gladiator who was equipped with a sword and
a small shield.

152

their prime, who would've fallen flat if you'd breathed on them; I've seen better men fighting wild beasts. He killed off some knights who could've stepped down from figurines on lamps; you would've thought these miniature gladiators were farmyard cocks: one as thin as a rake, the other bandy-legged, and the reserve fighter was a corpse taking the place of a corpse who was hamstrung. One man dressed as a Thracian gladiator[69] had some spirit, but he too fought according to his trainer. In short, they were all flogged afterward, indeed from the big crowd they all received shouts of 'Give 'em what for.' It was an absolute rout. 'Still,' said Norbanus, 'I did give you a show.' Yes, and I applaud you. Count it all up and I give you more than I got. One good turn deserves another. 46. Agamemnon, you seem to me to be saying: 'What's this bore complaining about?' I speak because you, who can speak, don't. You don't belong to our class, and so make fun of the way we poor folks talk. We know that you are off your head with all your education. What's there for me in response? Might I persuade you to come down to our country place some day and view our little house? We'll find something to eat there, chicken, eggs. It'll be very pleasant, even if the weather this year has ruined everything; we'll find the wherewithal to fill ourselves. My little lad is already growing into a follower of yours. He can divide now by four; if he stays well, you'll have a young servant at your side. For whatever spare time he has, he doesn't lift his head from the slate. He's a clever lad and made of good quality, even if he has an almost unhealthy interest in birds. I've already killed three of his finches and said that a weasel ate them. But he's found other hobbies, and has with great pleasure taken to painting. He's kicked out his Greek studies and

153

non male appetere, etiam si magister eius sibi placens fit[211]
6 nec uno loco consistit. | scit quidem[212] litteras, sed non vult
laborare. est et alter non quidem doctus, sed curiosus, qui
plus docet quam scit. itaque feriatis diebus solet domum
7 venire, et quicquid dederis, contentus est. | emi ergo nunc
puero aliquot libra rubricata, quia volo illum ad domusionem aliquid de iure gustare. habet haec res panem.
nam litteris satis inquinatus est. quod si resilierit, destinavi
illi[213] artificium[214] docere, aut tonstrinum[215] aut praeconem aut certe causidicum, quod illi auferre non possit
8 nisi Orcus. | ideo illi cotidie clamo: 'Primigeni, crede mihi,
quicquid discis, tibi discis. vides Phileronem causidicum:
si non didicisset, hodie famem a labris non abigeret. modo
modo collo suo circumferebat onera venalia, nunc etiam
adversus Norbanum se extendit. litterae thesaurum est, et
artificium numquam moritur.'"

47. eiusmodi fabulae vibrabant, cum Trimalchio intravit et detersa fronte unguento manus lavit spatioque mi-
2 nimo interposito | "ignoscite mihi" inquit "amici, multis
iam diebus venter mihi non respondit. nec medici se inve-
niunt. profuit mihi tamen malicorium[216] et taeda ex aceto.
3 | spero tamen, iam venter[217] pudorem sibi imponit. alio-
4 quin circa stomachum mihi sonat, putes taurum. | itaque
si quis vestrum voluerit sua re causa facere, non est quod
illum pudeatur. nemo nostrum solide natus est. ego nullum puto tam magnum tormentum esse quam continere.

---

[211] fit *Bücheler*: sit   [212] scit quidem *Jacobs*: sed venit dem
[213] illi *Öberg*: illum   [214] artificium *Scheffer*: artificii
[215] tonstrinum *Scheffer*: constreinum
[216] malicorium *Scheffer*: maleicorum
[217] venter *Giardina–Cuccioli Melloni*: ventrem

begun to attack his Latin with relish, even if his teacher's pleased with himself and doesn't finish what he starts. He's well educated but doesn't like to work. There's another teacher, not so learned, but with an inquiring mind, and he imparts more than he knows. On holidays he often comes to the house and is pleased with whatever you give him. I've now bought some law books for the boy, because I want him to get a taste of the law so that he can manage our household business. Law puts bread on the table. For he's contaminated enough by literature. But if he shrinks from studying law, I mean to make him learn a trade, as a barber or auctioneer, or at least an advocate, of which nothing but death can rob him. Therefore I daily shout at him: 'Primigenius, believe me, whatever you learn, you learn for your own benefit. Look at Phileros the advocate: if he hadn't learned his stuff, he wouldn't drive hunger from his lips today. It was just a little while ago he was carrying around goods for sale on his back, and now he stands up even against Norbanus. Education's a treasure, and a profession never dies.'"

47. Gossip of this kind was being passed back and forth, when Trimalchio came in, mopped his brow, and washed his hands with perfume. After a very brief pause he said: "My friends, excuse me. For many days now my stomach has not been responding to my needs. The doctors all feel lost. For me, however, the rind of pomegranate and resinous pine steeped in vinegar have done good. I hope that now my stomach will observe its former proprieties. Besides, round my stomach there's such loud rumbling that you'd think it was a bull. So if any of you want to relieve yourselves, there's no need to be ashamed. None of us was born solid inside. I can't imagine any torture as great as

5   hoc solum {vetare}[218] ne Iovis potest. | rides, Fortunata,
quae soles me nocte desomnem facere? nec tamen in triclinio ullum vetuo[219] facere quod se iuvet, et medici vetant
continere. vel si quid plus venit, omnia foras parata sunt:
6   aqua, lasani[220] et cetera minutalia. | credite mihi, anathy-
mia<s>is si[221] in cerebrum it, et in toto corpore fluctum
facit. multos scio sic periisse, dum nolunt sibi verum di-
7   cere." | gratias agimus liberalitati indulgentiaeque eius, et
8   subinde castigamus crebris potiunculis risum. | nec adhuc
sciebamus nos in medio {lautitiarum},[222] quod aiunt,
clivo[223] laborare. nam commundatis[224] ad symphoniam
mensis tres albi sues in triclinium adducti sunt capistris
et tintinnabulis culti, quorum unum bimum nomencu-
lator esse dicebat, alterum trimum, tertium vero iam
9   se<xen>nem.[225] | ego putabam petauristarios intrasse et
porcos, sicut in circulis mos est, portenta aliqua facturos;
10 | sed Trimalchio expectatione discussa "quem" inquit "ex
his vultis in cenam statim fieri? gallum enim gallinaceum,
penthiacum et eiusmodi nenias rustici faciunt: mei coci
11 etiam vitulos aeno coctos[226] solent facere." | continuoque
cocum vocari iussit, et non expectata electione nostra
12 maximum natu iussit occidi, et clara voce: | "ex quota de-

---

218 *deleted Kaibel*   219 vetuo *Bücheler*: vetui
220 lasani *Bücheler*: lassant   221 anathymia<s>is si *Mente-lius*: anathimia is si   222 *deleted Fraenkel*
223 quod aiunt clivo *Heinsius*: quo aiunt divo
224 commundatis *Heinsius*: cum mundatis
225 *added Wehle*   226 aeno coctos *Mentelius*: eno cocto

---

70 Suetonius claims that the emperor considered issuing an
edict permitting belching and farting at banquets (Suet. *Claud.*
52; for more on Claudius' personal habits, see Sen. *Apoc.* 4.3).

holding it in.[70] This is the one thing that even Jupiter can't do. Are you laughing, Fortunata? That's the way you keep me awake all night. So even in the dining room I don't forbid anyone from doing what helps him, for even the doctors forbid holding it in. But if anything more than gas is coming, everything's ready outside: water, chamber pots, and other little comforts. Believe me, vapors of stomach gas go to the brain and flood the whole body. I know many who have died this way, by refusing to admit the truth to themselves." We thanked him for his generosity and kindness, and then suppressed our laughter by frequent little drinks. We did not realize that we were still struggling halfway up the hill, as the saying goes. When the tables had been cleared to the sound of music, three white pigs adorned with halters and bells were led into the dining room. The announcer said that one of them was two years old, the second three, and the third as old as six. I was thinking that some acrobats had come in and the pigs would perform some tricks, as they do for crowds in the streets. But my anticipation was dashed when Trimalchio said: "Which of these would you like to be turned into a course for dinner this minute? Any peasant can prepare farmyard fowl or a beef hash or rubbish of that kind, but my cooks are accustomed to make whole calves cooked in a bronze pot." And right then he ordered the cook to be fetched, and without waiting for our choice, ordered that the oldest pig be slaughtered, and said in a loud voice to the cook: "Which division[71] of the household do you be-

71 Claiming to have thousands of slaves, Trimalchio must organize them into units.

curia es?" cum ille se ex quadragesima respondisset, "empticius an" inquit "domi natus?" "neutrum" inquit
13 cocus "sed testamento Pansae tibi relictus sum." | "vide ergo" ait "ut diligenter ponas; si non, te iubebo in decuriam viatorum conici." et cocum quidem potentia admonitum in culinam obsonium duxit, 48. Trimalchio autem miti ad nos vultu respexit et "vinum" inquit "si non placet,
2 mutabo; vos illud oportet bonum faciatis. | deorum beneficio non emo, sed nunc quicquid ad salivam facit, in suburbano nascitur eo, quod ego adhuc non novi. dicitur
3 confine esse Tarraciniensibus et Tarentinis. | nunc coniungere agellis Siciliam volo, ut cum Africam libuerit ire, per
4 meos fines navigem. | sed narra tu mihi, Agamemnon, quam controversiam hodie declamasti? ego etiam[227] si causas non ago, in domusionem[228] tamen litteras didici. et ne me putes studia fastiditum, tres[229] bibliothecas habeo, unam Graecam, alteram Latinam,—. dic ergo, si me amas,
5 peristasim declamationis tuae." | cum dixisset Agamemnon: "pauper et dives inimici erant," ait Trimalchio "quid est pauper?" "urbane" inquit Agamemnon et nescioquam
6 controversiam exposuit. | statim Trimalchio "hoc" inquit "si factum est, controversia non est; si factum non est,
7 nihil est." | haec aliaque cum effusissimis prosequeremur

---

[227] etiam *Wehle*: autem
[228] domusionem *Wehle*: divisione
[229] tres *H*: duas *Mentelius*

---

[72] He is named Daedalus (cf. ch. 70.2) after the clever designer of the wooden cow in which Pasiphaë hid herself to attract the sexual attentions of a bull.

long to?" When the cook answered that he came from the fortieth, he said: "Were you purchased or born on the estate?" "Neither," said the cook.[72] "I was left to you in the will of Pansa." Trimalchio said: "Be careful then to serve this course carefully, or I'll have you demoted to the division of messengers." Once the cook was reminded of the power of the master, our next meat course led him into the kitchen. 48. Trimalchio then looked at us with a mild expression and said: "I'll change the wine, if you don't like it; you ought to do justice to it by drinking it. Because of the kindness of the gods I don't buy it, but whatever is effective here in producing saliva is grown on a country estate that I haven't yet seen. I'm told it's on the boundary of Terracina and Tarentum.[73] Just now I want to join together Sicily with my little estates, so that when I take a fancy to go to Africa, I could sail along my own properties. But tell me, Agamemnon, what was the subject of your debate today? Even if I myself don't practice in the courts, still I've learned enough reading and writing for household use. And so that you don't think I despise learning, I have three libraries, one Greek, a second one is Latin,—. So, tell me the subject of your declamation, just as a favor." When Agamemnon had said "A poor man and a rich man were enemies," Trimalchio said: "What's a poor man?" Agamemnon said: "Very witty," and then expounded on some rhetorical debate. Trimalchio at once said: "If this happened, there's no disputing it; if it didn't happen, it's nothing." When we attended these and other comments

[73] These places are two hundred miles apart, and by citing them Trimalchio implies that his estates cover much of southern Italy.

laudationibus, "rogo" inquit "Agamemnon mihi carissime, numquid duodecim aerumnas Herculis tenes, aut de Ulixe fabulam, quemadmodum illi Cyclops pollicem forcipe[230] extorsit? solebam haec ego puer apud Homerum legere. |

8   nam Sibyllam quidem Cumis ego ipse oculis meis vidi in ampullam pendere, et cum illi pueri dicerent: Σίβυλλα, τί θέλεις; respondebat illa: ἀποθανεῖν θέλω."

49. nondum efflaverat omnia, cum repositorium cum

2   sue ingenti mensam occupavit. | mirari nos celeritatem coepimus et iurare, ne gallum quidem gallinaceum tam cito percoqui potuisse, tanto quidem magis, quod longe maior nobis porcus videbatur esse quam paulo ante appa-

3   ruerat.[231] | deinde magis magisque Trimalchio intuens

4   eum "quid? quid?" inquit. | "porcus hic non est exintera-tus? non mehercules est. voca, voca cocum in medio." |

5   cum constitisset ad mensam cocus tristis et diceret se obli-tum esse exinterare, "quid? oblitus?" Trimalchio exclamat "putares illum piper et cuminum non coniecisse. despo-

6   lia." | non fit mora, despoliatur cocus atque inter duos tortores maestus consistit. deprecari tamen omnes coepe-runt et dicere: "solet fieri; rogamus, mittas;[232] postea si

7   fecerit, nemo nostrum pro illo rogabit." | ego, crudelissi-mae severitatis, non potui me tenere, sed inclinatus ad aurem Agamemnonis "plane" inquam "hic debet servus

---

230 forcipe *Studer*: poricino
231 apparuerat *Heinsius*: aper fuerat
232 mittas *Heinsius*: mittes

---

74 In recounting well-known myths and historical events, Tri-malchio shows great ignorance and lack of formal education, but

with the most extravagant praises, he said: "I ask, my dear Agamemnon, do you know about the twelve labors of Hercules, or the story of Ulysses and how the Cyclops twisted off his thumb with pincers?[74] I used to read these things in Homer when I was a boy. For I myself with my own eyes saw the Sibyl at Cumae suspended in a flask, and when the boys said to her, 'Sibyl, what's your wish?,' she would reply, 'I want to die.'"[75]

49. He was still babbling on and on, when a tray containing a large pig took possession of the table. We began to express astonishment at the speed of the cooking, swearing that not even a cock could have been thoroughly cooked so quickly, especially as the pig seemed to us to be much larger than the boar had been a little while earlier. Looking at it more and more closely Trimalchio said: "What's all this? Hasn't this pig been gutted? By god, it hasn't been. Call the cook, get the cook here in our presence." When the sad cook stood at the table and said that he had forgotten to gut it, Trimalchio shouted: "What're you saying? You forgot? You'd think that he'd not added pepper and cumin. Off with his shirt!" Without delay the cook was stripped and stood there dolefully between two torturers. Then we all began to intercede for him and say: "This happens; we ask that you let him go; if he does it again, none of us will intercede on his behalf." I felt very hard-hearted and could not contain myself, but leaned over to Agamemnon's ear and said: "He just has to be the

he does entertain his guests with the gusto with which he relates false information.

[75] *nam Sibyllam . . . θέλω* was used by T. S. Eliot as the epigraph for *The Waste Land* (1922).

esse nequissimus; aliquis oblivisceretur porcum exinterare? non mehercules illi ignoscerem, si piscem prae-
8 terisset." | at non Trimalchio, qui relaxato in hilaritatem
vulto "ergo" inquit "quia tam malae memoriae es, palam
9 nobis illum exintera." | recepta cocus tunica cultrum ar-
ripuit porcique ventrem hinc atque illinc timida manu
10 secuit. | nec mora, ex plagis ponderis inclinatione crescen-
tibus thumatula[233] cum botulis[234] effusa sunt.

50. plausum post hoc automatum familia dedit et "Gaio
feliciter" conclamavit. nec non cocus potione honoratus[235]
est etiam argentea corona, poculumque in lance accepit
2 Corinthia. | quam cum Agamemnon propius consideraret,
ait Trimalchio: "solus sum qui vera Corinthea habeam." |
3 expectabam, ut pro reliqua insolentia diceret sibi vasa
4 Corintho afferri. | sed ille melius: "et forsitan" inquit
"quaeris, quare solus Corinthea vera possideam: quia scilicet aerarius, a quo emo, Corinthus vocatur. quid est au-
5 tem Corintheum, nisi quis Corinthum habet?[236] | et ne me
putetis nesapium esse, valde bene scio, unde primum
Corinthea nata sint. cum Ilium captum est, Hannibal,
homo vafer et magnus stelio,[237] omnes statuas aeneas et
aureas et argenteas in unum rogum congessit et eas incen-
6 dit; factae sunt in unum aera miscellanea. | ita ex hac massa
fabri sustulerunt et fecerunt catilla et paropsides ⟨et⟩[238]

---

[233] thumatula *H, cf. 31.11*
[234] botulis *Scheffer*: botulius
[235] honeratus *Scheffer*: oneratus
[236] habet *Bücheler*: habeat
[237] stelio *Heinsius*: scelio   [238] *added Scheffer*

---

[76] Another *porcus Troianus*; see also ch. 40.5.

most completely worthless slave; how could someone forget to gut a pig? By god, I would not forgive him, if he
forgot to gut a fish." But not so Trimalchio, his face softened into a smile and he said: "Well, because you're so
forgetful, gut it right here in front of us." The cook got
back his tunic, seized the knife, and with an apprehensive
hand slit the pig's belly on this side and that. At once the
slits widened from the pressure of the weight inside, and
sausages seasoned with thyme and black pudding tumbled
out.[76]

50. After this trick the slaves applauded and cried
"Long live Gaius!" The cook too was rewarded with a drink
and a silver crown, and he accepted the cup on a Corinthian plate. When Agamemnon had taken a closer look at
it, Trimalchio said: "I'm the only man who has genuine
Corinthian ware." I expected he would say with his usual
effrontery that his dishes were imported from Corinth.
But he went one better: "Perhaps you inquire," he said,
"how I alone possess genuine Corinthian ware: to be sure
it's because the bronze smith I buy it from is named Corinthus. How can it be real Corinthian, unless one has a
Corinthus to provide it? But in case you think I'm an ig-
noramus, I know perfectly well how Corinthian bronze
came into the world. At the capture of Ilium, Hannibal, a
trickster and a sly snake, piled all the bronze, gold, and
silver statues on to one pyre and set fire to them; they were
all turned into one substance, an amalgam of bronze.[77]
Craftsmen then took pieces of this lump and made plates,
dishes, and statuettes. In that way Corinthian ware was

[77] Trimalchio's confusion about items of Roman history are
more entertaining than actual history.

statuncula. sic Corinthea nata sunt, ex omnibus in unum,
7 nec hoc nec illud. | ignoscetis mihi quid dixero: ego malo
mihi vitrea, certe non olunt.[239] quod si non frangerentur,
mallem mihi quam aurum; nunc autem vilia sunt. 51. fuit
2 tamen faber qui fecit phialam vitream, | quae non frange-
batur. admissus ergo Caesarem est cum suo munere. <. . .>
deinde fecit reporrigere Caesarem[240] et illam in pavimen-
3 tum proiecit. | Caesar non pote valdius quam expavit. at
ille sustulit phialam de terra; collisa erat tamquam vasum
4 aeneum; | deinde martiolum de sinu protulit et phialam
5 otio belle correxit. | hoc facto putabat se coleum Iovis te-
nere, utique postquam ille[241] dixit: 'numquid alius scit
6 hanc condituram vitreorum?' | vide modo. postquam ne-
gavit, iussit illum Caesar decollari. quid enim?[242] si scitum
esset, aurum pro luto haberemus. 52. in argento plane
studiosus sum. habeo scyphos urnales plus minus <C. cae-
latos>,[243] quemadmodum Cassandra occidit filios suos, et
2 pueri mortui iacent sic ut vivere[244] putes. | habeo capidem
quam <mihi>[245] reliquit patronus meus, ubi Daedalus
3 Niobam in equum Troianum includit. | nam Hermerotis
pugnas et Petraitis in poculis habeo, omnia ponderosa;
4 meum enim intellegere nulla pecunia vendo." | haec dum

239 non olunt *Bücheler*: nolunt
240 Caesarem *Scheffer*: Caesari   241 ille *Heinsius*: illi
242 quid enim *Bailey*[2]: quia enim
243 <C.> *added Wehle*, <caelatos> *added Schmeling*
244 sic ut vivere *Heinsius*: sicuti vere
245 *added Schmeling*

78 Pliny tells a similar story about the invention of unbreakable glass in the reign of Tiberius (Plin. *NH* 36.195).

born, many things were used to make one, neither this nor that. You will forgive me for what I say, but I personally prefer glass, at least it doesn't give off a smell. If it were not so breakable, I'd prefer it to gold, and now as it is, it's cheap. 51. There was once a craftsman who made a glass goblet that was unbreakable.[78] Therefore he with his gift was given an audience with Caesar . . . he caused Caesar to give it back to him and then dropped it on the floor. Caesar could not have been more upset than he was. But the craftsman picked up the goblet from the floor; it was dented like a bronze vessel; he then took a little hammer out of his clothing and without any trouble neatly straightened the goblet. After doing this he thought that he had Jupiter by the balls, especially when Caesar said: 'Does anyone else know about this technique of making glass?' Notice now what happened. After the craftsman said no, Caesar ordered him to be beheaded. But why? Because if this technique were known, we'd have gold as cheap as dirt. 52. I myself am very fond of silver. I've about a hundred three-gallon urns done in relief showing how Cassandra killed her own children, and the boys are lying there so dead that you would think that they were alive. I've a bowl that my patron bequeathed to me, on which Daedalus is shutting Niobe in the Trojan horse.[79] And I've got the fights of Hermeros and Petraites[80] engraved on goblets, all of which are heavy; of course I don't sell products of my expertise for any amount of money." As he was

[79] The description of Trimalchio's confusion in retelling myths is brilliant.

[80] The name Hermeros appears on a first-century lamp from Puteoli, Petraites on several cups dated to the age of Nero.

refert, puer calicem proiecit. ad quem respiciens Trimal-
chio "cito" inquit "te ipsum caede, quia nugas[246] es." |
5 statim puer demisso labro ‹ora›re ‹coepit›.[247] at ille "quid
me" inquit "rogas? tamquam ego tibi molestus sim. |
6 suadeo, a te impetres, ne sis nugas."[248] tandem ergo ex-
oratus a nobis missionem dedit puero. ille dimissus circa
mensam percucurrit. ‹. . .› et "aquam foras, vinum intro"
7 clamavit. | excipimus urbanitatem iocantis, et ante omnes
Agamemnon qui sciebat quibus meritis revocaretur ad
8 cenam. | ceterum laudatus Trimalchio hilarius bibit et iam
ebrio proximus "nemo" inquit "vestrum rogat Fortunatam
meam ut saltet? credite mihi: cordacem nemo melius
9 ducit." | atque ipse erectis supra frontem manibus Syrum
histrionem exhibebat concinente tota familia: madeia
10 perimadeia. | et prodisset in medium, nisi Fortunata ad
aurem accessisset; {et}[249] credo, dixerit non decere gravi-
11 tatem eius tam humiles ineptias. | nihil autem tam inae-
quale erat; nam modo Fortunatam ‹verebatur›,[250] modo
ad naturam suam revertebatur.[251]

53. et plane interpellavit saltationis libidinem actua-
2 rius, qui tamquam urbis acta recitavit: | "VII. Kalendas
Sextiles: in praedio Cumano quod est Trimalchionis nati
sunt pueri XXX, puellae XL; sublata in horreum ex area
tritici millia modium quingenta; boves domiti quingenti. |

---

[246] nugas *Adams*[1], *citing CIL 4.5279, 5282*: nugax
[247] ‹ora›re *added Scheffer*, ‹coepit› *added Strelitz*
[248] nugas *Adams*[1], *citing CIL 4.5279, 5282*: nugax
[249] *deleted Bücheler*
[250] *added Heinsius*
[251] suam revertebatur *placed here by Bücheler*; *after* Fortunatam *in* H

recounting these things, a slave boy dropped a goblet. Trimalchio looked at him and said: "Kill yourself right now for being so stupid." The boy's lip immediately plunged and he began to beg for mercy. But Trimalchio said: "Why do you ask me, as if I were giving you trouble? I advise you to convince yourself not to be stupid." In the end we prevailed upon him to let the slave off. Once he was acquitted, the boy celebrated by running around the table. . . . Then Trimalchio shouted: "Out with the water, in with the wine." We applauded the jesting wit, led above all by Agamemnon who knew how to get invited again to dinner. Because of our praise Trimalchio drank more cheerfully and now was nearly drunk when he said: "Does none of you ask my Fortunata to dance? Believe me nobody can dance the cordax better." He himself with his hands over his brow portrayed the actor Syrus, while the whole company of servants sang: "Madeia, perimadeia." And he would have advanced to the center of the room, if Fortunata had not whispered in his ear; I suppose that she told him that such humiliating nonsense was beneath his dignity. But nothing was ever so inconsistent, for at one moment he was afraid of Fortunata, and at the next would revert to his natural self.

53. In an obvious move his accountant interrupted his passion for dancing and read out the records of the estate, as if they were the daily gazette[81] of the City: "July 26: on the estate at Cumae belonging to Trimalchio were born thirty boys and forty girls; five hundred thousand *modii* of

[81] This is staged here to imitate the gazette (*acta*) of the City of Rome. Trimalchio wants his estates compared with the *Urbs*.

3   eodem die: Mithridates servus in crucem actus est, quia
4   Gai nostri genio male dixerat. | eodem die: in arcam rela-
     tum est quod collocari non potuit, sestertium centies. |
5   eodem die: incendium factum est in hortis Pompeianis,
6   ortum ex aedibus Nastae vilici." | "quid?" inquit Trimal-
7   chio "quando mihi Pompeiani horti empti sunt?" | "anno
     priore" inquit actuarius "et ideo in rationem nondum
8   venerunt." | excanduit Trimalchio et "quicumque" inquit
     "mihi fundi empti fuerint, nisi intra sextum mensem
9   sciero, in rationes meas inferri vetuo." | iam etiam edicta
     aedilium recitabantur et saltuariorum testamenta, quibus
10 Trimalchio cum elogio exheredabatur; | iam nomina vili-
     corum et repudiata a circ{um}itore[252] liberta in balneato-
     ris contubernio deprehensa et atriensis Baias relegatus;
     iam reus factus dispensator et iudicium inter cubicularios
     actum.
11   petauristarii autem tandem venerunt. | baro insulsissi-
     mus cum scalis constitit puerumque iussit per gradus et
     in summa parte odaria saltare, circulos deinde ardentes
12 trans‹il›ire[253] et dentibus amphoram sustinere. | miraba-
     tur haec solus Trimalchio dicebatque ingratum artificium
     esse. ceterum duo esse in rebus humanis quae libentis-
     sime spectaret, petauristarios et cornic‹in›es;[254] reliqua
13 animalia acroamata tricas[255] meras esse. | "nam et comoe-

[252] *deleted Bücheler*
[253] *added Heinsius*   [254] *added Heinsius*
[255] acroamata tricas *Scheffer*: cromataricas

---

[82] A *modius* = 9 liters, about a peck or 8 dry quarts. It is esti-
mated that 500,000 *modii* of wheat could feed two legions for a
year. Trimalchio and his spokesmen speak only via exaggerations.

wheat[82] were taken up from the threshing floor to the warehouse; five hundred oxen were broken in. On the same day: the slave Mithridates was crucified for cursing the guardian spirit of our master Gaius. On the same day: ten million sesterces were brought back to the strongbox, because they could not be put to use in investments. On the same day: a fire occurred on the suburban estates at Pompeii, which broke out in the house of the manager Nasta." Trimalchio interrupted: "What's all this? When were suburban estates at Pompeii bought for me?" "Last year," said the accountant, "and so they're not yet entered into the accounts." Trimalchio became livid with anger and said: "Unless I'm informed within six months about any farms bought for me, I forbid that they be entered in my accounts." There was now also a recital of the edicts of the aediles, and wills of foresters in which Trimalchio was disinherited via codicil; then the lists of bonds kept by bailiffs. Then notices about a freedwoman divorced by her husband, a watchman, after she had been caught in the quarters of a bathman; about a hall porter exiled to Baiae; about a steward who was prosecuted; and about a court action between valets.

Then at last the acrobats came in. A most absurd brute stood there with a ladder and ordered a boy to go up the rungs and at the top to do a dance sequence to music, then to jump through burning hoops, and to pick up a wine jug with his teeth. Trimalchio alone admired all this and kept saying that it was a thankless occupation. He said that there were two things in the world that he could watch with great pleasure, acrobats and trumpeters; the rest, such as trained animals or musical or poetical performances were worthless trifles. "Once I bought some comic

dos" inquit "emeram, at malui illos Atell‹ani›am[256] facere,
et choraulen meum iussi Latine cantare."

54. cum maxime haec dicente eo[257] puer ‹. . .› Trimalchionis delapsus est. conclamavit familia, nec minus
convivae, non propter hominem tam putidum, cuius etiam
cervices fractas libenter vidissent, sed propter malum exitum cenae, ne necesse haberent alienum mortuum plo-
2 rare. | ipse Trimalchio cum graviter ingemuisset superque
bracchium tamquam laesum incubuisset, concurrere medici, et inter primos Fortunata crinibus passis cum scypho,
3 miseramque se atque infelicem proclamavit. | nam puer
quidem qui ceciderat circumibat iam dudum pedes nos-
tros et missionem rogabat. pessime mihi erat, ne his precibus per i‹o›culum[258] aliquid catastropha quaereretur.
nec enim adhuc exciderat cocus ille qui oblitus fuerat por-
4 cum exinterare. | itaque totum circumspicere triclinium
coepi, ne per parietem automatum aliquod exiret, utique
postquam servus verberari coepit, qui bracchium domini
contusum alba potius quam conchyliata involverat lana. |
5 nec longe aberravit suspicio mea; in vicem enim poenae[259]
venit decretum Trimalchionis quo puerum iussit liberum
esse, ne quis posset dicere tantum virum esse a servo vulneratum.[260]

[OHL]55. comprobamus nos factum [H]et quam in praecipiti
2 res humanae essent [OHL]vario sermone garrimus. | [H]"ita"
inquit Trimalchio "non oportet hunc casum sine inscrip-

---

256 added *Bücheler*
257 eo *Müller*: Gaio
258 per ioculum *Öberg*: periculo
259 poenae *Hadrianides*: cene
260 vulneratum *Scheffer*: liberatum

170

performers," he said, "but I preferred them to do Atellane farces,[83] and I told my flute player to play in Latin."

54. Just as Trimalchio was speaking, <the ladder suddenly broke and the boy fell on to his couch>. The slaves cried out, as did the guests, not over such a disgusting creature, whose neck they would gladly have seen broken, but because they feared that after a gloomy conclusion to the dinner, they would have to mourn the death of someone they did not know. When Trimalchio himself groaned aloud and nursed his arm as if it were injured, doctors rushed in, and Fortunata was among the first to arrive, her hair disheveled, cup in hand, proclaiming how wretched and unlucky she was. The boy who had fallen was already crawling around at our feet and begging to be let off. I had an uneasy feeling that with these pleas some theatrical trick was being arranged for the sake of a joke, for the incident of the cook who had forgotten to gut the pig had not yet faded from my mind. So I began to look all around the dining room in case some surprise trick should come out of the wall, especially after a slave began to be flogged for having bandaged his master's wounded arm with white wool instead of purple. My suspicions were not far off the mark; instead of punishment there came a decree of Trimalchio in which he ordered the slave to be freed, so that no one could say that such a great man had been wounded by a slave.

55. We approved his action and in wide-ranging conversations chattered on about how uncertain human affairs were. "So then," said Trimalchio, "we shouldn't let this occasion slip by without some record of it." And im-

[83] Indigenous Italian comedy.

tione transire" statimque codicillos poposcit et non diu
cogitatione distorta haec recitavit: |

3   ^{HφL}"quod non expectes, ex transverso fit ‹ubique›,[261]
     et ‹sua›[262] supra nos Fortuna negotia curat.
       ^Hquare da nobis vina Falerna, puer." |

4 ab hoc epigrammate ^{OHL}coepit poetarum esse mentio
diuque summa carminis penes Mopsum Thraecem memorata est, donec Trimalchio "rogo" inquit "magister,
quid putas inter Ciceronem et Pub‹li›lium[263] interesse? |
5 ego alterum puto disertiorem fuisse, alterum hones-
tiorem. quid enim his melius dici potest? |

6   'luxuriae rictu Martis marcent moenia.
     tuo palato clausus pavo pascitur[264]
     plumato amictus aureo Babylonico,
     gallina tibi Numidica, tibi gallus spado;
    5 ciconia etiam, grata peregrina hospita
     pietaticultrix gracilipes crotalistria,
     avis exul hiemis, titulus tepidi temporis,
     nequitiae nidum in caccabo fecit tuae.[265]
     quo margaritam caram[266] tibi, bacam Indicam?[267]
   10 an ut matrona ornata phaleris pelagiis
     tollat pedes indomita in strato extraneo?
     zmaragdum ad quam rem viridem, pretiosum
       vitrum?
     quo Carchedonios optas ignes lapideos?

---

[261] ubique, / nostra *added Heinsius*   [262] *added Campanile*
[263] *added Bücheler*   [264] pascitur *l*^{mg}: nascitur
[265] tuae *Fraenkel*: meo

mediately he called for writing materials, and after straining his imagination for only a moment, declaimed these verses: "What you do not expect comes at you always from the blind side, and above us Fortune directs her own affairs. And therefore, my slave, pass us the Falernian wine." From this epigram there arose a discussion about poets, and for some time the crown of poetry was in the possession of Mopsus of Thrace,[84] until Trimalchio said: "I ask you, master, what do you think is the difference between Cicero and Publilius?[85] I think that the first one is more eloquent, the second more honorable. For what could be better than these lines? 'The walls of Mars crumble beneath the gaping jaws of luxury. To please your palate the peacock clad in Babylonian golden plumage is fed in cages, for you the guinea hen, for you the capon; even the stork, the beloved foreign guest, devotion-filled, graceful-stepping, castanet-dancer, winter's exile, warrant of warm weather, has made its nest in the cooking pot of your worthlessness. Why seek costly pearls for yourself, why Indian pearl berries? (10) That your wife adorned with sea spoils might spread her legs, unchecked on the bed of a stranger? For what purpose do you seek green emeralds, the precious crystal? For what purpose the Carthaginian

---

[84] Trimalchio apparently gets the name wrong; the correct one could be Orpheus.

[85] Publilius is a first-century BC composer of mimes.

---

[266] margaritam caram *Ribbeck*: margarita cara
[267] tibi bacam Indicam *Heinsius*: tribaca indica

nisi ut scintillet probitas e[268] carbunculis.[269]
15 aequum est induere nuptam ventum textilem,
palam prostare nudam in nebula linea?'

[H]56. quod autem" inquit "putamus secundum litteras
2 difficillimum esse artificium? | ego puto medicum et num-
mularium: medicus, qui scit quid homunciones intra prae-
cordia sua habeant et quando febris veniat, etiam si illos
3 odi pessime, | quod mihi iubent saepe anatinam parari;
4 nummularius, qui per argentum aes videt. | nam mutae
bestiae laboriosissimae boves et oves: boves, quorum
beneficio panem manducamus; oves, quod lana illae nos
5 gloriosos faciunt. | et facinus indignum, aliquis ovillam est
6 et[270] tunicam habet. | apes enim ego divinas bestias puto,
quae mel vomunt, etiam si dicuntur illud a Iove afferre;
[HφL]ideo autem pungunt, quia ubicumque dulce est, ibi et
7 acidum invenies." | [H]iam etiam philosophos de negotio
deiciebat, cum pittacia in scypho circumferri coeperunt, puerque super hoc positus officium apophoreta reci-
8 tavit. | "argentum sceleratum": allata est perna, supra
quam acetabula erant posita. "cervical": offla collaris allata
est. "serisapia et contumelia": xerophagiae[271] e sale[272] da-
9 tae sunt et contus[273] cum malo. | "porri et persica": flagel-
lum et cultrum accepit; "passeres et muscarium": uvam

268 probita se *B*
269 carbunculis *Bücheler*: cabunculus
270 est et *Scheffer*: esset
271 xerophagiae *Reiske*: aecrophagie
272 e sale *Burman*: saele
273 contus *Burman*: centus

fiery red rubies, unless honesty is reflected in the jewels? Is it fitting that a bride wear a woven breeze, or stand publicly naked in misty linen?'

56. What profession," he asked, "do we think is the most difficult after that of writing? I myself think it's that of a doctor or of a money changer: the doctor, because he knows what poor human beings have in their insides, and when a fever might come—even if I loathe them, because they often prescribe a diet of duck for me; and the money changer because he sees the copper under the silver. As for the dumb animals, the hardest workers are the oxen and sheep: the oxen, because thanks to them we have bread to eat; the sheep, because with their wool they make us vain. It's a terrible disgrace when someone eats sheep and then wears a woolen tunic. Now bees I take to be heavenly creatures, for they spew out honey, even if they are said to bring it from Jupiter; but the reason they sting is because wherever there is something sweet, there you will also find something bitter." He was just now throwing even the philosophers out of work, when labels began to be carried around in a goblet, and the slave boy appointed to this task read aloud a list of departure gifts:[86] "Leggy silver"—a ham was brought in topped with vinegar bottles: "Neck pillow"—what was brought in was a scrap of meat from the neck; "Late learning and assault with a rod"—dry salt-biscuits and a pole with an apple were given to the recipient; "Leeks and peaches"—he got a whip and a knife; "Sparrows and flypaper"—raisins and honey;

---

[86] These are called *apophoreta*, consisting of a short text attached to a departure gift for the guest. Books 13 and 14 of Martial are filled with such short texts.

passam et mel Atticum. "canale et pedale": lepus et solea
est allata.[274] "cenatoria et forensia": offlam et tabulas accepit; "muraena et littera": murem cum rana alligata[275]
10 fascemque betae. | diu risimus: sexcenta huiusmodi fue-
runt, quae iam exciderunt[276] memoriae meae.

57. ceterum Ascyltos, intemperantis licentiae, cum omnia sublatis manibus eluderet et usque ad lacrimas rideret,
unus ex conlibertis Trimalchionis excanduit—is ipse qui
2 supra me discumbebat—et | "quid rides" inquit "vervex?
an tibi non placent lautitiae domini mei? tu enim beatior
es et convivare melius soles. ita tutelam huius loci habeam
propitiam, ut ego si secundum illum discumberem, iam illi
3 balatum clusissem.[277] | bellum pomum, qui rideatur alios;
larifuga nescioquis, nocturnus, qui non valet lotium suum.
ad summam, si circumminxero illum, nesciet qua fugiat.
non mehercules soleo cito fervere, sed in molle carne ver-
4 mes nascuntur. ridet. | quid habet quod rideat? numquid
pater fetum emit lamna? eques Romanus es: et ego regis
filius. 'quare ergo servivisti?' quia ipse me dedi in servitutem et malui civis Romanus esse quam tributarius. et nunc
5 spero me sic vivere, ut nemini iocus sim. | homo inter
homines sum,[278] capite aperto ambulo; assem aerarium
nemini debeo; constitutum habui numquam; nemo mihi

274 ⟨canale⟩ *added Bücheler*; ⟨pedale⟩ *added Hadrianides*;
lepus . . . allata *moved here by Fraenkel; it stands before* muraena
in H

275 muraena . . . littera . . . alligata *Bücheler*: -am . . . -am . . .
-am

276 exciderunt *Hadrianides*: ceciderunt

277 clusissem *Friedländer*: duxissem

278 sum *Burman*: suos

"Something for a dog and something for a foot"—a hare and a slipper were brought in; "Cloths for dinner and cloths for court"—the recipient got a piece of meat and writing tablets; "Lamprey and a letter"—a mouse with a frog tied to it and a bunch of beets. We laughed for some time: there were any number like these, which have now escaped my memory.

57. Ascyltos with his lack of restraint kept throwing up his hands, making fun of everything, and laughed until the tears ran. One of Trimalchio's fellow freedmen—in fact the one who sat next above[87] me—flared up in anger and said: "What are you laughing at, mutton head? Don't the elegant things of my host please you? I suppose you're richer and accustomed to better dining. As certain as I hope to have the holy guardian of this house standing with me, so that if I should ever recline next to this one, I'd have stopped his bleating by now. A fine specimen he is to be laughing at others; some vagrant fly-by-night, not worth his own piss. In short, if I were to pee all round him, he wouldn't know where to run. By god, I'm not one to boil over quickly, but in rotten flesh worms breed. He's laughing. What's he got to laugh about? Did his father pay cash for him when he was born? Are you a Roman knight? Well, I'm a king's son. 'Why then have you been a slave?' It was because I sold myself into slavery, preferring to be a Roman citizen rather than a taxpayer. And now I hope to live such a life that I'm a joke to no one. I'm a man among men, I walk about with my head uncovered; I owe nobody a copper *as*; I've never been sued for failure to pay an obli-

87 The autobiography of Hermeros is similar to that of Trimalchio.

177

6   in foro dixit 'redde quod debes.' | glebulas emi, lamellulas
paravi; viginti ventres pasco et canem; contubernalem
meam redemi, ne quis in illius ‹capillis›[279] manus terge-
ret; mille denarios pro capite solvi; sevir gratis factus sum;
7   spero, sic moriar, ut mortuus non erubescam. | tu autem
tam laboriosus es, ut post te non respicias? in alio pedu-
8   clum vides, in te ricinum non vides. | tibi soli ridicl{e}i[280]
videmur; ecce magister tuus, homo maior natus: placemus
illi. tu lacticulosus,[281] nec mu nec ma argutas, vasus fictilis,
9   immo lorus in aqua, lentior, non melior. | tu beatior es: bis
prande, bis cena. ego fidem meam malo quam thesauros.
ad summam, quisquam me bis poposcit? annis quadra-
ginta servivi; nemo tamen sciit[282] utrum servus essem an
liber. et puer capillatus in hanc coloniam veni; adhuc basi-
10   lica non erat facta. | dedi tamen operam ut domino satis
facerem, homini maiesto[283] et dignitos{s}o, cuius pluris
erat unguis quam tu totus es. et habebam in domo qui mihi
pedem opponerent hac illac; tamen—genio illius gratias—
11   enatavi. | haec sunt vera athla; nam {in}[284] ingenuum nasci
tam facile est quam 'accede istoc.' quid nunc stupes tamquam hircus in ervilia?"

     58. post hoc dictum Giton, qui ad pedes stabat, risum
2   iam diu compressum etiam indecenter effudit. | quod cum
animadvertisset adversarius Ascylti, flexit convicium in
puerum et "tu autem" inquit "etiam tu rides, cepa cir-

[279] added *Watt*
[280] deleted *Müller*
[281] lacticulosus *Scheffer*: laeticulosos
[282] sciit *Scheffer*: scit
[283] maiesto *Muncker*: mali isto
[284] deleted *Bücheler*

gation; no one has ever said to me in the forum 'Pay me what you owe.' I've bought a bit of land, I put away a bit of silver plate; I feed twenty mouths plus a dog; I bought the freedom of my common-law wife, so that no one could wipe his hands in her hair; I bought back my own freedom for a thousand *denarii*; I was made *sevir*, and the fees were waived; I expect thus to die so that I need not blush when dead. You, however, are so busy judging others that you don't look behind you? You see a louse on another man, but you don't see the flee on yourself. Only to you do we seem comic. Look at your teacher, a man older than you: he likes us. You are just barely weaned, you have not yet said your first words, you are as cheap as a clay pot, and as useless as leather in water, limper, not better. If you are richer, then eat two lunches, two dinners. I prefer my reputation to riches. In short, has anyone had to ask me twice to pay up? I was a slave for forty years, but no one knew whether I was a slave or free. And I came as a long-haired boy to this colony; the town hall had not yet been built. I did my best to please my master, a dignified and respectable man, whose fingernail was worth more than your whole self. There were some people in his household who tried to trip me up one way or another; but still—thanks to the master's guardian spirit—I steered clear of trouble. These are the real accomplishments in life; being born free is as easy as saying 'come hither' to a slave. Why do you look stunned like a goat in a vetch field?"

58. After these remarks Giton, who was standing at my feet, burst out into an unseemly laugh, which he had repressed for some time. When the adversary of Ascyltos had noticed this, he turned his abuse toward the boy and said: "But as for you, are you laughing too, you curly-

rata?[285] io Saturnalia, rogo, mensis December est? quando
vicesimam numerasti? quid faciat crucis offla, corvorum
cibaria? curabo, iam tibi Iovis iratus sit, et isti qui tibi non
3 imperat. | ita satur pane fiam, ut ego istud conliberto meo
dono; alioquin iam tibi depraesentiarum reddidissem. bene
nos habemus, at isti nugae[286] qui tibi non impera{n}t[287]—.
4 | plane qualis dominus, talis et servus. vix me teneo, nec[288]
sum natura caldicerebrius,[289] ⟨sed⟩[290] cum coepi, matrem
5 meam dupundii non facio. | recte, videbo te in publi-
cum, mus, immo terrae tuber: nec sursum nec deor-
sum non cresco, nisi dominum tuum in rutae folium non
conieci{t},[291] nec tibi parsero,[292] licet mehercules Iovem
Olympium clames. curabo, longe tibi sit comula ista besa-
6 lis et dominus dupunduarius. | recte, venies sub dentem:
aut ego non me novi, aut non deridebis, licet barbam au-
7 ream habeas. | Athana tibi irata sit, curabo, et ⟨ei⟩[293] qui
te primus 'deuro de' fecit. non didici geometrias, critica[294]
et alogas nenias,[295] sed lapidarias litteras scio, partes cen-
8 tum dico ad aes, ad pondus, ad nummum. | ad summum,
si quid vis, ego et tu sponsiunculam: exi, defero

---

[285] cirrata *Reinesius*: pirrata
[286] nugae *Bücheler*: geuge
[287] *deleted Scheffer*
[288] nec *Jahn*: et
[289] caldicerebrius *Jahn*: caldus cicer eius
[290] *added Bücheler*
[291] *deleted Scheffer*
[292] parsero *Reinesius*: per ero
[293] *added Reinesius*
[294] critica *Reiske*: cretica
[295] alogas nenias *Scheffer*: alogias menias

headed onion? Behold the Saturnalia, I ask if this is the month of December? When did you pay the five per cent tax[88] on your freedom? How should he act, this gallows meat, this crows' food? I'll see to it that the wrath of Jupiter falls on you, and on that one there who can't control you. Just as I pray that I get my share of bread, so I'll overlook this event for the sake of my freedman friend, otherwise I would've already given you what you deserve now on the spot. We're doing well, but then there's that wastrel who doesn't control you—clearly like master, like slave. I can barely restrain myself. I'm not naturally hot-headed, but once I get started, I don't care two *asses* for my mother. All right, I'll take care of you outside, you mouse, or rather dirtbag: I'll not grow upward, nor downward, unless I've thrown your master into real trouble, and by god I'll not spare you, though you call upon Olympian Jupiter. I'll see to it that your cheap curls and your master worth two *asses* won't be much use to you. All right, I'll get my teeth into you: either I don't know myself, or you'll not sneer, though you've a golden beard like a god. I'll see to it that the wrath of Athena falls on you, and on that one who first made you his come-hither boy. I didn't learn geometry, critical theory and meaningless nonsense, but I know capital letters, I do percentages in measures, weights, and money. In short, if you like, I and you'll have a little bet: come on, I'm putting my money down. You'll

---

[88] When an owner freed a slave he was required to pay a 5 percent tax on the value of that slave. See also ch. 65.10. Note that in his anger Hermeros addresses Ascyltos and Giton in the second and third person.

lamna\<m\>.[296] iam scies patrem tuum mercedes perdidisse, quamvis et rhetoricam scis.[297] ecce:

'qui de[298] nobis longe venio, late venio? solve me.' |

9 dicam tibi, qui de nobis currit et de loco non movetur; qui de nobis crescit et minor fit. curris, stupes, satagis, tam-
10 quam mus in matella. | ergo aut tace aut meliorem noli molestare, qui te natum non putat; nisi si me iudicas anu-
11 los buxeos curare, quos amicae tuae involasti. | Occuponem propitium. eamus in forum et pecunias mutuemur:
12 iam scies hoc ferrum fidem habere. | vah, bella res est volpis uda. ita lucrum faciam et ita bene moriar ut[299] populus per exitum meum iuret, nisi te ubique toga[300] perversa
13 fuero persecutus. | bella res e\<s\>t[301] iste qui te haec docet, mufrius, non magister. \<nos aliter\>[302] didicimus, dicebat enim magister: 'sunt vestra salva? recta domum; cave, cir-
14 cumspicias; cave, maiorem maledicas.' | at nunc mera[303] mapalia: nemo dupondii evadit. ego, quod me sic vides, propter artificium meum diis gratias ago."

59. coeperat Ascyltos respondere convicio, sed Trimalchio delectatus colliberti eloquentia "agite" inquit "scordalias de medio. suaviter sit potius, et tu, Hermeros, parce

---

[296] *added Heinsius*   [297] scis *Reiske*: scio
[298] qui de *Bücheler*: quidem   [299] ut *Heinsius*: aut
[300] ubique toga *Bücheler*: toga ubique
[301] *added Fuchs*   [302] *added Heraeus*
[303] at nunc mera *Heraeus*: aut numera

---

[89] A logical answer to the format of one riddle plus two clues is penis or shadow; if there are three riddles, the answers would

soon realize that your father wasted his education fees, even if you know rhetoric. Look here at the riddle: 'I'm someone of us, I come long and wide. Solve me.' I will ask: 'What part of us runs and does not move from its place?' 'What grows out of us and becomes smaller?'[89] You run about, you're bewildered, you're troubled, like a mouse in a chamber pot. So either keep your mouth shut or don't bother your betters, who think that you don't even exist; unless you think I'm impressed by boxwood rings you stole from your girlfriend. May the god of Opportunity be good to me. Let's go to the market and borrow some money: you'll soon realize that this iron ring[90] commands credit. So there you are, a pretty sight, like a fox caught in the rain. As sure as I hope to make a fortune and die in such style so that people swear by my death, if I don't put my toga the wrong way round[91] and hound you everywhere. What a fine thing this fellow is who teaches you to behave like this, a blockhead not a master. We were taught differently, for the master said: 'Are all your belongings safe? Now straight home; don't stop and look around; don't bad-mouth your elders.' But now it is all disorderly conduct: no one worth two *asses* is produced. I thank the gods for my craft skills which made me what you see."

59. Ascyltos had begun to reply to this abuse, but Trimalchio, delighted with his fellow freedman's way with words, said: "Come now, that's enough brawling. It's better for us to act pleasantly, and you, Hermeros, don't be so

be foot, eye, hair. Many riddles have both obscene and decent answers.
[90] Iron rings were for slaves, gold for *equites* and senators.
[91] The *toga perversa* is the dress of a judge presiding at a trial.

2 adulescentulo. sanguen illi fervet, tu melior esto. | $^{H\phi L}$semper in hac re qui vincitur vincit. ^{H}et tu cum esses capo, cocococo, aeque[304] cor non habebas.[305] simus ergo, quod melius est, ut primitus[306] hilares et Homeristas specte-
3 mus." | intravit factio statim hastisque scuta concrepuit. ipse Trimalchio in pulvino consedit, et cum Homeristae Graecis versibus colloquerentur, ut insolenter solent, ille canora voce Latine legebat librum. mox silentio facto "scitis" inquit "quam fabulam agant? Diomedes et Gany-
4 medes duo fratres fuerunt. | horum soror erat Helena. Agamemnon illam rapuit et Dianae cervam subiecit. ita nunc Homeros dicit quemadmodum inter se pugnent
5 Troiani et Tarentini.[307] | vicit scilicet <Agamemnon>[308] et Iphigeniam, filiam suam, Achilli dedit uxorem. ob eam
6 rem Aiax insanit et statim argumentum explicabit." | haec ut dixit Trimalchio, clamorem Homeristae sustulerunt, interque familiam discurrentem vitulus in lance du<ce>na-
7 ria[309] elixus allatus est, et quidem galeatus. | secutus est Aiax strictoque gladio, tamquam insaniret, <vitulum>[310] concidit, ac modo versa modo supina[311] gesticulatus mucrone frusta collegit mirantibusque {vitulum} partitus est.

---

304 aeque *Heinsius*: atque
305 habebas *Mentelius*: habeas
306 ut primitus *Watt*: a primitis
307 Tarentini *Scheffer*: Parentini
308 *added Scheffer*
309 *added Burman*
310 <vitulum> . . . {vitulum} *transposed Müller*
311 supina *Scheffer*: spuma

hard on the young man. He's got hot blood, and you should be more indulgent. In these affairs the one who backs off is always the winner. And you, when you were a young cock, you used to crow, and just like him you hadn't any sense. Therefore, what's better, let's be cheerful as we were at the beginning, and let's watch the troupe of actors reciting Homer." At once the company entered and struck their shields with spears. Trimalchio himself sat up on a cushion, and when the Homeric performers spoke to each other in Greek verses, as they were immoderately accustomed to do, he recited the text in Latin in a singsong voice. Soon he asked for silence and then said: "Do you know the story they're doing? Diomedes and Ganymede were two brothers.[92] Helen was their sister. Agamemnon carried her off and substituted a deer as a sacrifice to Diana. So Homer's now telling the story of how the Trojans and the Tarentines fought with each other. Of course Agamemnon won and gave his daughter Iphigenia to Achilles in marriage. This drives Ajax mad, and he'll explain the plot right now." As Trimalchio said this, the Homeric players raised a shout, and among the slaves running in different directions a boiled calf was brought in on a presentation dish weighing two hundred pounds, and on its head was a helmet. Ajax followed after it and, as if he were mad, used his drawn sword to cut it to pieces, and after making first forehand then backhand sweeps, collected pieces on his sword point and divided them among the astonished guests.

[92] Trimalchio's confused retelling of myths continues to be entertaining.

60. nec diu mirari licuit tam elegantes strophas; nam repente lacunaria sonare coeperunt totumque triclinium
2 intremuit. | consternatus ego exsurrexi et timui, ne per tectum petauristarius aliquis descenderet. nec minus reliqui convivae mirantes erexere vultus, expectantes quid
3 novi de caelo nuntiaretur. | ecce autem diductis[312] lacunaribus subito circulus ingens, de cupa videlicet grandi excussus, demittitur, cuius per totum orbem coronae aureae
4 cum alabastris unguenti pendebant. | dum haec apophoreta iubemur sumere, respiciens ad mensam <. . .> iam illic repositorium cum placentis aliquot erat positum, quod medium Priapus a pistore factus tenebat, gremioque satis amplo omnis generis poma et uvas sustinebat more
5 vulgato. | avidius ad pompam manus porreximus, et repente nova ludorum commissio[313] hilaritatem hic refecit.
6 | omnes enim placentae omniaque poma etiam minima vexatione contacta coeperunt effundere crocum, et usque
7 ad os[314] molestus umor accidere.[315] | rati ergo sacrum esse fer{i}culum[316] tam religioso apparatu perfusum, consurreximus altius et "Augusto, patri patriae, feliciter" diximus. quibusdam tamen etiam post hanc venerationem poma rapientibus et ipsi[317] mappas implevimus, ego praecipue, qui nullo satis amplo munere putabam me onerare
8 Gitonis sinum. | inter haec tres pueri candidas succincti tunicas intraverunt, quorum duo Lares bullatos super

---

312 diductis *Scheffer*: deductis   313 commissio *Delz*: remissio
314 os *Bücheler*: nos   315 accidere *Bücheler*: accedere
316 fericulum *Reinesius*: periculum   317 ipsi *Heinsius*: ipsas

---

93 Suetonius notes that Nero had dining rooms with retractable ceiling panels (Suet. *Ner.* 31.2).

60. We were not given long to admire such refined twists and turns, for suddenly the coffered ceiling panels began to rumble, and the whole dining room shook.[93] In a panic I jumped up, fearing that some acrobat would come down through the roof. No less startled the other guests looked up, waiting to see what new portent from heaven was being announced. Suddenly the ceiling panels parted and a giant hoop, apparently knocked off a huge cask, was let down, and all around the circumference were hung golden crowns with alabaster jars full of ointment. While we were being told to take these away as departure gifts, I looked back at the table . . . A tray with several cakes had now been placed there. An image of Priapus fashioned by the confectioner occupied the middle of the tray, and in his large apron he held fruit of every kind and grapes in a manner common to images of Priapus. With more than a little greed we reached out our hands toward the theatrical display, and suddenly a fresh start to the spectacles renewed our merriment. For all the cakes and all the fruit, when touched even lightly, began to spray out saffron, and the nasty juice flew even into our faces.[94] So, thinking that this was a sacred dish because it was drenched with such holy appointments, we rose to our feet and said: "Good health to Augustus, father of his country." But as some of the guests even after this solemn moment snatched the fruit, we also filled our napkins, especially I did so, for I thought that I could not load the lap of Giton with a large enough gift. Meanwhile three boys with their white tunics tucked up high came in, and two of them placed on the

[94] This scene shows a yellow liquid shooting out from the lap of Priapus, whose penis is always portrayed as erect.

mensam posuerunt, unus pateram vini circumferens "dii
propitii" clamabat ⟨. . .⟩ aiebat autem unum Cerdonem,
9 alterum Felicionem, tertium Lucrionem[318] vocari. | nos
etiam auream[319] imaginem ipsius Trimalchionis, cum iam
omnes basiarent, erubuimus praeterire.

61. postquam ergo omnes bonam mentem bonamque
2 valetudinem sibi optarunt, | Trimalchio ad Nicerotem re-
spexit et "solebas" inquit "suavius esse in convictu; nescioquid nunc[320] taces nec muttis.[321] oro te, sic felicem me
3 videas, narra illud quod tibi usu venit." | Niceros delecta-
tus affabilitate amici "omne me" inquit "lucrum transeat,
nisi iam dudum gaudimonio dissilio, quod te talem video.
4 | itaque hilaria mera sint, etsi timeo istos scholasticos, ne
me {de}rideant.[322] viderint: narrabo tamen; quid enim
mihi aufert qui ridet? satius est rideri quam derideri." |
5 "haec ubi dicta dedit,"[323] talem fabulam exorsus est: |
6 "cum adhuc servirem, habitabamus in vico angusto; nunc
Gavillae domus est. ibi, quomodo dii volunt, amare coepi
uxorem Terentii coponis: noveratis Melissam Tarentinam,
7 pulcherrimum baccibalium. | sed ego ⟨illam⟩[324] non
mehercules corporaliter {autem} aut propter res vene{ra}-
8 rias[325] curavi, sed magis quod benemoria[326] fuit. | si quid
ab illa petii, numquam mihi negatum fuit.[327] fecit assem,
semissem habui: in illius sinum demandavi, nec umquam
9 fefellitus sum. | huius contubernalis ad villam supremum

---

[318] Lucrionem *Reinesius*: lucronem   [319] auream *Jahn*: veram
[320] nunc *Scheffer*: nec   [321] muttis *Scheffer*: mutes H
[322] *deleted Mentelius*   [323] haec . . . dedit *Virgil uses
this eight times in the Aeneid*   [324] ⟨illam⟩ *added here
Schmeling, after* corporaliter *Bücheler*   [325] *deleted Scheffer*
[326] benemoria *Orelli*: bene moriar   [327] fuit *patav.: omitted*

table images of the Lares[95] wearing amulets, while the third carried round a wine bowl and shouted "May the gods be gracious." . . . But he said that one image was called Gain, a second Luck, and a third Profit. There was even a golden image of Trimalchio himself, and now since everyone was kissing it, we were embarrassed not to do the same.

61. So after they all had wished happiness and good health for themselves, Trimalchio looked at Niceros and said: "You used to be more entertaining at dinner; I don't know why you're quiet and don't utter a squeak. I ask you a favor to make me happy: tell us about that adventure you had." Niceros was delighted by his friend's affable request and said: "May I never make another profit, if all this time I've not been fairly bursting with joy to see you in such good form. So let's have some undiluted fun, even if I fear these scholars will laugh at me. That's up to them: I'll tell my story all the same; what do I lose if someone laughs at me? It's better to be laughed at than jeered at." 'After he had uttered these words,' he began this story: "When I was still a slave, we lived on a narrow alley in the house now belonging to Gavilla. There, as the gods arranged it, I fell in love with the wife of Terentius, the innkeeper; you all knew Melissa of Tarentum, a round thing of pure beauty. But I swear that I was drawn to her not for her physical beauty or because of sexual attraction, but rather because she was sweet-natured. She never refused anything I asked of her. If she made an *as*, I got a half: I entrusted it all to her keeping, and she never cheated me. Then her

95 The household gods.

diem obiit. itaque per scutum per ocream egi aginavi,
quemadmodum ad illam pervenirem: <scitis>[328] autem, in
angustiis amici apparent. 62. forte dominus Capuae exie-
2 rat ad scruta scita expedienda. | nactus ego occasionem
persuadeo hospitem nostrum ut mecum ad quintum mi-
liarium veniat. erat autem miles, fortis tamquam Orcus. |
3 apoculamus[329] nos circa gallicinia, luna lucebat tamquam
4 meridie. | venimus inter monumenta: homo meus coepit
ad stelas[330] facere, sed ego <pergo>[331] cantabundus et ste-
5 las[332] numero. | deinde ut respexi ad comitem, ille exuit se
et omnia vestimenta secundum viam[333] posuit. mihi {in}[334]
6 anima in naso esse, stabam tamquam mortuus. | at ille
circumminxit vestimenta sua, et subito lupus factus est.
nolite me iocari putare; ut mentiar, nullius patrimonium
7 tanti facio. | sed, quod coeperam dicere, postquam lupus
8 factus est, ululare coepit et in silvas fugit. | ego primitus
nesciebam ubi essem, deinde accessi, ut vestimenta eius
tollerem: illa autem lapidea facta sunt. qui mori timore nisi
9 ego? | gladium tamen strinxi et matutinas[335] umbras ce-
10 cidi, donec ad villam amicae meae pervenirem. | in larvam
intravi, paene animam ebullivi, sudor mihi per bifurcum
11 volabat, oculi mortui, vix umquam refectus sum. | Melissa
mea mirari coepit, quod tam sero ambularem, et 'si ante'
inquit 'venisses, saltem nobis adiutasses; lupus enim vil-
lam intravit et omnia pecora tamquam lanius sanguinem
illis misit. nec tamen derisit, etiam si fugit; servus enim

[328] *added Bücheler*   [329] apoculamus *Scheffer*: apoculanius
[330] stelas *Reiske*: stellas   [331] *added Heraeus*
[332] stelas *Bücheler*: stellas   [333] viam *Scheffer*: iam
[334] {in} anima *Scheffer*: in animo   [335] *Heraeus (only for
an example of the hundreds of conjectures)*: matavitatau

common-law partner died on the estate, and so by might and main I did everything in my power to get to her: as you know, friends turn up in tight places. 62. By chance my master had gone off to Capua to settle some neat odds and ends, so I seized my opportunity and persuaded my guest that he should come with me as far as the fifth milestone. He was a soldier and brave as hell. At about cock-crow we hauled ass; the moon shone like high noon. We came in among the tombs: my companion began to relieve himself against the gravestones, but I walked on, singing and counting the monuments. Then when I looked back at my companion, he stripped himself and placed all his garments by the side of the road. My heart was in my nose, and I stood there like a dead man. He pissed a circle round his clothes, and suddenly turned into a wolf. Don't think I am joking; I value no one's fortune so high that I'd lie about this. But as I was saying, after he turned into a wolf, he began to howl and fled into the woods. At first I was unaware of where I was, then I went over to pick up his clothes, but they had turned into stone. If anyone ever died of fright, I did so at that moment. But I drew my sword and slashed at morning shadows, until I came to the country estate of my girlfriend. I went in looking like a ghost, I was close to giving up my life, sweat was running down my legs, my eyes were glazed over, and only with difficulty was I revived. My dear Melissa was surprised that I was out walking so late, and she said: 'If you'd come earlier, you could at least have helped us. A wolf penetrated the estate and like a butcher drained the blood of all the sheep. He did not, however, have the last laugh, even if he got away, for one of our slaves pierced his neck

191

12 noster lancea collum eius traiecit.' | haec ut audivi, operire
oculos amplius non potuit, sed luce clara ad[336] nostri domum fugi tamquam copo compilatus, et postquam veni in
illum locum in quo lapidea vestimenta erant facta, nihil
13 inveni nisi sanguinem. | ut vero domum veni, iacebat miles
meus in lecto tamquam bovis, et collum illius medicus
curabat. intellexi illum versipellem esse, nec postea cum
14 illo panem gustare potui, non si me occidisses. | viderint
alii qui de hoc aliae opinionis sint;[337] ego si mentior, genios
vestros iratos habeam."

63. attonitis admiratione universis "salvo" inquit "tuo
sermone" Trimalchio "si qua fides est, ut mihi pili inhor-
ruerunt, quia scio Nicerotem nihil nugarum narrare:
2 immo certus est et minime linguosus. | nam et ipse vobis
3 rem horribilem narrabo: asinus in tegulis. | cum adhuc
capillatus essem, nam a puero vitam Chiam gessi, ipsimi
nostri[338] delicatus decessit, mehercules margaritum, cata-
4 mitus[339] {et}[340] omnium numerum. | cum ergo illum mater
misella plangeret et nos complor‹ant›es[341] in tristimonio
essemus, subito strigae coeperunt: putares canem leporem
5 persequi. | habebamus tunc hominem Cappadocem, lon-
gum, valde audaculum et qui valebat {poterat}[342] bovem[343]
6 iratum tollere. | hic audacter stricto gladio extra ostium
procucurrit, involuta sinistra manu curiose, et mulierem
tamquam hoc loco—salvum sit quod tango—mediam

---

336 ad *Müller*: hac   337 alii qui . . . sint *Schmeling*[5]: alii qui
hoc de alibi exopinissent   338 ipsimi nostri *Scheffer*: ipim mostri
339 catamitus *Jacobs*: caccitus   340 *deleted Jacobs*
341 nos complor‹antes› *Müller*: nos tum plures
342 poterat *omitted patav.*, *deleted Bücheler*
343 bovem *Reiske*: iovem

with a spear.' When I heard this, I was unable any longer to close my eyes, but at break of day I rushed back to the house of my master like an innkeeper who's been robbed. And when I came to the place where the clothes had been turned to stone, I found nothing but blood. But when I got home, my soldier was lying on the bed like a knocked down ox, and a doctor was looking after his neck. I realized that he was a werewolf, and afterward I was not able to share bread with him, not even if you'd killed me. Those of a different opinion can think what they like about this; but if I'm lying, may your guardian spirits rage against me."

63. With everyone dumbfounded, Trimalchio said: "In all respect for the truth of your story, if you'll believe me, my hair stood on end. For I know that Niceros doesn't narrate nonsense, but he's reliable and doesn't exaggerate. But I too will tell you a hair-raising tale, as strange and impossible as 'the donkey on the roof.' When I was still a long-haired boy—already from my youth on I lived a Chian[96] life—the sexual favorite of the master himself died. I swear that he was a gem, a one in a million catamite. So while his poor mother wept over him, and several of us shared in her sadness, all of a sudden the witches began to howl: you'd have thought it was a dog chasing a hare. We had at that time a Cappadocian in the house, a tall man, quite brave, someone who could lift a raging bull. After boldly drawing his sword he rushed outside, and with his left hand carefully wrapped up, ran a woman through the middle, just about here where I'm pointing—

[96] People of the island of Chios were notorious for their degenerate lifestyle.

traiecit. audimus gemitum, sed[344]—plane non mentiar—
7 ipsas non vidimus. | baro autem noster introversus se
proiecit in lectum, et corpus totum lividum habebat quasi
flagellis caesus, quia scilicet illum tetigerat mala manus. |
8 nos cluso ostio redimus iterum ad officium, sed dum mater
amplexaret corpus filii sui, tangit et videt manuciolum de
stramentis factum. non cor habebat, non intestina, non
quicquam: scilicet iam puerum strigae involaverant et
9 supposuerant stamenticium vavatonem. | rogo vos, oportet
credatis, sunt mulieres plussciae, sunt Nocturnae, et quod
10 sursum est, deorsum faciunt. | ceterum baro ille longus
post hoc factum numquam coloris sui fuit, immo post pau-
cos dies phreneticus periit." 64. miramur nos et pariter
credimus, osculatique mensam rogamus Nocturnas ut suis
se teneant, dum redimus a cena. |

2   et sane iam lucernae mihi plures videbantur ardere
totumque triclinium esse mutatum, cum Trimalchio "tibi
dico" inquit "Plocame, nihil narras? nihil nos delectaris?
et solebas suavius[345] esse, canturire belle deverbia, adicere
3 melica{m}.[346] | heu, heu, abistis dulces caricae."[347] "iam"
inquit ille "quadrigae meae decucurrerunt, ex quo poda-
gricus factus sum. alioquin cum essem adulescentulus,
4 cantando paene tisicus factus sum. | quid saltare? quid
deverbia? quid tonstrinum? quando parem habui nisi

---

344 sed *Jacobs*: et
345 suavius *Bücheler*: suavis
346 *deleted Scheffer*
347 dulces caricae *Scheffer*: dulcis carica

may that part of me be safe which I now touch. We heard a groan—I surely wouldn't lie—but we didn't see them. Our big strong fellow came back in and threw himself on the bed. His whole body was black and blue, as if he'd been cut up by whips; of course it was because the evil hand had touched him. After the door had been shut, we returned to the wake, but when the mother had put her arms around her son, she felt it and realized that it had become a small bundle of straw. It had no heart, no stomach and bowels, nothing. To be sure the witches had already carried off the boy and put a changeling of straw in his place. I beg you to believe that there are women round about who know everything, who're night witches, and bring down low what was up high. But that tall fellow never regained his normal color after this incident; on the contrary after a few days of suffering from delirium, he died." 64. We were all astonished and at the same time believed the story, and having kissed the table, we asked that the night witches keep themselves to themselves, until we returned from the banquet.

By this time the flaming lamps clearly seemed to me to have multiplied, and the whole dining room was altered, when Trimalchio said: "I say, Plocamus, haven't you got a story to tell us? Do you have nothing to entertain us? And yet you used to be better company, you used to recite verses beautifully and then add the lyrics. How sad it all is, the sweet Carian figs of yesterday are no more." He said: "My chariot-racing days have now run their course, ever since I got the gout. It was a different matter when I was a young man; I almost came down with consumption from singing so much. How I could dance, how I could recite, and what about my barbershop act? When did I

5 unum Apelletem?" | oppositaque ad os manu nescioquid
taetrum exsibilavit, quod postea Graecum esse affirmabat.
nec non Trimalchio ipse cum tubicines esset imitatus, ad
6 delicias suas respexit, quem Croesum appellabat. | puer
autem lippus, sordidissimis dentibus, catellam nigram atque indecenter pinguem prasina involvebat fascia pa-
nemque semissem ponebat supra torum atque ha‹n›c[348]
7 nausea recusantem saginabat. | quo admonitus officio
Trimalchio Scylacem iussit adduci "praesidium domus
familiaeque." nec mora, ingentis formae adductus est canis catena vinctus, admonitusque ostiarii calce ut cubaret,
8 ante mensam se posuit. | tum Trimalchio iactans candi-
dum panem "nemo" inquit "in domo mea me plus amat."
9 | indignatus puer quod Scylacem tam effuse laudaret, ca-
tellam in terram deposuit hortatusque ‹est›[349] ut ad rixam
properaret. Scylax, canino scilicet usus ingenio, taeterrimo
latratu triclinium implevit Margaritamque Croesi paene
10 laceravit. | nec intra rixam tumultus constitit, sed cande-
labrum etiam supra mensam eversum et vasa omnia crys-
tallina comminuit et oleo ferventi aliquot convivas resper-
11 sit. | Trimalchio ne videretur iactura motus, basiavit
12 puerum ac iussit supra dorsum ascendere suum. | non
moratus ille usus ‹est›[350] equo manuque plana[351] scapulas
eius subinde verberavit, interque risum proclamavit:
13 "bucca, bucca, quot sunt hic?" | repressus ergo aliquamdiu

---

[348] *added Hadrianides*
[349] *added Bücheler*
[350] *added Bücheler*   [351] plana *Scheffer*: plena

---

[97] Perhaps the Asianic tragic actor popular under Caligula
(Suet. *Calig.* 33).

ever have my equal except for Apelles[97] alone?" He put
his hand to his mouth and whistled out something foul,
afterward claiming that it was Greek. After Trimalchio
himself had imitated some trumpeters, he looked back at
his favorite young boy whom he called Croesus, a watery-
eyed boy with very rotten teeth, who was wrapping up a
black grossly fat puppy in a green cloth. He placed a half-
pound loaf of bread on the couch, and with it was trying
to stuff the dog who did not want it, and who threw it up.
Trimalchio was reminded by this of his duties and ordered
that Scylax, "the guardian of home and household," be
brought in. At once an enormous dog on a chain was led
in, and, nudged by the heel of the porter to lie down,
settled himself in front of the table. Then Trimalchio
threw it some white bread and said: "No one in my house
loves me more." The favorite boy Croesus took offense,
because he praised Scylax so lavishly, put his puppy on the
floor, and encouraged it to start a fight. Doubtless revert-
ing to a dog's nature, Scylax filled the dining room with the
most offensive barking and almost tore Croesus' Pearl to
pieces. The uproar was not confined to the fighting dogs,
for a lamp was overturned on the table and smashed all
the crystal glasses, and sprayed some of the guests with
hot oil. Trimalchio did not want to seem upset by the
havoc, so he kissed his boy and told him to jump on his
back. Without delay he mounted his horse and repeatedly
struck Trimalchio's shoulders with the flat of his hand, and
while laughing shouted out: "Big mouth, big mouth, how
many fingers do I have up?"[98] For some time Trimalchio

[98] Game similar to *morra*; cf. ch. 44.

Trimalchio camellam grandem iussit misceri ‹et›[352] potiones dividi omnibus servis, qui ad pedes sedebant, adiecta exceptione: "si quis" inquit "noluerit accipere, caput illi perfunde. interdiu severa, nunc hilaria."

65. hanc humanitatem insecutae sunt matteae, quarum etiam recordatio me, si qua est dicenti fides, offendit. |
2   singulae enim gallinae altiles pro turdis circumlatae sunt et ova anserina pilleata, quae ut comessemus ambitiosissime ‹a›[353] nobis Trimalchio petiit dicens exossatas esse
3   gallinas. | inter haec triclinii valvas lictor percussit, amictusque veste alba cum ingenti frequentia comissator
4   intravit. | ego maiestate conterritus praetorem putabam venisse. itaque temptavi assurgere et nudos pedes in ter-
5   ram deferre. | risit hanc trepidationem Agamemnon et "contine te" inquit "homo stultissime. Habinnas sevir est idemque lapidarius, qui vide{re}tur[354] monumenta optime
6   facere." | recreatus hoc sermone reposui cubitum, Habinnamque intrantem cum admiratione ingenti spectabam. |
7   ille autem iam ebrius uxoris suae umeris imposuerat manus, oneratusque aliquot coronis et unguento per frontem in oculos fluente praetorio loco se posuit continuoque vi-
8   num et caldam poposcit. | delectatus hac Trimalchio hilaritate et ipse capaciorem poposcit scyphum quaesivitque
9   quomodo acceptus esset. | "omnia" inquit "habuimus praeter te; oculi enim mei hic erant. et mehercules bene

---

352 *added Anton*   353 *added Scheffer*   354 *deleted Scheffer*

---

99 This scene recalls the entrance of Alcibiades in Plato's *Symposium* (212d–e).   100 *imus in imo*, also called the *locus consularis*. See Appendix.

was restrained by this effort but then ordered a large bowl of wine to be mixed and drinks to be distributed to all the slaves sitting at our feet, adding this provision: "If anyone refuses to take it, pour it over his head. The daytime's for business, the night's for pleasure."

65. After this display of refinement, savories were brought in, even the memory of which, if there is any reliability in the speaker, makes me sick. Instead of thrushes, fat chickens were brought round, one for each guest, and goose eggs wearing caps, which with utmost insistence Trimalchio begged us to eat, saying that they were boneless chickens. Just then a lictor knocked on the dining-room doors, and a reveler dressed in white followed by a large entourage came in. I was terrified by this appearance of greatness and thought that a praetor had arrived, so I tried to get up and place my bare feet down to the ground. Agamemnon laughed at my show of alarm and said: "Control yourself, you silly fool. It is Habinnas, the *sevir* and also a stonemason, who has a reputation for making superior tombstones." I was restored to my old self by this information, leaned back on my elbow, and with great wonder watched Habinnas' entrance.[99] He was already drunk and had put his hands on his wife's shoulders; he was covered by some wreaths, and with perfume pouring down his forehead into his eyes, settled himself in the consular seat of honor[100] and straightway ordered wine and hot water. Trimalchio was delighted at this good humor, and he himself demanded a larger cup, and asked how he had been treated. Habinnas said: "We had everything we wanted except you; the apple of my eye was here. And I

10   fuit. | Scissa lautum novendiale[355] servo suo misello facie-
bat, quem mortuum manu miserat. et puto, cum vicensi-
mariis magnam mantissam habet; quinquaginta enim mil-
11   libus aestimant mortuum. | sed tamen suaviter fuit, etiam
si coacti sumus dimidias potiones supra ossucula eius ef-
fundere." 66. "tamen" inquit Trimalchio "quid habuistis in
cena?" "dicam" inquit "si potuero; nam tam bonae memo-
2   riae sum, ut frequenter nomen meum obliviscar. | habui-
mus tamen in primo porcum botulo[356] coronatum et circa
sangunculum[357] et gizeria optime facta et certe betam et
panem autopyrum de suo sibi, quem ego malo candidum;
et vires facit, et cum mea re causa facio, non ploro. |
3   sequens ferculum fuit sc{i}rib{i}lita frigida et supra mel
caldum infusum excellente Hispanum. itaque de sc{i}-
rib{i}lita[358] quidem non minimum edi, de melle me usque
4   tetigi. | circa cicer et lupinum, calvae arbitratu et mala
singula. ego tamen duo sustuli et ecce in mappa alligata
habeo; nam si aliquid muneris meo vernulae non tulero,
5   habebo convicium. | bene me admonet domina mea. in
prospectu habuimus ursinae frust{r}um, de quo cum imprudens Scintilla gustasset, paene intestina sua vomuit;
ego contra plus libram comedi, nam ipsum aprum sapie-
6   bat. | et si, inquam, ursus homuncionem comest, quanto
7   magis homuncio debet ursum comesse? | in summo habui-
mus caseum mollem ex[359] sapa et cocleas singulas et cor-
dae frusta et hepatia in catillis et ova pilleata et rapam et

---

355 lautum novendiale *Bücheler*: laucum novendialem
356 botulo *Jac. Gronovius*: poculo
357 sangunculum *Heraeus*: saucunculum
358 scriblita (*bis*) *patav.*: sciribilita
359 ex *Bücheler*: et

swear it was really splendid. Scissa held a sumptuous
ninth-day funeral feast in memory of her poor dear slave,
whom she set free on his deathbed. And I think she has a
great load to pay to the five percent tax collector, for they
reckon that the dead man was worth fifty thousand sesterces. But anyway it was a pleasant affair, even if we were
forced to pour half our drinks over his poor bones." 66.
"So what'd you have for dinner?" said Trimalchio. "I'll tell
you, if I can," he answered. "I've such a good memory that
I often forget my own name. First we had pork topped
with sausage, and around this was black pudding, and gib-
lets very nicely done, and of course beets, and pure whole-
meal bread which I myself prefer to white, because it
makes me strong, and when I do my business in the lavatory, I don't groan.

The next dish was a cold tart and over it was poured
warm honey, then on top of that an excellent Spanish wine.
To be sure I ate a large helping of the tart, and I fairly
wallowed in the honey. There were chickpeas and lupines,
a choice of smooth nuts, an apple apiece, but I took two,
and I have them wrapped up right here in my napkin,
because if I don't bring some gift for my pet slave boy, I'll
have a protest on my hands. My good mistress kindly re-
minds me that we also had on offer a chunk of bear meat.
When Scintilla rashly tasted some of it, she nearly threw
up her insides. On the other hand I ate more than a pound,
for it tasted just like wild boar. What I say is this, if a bear
eats poor little men, how much more ought poor little men
eat bear? At the end we had soft cheese soaked in new
wine, a snail for each and pieces of tripe and liver in little
dishes and eggs in caps and turnips and mustard and a dish

senape et catillum concacatum,[360] pax Palamedes. etiam
in alveo circumlata sunt oxycomina, unde quidam etiam
improbe ternos pugnos[361] sustulerunt. nam pernae missionem dedimus. 67. sed narra mihi, Gai, rogo, Fortunata

2 quare non recumbit?" | "quomodo nosti" inquit "illam"
Trimalchio "nisi argentum composuerit, nisi reliquias pue-

3 ris diviserit, aquam in os suum non coniciet." | "atqui"
respondit Habinnas "nisi illa discumbit, ego me apoculo"
et coeperat surgere, nisi signo dato Fortunata quater am-

4 plius a tota familia esset vocata. | venit ergo galbino suc-
cincta cingillo, ita ut infra cerasina appareret tunica et

5 periscelides tortae phaecasiaeque inauratae. | tunc sudario
manus tergens, quod in collo habebat, applicat se illi toro,
in quo Scintilla Habinnae discumbebat uxor, osculataque

6 plaudentem "est te" inquit "videre?" | eo deinde perven-
tum est, ut Fortunata armillas suas crassissimis detraheret
lacertis Scintillaeque miranti ostenderet. ultimo etiam
periscelides resolvit et reticulum aureum, quem ex

7 obrussa[362] esse dicebat. | notavit haec Trimalchio iussitque
afferri omnia et "videtis" inquit "mulieris[363] compedes: sic
nos barcalae despoliamur. sex pondo et selibram debet
habere. et ipse nihilo minus habeo decem pondo armillam

8 ex millesimis Mercurii factam." | ultimo etiam, ne mentiri
videretur, stateram iussit afferri et circumlatum approbari

360 concacatum *Burman*: concagatum
361 improbe ternos pugnos *Jac. Gronovius*: improbiter nos
pugno
362 obrussa *Scheffer*: sobriissa
363 mulieris *Mentelius*: mulieres

of hash, that's enough, Palamedes! Also olives pickled in cumin seed were brought round on a large tray, from which some guests even to the point of brazenness took three fistfuls each. When the ham came, we gave it a pass. 67. But tell me, Gaius, why's Fortunata not reclining here at dinner?" Trimalchio said: "You know how it is with her. If she hasn't put away the silver, if she hasn't divided the leftovers among the slaves, she'll not toss even a drink of water into her mouth." Habinnas replied: "Yes, but unless she reclines at her couch, I'm trotting off." He began to get up, but at a given signal Fortunata was summoned four times or more by the whole household. So in she came, her dress was tucked up with a greenish-yellow belt with the result that her cherry-red tunic showed underneath, as well as her coiled anklets and gold-embroidered slippers. Just then she wiped her hands on the napkin which she had round her neck, took her place on the couch where Habinnas' wife Scintilla was reclining, and having kissed the clapping woman said: "Can I believe my eyes? Is it really you?" The situation developed then to the point that Fortunata took the bracelets from her fat arms and displayed them to Scintilla's admiring gaze. In the end she took off even her anklets and golden hairnet which she said was pure gold. Trimalchio noted these actions and ordered that all the jewelry be brought to him and said: "What you see here are a woman's fetters: this is the way we poor fools are robbed. The gold she wears must weigh six and a half pounds. I myself have a bracelet weighing not one ounce less than ten pounds, which represents one tenth of one per cent of the gold I owe Mercury." At last, for fear that he should seem to be lying, he ordered even scales to be brought in, and the weight of his jewelry was

9 pondus. | nec melior Scintilla, quae de cervice sua capsellam detraxit aureolam, quam Felicionem appellabat. inde duo crotalia protulit et Fortunatae in vicem consideranda dedit et "domini" inquit "mei beneficio nemo habet meliora." | "quid?" inquit Habinnas "excatarissasti me, ut tibi
10 emerem fabam vitream. plane si filiam haberem, auriculas illi praeciderem. mulieres si non essent, omnia pro luto haberemus; nunc hoc est caldum meiere et frigidum
11 potare." | interim mulieres sauciae inter se riserunt ebriaque[364] iunxerunt oscula, dum altera diligentiam matris familiae[365] iactat, altera delicias et indiligentiam viri. |
12 dumque sic cohaerent, Habinnas furtim consurrexit pedesque Fortunatae correptos[366] super lectum immisit. |
13 "au au" illa proclamavit aberrante tunica super genua. composita ergo in gremio Scintillae incensissimam[367] rubore faciem sudario abscondit.

68. interposito deinde spatio cum secundas mensas Trimalchio iussisset afferri, sustulerunt servi omnes mensas et alias attulerunt, sc{r}obemque[368] croco et minio tinctam sparserunt et, quod numquam ante videram, ex
2 lapide speculari pulverem tritum. | statim Trimalchio "poteram quidem" inquit "hoc fericulo esse contentus; secundas enim mensas habetis. <sed>[369] si quid belli

---

364 ebriaque *Müller*: ebrieque
365 matris familiae *Mentelius*: matrifamilie
366 correptos *Scheffer*: correctos
367 incensissimam *Reinesius*: indecens imam
368 *deleted Scheffer*
369 *added Bücheler*

verified by being carried round. Scintilla was just as bad. From her neck she took a little gold box, which she called Felicio, her lucky box. From it she brought out two earrings and gave them in turn to Fortunata to examine and said: "Thanks to my husband, no one has a finer set." "What's this?" said Habinnas. "You cleaned me out so that I could buy you a glass bean. Surely if I had a daughter, I'd cut off her dear little ears. If there were no women, everything round us would be dirt cheap. Now as it is, what we piss out is hot, what we drink in is cold." Meanwhile the women affected by the wine laughed at each other and exchanged drunk kisses, as one boasted about her attentiveness as female head of house, and the other complained about her husband's favorite young boy and his inattentiveness of her. While the women thus stuck together, Habinnas quietly rose and grabbed the feet of Fortunata and threw her over the couch. "Oh, oh," she said in astonishment, as her tunic went astray above her knees. She took refuge on the bosom of Scintilla and buried her blushing red face in her napkin.

68. Then after a brief interval when Trimalchio ordered that the dessert course—second tables[101]—be brought in, the servants removed even the tables and brought in others, then sprinkled sawdust colored with saffron and vermilion, and a thing I had never seen before, powdered mica on the floor. At once Trimalchio said: "I could in fact be satisfied with this course, for you've got your second tables. But if you've anything nice, my boy,

[101] second tables = desert; the servants on cue from Trimalchio intentionally misunderstand the order and remove also the tables themselves. This is supposedly amusing.

3 habes, ⟨puer,⟩[370] affer." | interim puer Alexandrinus, qui
caldam ministrabat, luscinias coepit imitari clamante Tri-
4 malchione subinde: "muta." | ecce alius ludus. servus qui
ad pedes Habinnae sedebat, iussus, credo, a domino suo
proclamavit subito canora voce: "interea medium Aeneas
5 iam classe tenebat." | nullus sonus umquam acidior per-
cussit aures meas; nam praeter errantis barbariae aut
adiectum[371] aut deminutum clamorem miscebat Atellani-
cos versus, ut tunc primum me etiam Vergilius offenderit.
6 | lassus tamen cum aliquando desisset,[372] adiecit Habin-
nas: "et num⟨quam" in⟩quit[373] "didicit, sed ego ad circu-
7 latores eum mittendo erudibam.[374] | itaque parem non
habet, sive muliones volet sive circulatores imitari. desperatum[375] valde ingeniosus est: idem sutor est, idem cocus,
8 idem pistor, omnis musae mancipium. | duo tamen vitia
habet, quae si non haberet, esset omnium numerum:[376]
recutitus est et stertit. nam quod strabonus est, non curo:
sicut Venus spectat. ideo nihil tacet, vix oculo mortuo
umquam. illum emi trecentis[377] denariis." 69. interpellavit
loquentem Scintilla et "plane" inquit "non omnia artificia
2 servi nequam narras. | agaga est; at curabo, stigmam ha-
beat." risit Trimalchio et "adcognosco" inquit "Cappado-
cem: nihil sibi defraudat,[378] et mehercules laudo illum;
hoc enim nemo parentat. tu autem, Scintilla, noli zelotypa
3 esse. | crede mihi, et vos novimus. sic me salvum habeatis,

---

[370] *added Walsh*[2]   [371] adiectum *Scheffer*: abiectum
[372] desisset *Scheffer*: dedisset   [373] numquam inquit
Bücheler: numquid   [374] erudibam *Jahn*: audibant
[375] desperatum *Bücheler*: desperatus   [376] numerum
Scheffer: nummorum   [377] emi trecentis *Scheffer*: emit
retentis   [378] defraudat *Hadrianides*: defraudit

bring it in." Meanwhile a slave from Alexandria who was providing hot water began to imitate nightingales, while Trimalchio repeatedly shouted: "Change the tune." And then there was another form of amusement. The slave sitting at the feet of Habinnas, prompted I am sure by his master, suddenly declaimed in a singsong voice: "Meanwhile Aeneas held midocean with his fleet."[102] No more disagreeable sound ever struck my ears; apart from the way he raised or lowered his yapping voice in his barbarous meanderings, he inserted Atellane verses so that then for the first time even Virgil set my teeth on edge. When at last he grew tired and stopped, Habinnas added a comment: "He never went to school, but I saw to his education by sending him to street entertainers. So whether he wishes to imitate muleteers or hawkers, he's got no equal. He's desperately clever: he's a cobbler, cook, baker, a good all-purpose slave. He, however, has two faults, which if he didn't have, he'd be one in a million: he's circumcised, and he snores. I don't mind his being squint-eyed: Venus looks the same way.[103] He keeps nothing secret from me, he tells me everything he sees. I bought him for three hundred *denarii*." 69. Scintilla interrupted his comments and said: "For sure you are not telling the whole truth about all the tricks of that worthless slave. He's a pimp, and I'll see to it that he's branded." Trimalchio laughed and said: "I know a Cappadocian when I see one: he takes care of himself first, and I swear I admire him; no one can give happiness to the dead. You, Scintilla, don't be jealous. Believe me, we know you women. By my hope that I stay healthy, how

102 Verg. *Aen*. 5.1.
103 On Venus' squint, cf. Ov. *Ars am*. 2.659.

ut ego sic solebam ipsumam meam debattuere, ut etiam
dominus suspicaretur; et ideo me in vilicationem relega-
4 vit. sed tace, lingua{m},[379] dabo panem." | tamquam lau-
datus esset nequissimus servus, lucernam de sinu fictilem
protulit et amplius semihora tubicines imitatus est suc-
cinente Habinna et inferius labrum manu deprimente. |
5 ultimo etiam in medium processit et modo harundinibus
quassis choraulas imitatus est, modo lacernatus cum fla-
gello mulionum fata egit, donec vocatum ad se Habinnas
basiavit, potionemque illi porrexit et "tanto melior" inquit
"Massa, dono tibi caligas." |

6 nec ullus tot malorum finis fuisset, nisi epidipnis esset
allata, turdi siliginei[380] uvis passis nuceribusque farsi.[381] |
7 insecuta sunt Cydonia etiam mala spinis confixa, ut echinos
efficerent. et haec quidem tolerabilia erant, si non ferculum longe monstrosius effecisset ut vel fame perire
8 mallemus. | nam cum positus esset, ut nos putabamus,
anser altilis circaque pisces et omnium genera avium,
"<amici,>"[382] inquit Trimalchio "quicquid videtis hic
9 positum, de uno corpore est factum." | ego, scilicet homo
prudentissimus, statim intellexi quid esset, et respiciens
Agamemnonem "mirabor" inquam "nisi omnia ista de
<faece>[383] facta sunt aut certe de luto. vidi Romae Satur-
nalibus eiusmodi cenarum imaginem fieri." 70. necdum
finieram sermonem, cum Trimalchio ait: "ita crescam pa-
trimonio, non corpore, ut ista cocus meus de porco fecit.
2 | non potest esse pretiosior homo. volueris, de vulva[384]

---

[379] deleted *Scheffer*   [380] turdi silignei *Heinsius*: turdis iligine
[381] farsi *Heinsius*: farsis   [382] *added Bücheler*
[383] *added Lowe*
[384] vulva *Scheffer*: bulla

I used to bang my own mistress to such an extent that even my master became suspicious, and therefore he banished me to the stewardship of his country estate. But, 'my tongue, shut up and I'll give you some bread.'" This most worthless slave acted as if he had been complimented, took a clay lamp out of his pocket, and for more than half an hour gave imitations of trumpeters, while Habinnas chimed in, pulling down his lower lip with his hand. Finally the boy came right into the center of the room: now using broken reeds he imitated flute players, now wearing a cloak and holding a whip, he acted episodes from the lives of muleteers, until Habinnas called him over and kissed him, and offered him a drink and said: "Bravo, Massa, I'll give you a pair of boots for that."

There would have been no end to our discomfort, if an extra course had not been brought in, consisting of pastry thrushes stuffed with raisins and nuts. Quinces came next, inserted into which were thorns to give the impression of sea urchins. We could have endured also all this, if a far more pretentious dish had not driven us to prefer death even by starvation. When what we took to be a fat goose surrounded by fish and all kinds of birds was set before us, Trimalchio commented: "Friends, whatever you see served here is made from one substance." Being an intelligent man, I immediately understood what it was, and looked over to Agamemnon and said: "I will be surprised if all these are not made of dregs or, at any rate, of clay. I have seen fake dinners of this kind served at Rome during the Saturnalia." 70. I had not yet finished my statement when Trimalchio said: "As sure as I hope to expand in wealth, not in body size, my cook has made all these out of pork. There can't be a more valuable man. If you so

209

faciet piscem, de lardo palumbum, de perna turturem, de colepio gallinam. et ideo ingenio meo impositum est illi
3 nomen bellissimum; nam Daedalus vocatur. | et quia bonam mentem habet, attuli[385] illi Roma munus[386] cultros Norico ferro." quos statim iussit afferri inspectosque miratus est. etiam nobis potestatem fecit, ut mucronem ad buccam probaremus. |
4 subito intraverunt duo servi, tamquam qui rixam ad lacum fecissent; certe in collo[387] adhuc amphoras habe-
5 bant. | cum ergo Trimalchio ius inter litigantes diceret, neuter sententiam tulit decernentis, sed alterius ampho-
6 ram fuste percussit. | consternati nos insolentia ebriorum intentavimus oculos in proeliantes notavimusque ostrea pectinesque e gastris[388] labentia, quae collecta puer lance
7 circumtulit. | has lautitias aequavit ingeniosus cocus; in craticula enim argentea cochleas attulit et tremula taeter-
8 rimaque voce cantavit. | pudet referre quae secuntur: inaudito enim more pueri capillati attulerunt unguentum in argentea pelve pedesque recumbentium unxerunt, cum
9 ante crura talosque corollis vinxissent. | hinc ex eodem unguento in vinarium atque lucernam aliquantum[389] est
10 infusum. | iam coeperat Fortunata velle saltare, iam Scintilla frequentius plaudebat quam loquebatur, cum Trimalchio "permitto" inquit "Philargyre {et Carrio},[390] etsi pra-

---

385 attuli *Heinsius*: attulit   386 Roma munus *Heinsius*: romā unus   387 collo *Heinsius*: loco

388 gastris *Muncker*: castris   389 aliquantum *Heinsius*: liquatum   390 *deleted Kaibel*

---

104 A territory roughly corresponding to modern Austria and famous for producing high-quality iron.

wish, he will make a fish out of sow's belly, a pigeon out of bacon, a turtledove out of ham, a chicken out of pork knuckle. And so using my mental gifts, I selected a most suitable name: he is called Daedalus. Because he has talent, I brought him a gift from Rome of steel knives made in Noricum."[104] He at once ordered that they be brought in, and having looked them over and admired them, he gave us the chance to test the edges against our cheeks.

Suddenly two slaves entered who looked as if they had been fighting at a public fountain; at least they still had water jugs on their shoulders. Of course when Trimalchio assumed the role of magistrate between litigants, neither accepted his decision, but struck the other's pot with a stick. We were startled by the arrogance of the drunks, stared at them as they did battle, and then noticed oysters and scallops falling from the jugs, which a boy gathered up and carried round on a dish. The clever cook matched these refinements: he carried round snails on a silver gridiron and sang in a wavering and most hideous voice. I am ashamed to repeat what followed: in defiance of convention, long-haired boys brought round perfume in a silver bowl and rubbed it on the feet of those reclining, first having wound garlands round our legs and ankles. Then some of the same perfume was poured into the wine bowl and also into a lamp. Fortunata had already begun to show a desire to dance, and Scintilla was now clapping more than speaking, when Trimalchio said: "Philargyrus, even if you are an infamous supporter of the Greens,[105] I give you

[105] There were four teams (*factiones*) of charioteers in the Circus, and they were distinguished by their colors: green, blue, red, white.

sinianus es famosus, dic et Menophilae, contubernali tuae,
11 discumbat." | quid multa? paene de lectis deiecti sumus,
12 adeo totum triclinium familia occupaverat. | certe ego
notavi super me positum cocum, qui de porco anserem
13 fecerat, muria condimentisque fetentem. | nec contentus
fuit recumbere, sed continuo Ephesum tragoedum coepit
imitari et subinde dominum suum sponsione provocare "si
prasinus proximis circensibus primam palmam."

71. diffusus hac contentione Trimalchio "amici," inquit
"et servi homines sunt et aeque unum lactem biberunt,
etiam si illos malus fatus oppresserit. tamen me salvo cito
aquam liberam gustabunt. ad summam, omnes illos in
2 testamento meo manu mitto. | Philargyro etiam fundum
lego et contubernalem suam, Carioni[391] quoque insulam
3 et vicesimam et lectum stratum. | nam Fortunatam meam
heredem facio, et commendo illam omnibus amicis meis.
et haec ideo omnia publico, ut familia mea iam nunc sic
4 me amet tamquam mortuum." | gratias agere omnes indul-
gentiae coeperant domini, cum ille oblitus nugarum exemplar testimenti iussit afferri et totum a primo ad ultimum
5 ingemescente familia recitavit. | respiciens deinde Habin-
nam "quid dicis" inquit "amice carissime? aedificas monu-
6 mentum meum, quemadmodum te iussi? | valde te rogo
ut secundum pedes statuae meae catellam fingas[392] et
coronas et unguenta et Petraitis omnes pugnas, ut mihi
contingat tuo beneficio post mortem vivere; praeterea ut

391 Carioni *Bücheler*: Carrioni
392 fingas *Scheffer*: pingas

permission—invite also your common-law wife Menophila—to recline on a couch." What more need I say? We
were almost pushed off the couches, so completely had
the household staff taken over the dining room. Of course
I noticed that the cook, who had made the goose from
pork, was reclining just above me and stinking of pickles
and spices. Not satisfied with having a place at the table,
he at once began to imitate the tragic actor Ephesus[106] and
then to call out his master to settle up, if the charioteer of
the Greens won first place at the next races.

71. Trimalchio became affable in this dispute and said:
"Friends, even slaves are men and have drunk the same
milk as everyone else, even if an evil fate has overwhelmed
them. But if things go my way, they'll soon taste the water
of freedom. In fact, I'm setting them all free in my will. To
Philargyrus I also bequeath a farm and his common-law
wife, and to Cario a block of flats, his manumission tax, and
bed and bedding. Now as to Fortunata, I make her my
heir, and commend her to all my friends. And I'm making
all these things public so that my household might so love
me now as if I were dead." They all began to thank their
master for his generosity, when he turned serious and ordered a copy of his will to be brought in, which he read
out from beginning to end, while the household groaned.
Looking over at Habinnas, he said: "Tell me, my dearest
friend, are you building my tomb in the way that I ordered
you? I ask you earnestly to mold an image of my dog round
the feet of my statue, as well as garlands and perfumes and
all the fights of Petraites, so that by your kindness I might
live on after death; I ask moreover that my tomb complex

---

[106] Unknown person.

sint in fronte pedes centum, in agrum pedes ducenti. |
7   omne genus autem[393] poma volo sint circa cineres meos,
et vinearum largiter. valde enim falsum est vivo quidem
domos cultas esse, non curari eas, ubi diutius nobis habi-
tandum est. et ideo ante omnia adici volo: 'hoc monumen-
8   tum heredem non sequatur.' | ceterum erit mihi curae ut
testamento caveam ne mortuus iniuriam accipiam. prae-
ponam enim unum ex libertis sepulcro meo custodiae
causa, ne in monumentum meum populus cacatum currat.
9 | te rogo ut naves etiam {monumenti mei}[394] facias plenis
velis euntes, et me in tribunali sedentem praetextatum
cum anulis aureis quinque et nummos in publico de sac-
culo effundentem; scis enim quod epulum dedi binos
10 denarios. | faciantur,[395] si tibi videtur, et triclinia. facies et
11 totum populum sibi suaviter facientem. | ad dexteram
meam pones statuam Fortunatae meae columbam te-
nentem—et catellam cingulo alligatam ducat—et cica-
ronem meum, et amphoras copiosas gypsatas, ne effluant
vinum. et unam licet fractam sculpas, et super eam puerum plorantem. horologium in medio, ut quisquis horas
12 inspiciet, velit nolit, nomen meum legat. | inscriptio quo-
que vide diligenter si haec satis idonea tibi videtur: 'C.
Pompeius Trimalchio Maecenatianus hic requiescit. huic
seviratus absenti decretus est. cum posset in omnibus

---

393 autem *Holford-Strevens*: enim
394 *deleted Müller*
395 faciantur *Goesius*: faciatur

---

107 A toga with a purple stripe was perhaps Trimalchio's due
as a *sevir Augustalis*; it is not clear what five gold rings signify
except perhaps to hint at some unspecified dignity; he is not ac-

have a frontage of one hundred feet and to be two hundred feet in depth. I want to have all kinds of fruit trees growing round my ashes, and plenty of vines. It's quite wrong for a man to have a handsome house while he's alive, and not to be concerned about the house where we have to live for a longer time. And so above all I want this added to the inscription: 'This tomb must not pass to an heir.' Certainly I will take care to provide in my will that I suffer no damage, when I'm dead. I'll appoint one of my freedmen to guard my tomb and prevent the common people from running there to shit. I ask you also to show ships in full sail, and portray me sitting on a dais in a toga with a purple stripe, wearing five gold rings and pouring out coins in public from a bag; for you know that I sponsored a free dinner for them at two *denarii* a head.[107] If you can arrange it, add some dining rooms. Portray also all the citizens enjoying each other. On my right hand put a statue of my Fortunata holding a dove—and have her lead her puppy tied to her belt—and my boy-favorite, and lots of wine jars sealed with gypsum so that they can keep the wine from flowing out. And show one of the jars as broken and a slave weeping over it. Place a sundial in the middle so that whoever looks at the time will read my name, whether he wants to or not. Also consider carefully whether this inscription seems suitable enough to you: 'Here rests Gaius Pompeius Trimalchio who belonged to the household of Maecenas. The Sevirate was conferred upon him in his absence. Though he could have been a

tually distributing money to the people, a privilege he did not have; a free dinner was regularly given by a *sevir* upon entering office.

decuriis Romae esse, tamen noluit. pius,[396] fortis, fidelis,
ex parvo crevit; sestertium reliquit trecenties, nec umquam philosophum audivit. vale: et tu.'"

72. haec ut dixit Trimalchio, flere coepit ubertim. flebat
et Fortunata, flebat et Habinnas, tota denique familia,
tamquam in funus rogata, lamentatione triclinium imple-
2 vit. | immo iam coeperam etiam ego plorare, cum Trimal-
chio "ergo" inquit "cum sciamus nos morituros esse, quare
3 non vivamus? | sic vos felices videam, coniciamus nos in
4 balneum, meo periculo, non paenitebit. | sic calet tam-
quam furnus." "vero, vero" inquit Habinnas "de una die
duas facere, nihil malo" nudisque consurrexit pedibus et
5 Trimalchionem plaudentem[397] subsequi ‹coepit›.[398] | ego
respiciens ad Ascylton "quid cogitas?" inquam "ego enim
6 si videro balneum, statim expirabo." | "assentemur" ait ille
7 "et dum illi balneum petunt, nos in turba exeamus." | cum
haec placuissent, ducente per porticum Gitone ad ianuam
venimus, ubi canis catenarius tanto nos tumultu excepit,
ut Ascyltos etiam in piscinam ceciderit. nec non ego quoque ebrius ‹et›[399] qui etiam pictum timueram canem,
dum natanti opem fero, in eundem gurgitem tractus sum.
8 | servavit nos tamen atriensis, qui interventu suo et canem
9 placavit et nos trementes extraxit in siccum. | et Giton
quidem iam dudum se ratione[400] acutissima redemerat a
cane; quicquid enim a nobis acceperat de cena, latranti
sparserat, at ille avocatus cibo furorem suppresserat. |

396 pius *Reinesius*: plus
397 plaudentem *Jacobs*: gaudentem
398 *added Burman*
399 *added Müller*
400 se ratione *Scheffer*: servatione

member of every guild in Rome, he refused. God-fearing, brave, faithful, he grew from a small beginning. He left thirty million sesterces, and he never heard a philosopher. Farewell, Trimalchio; and farewell, passerby.'"

72. As he said these words, he began to weep copiously. Fortunata also wept, Habinnas also wept, finally the whole household, as though invited to a funeral, filled the dining room with weeping. By now even I had begun to wail, when Trimalchio said: "Therefore since we know we'll die, why shouldn't we live now? Because I would thus wish to see you happy, let's throw ourselves into the bath. I'll bet my life that you won't regret it. The water's as hot as an oven." Habinnas said: "Very true, very true. I like nothing more than making two days out of one," and with his bare feet on the floor he rose and began to follow Trimalchio who was applauding his guests. Looking over at Ascyltos, I said: "What are you thinking? For if I even see a bath, I will die on the spot." He said: "Let us agree to their plan, and while they are making for the bath, we can slip away in the crowd." After this was agreed on, Giton led us through a colonnade until we came to the door, where a dog on a chain welcomed us with such a loud noise that Ascyltos fell into the fishpond. I too was drunk and had earlier been scared even of a painted dog, and while I was helping my swimming friend, I was dragged into the same deep water. The doorman, however, rescued us, and by his intervention both calmed the dog and pulled us out shivering onto the dry floor. In fact in a very clever ploy Giton had already bought off the dog: he had thrown all the pieces of food from the banquet, which he had received from us, to the dog, who was distracted by the edibles and had allayed his frenzy.

10 ceterum cum algentes udique[401] petissemus ab atriense
ut nos extra ianuam emitteret, "erras" inquit "si putas te
exire hac posse qua venisti. nemo umquam convivarum
per eandem ianuam emissus est; alia intrant, alia exeunt."
73. quid faciamus homines miserrimi et novi generis laby-
rintho inclusi, quibus lavari iam coeperat votum esse? |

2 ultro ergo rogavimus ut nos ad balneum duceret, proiec-
tisque vestimentis, quae Giton in aditu siccare coepit,
balneum intravimus, angustum scilicet et cisternae frigi-
dariae simile, in quo[402] Trimalchio rectus stabat. ac ne sic
quidem putidissimam eius iactationem[403] licuit effugere;
nam nihil melius esse dicebat quam sine turba lavari, et eo

3 ipso loco aliquando pistrinum fuisse. | deinde ut lassatus
consedit, invitatus balnei sono diduxit usque ad cameram
os ebrium et coepit Menecratis cantica lacerare, sicut

4 illi dicebant qui linguam eius intellegebant. | ceter⟨um
ali⟩i[404] convivae circa labrum manibus nexis currebant et
gingilipho ingenti clamore exsonabant. alii autem {aut}[405]
restrictis manibus anulos de pavimento ⟨dentibus⟩[406]
conabantur tollere aut posito genu cervices post terga flec-

5 tere et pedum extremos pollices tangere. | nos, dum illi[407]
sibi ludos faciunt, in solium,[408] quod Trimalchioni servabatur,[409] descendimus.

ergo ebrietate discussa in aliud triclinium deducti sumus, ubi Fortunata disposuerat lautitias suas ita ut supra

---

[401] udique *Bücheler*: utique   [402] quo *Bücheler*: qua
[403] eius iactationem *Heinsius*: ei actionem
[404] *added Müller*   [405] *deleted Bücheler*
[406] *added Burman*   [407] illi *Bücheler*: alii
[408] solium *Bücheler*: solo
[409] servabatur *Novák*: pervapatur

But when cold and wet we asked the doorman to let us out the door, he said: "You're mistaken if you suppose that you can go out the door by which you came in. None of the guests is ever let out by the same door; they come in at one and go out another." 73. What could we poor victims do, trapped in a new kind of labyrinth, to whom the idea of washing now began to be our own wish? So of our own accord we asked him to lead us to the bath. We threw off our clothes which Giton began to dry in the doorway, and entered the baths. To be sure, it was a narrow bath, like a cold-water cistern, and Trimalchio was standing upright in it. And not even here were we allowed to escape his nauseating boasting; he kept saying there was nothing better than a bath away from the crowds, and on this very spot at one time there had been a bakery. Then, as though exhausted, he sat back, and encouraged by the acoustics of the bath opened up his drunk mouth toward the ceiling and began to butcher the songs of Menecrates,[108] so those reported who could understand his words. But some guests joined hands and ran round the bath and with peals of laughter raised an uproar, while others with their hands tied behind them tried to pick up rings from the floor with their teeth, or on their knees, tried to bend their necks backward and touch the tips of their big toes. While they were amusing themselves, we went down toward the seat in the bath which was reserved for Trimalchio.

Once the effects of our drunkenness were shaken off, we were led into another dining room, where Fortunata had displayed her luxury items in such a way that over the

[108] Name of a harp player in the reign of Nero (Suet. *Ner.* 30).

lucernas < . . . > aeneolosque piscatores notaverim< us >[410] et
mensas totas argenteas calicesque circa fictiles inauratos
6 et vinum in conspectu sacco defluens. | tum Trimalchio
"amici," inquit "hodie Croesus[411] meus barbatoriam[412]
fecit, homo praefiscini frugi et micarius. itaque tangomenas faciamus et usque in lucem cenemus." 74. haec dicente eo gallus gallinaceus cantavit. qua voce confusus
Trimalchio vinum sub mensa iussit effundi lucernamque
2 etiam mero spargi. | immo anulum traiecit in dexteram
manum et "non sine causa" inquit "hic bucinus signum
dedit; nam aut incendium oportet fiat, aut aliquis in vicinia
3 animam abiciet. | longe a nobis. itaque quisquis hunc indi-
4 cem attulerit, corollarium accipiet." | dicto citius de vicinia
gallus allatus est, quem Trimalchio iussit < occidi >[413] ut
5 aeno coctus fieret. | laceratus igitur ab illo doctissimo coco,
qui paulo ante de porco aves piscesque fecerat, in cacca-
bum est coniectus. dumque Daedalus potionem ferventis-
6 simam haurit, Fortunanta mola buxea piper trivit. | sump-
tis igitur matteis respiciens ad familiam Trimalchio "quid?
vos" inquit "adhuc non cenastis? abite, ut alii veniant ad
7 officium." | subiit igitur alia classis, et illi quidem exclama-
8 vere: "vale Gai," hi autem: "ave Gai." | hinc primum hila-
ritas nostra turbata est; nam cum puer non inspeciosus
inter novos intrasset ministros, invasit eum Trimalchio
9 osculari diutius coepit. | itaque Fortunata, ut ex aequo ius
firmum approbaret, male dicere Trimalchioni[414] coepit et
purgamentum dedecusque praedicare, qui non contineret

[410] *added Schmeling*   [411] Croesus *Wehle*: servus
[412] barbatoriam *Scheffer*: babatoriam
[413] *added Bücheler*
[414] Trimalchioni *Anton*: Trimalchionem

lamps . . . and we noted bronze fishermen, solid silver tables, pottery cups gilded all round, and wine being strained through a cloth for everyone to see. Then Trimalchio said: "Friends, today my Croesus celebrated his first shave: he's an honest fellow, so help me, frugal and economical. So let's drink our fill and eat till dawn." 74. Just as he was saying these things, a cock crowed. Upset by this sound, Trimalchio ordered wine to be poured under the table and the lamp to be sprinkled with pure wine. Further, he transferred his ring to his right hand and said: "For some reason that trumpeter gave a signal: either a fire is about to occur, or someone in the neighborhood will give up the ghost. Keep all evil away from us. So whoever brings in that informer will get a reward." No sooner were the words out of his mouth than a cock was brought in from the neighborhood, and Trimalchio ordered it to be killed, so that it could be cooked in a pot. Therefore it was cut up by that learned cook, who shortly before had made birds and fish from pork, and thrown into a pot. And while Daedulus scooped up the scalding broth, Fortunata ground up pepper in a boxwood mill. After the delicacies were eaten, Trimalchio looked over at his household of slave waiters and said: "What? Haven't you had your dinner yet? Off you go so others can come and serve." So a second shift advanced, and those leaving shouted "Goodbye, Gaius," and those coming in "Greetings, Gaius." But then our good humor received its first shock. For when a not unhandsome slave lad entered among the incoming waiters, Trimalchio fell upon him and began to kiss him for an unseemly long time. This persuaded Fortunata to assert her legal connubial rights, and she began to curse Trimalchio, calling him a disgraceful bag of garbage for not con-

10 libidinem suam. ultimo etiam adiecit: "canis." | Trimalchio
contra offensus convicio calicem in faciem Fortunatae
11 immisit. | illa tamquam oculum perdidisset exclamavit
12 manusque trementes ad faciem suam admovit. | conster-
nata est etiam Scintilla trepidantemque sinu suo texit.
immo puer quoque officiosus urceolum frigidum ad malam eius admovit, super quem incumbens Fortunata ge-
13 mere ac flere coepit. | contra Trimalchio "quid enim?"
inquit "ambubaia non meminit se? de[415] machina[416] illam
sustuli, hominem inter homines feci. at inflat se tamquam
rana, et in sinum suum non spuit,[417] codex, non mulier. |
14 sed hic qui in pergula natus est aedes non somniatur. ita
genium meum propitium habeam, curabo domata sit Cas-
15 sandra caligaria. | et ego, homo dipundiarius, sestertium
centies accipere potui. scis tu me non mentiri. Agatho
unguentarius hic[418] proxime seduxit me et 'suadeo' inquit
16 'non patiaris genus tuum interire.' | at ego dum bonatus
ago et nolo videri levis, ipse mihi asciam in crus impegi. |
17 recte, curabo me unguibus quaeras. et tu depraesentiarum intellegas quid tibi feceris: Habinna, nolo statuam
eius in monumento meo ponas, ne mortuus quidem lites
habeam. immo, ut sciat me posse malum dare, nolo me
mortuum basiet."

75. post hoc fulmen Habinnas rogare coepit ut iam
desineret irasci et [HφL]"nemo" inquit "nostrum non peccat.
2 homines sumus, non dii."[419] | [H]idem et Scintilla flens dixit
ac per genium eius Gaium appellando rogare coepit ut se

---

415 meminit se de *Heinsius*: me misit se de
416 machina *Reiske*: machillam
417 non spuit *Reiske*: conspuit
418 hic *Fuchs*: here   419 dii *L*: dei

trolling his lustful passions. For a final abuse she added: "You dog." Trimalchio was stung by her invective and in reply threw a cup at her face. She shrieked as though she had lost an eye, and raised her trembling hands to her face. Scintilla also was alarmed and protected her quivering friend in her lap. Then a slave dutifully applied a cold jar to her cheek, and Fortunata leaned over it and began to groan and cry. Trimalchio's reaction was to comment: "What's all this? Does my flute girl not remember who she is? I took her from the slave block and made her as good as the next person. But she puffs herself up like a frog and doesn't spit into her own lap, a log not a woman. But a person born in a hut doesn't dream about living in a mansion. Just as I hope to have a kindly disposed guardian spirit, I'll take care to tame my jackbooted Cassandra. A fool worth two *asses* that I am, I could've married into ten million sesterces. You know I'm not lying. Agatho the parfumier took me aside recently and said: 'I urge you not to let your line die out.' But I, like a good man, and not wishing to seem fickle, drove the ax myself into my own leg. Very well then, I'll make you want to go for me with your bare nails. And so that you know here and now what you've done: Habinnas, I don't want you to put a statue of her on my tomb, otherwise I'll have nothing but nagging when I'm dead. In fact, to show that I can do her a bad turn, I don't want her to kiss me when I'm dead."

75. After this bolt out of the blue, Habinnas began to beg him to abandon his anger and said: "We've all made mistakes. We're humans, not gods." In her tears Scintilla said the same thing, and in calling him Gaius began to beg

3 frangeret.[420] | non tenuit ultra lacrimas Trimalchio et
   "rogo" inquit "Habinna, sic peculium tuum fruniscaris: si
4 quid perperam feci, in faciem meam inspue. | puerum
   basiavi frugalissimum, non propter formam, sed quia frugi
   est: decem partes dicit, librum ab oculo legit, thraecium[421]
   sibi de diariis fecit, arcisellium de suo paravit et duas trul-
   las. non est dignus quem in oculis feram? sed Fortunata
5 vetat. | ita tibi videtur, fulcipedia? | suadeo bonum tuum
6 concoquas, milva, et me non facias[422] ringentem, ama-
7 siuncula: alioquin experieris cerebrum meum. | nosti me:
   quod semel destinavi, clavo trabali[423] fixum est. sed vivo-
8 rum meminerimus. | vos rogo, amici, ut vobis suaviter sit.
   nam ego quoque tam fui quam vos estis, sed virtute mea
   ad hoc perveni. coricillum est quod homines facit, cetera
9 quisquilia omnia. | 'bene emo, bene vendo'; alius alia vobis
   dicet. felicitate dissilio. tu autem, sterteia, etiamnum plo-
10 ras? iam curabo fatum tuum plores. | sed, ut coeperam
   dicere, ad hanc me fortunam frugalitas mea perduxit. tam
   magnus ex Asia veni quam hic candelabrus est. ad sum-
   ma⟨m⟩,[424] quotidie me solebam ad illum metiri,[425] et ut
   celerius rostrum barbatum haberem, labra de lucerna
11 ungebam. | tamen ad delicias {femina} ipsimi {domini}
   annos quattuordecim fui. nec turpe est quod dominus
   iubet. ego tamen et ipsimae {dominae}[426] satis faciebam.
   scitis quid dicam: taceo, quia non sum de gloriosis.

[420] se frangeret *Heinsius*: effrangeret
[421] thraecium *Orelli*: thretium   [422] facias *Mentelius*: facies
[423] trabali *Scheffer*: tabulari
[424] *added Mentelius*
[425] metiri *Scheffer*: me uri
[426] {femina} ... {domini} ... {dominae} *deleted Bücheler*

him by his guardian spirit to relent. No longer did Trimalchio hold back his tears and said: "I ask you, Habinnas, as you hope to enjoy your savings, if I've done anything wrong, spit in my face. I kissed this most prudent slave boy not because of his beauty, but because he has merit: he knows his ten-times tables, reads a book at sight, from his own allowance he's got toy armor in the style of a Thracian gladiator, and with his own money purchased an arched-back chair and two ladles. Isn't he worthy to be kept in my thoughts? But Fortunata forbids it. Is that the way you see it, you in the high heels? I urge you to consider well the blessings you have, you kite, and don't make me show my teeth, my little darling, otherwise you'll taste my anger. You know what I am: once I've determined to do something, it is fastened with a construction nail. But let's remember the living. My friends, I beg you to enjoy yourselves. For I also was once what you are, but by my own merits I've reached to this level. A little brains is what makes people successful, the rest is just rubbish. 'I buy well, I sell well,' that's my rule; another person will tell you something else. I'm bursting with happiness. But you, the snorer, are you still whining? Soon I'll see to it that you've something to whine about. As I had begun to say, my own hard work brought me to success. When I came here from Asia, I was about as tall as that lampstand. In short, everyday I used to measure myself against it, and to raise a mustache under my beak more quickly I'd often grease my lips from the lamp oil. Still, I was my master's favorite at the age of fourteen. It's not disgraceful to do what your master demands. Then too, I used to satisfy my mistress. You know what I'm talking about: I say no more because I'm not one of the braggarts.

225

76. ceterum, quemadmodum di volunt, dominus in
2 domo factus sum, et ecce cepi ipsimi cerebellum. | quid
multa? coheredem me Caesari fecit, et accepi[427] patrimo-
3 nium laticlavium. | nemini tamen nihil satis est. concupivi
negotiari. ne multis vos morer, quinque naves aedificavi,
oneravi vinum—et tunc erat contra aurum—misi Romam.
4 | putares me hoc iussisse: omnes naves naufragarunt, fac-
tum, non fabula. uno die Neptunus trecenties sestertium
5 devoravit. putatis me defecisse? | non meherules mi haec
iactura gusti fuit, tamquam nihil facti. alteras feci maiores
et meliores et feliciores, ut nemo non me virum fortem
6 diceret. | sc<it>is,[428] magna navis magnam fortitudinem
habet. oneravi rursus vinum, lardum, fabam, seplasium,
7 mancipia. | hoc loco Fortunata rem piam fecit; omne enim
aurum suum, omnia vestimenta vendidit et mi centum
8 aureos in manu posuit. | hoc fuit peculii mei fermentum.
cito fit[429] quod di volunt. uno cursu centies sestertium
corrotundavi. statim redemi fundos omnes, qui patroni
mei fuerant. aedifico domum, venalicia coemo, <com-
paro>[430] iumenta; quicquid tangebam, crescebat tamquam
9 favus. | postquam coepi plus habere quam tota patria mea
habet, manum de tabula: sustuli me de negotiatione et
10 coepi <per>[431] libertos faenerare. | et sane nolente<m>[432]
me negotium meum agere exhortavit mathematicus, qui
venerat forte in coloniam nostram, Graeculio, Serapa no-
11 mine, consiliator deorum. | hic mihi dixit etiam ea quae
oblitus eram; ab acia et acu mi omnia exposuit;[433] intesti-

---

[427] accepi *Scheffer*: accepit   [428] *added Bücheler*
[429] fit *Scheffer*: fio   [430] *added Müller*
[431] *added Heinsius*   [432] *added Scheffer*
[433] exposuit *Scheffer*: exposcit

76. Then just as the gods willed it, I became the real master in the house, and I captured my master's heart and soul. What can I add, except that he made me joint heir with Caesar, and I came into an estate fit for a senator. Yet nothing's ever enough for nobody. I conceived a passion for business. To keep a long story short, I built five ships, loaded them with a cargo of wine—then it rivaled gold in value—and sent them to Rome. All the boats were wrecked, a fact not a fairy tale; you'd have thought I arranged it. In one day Neptune ate up thirty million sesterces. Do you think I lost heart? I swear this loss meant nothing to me; it was as if nothing happened. I built a second fleet of ships, bigger, better, and luckier, so that no one could say I was not a brave man. You know this, that a big ship has it own strength. I again loaded them with wine, bacon, beans, perfumes, slaves. At this point Fortunata did her helpmate best, for she sold all her gold and her clothes, and placed the proceeds, a hundred *aurei*, in my hands. This was the leaven that gave rise to my fortune. What the gods wish for happens quickly. On one voyage I rounded out ten million sesterces. I at once bought back all the estates which had belonged to my patron. I built a house, bought slaves, purchased cattle; whatever I touched grew like a honeycomb. Once I came to have more money than my whole community, I removed my hand from the game: I retired from active business and began to lend money at interest through freedmen intermediaries. Actually I was tired of trading on my own account, and it was an astrologer who convinced me to quit. He happened to come to our colony, a sort of Greek by the name of Serapa, one who shares in the counsel of the gods. He told me even things that I'd forgotten. He went through every-

nas meas noverat; tantum quod mihi non dixerat quid pridie cenaveram. putasses illum semper mecum habitasse.
77. rogo, Habinna—puto, interfuisti –: 'tu dominam tuam
de rebus illis fecisti. tu parum felix in amicos es. nemo
2 umquam tibi parem gratiam refert. | tu latifundia possides.
tu viperam sub ala nutricas,' et, quod vobis non dixerim,
etiam nunc mi restare vitae annos triginta et menses quat-
3 tor et dies duos. praeterea cito accipiam hereditatem. | hoc
mihi dicit fatus meus. quod si contigerit fundos Apuliae
4 iungere, satis vivus pervenero. | interim dum Mercurius
vigilat, aedificavi hanc domum. ut scitis, casa adhuc[434]
erat; nunc templum est. habet quattuor cenationes, cubi-
cula viginti, porticus marmoratos[435] duos, susum cella-
tionem, cubiculum in quo ipse dormio, viperae huius ses-
sorium, ostiarii cellam perbonam; hospitium hospites
5 ⟨C⟩[436] capit. | ad summa⟨m⟩,[437] Scaurus cum huc venit,
nusquam mavoluit hospitari, et habet ad mare paternam
6 hospitium. | et multa alia sunt, quae statim vobis ostendam.
credite mihi: assem habeas, assem valeas; habes, habebe-
7 ris. sic amicus vester, qui fuit rana, nunc est rex. | interim,
Stiche, profer vitalia, in quibus volo me efferri. profer et

---

434 casa adhuc *Corbett*: cusuc
435 marmoratos *Bücheler*: marmoratis
436 *added Heinsius*   437 *added Scheffer*

---

109 The *domina* here is probably not Fortunata, but the wife
of Trimalchio's former master; "those things" might be thought of
as sex toys.
110 Add this reference to the place-names in ch. 48, and Trimalchio would extend his farms to the southeast and thus over
much of southern Italy.

thing for me in great detail; he knew me inside out; the only thing he didn't tell me was what I'd eaten the day before. You'd have thought that he'd always lived with me. 77. I ask you, Habinnas, to endorse my recollection of what he told me—I think you were there: 'You made your mistress your own, using (we all know) those things.[109] You're not lucky in your friends. No one ever thanks you enough for your trouble. You own large estates. You're nourishing a viper under your wing.' And something else that he told me and I shouldn't tell you, that even now I've thirty years, four months, and two days of my life left. Moreover I'll soon receive a legacy, as my horoscope tells me. If only I could extend my farms to Apulia,[110] I'll have gone far enough and lived long enough. Meanwhile under the protection of Mercury I built this house. As you know, it was still a cottage; now it is a temple. It has four dining rooms, twenty bedrooms, two marble colonnades, a series of rooms upstairs, a bedroom where I sleep, the boudoir of this viper, a nice office for the doorman; the guest area has room for a hundred. In short, when Scaurus[111] comes here, there's nowhere else he prefers to stay, even though he has his father's guest house by the sea. And there are many other things that I'll show you right away. Believe me, if you've an *as*, you're valued at an *as*; if you've something, you're valued as someone. Thus your friend here, he was a frog but now is a king. In the meantime, Stichus, bring out the grave clothes in which I wish to be buried.

[111] Trimalchio seems to imply here that this Scaurus was a member of the senatorial Aemilii Scauri, and not the Pompeian purveyor of garum sauce.

unguentum et ex illa amphora gustum, ex qua iubeo lavari ossa mea." 78. non est moratus Stichus, sed et stragulum albam et praetextam in triclinium attulit ⟨. . .⟩ iussitque
2 nos temptare an bonis lanis essent confecta. | tum subridens "vide tu" inquit "Stiche, ne ista mures tangant aut tineae; alioquin te vivum comburam. ego gloriosus volo
3 efferri, ut totus mihi populus bene imprecetur." | statim ampullam nardi aperuit omnesque nos unxit et "spero" inquit "futurum ut aeque me mortuum iuvet tamquam
4 vivum." | nam vinum quidem in vinarium iussit infundi et "putate vos" ait "ad parentalia mea invitatos esse." |
5 ibat res ad summam nauseam, cum Trimalchio ebrietate turpissima gravis novum acroama, cornicines, in triclinium iussit adduci, fultusque cervicalibus multis extendit se supra torum extremum et "fingite me" inquit "mortuum esse. dicite aliquid belli." consonuere corni-
6 cines funebri strepitu. | unus praecipue servus libitinarii[438] illius, qui inter hos honestissimus erat, tam valde intonuit,
7 ut totam concitaret viciniam. | itaque vigiles, qui custodiebant vicinam regionem, rati ardere Trimalchionis domum effregerunt ianuam subito et cum aqua securibusque tu-
8 multuari suo iure coeperunt. | nos occasionem opportunissimam nacti Agamemnoni verba dedimus raptimque plane tamquam[439] ex incendio fugimus.

[438] libitinarii *Scheffer*: libertinarii
[439] plane tamquam *Jahn*: tam plane quam

---

[112] Proculus.

Bring out also the ointment and a sample of wine from that jar with which I want my bones to be washed." 78. Stichus did not delay but brought the white winding-sheet and toga with the purple stripe into the dining room . . . and Trimalchio asked us to test by touching that they were made of the best quality wool. Then with the hint of a smile he said: "Stichus, see to it that the mice and moths don't touch these; otherwise I'll have you burned alive. I want to be carried out to my tomb in style, so that all the people bless me." At once he opened the flask of nard oil and sprinkled some on all of us and said: "I hope this pleases me as much when I'm dead, as it does when I'm alive." Besides this he ordered wine poured into a bowl and said: "Imagine you've been invited to the annual commemoration of the dead in my honor."

The whole thing was absolutely sickening, when Trimalchio now deep in repulsive drunkenness ordered fresh entertainment, trumpeters, to be brought into the dining room. And propping himself up on a heap of pillows, he stretched out along the edge of the couch and said: "Imagine I'm dead. Play something pretty." The trumpeters all together blasted out a funeral march. One of the trumpeters, a slave of the undertaker,[112] who was the most respectable man among them, blew his trumpet so loudly that he roused the whole neighborhood. So the night sentinels who were patrolling the area round about, thinking that the house of Trimalchio was on fire, suddenly broke down the door, and with water and axes began to create a disturbance to the full extent of their rights. We seized this most opportune time, gave Agamemnon the slip, and took to our heels as quickly as though there were a real fire.

^{L}79. neque fax ulla in praesidio erat, quae iter aperiret errantibus, nec silentium noctis iam mediae promittebat
2 occurrentium lumen. | accedebat huc ebrietas et impru-
3 dentia locorum etiam interdiu obfutura.[440] | itaque cum hora paene tota per omnes scrupos[441] gastrarumque eminentium fragmenta traxissemus cruentos pedes, tan-
4 dem expliciti acumine Gitonis sumus. | prudens enim puer,[442] cum luce etiam clara timeret errorem, omnes pilas columnasque notaverat cretaeque[443] lineamenta evicerunt spississimam noctem et notabili candore ostenderunt er-
5 rantibus viam. | quamvis non minus sudoris habuimus
6 etiam postquam ad stabulum pervenimus. | anus enim ipsa inter deversitores diutius ingurgitata ne ignem quidem admotum sensisset. et forsitan pernoctassemus in limine, ni tabellarius Trimalchionis intervenisset ex vehiculis re-
7 diens.[444] | non diu ergo tumultuatus stabuli ianuam effregit et nos per eam tandem[445] admisit. |

⟨ * * * ⟩

8   qualis nox fuit illa, di deaeque,
    quam mollis torus. haesimus calentes
    et transfudimus hinc et hinc labellis
    errantes animas. valete, curae
   5 mortales. ego sic perire coepi.

9 sine causa gratulor mihi. | nam cum solutus mero remisis-
sem[446] ebrias manus, Ascyltos, omnis iniuriae inventor,

440 obfutura *Bücheler*: obscura
441 scrupos *l*^{mg}: scirpos
442 puer *Nisbet*: prudens *or* pridie
443 cretaeque *Schmeling*[5]: certaque
444 ex vehiculis rediens *Blommendaal*: X vehiculis dives

79. There was no torch to aid us and show us the way as we wandered about, nor did the silence of the midnight hour give promise of the likelihood of meeting anyone with a light. Added to this, our drunkenness and ignorance of the places would have been dangerous weaknesses even in daylight. And so for almost an hour we dragged our bleeding feet over all the sharp stones and pointed pieces of broken pots, until finally we were rescued by the ingenuity of Giton. Since he was afraid of losing his way even in daylight, the boy had shrewdly marked all the posts and columns, and the lines of chalk prevailed over the blackest night, and with their brilliant whiteness showed the way for us as we were wandering about. But even when we reached our lodgings, we still had to work and sweat, for the old woman had been soaking herself in wine in together with her lodgers, and would not have felt it even if someone had set her on fire. Perhaps we might have had to spend the night on the doorstep, had Trimalchio's courier not come on the scene, returning from his carts. He did not make shouting noises for long, but broke down the door of our lodgings and then let us in through it. . . .

"You gods and goddesses, what a night that was, how soft was the bed. We clung together in heated passion, and in reciprocity decanted our souls-in-a-kiss. Farewell mortal cares. Thus I began to die." Without any good reason I congratulated myself. For when I was numb with wine and had relaxed my drunken hands, Ascyltos, the discov-

---

445 per eam tandem *Gurlitt*: per eandem terram
446 remisissem *Jabobs*: amisissem

subduxit mihi nocte puerum et in lectum transtulit suum,
volutatusque liberius cum fratre non suo, sive non sen-
tiente iniuriam sive dissimulante, indormivit alienis am-
10   plexibus oblitus iuris humani. | itaque ego ut experrectus
pertrectavi gaudio despoliatum torum. <. . .> si qua est
amantibus fides, ego dubitavi an utrumque traicerem gla-
11   dio somnumque morti iungerem. | tutius deinde[447] secu-
tus consilium Gitona quidem verberibus excitavi, Ascylton
autem truci intuens vultu "quoniam" inquam "fidem sce-
lere violasti et communem amicitiam, res tuas ocius tolle
et alium locum quem polluas quaere." |

12   non repugnavit ille, sed postquam optima fide partiti
manubias sumus, "age" inquit "nunc et puerum divida-
mus." 80. iocari putabam discedentem. at ille gladium
parricidali manu strinxit et "non frueris" inquit "hac
praeda, super quam solus incumbis. partem meam ne-
2   cesse est vel hoc gladio contemptus[448] abscidam."[449] | idem
ego ex altera parte feci et intorto circa bracchium pallio
3   composui ad proeliandum gradum. | inter hanc misero-
rum dementiam infelicissimus puer tangebat utriusque
genua cum fletu petebatque suppliciter ne Thebanum par
humilis taberna spectaret neve sanguine mutuo polluere-
4   mus familiaritatis clarissimae sacra. | "quod si utique" pro-
clamabat "facinore opus est, nudo ecce iugulum, conver-
tite huc manus, imprimite mucrones. ego mori debeo, qui

[447] deinde *Novák*: dein *l*
[448] contemptus *Burman*: contentus
[449] abscidam *l^c r^c*: abscindam

[113] A reference to the fight between Oedipus' sons, Eteocles
and Polynices.

234

erer of all kinds of gross injustice, stole my young boy-partner at night and transferred him to his own bed. Wallowing freely in sex with a young partner not his own, who either did not feel the sexual assault or pretended that he did not, Ascyltos fell asleep in the illicit embraces of another man's lover, in defiance of various unwritten laws. And so when I awoke, I felt all over my bed now stripped of its joy. . . . While wondering if there is any trust among lovers, I hesitated whether to run them both through with my sword and join their sleep to death. Next in order I followed a safer plan and awakened Giton with my blows, but I looked savagely at Ascyltos and said: "Since you have broken the trust and friendship between us with your wicked behavior, collect your things at once and find some other place whose sanctity you can destroy."

He did not resist, but after we had scrupulously divided our spoils, he said: "Come now, we must divide the boy." 80. I thought that this was his parting joke, but he drew his sword with a murderous hand and said: "You will not enjoy this prize over which you alone have control. Since you despise me, I must have my share, even if I cut if off with my sword." I acted the same way on my side, and having wrapped my cloak around my arm prepared my position for battle. In the midst of the madness of the pitiful pair of us, that most unhappy boy tearfully touched the knees of both of us and like a suppliant begged us not to let that humble lodging be the scene of a Theban duel,[113] or stain the sanctity of a beautiful friendship with each other's blood. "But if by all means," he cried, "you must commit your crime, look here, I bare my throat. Turn your hands this way, thrust your daggers here. I am the one who deserves to die for destroying your oath of sacred

235

5 amicitiae sacramentum delevi." | inhibuimus ferrum post
has preces, et prior Ascyltos "ego" inquit "finem discor-
diae imponam. puer ipse quem vult sequatur, ut sit illi
6 saltem in eligendo fratre salva[450] libertas." | ego qui[451] ve-
tustissimam consuetudinem putabam in sanguinis pignus
transisse, nihil timui, immo condicionem praecipiti festi-
natione rapui commisique iudici litem. qui ne deliberavit
quidem, ut videretur cunctatus, verum statim ab extrema
parte verbi consurrexit ⟨et⟩[452] fratrem Ascylton elegit. |
7 fulminatus hac pronuntiatione sic ut eram sine gladio in
lectulum decidi, et attulissem mihi damnatus manus, si
8 non inimici victoriae inviderem.[453] | egreditur superbus
cum praemio Ascyltos et paulo ante carissimum sibi com-
militonem fortunaeque etiam similitudine parem in loco
peregrino destituit abiectum. |

9   [OφL]nomen amicitiae si quatenus expedit haeret,
          calculus in tabula mobile ducit opus.
       dum[454] fortuna manet, vultum servatis, amici;
          cum cecidit, turpi vertitis ora fuga.
   5   [OL]grex agit in scaena mimum: pater ille vocatur,
          filius hic, nomen divitis ille tenet.
       mox ubi ridendas inclusit pagina partes,
          vera redit facies, assimulata[455] perit.

   81. nec diu tamen lacrimis indulsi, sed veritus ne Menelaus etiam antescholanus inter cetera mala solum me in

---

[450] salva *rtp*: omittted *lm*
[451] qui *p²*: *omitted others*   [452] *added Bücheler*
[453] inviderem *l*: invidissem
[454] dum *Jahn*: cum
[455] assimulata *Dousa*: dissimulata

friendship." After these pleas we put up our swords, and
then Ascyltos spoke first: "I will put an end to this quarrel.
Let the boy follow the one he wants. That way he has
perfect freedom at any rate in choosing his older partner."
I had no fears in this matter, because I thought our long-
standing love affair had come to mean as much as ties of
blood. On the contrary, I seized the proposal in headlong
haste and entrusted the matter in dispute to the judge. He
did not think it over long enough even to pretend to delay,
but as soon as I finished speaking, got up and chose Ascyltos for his older partner. I was thunderstruck at his decision, and fell down on the bed, just as I was without a
sword.[114] With the verdict against me, I would have turned
my hands violently against myself, had I not begrudged
such a triumph to my enemy. Proud in his prize winnings,
Ascyltos departed and abandoned his comrade, now in
despair in a foreign place, who shortly before had been his
dearest partner and whose fortunes had been so like his
own. "If the name of friendship lasts only as long as it is
expedient, it is like a marker which weaves a fickle pattern
on the game board. While my luck holds, you preserve
your smiles, my friends, but when it has fallen, you turn
your faces away in shameful flight. A company acts a farce
on the stage: that one is called the father, this one the son,
a third has the name of rich man. Soon the page has enclosed the comic parts, the true face returns, and theatrical pretense dies."

81. I did not, however, give way to tears for long. I was
afraid that Menelaus, the assistant at the school of rheto-

114 Encolpius perhaps references his impotent member by
saying that he is without a sword.

deversorio inveniret, collegi sarcinulas locumque secre-
2 tum et proximum litori maestus conduxi. | ibi triduo inclu-
sus redeunte in animum solitudine atque contemptu ver-
berabam aegrum planctibus pectus ^Let inter tot altissimos
gemitus frequenter etiam proclamabam: "ergo me non
3 ruina terra potuit haurire? | non iratum etiam innocenti-
bus mare? effugi iudicium, harenae imposui, hospitem
occidi, ut inter ⟨tot⟩[456] audaciae nomina mendicus, exul,
in deversorio Graecae urbis iacerem desertus? et quis
4 hanc mihi solitudinem[457] imposuit? | adulescens omni libi-
dine impurus et sua quoque confessione dignus exilio,
stupro liber, stupro ingenuus, cuius anni ad tesseram venierunt,[458] quem tamquam puellam conduxit etiam qui
5 virum putavit. | quid ille alter? qui tamquam die[459] togae
virilis stolam sumpsit, qui ne vir esset a matre persuasus
est, qui opus muliebre in ergastulo fecit, qui postquam
conturbavit et libidinis suae solum vertit, reliquit veteris
amicitiae nomen et, pro pudor, tamquam mulier secutu-
6 leia unius noctis tactu omnia vendidit. | iacent nunc ama-
tores adligati[460] noctibus totis, et forsitan mutuis libidini-
bus attriti derident solitudinem meam. sed non impune.
nam aut vir ego liberque non sum, aut noxio sanguine
parentabo iniuriae meae."

456 *added Jacobs*
457 solitudinem *lt*^{mg}*p*²: solicitudinem
458 venierunt *t*^{mg}: venerunt
459 qui tamquam die *l*^{mg}: die qui tamquam
460 adligati *Bücheler*: obligati

---

115 Reference to ch. 9.
116 *tessera* = ticket. Such tickets (good for gifts, meals, entrance to the games and brothels) were distributed at places like

ric, might increase my troubles by finding me alone in the lodgings, so I gathered my bags and sadly rented a remote place near the sea. I shut myself up there for three days; I was haunted by the realization that I was deserted and humiliated; I beat my breast, already worn with blows, and among so many very deep groans even cried aloud many times: "Why could the earth not swallow me in some sort of catastrophe, or the sea that is angry even with the innocent? Did I flee justice, cheat a brothel[115] and kill a guest, so that among so many badges of courage, I would lie here a beggar and an exile, abandoned in lodgings in a Greek city? And who inflicted this loneliness on me? A youngster sullied by every kind of sexual desire, who by his own admission deserves banishment, free for sex, freeborn for sex, whose youthful charms were sold to the man with a ticket;[116] even the one who thought he was a man, hired him as a girl. What about the other one, who almost on the day he became eligible for the manly toga, put on a woman's robe, was persuaded by his mother that he was not a man, played the part of a woman in a slaves' prison, and after running out of money, changed the basis of his sexual desires? He abandoned the name of an old friendship, and, for shame, as if he were a street whore, sold everything in a one-night stand. Now the lovers lie together wallowing in bed whole nights on end, and perhaps laughing at my loneliness, when they are exhausted by each other's demands for sex. But this will not continue with impunity. Either I am not a man and no free citizen, or I will avenge their outrages against me with their guilty blood."

the Circus by patrons to clients, by the wealthy to the masses, and by candidates for public offices to voters.

82. haec locutus gladio latus cingor, et ne infirmitas
militiam perderet, largioribus cibis excito vires. mox in
publicum prosilio furentisque more omnes circumeo por-
2 ticus. | sed dum attonito vultu efferatoque nihil aliud
quam caedem et sanguinem cogito frequentiusque manum ad capulum quem devoveram refero, notavit me
miles, sive ille planus fuit sive nocturnus grassator, et |
3 "quid? tu" inquit "commilito, ex qua legione es aut cuius
centuria?" cum constantissime et centurionem et legi-
onem essem ementitus, "age ergo" inquit ille "in exercitu
4 vestro phaecasiati milites ambulant?" | cum deinde vultu
atque ipsa trepidatione mendacium prodidissem, ponere
iussit arma et malo cavere. despoliatus ergo armis[461] prae-
cisa ultione retro ad deversorium tendo paulatimque te-
meritate laxata[462] coepi grassatoris audaciae gratias agere. |

〈 * * * 〉

5      $^{\phi L}$non bibit inter aquas poma aut pendentia carpit
       Tantulus infelix, quem sua vota premunt.
       divitis haec magni facies erit, omnia cernens
       qui timet et sicco concoquit ore famem. |

〈 * * * 〉

6 ^{L}non multum oportet consilio credere, quia suam habet
fortuna rationem.

〈 * * * 〉

83. in pinacothecam perveni vario genere tabularum
mirabilem. nam et Zeuxidos manus vidi nondum vetustatis
iniuria victas, et Protogenis rudimenta cum ipsius naturae

---

[461] armis *Bücheler*: immo
[462] laxata *Muncker*: lassata

82. With these words I put on my sword, and to build up my strength ate an extra hearty meal to prevent losing the battle because of weakness. Then I rushed outdoors and like a madman visited all the colonnades. My face had a frenzied and savage aspect, and I thought of nothing other than slaughter and blood, and kept putting my hand on the sword hilt, on which I had uttered my vow of revenge. Then a soldier, who might have been an imposter or a night-prowling thief, spotted me and said: "What are you up to there, comrade? From what legion are you and who's your centurion?" When I lied most brazenly both about my centurion and the legion, he said: "Come now, in your army do the soldiers walk round dressed in white slippers?" When by my expression and alarm I had showed that I had lied, he ordered me to hand over my arms and stay out of trouble. So not only was I stripped of my sword, but my method of revenge was cut short. I made my way back to the lodgings and little by little as my rashness abated, I began to feel grateful for the impudence of the thief. . . . "Poor Tantalus in water never gets to drink, does not pluck the hanging fruit, and his longings torment him. That is the face of a great rich man, who, seeing everything around him, is afraid and in a dry mouth has nothing to digest but his own hunger." . . . One should not put much trust in planning, because Fortune has her own way of doing things. . . .

83. I came into an art gallery with an extraordinarily wide collection of pictures. The exhibition I saw included works by Zeuxis' hand, not yet overcome by the ravages of time, and with a shiver of awe I examined a rough drawing by Protogenes that competed with the truth of Nature

veritate certantia non sine quodam horrore tractavi. |
2 iam vero Apellis quem Graeci monocnemon[463] appellant,
etiam adoravi. tanta enim subtilitate extremitates imagi-
num erant ad similitudinem praecisae, ut crederes etiam
3 animorum esse picturam. | hinc aquila ferebat caelo subli-
mis Idaeum,[464] illinc candidus Hylas repellebat improbam
Naida. damnabat Apollo noxias manus lyramque resolu-
4 tam modo nato flore honorabat. | inter quos {etiam}[465]
pictorum amantium vultus tamquam in solitudine excla-
mavi: "ergo amor etiam deos tangit. Iuppiter in caelo suo
non invenit quod eligeret, et peccaturus in terris nemini
5 tamen iniuriam fecit. | Hylan Nympha praedata imperas-
set amori suo, si venturum ad interdictum Herculem cre-
didisset. Apollo pueri umbram revocavit in florem, et
omnes fabulae—⟨picturae⟩ quoque—[466] habuerunt sine
6 aemulo complexus. | at ego in societatem recepi hospitem
7 Lycurgo crudeliorem." | ecce autem, ego dum cum ventis
litigo, intravit pinacothecam senex canus, exercitati vultus
et qui videretur nescioquid magnum promittere, sed cultu
non proinde speciosus, ut facile appareret eum ⟨ex⟩[467] hac

[463] monocnemon *l*: monocremon *L. Meaning uncertain.*
[464] Idaeum *Wehle*: deum   [465] *deleted Müller*
[466] —⟨picturae⟩ quoque— *Schmeling*
[467] *added Dousa*

---

[117] Three painters usually grouped together: Zeuxis was in
Athens during the Peloponnesian War and known for his treatment of light and shade; Protogenes, fourth century, detailed
workmanship and accuracy of line and color; Apelles, fourth century, at the court of Alexander the Great, creator of "Aphrodite
Rising from the Sea," and the most famous painter of the three.

242

herself. But when I came to the paintings by Apelles,[117] whom the Greeks call *monocnemos*,[118] I positively worshipped them. The outlines of his figures were so skillfully defined in imitation, that you would have believed he painted their souls as well. In one picture a high-flying eagle was carrying the youth Ganymede from Mount Ida to heaven; in another fair Hylas was trying to fend off a cruel Naiad; in another Apollo was denouncing his guilty hands and adorning his unstrung lyre with a newborn flower. Among these portraits of lovers, I cried out as if in hopeless isolation: "So love touches even the gods. Jupiter found no object for his passion in heaven, and came down to earth to transgress, but did no one any harm. The Nymph who ravished Hylas would have restrained her passion, had she believed that Hercules would come to dispute her claim. Apollo called the departed shade of the youth Hyacinthus back to become a flower, and all the stories—but also the pictures—show erotic embraces enjoyed without a rival. But I took into my company a guest more cruel than Lycurgus."[119] Then, lo and behold, as I was bandying words with the winds, a white-haired old man[120] entered the gallery. There was an expression of concentration on his face, and he seemed to promise something great. But because of the state of his clothes he was not handsome, and so it was quite clear from this

118 The meaning of this word is obscure.

119 Character from a lost episode, mentioned also in ch. 117.

120 The *senex canus*, old white-haired man, is Eumolpus, who replaces Ascyltos and becomes the second member of the second triad of core actors. Ascyltos makes several more appearances but is no longer a central character.

8   nota litteratorum[468] esse, quos odisse divites solent. | is
ergo ad latus constitit meum. "ego" inquit "poeta sum et
ut spero non humillimi spiritus, si modo coronis aliquid
credendum est, quas etiam ad immeritos[469] deferre gratia
9   solet. | 'quare ergo' inquis 'tam male vestitus es?' propter
hoc ipsum: amor ingenii neminem umquam divitem fe-
cit. |

10   [OφL]qui pelago credit, magno se faenore tollit;
          qui pugnas et castra petit, praecingitur auro;
          vilis adulator picto iacet ebrius ostro,
          et qui sollicitat nuptas, ad praemia peccat:
    5   sola pruinosis horret facundia pannis
          atque inopi lingua desertas invocat artes.

84. non dubie ita est: si quis vitiorum omnium inimicus
rectum iter vitae coepit insistere,[470] primum propter mo-
rum differentiam odium habet; quis enim potest probare
2   diversa? | deinde qui solas extruere divitias curant, nihil
volunt inter homines melius credi quam quod ipsi tenent.
3 | [OL]inescant[471] itaque, quacumque ratione possunt, littera-
rum amatores, ut videantur illi quoque infra pecuniam
positi." |

                 ⟨ * * * ⟩

4   "[φL]nescioquomodo bonae mentis soror est paupertas." |

                 ⟨ * * * ⟩

5   [L]"vellem tam innocens esset frugalitatis meae hostis, ut
deliniri posset. nunc veteranus est latro et ipsis lenonibus[472] doctior."

                 ⟨ * * * ⟩

---

[468] litteratorum *Dousa*: litteratum
[469] immeritos *Bücheler*: imperitos

standard that he was a man of letters, a class of people whom the rich love to hate. This man came and stood next to me and said: "I am a poet, and one, I hope, of no commonplace genius, if one can give any credence to the awards, which influence is accustomed to bestow on the unworthy. 'Why then,' you say, 'are you so shabbily dressed?' For this reason: passion for the intellect never made anyone rich. The man who puts his trust in the sea makes huge profits; the man who seeks battles and camps is dressed in gold; the cheap flatterer lies drunk in dyed purple coverings; and the man who seduces brides takes money for his corruption; eloquence alone shivers in cold rags, and with a destitute tongue calls upon neglected arts. 84. This is undoubtedly the situation: if anyone dislikes all vices and begins to tread an upright path in life, he first meets hatred because of the difference of ways of living; for who can approve a conduct different from his own? Further, those who are interested only in heaping up riches want nothing to be considered better among men than what they themselves hold. And so they entice, by whatever way they can, the lovers of literature, trying to make them appear also subservient to money." . . . "Somehow or other, poverty is the sister of talent." . . . "I could only wish that the one who hates me for my honesty were so guiltless that he could be won over to my views. As it is he is a confirmed robber and more clever than the pimps themselves." . . .

---

470 insistere *Brassicanus*: inspicere
471 inescant *Müller*: iactantur
472 lenonibus *Bongars, p^2*: leonibus

85. {*Eumolpus*} "in Asiam cum a quaestore essem stipendio eductus, hospitium Pergami accepi. ubi cum libenter habitarem non solum propter cultum aedicularum, sed etiam propter hospitis formosissimum filium, excogitavi rationem, qua non essem patri familiae suspectus amator.

2 | quotiescumque enim in convivio de usu formosorum mentio facta est, tam vehementer excandui, tam severa tristitia violari aures meas obsceno sermone nolui, ut me mater praecipue tamquam unum ex philosophis intuere-

3 tur. | iam ego coeperam ephebum in gymnasium deducere, ego studia eius ordinare, ego docere ac praecipere, ne quis praedator corporis admitteretur in domum. |

⟨ * * * ⟩

4 forte cum in triclinio iaceremus, quia dies sollemnis ludum adiuverat[473] pigritiamque recedendi imposuerat hilaritas longior, fere circa mediam noctem intellexi puerum

5 vigilare. | itaque timidissimo murmure votum feci et 'domina' inquam 'Venus, si ego hunc puerum basiavero ita ut

6 ille non sentiat, cras illi par columbarum donabo.' | audito voluptatis pretio coepit puer stertere.[474] itaque aggressus ⟨dis⟩simulantem[475] aliquot basiolis invasi. contentus hoc principo bene mane surrexi electumque par columbarum attuli expectanti ac me voto exsolvi. 86. proxima nocte cum idem liceret, mutavi opinionem et 'si hunc' inquam 'tractavero improba manu et ille non senserit, gallos galli-

2 naceos pugnacissimos duos donabo patienti.' | ad hoc votum ephebus ultro se admovit et, puto, vereri coepit ne

473 adiuverat *Vannini*[1]: artaverat
474 coepit puer stertere *Fraenkel*: puer stetere coepit
475 *added Holford-Strevens*

85. [Eumolpus] "When I had been brought out to Asia on salary by a quaestor, I accepted accommodation in Pergamum. Here I settled in, pleased not only because of the elegance of the residence but also because of the very handsome son of my host. I thought of a way by which I would not be suspected by the father as a lover of the boy. Whenever the talk at the table turned to the subject of sex with handsome boys, I burned with such anger, and with such terrible sadness I refused to have my ears offended by obscene talk, that the boy's mother in particular looked on me as one of the philosophers. Soon I had begun to escort the boy to the gymnasium, I arranged his studies, I taught him, and I especially saw to it that no seducer of his body be admitted to the house. . . . It so happened that we were relaxing in the dining room, because the holiday had encouraged our sport, and prolonged merrymaking had made us too lazy to retire. It was about midnight and I noticed that the boy was awake, and so with a very shy whisper I offered a prayer and said: 'Dear Venus, if I can kiss this boy in such a way that he does not realize it, I will give him a pair of doves tomorrow.' When the boy had heard the value of the offer for pleasure, he began to snore. And so I approached the boy who pretended not to notice, and I pressed several kisses on him. Satisfied with this beginning I got up very early in the morning and fulfilled my vow by bringing the expectant boy a choice pair of doves. 86. When on the next night I had another opportunity, I increased the level of my options and said: 'If I can caress him with my naughty hand without his feeling it, I will repay him for his experience with two really aggressive fighting-cocks.' When the boy heard my vow he voluntarily drew himself into a comfortable posi-

3 ego obdormissem. | indulsi ergo sollicito, totoque corpore
citra summam voluptatem me ingurgitavi. deinde ut dies
4 venit, attuli gaudenti quicquid promiseram. | ut tertia nox
‹eandem›[476] licentiam dedit, consurrexi ‹et›[477] ad aurem
male dormientis 'dii' inquam 'immortales, si ego huic dormienti abstulero coitum plenum et optabilem, pro hac
felicitate cras puero asturconem Macedonicum optimum
donabo, cum hac tamen exceptione, si ille non senserit.' |
5 numquam altiore somno ephebus obdormivit. itaque
primum implevi lactentibus papillis manus, mox basio
6 inhaesi, deinde in unum omnia vota coniunxi. | mane
‹puer›[478] sedere in cubiculo coepit atque expectare consuetudinem meam. scis quanto facilius sit columbas gal-
losque gallinaceos emere quam asturconem, et praeter
hoc etiam timebam ne tam grande munus suspectam fac-
7 eret humanitatem meam. | ergo aliquot horis spatiatus in
hospitium reverti nihilque aliud quam puerum basiavi. at
ille circumspiciens ut cervicem meam iunxit amplexu,
'rogo' inquit 'domine, ubi est asturco?'

‹ * * * ›

87. cum ob hanc offensam praeclusissem mihi aditum
quem feceram, iterum ad licentiam redii. interpositis
enim paucis diebus cum similis nos casus in eandem fortunam rettulisset, ut intellexit stertere patrem, rogare
coepi ephebum ut reverteretur in gratiam mecum, id est
ut pateretur satis fieri sibi, et cetera quae libido distenta
2 dictat. | at ille plane iratus nihil aliud dicebat nisi hoc: |
3 'aut dormi, aut ego iam dicam patri.' $^{\phi L}$nihil est tam
arduum quod non improbitas extorqueat. ^{L}dum dicit:

476 *added Müller*   477 *added Fraenkel*
478 *added Müller*

248

tion, and, I think, began to fear that I had dropped off to sleep. So I made allowances for his impatience, and wallowed in enjoyment of his whole body, keeping just short of that final pleasure. Then as daylight came, I brought whatever I had promised to the delighted youth. When the third night gave me the same license, I rose and spoke into his ear as he pretended to sleep: 'Immortal gods, if I can snatch full and longed-for sex from this sleeping boy, tomorrow in return for this pleasure I will give him the finest Macedonian thoroughbred, on this condition only, that he does not feel anything.' Never had the youth slept more deeply. And so first I filled my hands with his milky-white breasts, then I clung to him in a long kiss, and finally I united all my prayers in that one action. Next morning the boy sat in his room and waited for my usual routine. You know how much easier it is to buy doves and cocks than a thoroughbred horse. And besides this I was afraid that such a large gift would make my generosity suspect. Therefore I walked about for a few hours, and when I returned to my lodging, I gave the boy nothing more than a kiss. As he threw his arms around my neck, he looked all around and said: 'Tell me, sir, where is my stallion?' . . .

87. By this breach of my word I had cut off the approach I had gained, but again I returned to my former wantonness. Not many days later when a similar chance brought us to the same position, and I heard his father snoring, I began to beg the boy to be friends again, that is, that he allow amends to be made to him, and all the other things that an aroused lust makes one say. But he was clearly angry and said nothing other than: 'Go to sleep or I will tell my father at once.' Nothing is so difficult that immodesty cannot extort it. While he was saying 'I will

'patrem excitabo,' irrepsi tamen et male repugnanti gau-
4 dium extorsi. | at ille non indelectatus nequitia mea, post-
quam diu questus est deceptum se et derisum traduc-
tumque inter condiscipulos, quibus iactasset censum
5 meum, | 'videris tamen' inquit 'non ero tui similis. | si quid
6 vis, fac iterum.'

ego vero deposita omni offensa cum puero in gratiam
redii ususque beneficio eius in somnum delapsus sum. |
7 sed non fuit contentus iteratione ephebus plenae maturi-
tatis et annis ad patiendum gestientibus. itaque excitavit
8 me sopitum et 'numquid vis?' inquit. | et {non}[479] paene[480]
iam molestum erat munus. utcumque igitur inter anheli-
tus sudoresque tritus, quod voluerat accepit, rursusque in
9 somnum decidi gaudio lassus. | interposita minus hora
pungere me manu coepit et dicere: 'quare non facimus?'
10 | tum ego totiens excitatus plane vehementer excandui
et reddidi illi voces suas: 'aut dormi, aut ego iam patri
dicam.'"

⟨ * * * ⟩

88. erectus his sermonibus consulere prudentiorem
coepi ⟨. . .⟩ aetates tabularum et quaedam argumenta
mihi obscura simulque causam desidiae praesentis excu-
tere, cum pulcherrimae artes perissent, inter quas pictura
2 ne minimum quidem sui vestigium reliquisset. | tum
ille "pecuniae" inquit "cupiditas haec tropica instituit.
[OφL]priscis enim temporibus, cum adhuc nuda virtus placeret, vigebant artes ingenuae summumque certamen inter
homines erat, ne quid profuturum saeculis diu lateret. |
3 itaque hercule herbarum omnium sucos Democritus ex-

[479] *deleted Blommendaal*
[480] paene *Müller*: plane

250

wake up my father,' I crept in, however, and extorted my pleasure in spite of his faint resistance. But he was not displeased with my naughty behavior, and after a long complaint that he was deceived and laughed at and made a figure of mockery among his classmates, to whom he had boasted about my wealth, he said: 'But you will see that I will not be like you. Do it again, if you want to.'

"So with all bad feelings laid aside, I was reconciled to the boy, and having made use of his goodwill I fell asleep. But the boy, fully mature and at an age when one is eager to take it on, was not satisfied with a single repetition. So he roused me from my sleep and said: 'Do you want anything?' Servicing him now was almost tiresome. But one way or another among my gasps and sweat, he was worn down and got what he had wanted, and again I fell asleep tired and happy. Less than an hour later he began to poke me with his hand and said: 'Why aren't we doing it?' Then I grew really angry at being disturbed so often, and I turned his own words back on him: 'Go to sleep, or I will tell your father.'" . . .

88. Encouraged by this conversation I began to draw on his greater knowledge . . . about the dating of the pictures and the subjects of some of those which puzzled me, and at the same time I began to puzzle over the reason for the present decadence, since the loveliest arts had died off, among which painting had left not even the smallest trace. Then he replied: "It was the greed for money that brought about this change. In the old days, when unadorned merit was acceptable, the liberal arts flourished, and there was the keenest competition among men to see to it that no benefit to posterity should lie hidden for long. That is why, by god, Democritus extracted the juice of

pressit, et ne lapidum virgultorumque vis lateret, aetatem
4 inter experimenta consumpsit. | Eudoxos quidem in cacu-
mine excelsissimi montis consenuit, ut astrorum caelique
motus deprehenderet, et Chrysippus, ut ad inventionem
5 sufficeret ‹rerum›,[481] ter elleboro animum detersit. | ve-
rum ut ad plastas convertar, Lysippum statuae unius
lineamentis inhaerentem inopia extinxit, et Myron, qui
paene animas hominum ferarumque aere comprehendit,
6 non invenit heredem. | at nos vino scortisque demersi ne
paratas quidem artes audemus cognoscere, sed accusa-
tores antiquitatis vitia tantum docemus [OL]et discimus. ubi
est dialectica? ubi astronomia? ubi sapientiae consum-
7 matissimae[482] via? | [OφL]quis umquam venit in templum et
votum fecit, si ad eloquentiam pervenisset? quis, si philo-
8 sophiae fontem attigisset? | ac ne bonam quidem mentem
aut bonam valetudinem petunt, sed statim antequam limen Capitolii tangant, alius donum promittit, si propin-
quum divitem extulerit, alius, si thesaurum effoderit,
9 alius, si ad trecenties sestertium salvus pervenerit. | ipse
senatus, recti bonique praeceptor, mille pondo auri Capi-
tolio promittere solet, et ne quis dubitet pecuniam concu-
10 piscere, Iovem quoque peculio exornat.[483] | [OL]noli ergo
mirari, si pictura deficit, cum omnibus diis hominibusque
formosior videatur massa auri quam quicquid Apelles Phi-
diasque, Graeculi delirantes, fecerunt. 89. sed video te

---

[481] *added l*[mg]
[482] consummatissimae *Müller*: consultissima
[483] exornat *s*[mg]: exorat

---

[121] Democritus, fifth-century atomic theorist; Eudoxus,
fourth-century astronomer; Crysippus, third-century Stoic philosopher; Lysippus, fourth-century sculptor and bronze caster;

every plant, and spent his life on experiments to make sure that the properties of stones and shrubbery should be known. Eudoxus grew old on the top of the highest mountain trying to discover the movements of the stars and the sky, and Chrysippus cleansed his mind thrice with hellebore to be adequate for the discovery of all things. Lysippus died in poverty, as he focused on the lines of a single statue, and Myron,[121] who almost captured in bronze the souls of men and beasts, found no heir. We now are besotted with wine and whores and do not venture to understand even the traditional arts, but we harshly criticize the past and learn and teach nothing but vices. Where is dialectic? Where astronomy? Where is the surest path to wisdom? Who ever comes to a temple and promises an offering, on the condition that he attains eloquence, or touches the fountainhead of philosophy? Not even good sense or good health do they ask for, but before they even step over the threshold of the Capitol, one promises a gift if he can bury a rich relative, another if he digs up a treasure, another if he can make thirty million sesterces safely. Even the Senate, our teacher of the right and the good, often promises a thousand pounds of gold for the Capitoline temple, and so that no one need hesitate about lusting after money, the Senate adorns Jupiter also with ancestral cash. So there is nothing surprising in the demise of painting, when to all the gods and men a clump of gold seems more beautiful than anything those poor crazy Greeks, Apelles and Phidias,[122] created. 89. But I see that you are

Myron, fifth-century sculptor. The attributes given to each of these by Eumolpus are eccentric in the extreme.

[122] Apelles, fourth-century painter; Phidias, fifth-century sculptor for the Parthenon.

totum in illa haerere tabula, quae Troiae halosin ostendit.
itaque conabor opus versibus pandere:

iam decuma maestos inter ancipites metus
Phrygas obsidebat messis et vatis fides
Calchantis atro dubia pendebat metu,
cum Delio profante caesi vertices
5   Idae trahuntur scissaque in molem cadunt
robora, minacem quae figurabunt[484] equum.
aperitur ingens antrum et obducti specus,
qui castra caperent. huc decenni proelio
irata virtus abditur, stipant graves
10 Danai recessus, in suo voto latent.
o patria, pulsas mille credidimus rates
solumque bello liberum: hoc titulus fero
incisus, hoc ad furta[485] compositus Sinon
firmabat et mens semper[486] in damnum potens.
15   iam turba portis libera ac bello carens
in vota properat.[487] fletibus manant genae
mentisque pavidae gaudium lacrimas habet.
quas metus abegit. namque Neptuno sacer
crinem solutus omne Laocoon replet
20 clamore vulgus. mox reducta cuspide
uterum notavit, fata sed tardant manus,
ictusque resilit et dolis addit fidem.
iterum tamen confirmat invalidam manum

[484] figurabunt *Lachmann*: figurabant
[485] furta *Bücheler*: fata
[486] mens semper p^{2v}: mendacium
[487] properat *r*: properant

completely enthralled by that picture which depicts the fall of Troy, so I will try to explain the work in verses: It was now the tenth harvest for the Trojans held under siege amid sad and dangerous fears, and the reliability of the prophet Calchas[123] hung wavering in dark fear, when at Apollo's bidding the wooded peaks of Ida were felled and dragged below, and the sawed planks fell in a heap to fashion a menacing horse. A great hollow space was created and concealed caves that could hold a camp of men. In this space after ten years of anger, men of valor were hidden, (10) the Greeks were loaded aboard and filled every corner, and they lay in wait in their own votive offering. Ah, my poor country. We thought the thousand ships had been beaten off and our land was free from war: the inscription carved into the beast, Sinon[124] complicit in defeat, and our mindset always driving toward our own doom, all strengthened our faulty perception. Now a crowd, free and unoppressed by war, hurries from the gate to pay its vows. Their cheeks are wet from crying, and the joy of their fearful minds produces tears, which fear had banished. Laocoon,[125] priest of Neptune, with hair unbound, incites the whole mob to cry aloud. (20) Then drawing back his spear he gashes the belly of the horse, but the fates restrained his hands, and after the spear struck, it recoiled, adding our trust to the fraud. Again he makes an effort with his feeble hand, and tests the lofty

[123] Chalchas foretold that the Trojan War would last nine years and that the city would fall in the tenth.

[124] Sinon pretended to be a deserter and convinced the Trojans to welcome the horse.   [125] The priest Laocoon warned the Trojans not to accept the horse.

altaque bipenni latera pertemptat. fremit
25 captiva pubes intus, et dum murmurat,
roborea moles spirat alieno metu.
ibat iuventus capta, dum Troiam capit,
bellumque totum fraude ducebat nova.
  ecce alia monstra: celsa qua Tenedos mare
30 dorso replevit, tumida consurgunt freta
undaque resultat scissa tranquillo minax,[488]
qualis silenti nocte remorum sonus
longe refertur, cum premunt classes mare
pulsumque marmor abiete imposita gemit.
35 respicimus: angues orbibus geminis ferunt
ad saxa fluctus, tumida quorum pectora
rates ut altae lateribus spumas agunt.
dat cauda sonitum, liberae ponto iubae
consentiunt luminibus, fulmineum iubar
40 incendit aequor sibilisque undae fremunt.[489]
stupuere mentes. infulis stabant sacri
Phrygioque cultu gemina nati pignora
Lauconte. quos repente tergoribus ligant
angues corusci. parvulas illi manus
45 ad ora referunt, neuter auxilio sibi,
uterque fratri: transtulit pietas vices
morsque ipsa miseros mutuo perdit metu.
accumulat ecce liberum funus parens,
infirmus auxiliator. invadunt virum
50 iam morte pasti membraque ad terram trahunt.
iacet sacerdos inter aras victima
terramque plangit. sic profanatis sacris
peritura Troia perdidit primum deos.

---

[488] minax *Helm*: minor   [489] fremunt *Haupt*: tremunt

sides with an ax. The soldiers enclosed within complain angrily, and while they grumble, the massive structure gasps with fear not its own. The young warriors who had been held captive went forward to take Troy captive, and they conducted the whole war with unprecedented deceit. There followed other portents: where Tenedos fills the sea with its high ridge, (30) the billowing sea rises, and the shattered wave leaps back threatening the calm. It is the kind of sound that oars make in the silent night, when it is carried back from afar, as ships press upon the sea, and the whitened surface of the sea groans as it is pounded by the fir keels of the ships. We look back: the waves carry twin coiling snakes toward the rocks, their swollen breasts like tall ships parting the sea foam with their flanks. Their tails crash loudly into the sea, their crests move free over the water and conspire with their eyes, whose lightning-like brightness ignites the sea, (40) and the waves resound with their hissing. Our minds grew numb. The priests were adorned with headbands, and the twin sons of Laocoon stood there in Phrygian raiment. Suddenly the glistening snakes envelop the boys with their coils. They raise their little hands to their faces, neither aiding himself, each helping his brother: brotherly love transforms the interchanges, and death itself destroys the poor boys with the assistance of their unselfish fear. The father is only a feeble helper and spreads his body over the corpses of his children. (50) The snakes having fed on death attack the man and drag his limbs to the ground. The priest lies a victim between the altars and thrashes the earth. After its rituals had been desecrated, Troy, doomed to fall, first loses her

iam plena Phoebe candidum extulerat iubar
55   minora ducens astra radianti face,
cum inter sepultos Priamidas nocte et mero
Danai relaxant claustra et effundunt viros.
temptant in armis se duces, veluti[490] solet
nodo[491] remissus Thessali quadrupes iugi
60   cervicem et altas quatere ad excursum iubas.
gladios retractant, commovent orbes manu
bellumque sumunt. hic graves alius mero
obtruncat et continuat in mortem ultimam
somnos, ab aris[492] alius accendit faces
65   contraque Troas invocat Troiae sacra."

⟨ * * * ⟩

[L]90. ex is, qui in porticibus spatiabantur, lapides in
Eumolpum recitantem miserunt. at ille, qui plausum ingenii sui noverat, operuit caput extraque templum profugit.
2 | timui ego ne me ⟨quoque⟩[493] poetam vocarent,[494] itaque
subsecutus fugientem ad litus perveni, et ut primum extra
3   teli coniectum licuit consistere, | "rogo" inquam "quid tibi
vis cum isto morbo? minus quam duabus horis mecum
moraris, et saepius poetice quam humane locutus es. ita-
4   que non miror, si te populus lapidibus persequitur. | ego
quoque sinum meum saxis onerabo, ut quotiescumque
coeperis a te exire, sanguinem tibi a capite mittam." movit
ille vultum et "o mi" inquit "adulescens, non hodie pri-
5   mum auspicatus sum. | immo quotiens theatrum, ut reci-
tarem aliquid, intravi, hac[495] me adventicia excipere fre-

---

490 veluti *Krohn*: ceu ubi   491 nodo *Dousa*: nudo
492 ab aris *Junius*: avaris   493 *added Fuchs*
494 vocarent *t*[mg]: vocaret   495 hac *Dousa*: haec

gods. Now the full moon had lifted up her white beam, leading the smaller stars with her glowing torch. The Greeks remove the bolts from the door and pour out their warriors among Priam's sons, who are buried in darkness and drowned in wine. The leaders test themselves with their weapons, just as a steed untied from the knot of its Thessalian yoke (60) is wont to toss its head and lofty mane, as it charges forward. They draw their swords, brandish their shields, and begin the battle. Here one slays Trojans lost in wine and merges their sleep into ultimate death, and another lights torches from the altars, and invokes the sacred rites of Troy against the Trojans." . . .

90. Some of the people who were strolling in the colonnades threw stones at Eumolpus, as he recited. But he recognized this as tribute to his genius, and covering his head, fled out of the temple. I was afraid that they would label me a poet also, and so having followed him as he flew, I arrived at the seashore, and as soon as we were out of range of the weapons and were permitted to stop, I said: "Tell me, what do you plan to do about this disease of yours? You have been in my company for less than two hours, and in that space of time you have spoken poetry more often than talked like a human. And so I am not surprised, if the people pursue you with stones. I too will load my pockets with stones, and whenever you begin to forget yourself, I will see to it that blood flows from your head." He nodded his head and said: "My dear young man, today is not the first time I have experienced this. In fact, whenever I enter the theater to recite something, the crowd is accustomed to receive me with this kind of wel-

6 quentia solet. | ceterum ne {et}[496] tecum quoque habeam
rixandum, toto die me ab hoc cibo abstinebo." "immo"
inquam ego "si eiuras hodiernam bilem, una cenabimus." |

⟨ * * * ⟩

7 mando aedicularum custodi cenulae officium.

⟨ * * * ⟩

91. video Gitona cum linteis et strigilibus parieti appli-
2 citum tristem confusumque. | scires non libenter servire.
itaque ut experimentum oculorum caperem ⟨. . .⟩ convertit ille solutum gaudio vultum et "miserere" inquit "frater.
ubi arma non sunt, libere loquor. eripe me latroni cruento
et qualibet saevitia paenitentiam iudicis tui puni. satis
magnum erit misero solacium, tua voluntate cecidisse." |
3 supprimere ego querelam iubeo, ne quis consilia deprehenderet, relictoque Eumolpo—nam in balneo carmen recitabat—per tenebrosum et sordidum egressum
extraho Gitona raptimque in hospitium meum pervolo. |
4 praeclusis deinde foribus invado pectus amplexibus et
5 perfusum os lacrimis vultu meo contero. | diu vocem neu-
ter invenit; nam puer etiam singultibus crebris amabile
6 pectus quassaverat. | "o facinus" inquam "indignum, quod
amo te quamvis relictus, et in hoc pectore, cum vulnus
ingens fuerit, cicatrix non est. quid dicis, peregrini amoris
7 concessio? dignus hac iniuria fui?" | postquam se amari
sensit, supercilium altius sustulit ⟨. . .⟩ "nec amoris arbi-
trium ad alium iudicem ⟨de⟩tuli.[497] sed nihil iam queror,
nihil iam memini, si bona fide sententiam[498] emendas." |
8 haec cum inter gemitus lacrimasque fudissem, detersit ille

[496] *deleted Bücheler*
[497] *added Bücheler*
[498] sententiam *Bücheler*: paenitentiam

come. But so as not to quarrel with you as well, I will abstain from this kind of food all day." I said: "Well, if you foreswear your madness for the day, we will dine together." . . . I gave the porter of the lodgings the task of providing a simple dinner. . . .

91. I saw Giton with some towels and scrapers leaning against a wall, and he looked sad and disoriented. You could see that he was not a willing slave. And so to get proof of what my eyes told me . . . He turned his face now relaxed with delight and said: "My brother, have pity on me. Since there are no weapons here, I speak freely. Take me away from this bloodstained robber, and punish your repentant judge as cruelly as you like. I will be adequately comforted in my grief, if I die at your wish." I ordered him to put a stop to his lament, fearing that someone might overhear our plans. We gave Eumolpus the slip—he was reciting a poem in the baths—and I dragged Giton out through a dark and dirty exit and hastily flew to my lodgings. After the door had been shut, I attacked his breast with embraces and with my face rubbed his cheek which was flooded with tears. For some time neither of us found words; the boy's lovable breast shook with frequent sobs. I said: "Your action was uncalled for, the fact was I loved you, although deserted by you. And in my breast there is no scar, though the wound was deep. What excuse do you have for giving in to a stranger's love? Did I deserve this insult?" After he realized that he was still loved, he raised an eyebrow. . . . "I did not lay the decision about my love before any other judge. But now I complain about nothing, now I remember nothing, if in all honesty you correct your behavior." When I had poured out such words amid groans and tears, he wiped his face with his cloak and said:

pallio vultum et "quaeso" inquit "Encolpi, fidem memoriae tuae appello: ego te reliqui an tu ‹me›[499] prodidisti?
equidem fateor et prae me fero: cum duos armatos vide-
9 rem, ad fortiorem confugi." | exosculatus pectus sapientia
plenum inieci cervicibus manus, et ut facile intellegeret
redisse me in gratiam et optima fide reviviscentem amicitiam, toto pectore adstrinxi.

92. et iam plena nox erat mulierque cenae mandata
2 curaverat, cum Eumolpus ostium pulsat. | interrogo ego:
"quot estis?" obiterque per rimam foris speculari diligen-
3 tissime coepi, num Ascyltos una venisset. | deinde ut so-
lum hospitem vidi, momento recepi. ille ut se in grabatum
reiecit viditque Gitona in conspectu ministrantem, movit
4 caput et "laudo" inquit "Ganymedem. | oportet hodie bene
sit." non delectavit me tam curiosum principium timuique
5 ne in contubernium recepissem Ascylti parem.[500] | instat
Eumolpus, et cum puer illi potionem dedisset, "malo te"
inquit "quam balneum totum" siccatoque avide poculo
6 negat sibi umquam acidius fuisse. | "nam et dum lavor" ait
"paene vapulavi, quia conatus sum circa solium sedentibus
carmen recitare, et[501] postquam de balneo tamquam de
theatro eiectus sum, circuire omnes angulos coepi et clara
7 voce Encolpion clamitare. | ex altera parte iuvenis nudus,
qui vestimenta perdiderat, non minore clamoris in-
8 dignatione Gitona flagitabat. | et me quidem pueri tam-
quam insanum imitatione petulantissima deriserunt, illum

499 *added t*
500 parem *t*[mg]: partem
501 et *Goldast*: at

"I ask you, Encolpius, I appeal to the honesty of your memory: did I desert you or did you betray me? I admit and I confess openly: when I saw two armed men, I took refuge with the stronger." After I had kissed that breast so full of wisdom, I threw my arms around his neck, and that he might really know that I had been reconciled to him, and that our friendship lived afresh in perfect trust, I hugged him with my whole breast.

92. It was now completely dark outside, and the woman given instructions about our dinner had taken care of it, when Eumolpus knocked on the door. I asked: "How many of you are there?" and began, as I spoke, to look very carefully through a chink in the door to see whether Ascyltos had come with him. When I saw that he was the only guest, I let him in at once. As he flung himself on the bed and saw Giton before his eyes waiting on table, he nodded and said: "I approve of your Ganymede. It should be a great day." Such an officious opening did not please me, and I was afraid that I had taken for a companion another Ascyltos. Eumolpus persisted, and when the boy had given him a drink, said: "I prefer you to a whole bath full of beautiful boys." Once he had greedily finished off his drink, he said that he had never been treated so disagreeably: "It was while I was bathing, and just because I tried to recite a poem to the men sitting round the rim of the bath, I was almost flogged. And after I had been thrown out of the bath, as if it were from the theater, I began to make the rounds of every nook and cranny and to cry out for Encolpius in a loud voice. On the other side of the place there was a nude young man who had lost his clothes, and in a no less angry voice was clamoring for someone named Giton. The boys there indeed were making fun of me with the most insolent imitations as if I were a lunatic,

autem frequentia ingens circumvenit cum plausu et admi-
9 ratione timidissima. ⌐ habebat enim inguinum pondus tam
grande, ut ipsum hominem laciniam fascini crederes. o
iuvenem laboriosum! puto illum pridie incipere, postero
10 die finire. | itaque statim invenit auxilium; nescioquis
enim, eques Romanus ut aiebant[502] infamis, sua veste er-
rantem circumdedit ac domum abduxit, credo, ut tam
11 magna fortuna solus uteretur. | at ego ne mea quidem
vestimenta ab officioso ⟨capsario⟩[503] recepissem, nisi notorem dedidissem. tanto magis expedit[504] inguina quam
12 ingenia fricare." | haec Eumolpo dicente mutabam ego
frequentissime vultum, iniuriis scilicet inimici mei hilaris,
13 commodis tristis. | utcumque tamen, tamquam non agnos-
cerem fabulam, tacui et cenae ordinem explicui.

⟨ * * * ⟩

93. "vile est quod licet, et animus errore laetus[505] iniu-
rias diligit. |

2   [φL]ales Phasiacis petita Colchis
atque Afrae[506] volucres placent palato,
quod non sunt faciles: at albus anser
et pictis anas involuta[507] pennis
5   plebeium sapit. ultimis ab oris
attractus scarus atque arata Syrtis
si quid naufragio dedit, probatur:
mullus iam gravis est. amica vincit
uxorem. rosa cinnamum veretur.
quicquid quaeritur, optimum videtur." |

---

502 aiebant *Dousa*: aiebat   503 *added Müller*: ⟨custode⟩
added Bücheler   504 expedit *Dousa*, p^2: impedit
505 laetus *Graevius*: lentus   506 Afrae *Puteanus*, $l^{mg}tp$:
aeriae   507 involuta *Busche*: renovata

but a huge crowd surrounded the nude youth, clapping their hands and looking on in humble admiration. For he had such enormous sexual organs, you would have thought that the man was an attachment to his penis. This youth must work hard at his job! I think he could start on the day before and finish on the day after. And for this reason he found assistance at once: some Roman knight or other, a disreputable fellow they said, put his own clothes on him as he wandered about, and took him off home, I think, to enjoy his good fortune alone. But as for me, I would not have recovered even my own clothes from the meddlesome bath attendant, had I not produced someone to vouch for me. It just goes to show how much more useful it is to rub groins than brains." While Eumolpus narrated these events, I kept changing my expressions, from delight at my enemy's injuries, to sadness at his good fortune. However, I kept quiet as if I did not recognize what the story was about, and I explained the order of the courses for dinner. . . .

93. "We hold cheap what is legitimate, and our minds delighting in delusion love to do wrong. The pheasant sought from Colchis on the Phasis river and the fowls from Africa are pleasing to the palate, because they are not easy to get: but the white goose and the duck covered with colorful feathers are readily available and thus appeal to plebeian tastes. The parrot wrasse brought from far-off shores and fish caught by ships plowing the Syrtis are praised, if first they lead to shipwreck; the mullet now is disagreeable. The mistress prevails over the wife. The rose fears the imported cinnamon. Whatever is hard to get seems the best." And I said:

3   ^L"hoc est" inquam "quod promiseras, ne quem hodie versum faceres? per fidem, saltem nobis parce, qui te numquam lapidavimus. nam si aliquis ex is, qui in eodem synoecio potant, nomen poetae olfecerit, totam concitabit viciniam et nos omnes sub eadem causa obruet. miserere

4   et aut pinacothecam aut balneum cogita." | sic me loquentem obiurgavit Giton, mitissimus puer, et negavit recte facere, quod seniori conviciarer simulque oblitus officii mensam, quam humanitate posuissem, contumelia tollerem, multaque alia moderationis verecundiaeque verba, quae formam eius egregie decebant

⟨ * * * ⟩

    ^{OL}94. {*Eumolpus ad Gitonem*} "o felicem" inquit "matrem tuam, quae te talem peperit: macte virtute esto.

2   ^{OφL}raram fecit mixturam cum sapientia forma. | ^{OL}itaque ne putes te tot verba perdidisse, amatorem invenisti. ego laudes tuas carminibus implebo. ego paedagogus et custos etiam quo non iusseris sequar. nec iniuriam Encolpius

3   accipit, alium amat." | profuit etiam Eumolpo miles ille, qui mihi abstulit gladium; alioquin quem animum adversus Ascylton sumpseram, eum in Eumolpi sanguinem

4   exercuissem. nec fefellit hoc Gitona. | itaque extra cellam processit tamquam aquam peteret, iramque meam pru-

5   denti absentia extinxit. | paululum ergo intepescente saevitia "Eumolpe" inquam "iam malo vel carminibus loquaris quam eiusmodi tibi vota proponas. et ego iracundus sum et tu libidinosus: vide quam non conveniat his mori-

6   bus. | puta igitur me furiosum esse, cede insaniae, id est

"This is how you keep your promise not to deliver a single line of poetry? After giving us your word of honor, at least spare us who have never stoned you. For if any of the drinkers in this lodging smells the suggestion of a poet, he will rouse the whole neighborhood and bury us alive for the same reason. Have some sympathy for us, and remember what happened in the picture gallery or at the baths." Giton, the gentlest of boys, scolded me for speaking this way, and said that I was wrong to rebuke an older man, and at the same time to forget my duty as host. He said that with my insults I was spoiling the table I had so kindly set out, and then added many other calm and gentle words of advice which added such grace to his good looks. . . .

94. "How fortunate your mother is," said Eumolpus, "to have given birth to a son like you. Well done! Beauty and wisdom have made a rare combination. So do not think that you have wasted all your words, since you have found a lover in me. I shall fill my verses with your praise. I shall escort you to school, be your guardian, and will follow you even where you do not ask me. Encolpius does not suffer an injustice, since he loves another." The soldier who took away my sword did Eumolpus a favor also, otherwise I would have used the anger that I had raised against Ascyltos to draw the blood of Eumolpus. The look in my eye did not escape Giton's attention, and so he went out of the room on the pretense of fetching some water. He quenched my anger by his tactful departure, and therefore with my rage cooling a little I said: "I would prefer now that you speak even in poetry rather than harbor hopes of this sort for yourself. I am hotheaded and you are lecherous: you must understand that these emotions are not compatible. Therefore think of me as a maniac,

7 ocius foras exi." | ^Lconfusus hac denuntiatione Eumolpus
non quaesiit iracundiae causam, sed continuo limen egres-
sus adduxit repente ostium cellae meque nihil tale expec-
tantem inclusit, exemitque raptim clavem et ad Gitona
8 investigandum cucurrit. | inclusus ego suspendio vitam
finire constitui. et iam semicinctio <lecti>⁵⁰⁸ stantis ad
parietem spondam vinxeram cervicesque nodo condebam,
cum reseratis foribus intrat Eumolpus cum Gitone meque
9 a fatali iam meta revocat ad lucem. | Giton praecipue ex
dolore in rabiem efferatus tollit clamorem, me utraque
10 manu impulsum praecipitat super lectum. | "erras" inquit
"Encolpi, si putas contingere posse ut ante moriaris. prior
11 coepi; in Ascylti hospitio gladium quaesivi. | ego si te non
invenissem, petiturus {per}⁵⁰⁹ praecipitia fui. et ut scias
non longe esse quaerentibus mortem, specta invicem
12 quod me spectare voluisti." | haec locutus mercennario
Eumolpi novaculam rapit et semel iterumque cervice per-
13 cussa ante pedes collabitur nostros. | exclamo ego attoni-
tus, secutusque labentem eodem ferramento ad mortem
14 viam quaero. | sed neque Giton ulla erat suspicione vulne-
ris laesus neque ego ullum sentiebam dolorem. rudis enim
novacula et in hoc retusa, ut pueris discentibus audaciam
15 tonsoris daret, instruxerat thecam. | ideoque nec mercen-
narius ad raptum ferramentum expaverat nec Eumolpus
interpellaverat mimicam mortem.

    ^{OL}95. dum haec fabula inter amantes luditur, deversitor
cum parte cenulae intervenit, contemplatusque foedissi-

---

⁵⁰⁸ *added Bücheler*
⁵⁰⁹ *omitted lr*

step aside before my madness—in short, get out right now." Eumolpus was upset by this warning, did not question the reason for my anger, but at once left the room and suddenly slammed the door. Taking me completely by surprise, he shut me in, swiftly removed the key, and ran out to look for Giton. Locked in my room I decided to end my life by hanging myself. I had just tied a belt to the frame of a bed standing against the wall and was plunging my neck into the noose, when the door was unlocked, and Eumoplus came in with Giton, recalling me to light and away from my lethal goal. Giton in particular went wild first in grief then in hysteria, raised a shout, and pushing with both hands threw me on to the bed. "You are wrong, Encolpius," he said, "if you suppose that you could possibly succeed in dying before me. I anticipated you in this: I searched for a sword in Ascyltos' lodgings. If I had not found you, I would have hurled myself over a precipice. And so that you realize death is nearby for those who seek it, you in your turn must now look at the scene you wanted me to see." With these words he grabbed the razor from Eumolpus' servant, slashed his throat once and then again, and tumbled down at our feet. Looking on in horror I cried out, rushed to him as he fell, and sought the road to death by use of the same steel. But Giton was not marked by any suggestion of a wound, and I was not feeling any pain. For it was a practice razor, blunted for this reason, and had a sheath to give boys learning the trade the courage of a real barber. And so the servant had not panicked when the steel was snatched, nor had Eumolpus interrupted our staged death scene.

95. While this drama among lovers was being played out, a porter came on the scene with a part of our little

2   mam iacentium volutationem | "rogo" inquit "ebrii estis an
fugitivi an utrumque? quis autem grabatum illum erexit,

3   aut quid sibi vult tam furtiva molitio? | vos mehercules ne
mercedem cellae daretis, fugere nocte in publicum voluis-
tis. sed non impune. iam enim faxo sciatis non viduae hanc

4   insulam esse sed M. Mannicii." | exclamat Eumolpus
"etiam minaris?" simulque os hominis palma excussissima

5   pulsat. | ille tot hospitum potionibus liber[510] urceolum fic-
tilem in Eumolpi caput iaculatus est solvitque clamantis

6   frontem et de cella se proripuit. | Eumolpus contumeliae
impatiens rapit ligneum candelabrum sequiturque abeun-

7   tem et creberrimis ictibus supercilium suum vindicat. | fit
concursus familiae hospitumque ebriorum frequentia. ego
autem nactus occasionem vindictae Eumolpon[511] excludo,
redditaque scordalo vice sine aemulo scilicet et cella utor

8   et nocte. | interim coctores insulariique mulcant exclusum
et alius veru extis stridentibus plenum in oculos eius in-
tentat, alius furca de carnario rapta statum proeliantis
componit. anus praecipue lippa, sordidissimo praecincta
linteo, soleis ligneis imparibus imposita, canem ingentis

9   magnitudinis catena trahit instigatque in Eumolpon. | sed
ille candelabro se ab omni periculo vindicabat. 96. vide-
bamus nos omnia per foramen valvae, quod paulo ante
ansa ostioli rupta laxaverat, favebamque ego vapulanti. |

---

[510] tot . . . liber *obelized Müller*
[511] Eumolpon *Müller*: Eumolpum

dinner, and after looking at the really filthy scene of us rolling about on the floor, said: "Tell me, are you drunk, or runaway slaves, or both? Who stood the bed up against the wall, and why this devious piling up of furniture? I swear that you intended to skip out into the open at night without paying your bill. But you will pay for it. For now I'll see to it that you realize that this block of flats does not belong to some widow, but to Marcus Mannicius." Eumolpus shouted out: "Are you threatening us?" And as he spoke, he hit the man violently in the face with his palm. Acting without fear of consequences by having drunk so much with the guests, the porter hurled an earthenware jug at Eumolpus' head, cut up the forehead of the shouting man, and bolted from the room. Eumolpus did not put up with the insult, but grabbed a wooden candlestick, followed the porter out of the room, and with a rain of blows avenged his damaged forehead. There was a gathering of the whole household and a crowd of drunken guests. Having acquired the opportunity for revenge, I locked Eumolpus out, and with the tables turned on the aggressor, I was of course without a rival, and enjoyed both the room and the night. Meanwhile the cooks and lodgers beat up the locked-out Eumolpus: one thrust a spit full of sizzling meat at his eyes, another after taking a fork from the meat rack struck a warrior's pose. Of special interest was an old hag with bleary eyes, dressed in a totally filthy linen wrap, supported on uneven wooden clogs, and dragging along an enormous dog on a chain, which she sicced on Eumolpus. But he defended himself from all danger with the candlestick. 96. We saw everything through a hole in the leaf of the door, which had been made a little while before, when the handle of the door was broken. I was cheering

2 Giton autem non oblitus misericordiae suae reserandum
3 esse ostium succurrendumque periclitanti censebat. | ego
   durante adhuc iracundia non continui manum, sed caput
4 miserantis stricto acutoque articulo percussi. | et ille
   quidem flens consedit in lecto. ego autem alternos oppo-
   nebam foramini oculos iniuriaque[512] Eumolpi *L*velut
   quodam cibo me replebam *OL*advocationemque commen-
   dabam, cum procurator insulae Bargates a cena excitatus
   a duobus lecticariis in mediam rixam perfertur; nam erat
5 etiam pedibus aeger. | is ut rabiosa barbaraque voce in
   ebrios fugitivosque diu peroravit, respiciens ad Eumolpon
6 | "o poetarum" inquit "disertissime, tu eras? et non disce-
   dunt ocius nequissimi servi manusque continent a rixa?" |

⟨ * * * ⟩

7 *L*{*Bargates procurator ad Eumolpum*} "contubernalis mea
   mihi fastum facit. ita, si me amas, maledic illam versibus,
   ut habeat pudorem."

⟨ * * * ⟩

97. dum Eumolpus cum Bargate in secreto loquitur,
   intrat stabulum praeco cum servo publico aliaque sane
   ⟨non⟩[513] modica frequentia, facemque fumosam magis
2 quam lucidam quassans haec proclamavit: | "puer in bal-
   neo paulo ante aberravit, annorum circa XVI, crispus,
   mollis, formosus, nomine Giton. si quis eum reddere aut
3 commonstrare voluerit, accipiet nummos mille." | nec
   longe a praecone Ascyltos stabat amictus discoloria veste
   atque in lance argentea indicium et fidem praeferebat. |
4 imperavi Gitoni ut raptim grabatum subiret annecte-

512 iniuriaque *t*: iniuriamque
513 *added Pithoeus 1565*

as Eumolpus got thrashed. Giton, however, did not forget his stance on compassion and declared that we ought to open the door and run to the aid of the endangered man. With my anger still hot, I did not restrain my hand, and with my clenched fist struck the compassionate boy a sharp knock on the head. He in fact began to cry and sat down on the bed. I glued each of my eyes in turn to the chink in the door, and gorged myself on the injuries dealt out to Eumolpus, as though they were rich foods. I was in favor of an extended duration of the fight, but then Bargates, who was manager of the apartment house, and had been disturbed at dinner, was carried right into the brawl by two litter bearers. For besides everything else, he had gout. In furious and vulgar language he spoke at length against drunkards and runaway slaves, but then looking around saw Eumolpus and said: " Most learned of poets, was that you? And these totally worthless slaves do not run away quickly and cease their brawling? . . . My common-law wife despises me. So, if you love me, curse her in verse, so that she learns to respect me." . . .

97. While Eumolpus was talking privately to Bargates, a crier accompanied by a municipal slave and a large crowd of others entered the house. Brandishing a torch that gave off more smoke than light, he made this an-nouncement: "A slave boy has recently wandered off at the baths, about sixteen years old, curly haired, effeminate, good-looking, going by the name of Giton. If anyone is willing to return him or to indicate his whereabouts, there will be a reward of a thousand sesterces." Not far from the crier stood Ascyltos dressed in multicolored clothes, and holding out a silver platter on which was information about Giton and the promised reward. I ordered Giton to

retque pedes et manus institis, quibus sponda culcitam
ferebat, ac sic ut olim Ulixes prono[514] arieti[515] adhaesisset,
extentus infra grabatum scrutantium eluderet manus. |
5 non est moratus Giton imperium momentoque temporis
6 inseruit vinculo manus et Ulixem astu simillimo vicit. | ego
ne suspicioni relinquerem locum, lectulum vestimentis
implevi uniusque hominis vestigium ad corporis mei men-
7 suram figuravi. | interim Ascyltos ut pererravit omnes cum
viatore cellas, venit ad meam, et hoc quidem pleniorem
spem concepit quo[516] diligentius oppessulatas invenit fo-
8 res. | publicus vero servus insertans commissuris secures[517]
9 claustrorum infirmitatem laxavit. | ego ad genua Ascylti
procubui et per memoriam amicitiae perque societatem
miseriarum petii ut saltem ostenderet fratrem. immo ut
fidem haberent fictae preces, "scio te" inquam "Ascylte, ad
occidendum me venisse. quo enim secures attulisti? itaque satia iracundiam tuam: praebeo ecce cervicem, funde
sanguinem, quem sub praetextu quaestionis petisti." |
10 amolitur Ascyltos invidiam et se vero nihil aliud quam
fugitivum suum dixit quaerere, nec mortem[518] hominis
concupisse {nec}[519] supplicis, utique eius quem ⟨etiam⟩[520]
post fatalem rixam habuerit[521] carissimum. 98. at non servus publicus tam languide agit, sed raptam cauponi harun-

514 prono *La Penna*: pro
515 arieti *Bücheler*: ariete
516 quo *l*[mg]: quod   517 commissuris secures *Pithoeus 1565*,
tp: commissuras secure
518 nec mortem *Bücheler*: mortem nec
519 *deleted Ernout*
520 *added Ernout*
521 habuerit *Jacobs*: habuit

get under the bed at once, and hook his feet and hands into the roping by which the bed frame held the mattress, and just as Ulysses[126] of old had clung to the headlong ram, to stretch out beneath the bed and elude the prying hands. Giton obeyed the order at once, and promptly inserted his hands into the webbing, surpassing Ulysses with almost identical cleverness. I did not want to leave any room for suspicious traces, so I piled up clothes on the little bed, and arranged them in the shape of a single person about my own size. Meanwhile Ascyltos toured all the rooms in the company of the process server, and when he came to mine he in fact fostered higher hopes, because he found the doors more carefully bolted. The municipal slave slid an ax into the door joints and loosened the already weakened bolts. I fell at the knees of Ascyltos and begged him, in recollection of our friendship and because of our fellowship in misfortune, that at least he should show me my boy-partner. That my fake prayers might sound more convincing, I said: "Ascyltos, I realize that you have come here to kill me. For were this not so, why have you brought axes? And so, appease your anger: here is my neck, pour out my blood, this is the real object you wanted in your pretended legal search." Ascyltos rebutted the charge of hatred, and said that he desired nothing other than his own runaway slave; he did not seek the death of any suppliant man, especially the one whom he held most dear, even after their deadly dispute was over. 98. The municipal slave, however, did not act so sluggishly, but grabbed

---

[126] The story of the Cyclops (Hom. *Od.* 9.431–505), a character mentioned again in chs. 48.7 and 101.5; Odysseus hides under a sheep and escapes the clutches of the Cyclops.

dinem subter lectum mittit omniaque etiam foramina
parietum scrutatur. subducebat Giton ab ictu corpus et
retento[522] timidissime spiritu ipsos sciniphes ore tange-
2 bat. ‹. . .› | Eumolpus autem, quia effractum ostium cellae
neminem poterat excludere, irrumpit perturbatus et
"mille" inquit "nummos inveni; iam enim persequar
abeuntem praeconem et in potestate tua esse Gitona[523]
3 meritissima proditione[524] monstrabo." | genua ego per-
severantis amplector, ne morientes vellet occidere, et
"merito" inquam "excandesceres, si posses perditum[525]
ostendere. nunc inter turbam puer fugit, nec quo abierit
suspicari possum. per fidem, Eumolpe, reduc puerum et
4 vel Ascylto redde." | dum haec ego iam credenti per-
suadeo, Giton collectione spiritus plenus ter continuo ita
5 sternutavit ut grabatum concuteret. | ad quem motum
Eumolpus conversus salvere Gitona iubet. remota etiam
culcita videt Ulixem, cui vel esuriens Cyclops potuisset
6 parcere. | mox conversus ad me "quid est" inquit "latro?
ne deprehensus quidem ausus es mihi verum dicere.
immo ni deus quidam humanarum rerum arbiter pendenti
puero excussisset indicium, elusus circa popinas erra-
rem." |

‹ * * * ›

7 Giton longe blandior quam ego, primum araneis oleo
madentibus vulnus, quod in supercilio factum erat, coar-
tavit. mox palliolo suo laceratam mutavit vestem, amplexus-

---

[522] retento *Müller*: reducto
[523] Gitona *Müller*: Gitonem
[524] proditione *Pithoeus in Notis*: propositione
[525] perditum *Jacobs*: proditum

a cane from the innkeeper and thrust it under the bed, and scrutinized everything, even the cracks in the walls. Giton twisted his body away from the blow of the stick, held his breath very nervously and pressed his face against the stinging insects themselves. . . . But because the broken door could not keep anyone out, Eumolpus burst in. He was offended and said: "I have found a thousand sesterces, for I mean to follow the crier as he goes out, and betray you as you so richly deserve by informing him that Giton is in your hands." He persisted, and I embraced his knees in supplication not to kill the dying. I said: "You would be justifiably angry, if you could reveal the scoundrel. As it is, the boy fled among the crowds, and I do not have the least idea where he has gone. By all that is right, Eumolpus, get the boy back or, if you wish, return him to Ascyltos." It was while I was persuading him about these things, and he was beginning to believe me, that Giton, who had been holding his breath and was now full of air, sneezed so violently three times in rapid succession that he shook the bed. Eumolpus turned toward this activity and ordered us to bless Giton. He lifted up the mattress and saw a Ulysses whom even a hungry Cyclops would have abstained from eating. Then he turned on me and said: "What is this all about, you thief? You did not venture to tell me the truth even when you were caught. In fact, unless some god who controls human affairs had not shaken a sign from the boy as he hung there, I would have been made a fool and be wandering around low-class eating houses." . . . Giton was far more charming than I, and first of all stanched the wound made on Eumolpus' forehead with spiders' webs soaked in oil. Then he gave him his own little cloak in exchange for his torn clothes, and having embraced him

que iam mitigatum osculis tamquam fomentis aggressus
8 est et | "in tua" inquit "pater carissime, in tua sumus custo-
9 dia. si Gitona tuum amas, incipe velle servare. | utinam me
solum inimicus ignis hauriret vel[526] hibernum invaderet
mare. ego enim omnium scelerum materia, ego causa
sum. si perirem, conveniret inimicis."

⟨ * * * ⟩

[φL]99. {*Eumolpus*}[527] "ego sic semper et ubique vixi, ut
ultimam quamque lucem tamquam non redituram consu-
merem." |

⟨ * * * ⟩

2 [L]profusis ego lacrimis rogo quaesoque ut mecum quoque
redeat in gratiam: neque enim in amantium esse potestate
furiosam aemulationem; daturum tamen operam ne aut
dicam aut faciam amplius quo possit offendi; tantum omnem scabitudinem animo tamquam bonarum artium ma-
3 gister delevet[528] sine cicatrice. | [φL]"incultis asperisque
regionibus diutius nives haerent, ast ubi[529] aratro dome-
facta tellus nitet, dum loqueris levis pruina dilabitur. simi-
liter in pectoribus ira considit: feras quidem mentes obsi-
4 det, eruditas praeterlabitur." | [L]"ut scias" inquit Eumolpus
"verum esse quod dicis, ecce etiam osculo iram finio. itaque, quod bene eveniat, expedite sarcinulas et vel sequi-
5 mini me vel, si mavultis, ducite." | adhuc loquebatur, cum
crepuit ostium impulsum, stetitque in limine barbis
horrentibus nauta et "moraris" inquit "Eumolpe, tam-
6 quam properandum[530] ignores." | haud mora, omnes
consurgimus, et Eumolpus quidem mercennarium suum
iam olim dormientem exire cum sarcinis iubet; ego cum

---

526 vel *Bücheler*: ut *lr*   527 *Names of characters so identified in some sources are deleted here as later additions.*

and softened him up with kisses as if they were poultices, said: "Dearest father, we are in your hands, yours entirely. If you love your Giton, start now to rescue him. I desire only that a cruel fire might devour me or that a wintry sea seize me, because I am the source of all these calamities, I am the cause. If I were to die, you two, who are enemies now, would be reconciled." . . .

99. [Eumolpus] "Always and everywhere I have so lived my life as though I were spending my last day, one that would never return." . . . After a flood of tears I asked and begged him to be friends again also with me: mad jealousy was outside the control of lovers; I would do my best to say or do nothing more, by which he would be offended; as if a master of all virtues, he should only smooth over the rancor in his mind and leave no scar behind. "On the uncultivated and rough country the snows stick longer, but where the earth is mastered by the plow and looks beautiful, the light frost passes even as you speak. The same thing happens to anger in the heart: it besieges the savage minds, but falls away from the educated." Eumolpus said: "So that you might know what you said is true, look, I will put an end to anger even with a kiss. And so, may it turn out all right. Pack your bags and follow me, or if you prefer, lead the way." He was still speaking when there was a knock on the door, and at the threshold stood a sailor with a bristling beard who said: "You're detaining us, Eumolpus, as if you didn't know we had to hurry." We all rose quickly and Eumolpus ordered his servant, who had been asleep for some time, to go out with the luggage.

---

528 delevet *Fraenkel*: deleret
529 ubi ϕ: ubi ea   530 properandum t^{mg}: propudium

Gitone quicquid erat in altum[531] compono et adoratis sideribus intro navigium.

〈 * * * 〉

100. "molestum est quod puer hospiti placet. [φL]quid autem? non commune est quod natura optimum fecit? sol omnibus lucet. luna innumerabilibus comitata sideribus etiam feras ducit ad pabulum. quid aquis dici formosius potest? in publico tamen manant. [L]solus ergo amor furtum potius quam praemium erit? immo vero nolo habere bona nisi quibus populus inviderit. unus, et senex, non erit gravis; etiam cum voluerit aliquid sumere, opus anhelitu pro-

2 det." | haec ut infra fiduciam posui fraudavique animum dissidentem, coepi somnum obruto tunicula capite men-

3 tiri. | sed repente quasi destruente fortuna constantiam meam eiusmodi vox super constratum puppis ingemuit:[532]

4 "ergo me derisit?" | et[533] haec quidem virilis et {paene}[534] auribus meis familiaris animum palpitantem 〈paene〉 percussit. ceterum eadem indignatione mulier lacerata ulterius excanduit et "si quis deus manibus meis" inquit "Gitona imponeret, quam bene exul eum[535] exciperet."[536]

5 | uterque nostrum tam inexpectato ictus sono amiserat sanguinem. ego praecipue quasi somnio quodam turbulento circumamictus diu vocem collegi tremebundisque manibus Eumolpi iam in soporem labentis laciniam traxi[537] et "per fidem" inquam "pater, cuius haec navis est, aut

6 quos vehat dicere potes?" | inquietatus ille moleste tulit et "hoc erat" inquit "quod placuerat tibi, ut subter[538] constra-

---

[531] altum *t*: alt̃ *L*: iter *Bücheler*   [532] ingemuit *Müller*: congemuit   [533] et *Bücheler*: at   [534] {paene} ... 〈paene〉 *transposed Schmeling*[5]   [535] exul eum *Strelitz*: exulem
[536] exciperet *L*: exciperem *t*[mg]   [537] traxi *t*[mg]: duxi
[538] subter *Müller*: super

I put together with Giton's help whatever was at hand for the sea voyage, and after praying to the stars, boarded the ship. . . .

100. "It is annoying that our new friend likes the boy. What about it? Are not nature's best works common property? The sun shines on all creatures alike; the moon accompanied by countless stars leads even the wild beasts to their food. What lovelier object can be discussed than water? yet it flows for all to use. Then will love alone be something stolen rather than a prize to be enjoyed? It is true, however, that I do not want goods unless the masses envy them. But one new acquaintance, and an old man at that, will not be troublesome; even if he wishes to take sexual pleasures, he will betray his efforts by his panting." As I itemized these points without much confidence, and deceived my skeptical spirit, I covered my head with my little tunic and pretended to sleep. But suddenly as if Fortune destroyed my resolution, a voice on the poop deck spoke in offended groans: "So he made a fool of me, did he?" This was indeed a man's voice, familiar to my ears, and it almost shocked my throbbing heart. Then a woman, tortured by similar indignation, became even more angry and said: "If some god delivered Giton into my hands, how warmly this exiled woman would welcome him." Both of us turned pale after we had been struck by such unexpected sounds. For me it was as if I had been trapped in some troubled dream. I could not find my voice for some time, and with shaking hands I pulled at the hem of Eumolpus' cloak, just as he was falling asleep. "Tell me the truth, father," I said, "whose ship is this, or who is on board, can you tell me?" He was annoyed at being disturbed and said: "Was this the reason you resolved that we

281

tum navis occuparemus secretissimum locum, ne nos pa-
7   tereris requiescere? | quid porro ad rem pertinet, si dixero
Licham Tarentinum esse dominum huiusce navigii, qui
Tryphaenam exulem Tarentum ferat?" 101. intremui post
hoc fulmen attonitus, iuguloque detecto "aliquando" inquam "totum me, Fortuna, vicisti." nam Giton quidem
2   super pectus meum positus diu animam egit. | deinde ut
effusus sudor utriusque spiritum revocavit, comprehendi
Eumolpi genua et "miserere" inquam "morientium, id est
pro consortio studiorum commoda manum; mors venit,
quae nisi per te non[539] licet, potest esse pro munere." |
3   inundatus hac Eumolpus invidia iurat per deos deasque se
neque scire quid acciderit nec ullum dolum malum consilio adhibuisse, sed mente simplicissima et vera fide in
navigium comites induxisse, quo ipse iam pridem fuerit
4   usurus. | "quae autem hic insidiae sunt" inquit "aut quis
nobiscum Hannibal navigat? Lichas Tarentinus, homo
verecundissimus et non tantum huius navigii dominus
quod regit, sed fundorum etiam aliquot et familiae nego-
5   tiantis, onus deferendum ad mercatum conducit. | hic est
Cyclops ille et archipirata, cui vecturam debemus; et praeter hunc Tryphaena, omnium feminarum formosissima,
6   quae voluptatis causa huc atque illuc vectatur." | "hi sunt"
inquit Giton "quos fugimus" simulque raptim causas odio-
rum et instans periculum trepidanti Eumolpo exponit. |
7   confusus ille et consilii egens iubet quemque suam sen-

---

[539] non l^c: *omitted* L

---

[127] The insults occurred in a lost episode, where Encolpius
seems to have robbed Lichas, stolen a sacred robe and rattle
dedicated to Isis, and seduced his wife; see also chs. 113–14.

282

should occupy the most secluded place below deck, to prevent us from getting any rest? Further, what does it matter if I tell you that Lichas of Tarentum is the master of this ship, and he is carrying Tryphaena into exile in Tarentum?" 101. I shook with fear after being hit by this bolt from the blue, bared my throat, and said: "Ah, Fortune, at last you have vanquished me completely." Giton indeed was sprawled over my chest, having long ago fainted. Then as sweat broke out on us, it revived us. I clutched the knees of Eumolpus and said: "Have pity on us, for we are as good as dead men. In consideration of our shared education, lend us a hand; our last hour has arrived, and unless you prevent it, death comes as a blessing." Eumolpus was overwhelmed by this wrongful accusation, and swore by gods and goddesses that he did not know what had happened previously, nor had he any sinister intention in his plan, but with the clearest conscience and in good faith he had led us aboard as his companions; he had decided already some time earlier to use this ship. "But what trap is there here?" he asked, "or who is the Hannibal sailing with us? Lichas of Tarentum is a very respectable person, and he is not only owner and captain of this ship, but even has several farms and underwrites his slaves in business, and is carrying cargo to market for his own account. So this is the one, that Cyclops and pirate king, to whom we owe our passage; and besides him there is Tryphaena, the most beautiful of all women, who is carried from one port to another for the sake of pleasure." "These are the two," said Giton, "we are running away from." At the same time he hastily explained to the frightened Eumolpus why they hated us and that danger was imminent.[127] In his state of shock and dearth of plans, he

283

tentiam promere et "fingite" inquit "nos antrum Cyclopis
intrasse. quaerendum est aliquod effugium, nisi naufra-
8 gium ponimus et omni nos periculo liberamus." | "immo"
inquit Giton "persuade gubernatori ut in aliquem portum
navem deducat, non sine praemio scilicet, et affirma ei
impatientem maris fratrem tuum in ultimis esse. poteris
hanc simulationem et vultus confusione et lacrimis[540]
obumbrare, ut misericordia permotus {gubernator}[541] tibi
9 indulgeat."[542] | negavit hoc Eumolpus fieri posse, "quia
magna" inquit "navigia portubus se curvatis insinuant, nec
10 tam cito fratrem defecisse veri simile erit. | accedit his
quod forsitan Lichas officii causa visere languentem desi-
derabit. vides quam valde nobis expediat ultro dominum
11 ad fugientes accersere![543] | sed finge navem ab ingenti
posse cursu deflecti et Licham non utique circumiturum
aegrorum cubilia: quomodo possumus egredi nave, ut non
conspiciamur a cunctis? opertis capitibus an nudis? opertis, et quis non dare manum languentibus volet? nudis, et
quid erit aliud quam se ipsos proscribere?" 102. "quin
potius" inquam ego "ad temeritatem confugimus et per
funem lapsi descendimus in scapham praecisoque vinculo
2 reliqua fortunae committimus? | nec ego in hoc periculum
Eumolpon arcesso. quid enim attinet innocentem alieno
periculo imponere? contentus sum, si nos descendentes
3 adiuverit casus." | "non imprudens" inquit "consilium"
Eumolpus "si aditum haberet. quis enim non euntes
notabit? utique gubernator, qui pervigil nocte siderum

540 et vultis . . . lacrimis *l*: et lacrimis et vultus confusione
541 *deleted Nisbet*
542 tibi indulgeat *Nisbet*: indulgeat tibi
543 accersere *Bücheler*: accedere

asked each of us to put forward our opinion about what to do, and said: "Imagine that we have entered the cave of the Cyclops. We must find some way of escaping, unless we stage a shipwreck and free ourselves from all danger." In answer Giton said: "On the contrary, persuade the helmsman to put the ship into some port, of course with a bribe, and assure him that your brother is seasick and on his last legs. You will be able to hide this deception by the troubled look and tears on your face, and he will be moved with sympathy and accede to your request." Eumolpus said that this was impossible: "Large ships can anchor only in deepwater bays enclosed by curved breakwaters, and the story that my brother has fallen ill so soon in the voyage will not be credible. Add to this the fact that Lichas in his role as captain will likely want to see the sick person. You realize how helpful this would be for us to summon the master voluntarily to meet the runaways. But suppose the ship could be diverted from its great voyage and Lichas would not carefully make the rounds of the beds of the sick: how can we leave the ship without being seen by all? Do we go with our heads covered or bare? If we cover them, who will not want to lend a hand to the sick? If we leave them bare, what does that amount to except to advertise ourselves?" 102. "Would it not be a better idea," I said, "to take refuge in bold actions, to slip down a rope and descend into the dinghy, cut the painter, and leave the rest to Fortune? I do not invite Eumolpus into this danger, for how is it proper to load an innocent person with other people's dangers? I am satisfied, if chance is on our side, as we descend." Eumolpus said: "It is not a bad plan, if it had a chance of success. But who will not take note of your departure, especially the helmsman, who stays awake all

4   quoque motus custodit. | et utcumque imponi vel ‹nil›[544]
dormienti posset, si per aliam partem navis fuga quoque
quaereretur: nunc per puppim, per ipsa gubernacula dela-
bendum est, a quorum regione funis descendit qui sca-
5   phae custodiam tenet. | praeterea illud miror, Encolpi, tibi
non succurrisse, unum nautam stationis perpetuae interdiu noctuque[545] iacere in scapha, nec posse inde custodem
6   nisi aut caede expelli aut praecipitari viribus. | quod an
fieri possit interrogate audaciam vestram. nam quod ad
meum quidem comitatum attinet, nullum recuso pericu-
7   lum quod salutis spem ostendit. | nam sine causa {qui-
dem}[546] spiritum tamquam rem vacuam impendere ne[547]
8   vos quidem existimo velle. | videte numquid hoc placeat:
ego vos in duas iam pelles coniciam vinctosque loris inter
vestimenta pro sarcinis habebo, apertis scilicet aliquate-
nus labris, quibus et spiritum recipere possitis et cibum. |
9   conclamabo deinde nocte servos poenam graviorem
timentes praecipitasse se in mare. deinde cum ventum
fuerit in portum, sine ulla suspicione pro sarcinis vos effe-
10   ram." | "ita vero" inquam ego "tamquam solidos alligatu-
rus, quibus non soleat venter iniuriam facere? an tamquam eos qui sternutare non soleamus nec stertere? an
11   quia hoc genus furti semel {mea}[548] feliciter cessit? | sed
finge una die vinctos posse durare: quid ergo si diutius aut
tranquillitas nos tenuerit aut adversa tempestas? quid fac-

---

[544] *added Müller*
[545] noctuque *l*[mg]: noctisque
[546] *deleted Bücheler*
[547] ne *Bücheler*: nec
[548] *deleted l*[c]

night to keep watch also on the courses of the stars. One way or another it might be possible to escape detection even if he were wide awake, if that escape were attempted in another part of the ship: as it is, you would have to slide down at the stern close to the steering oars, where the rope hangs which tethers the dinghy for the sentry. Moreover I am surprised that is has not occurred to you, Encolpius, that one sailor lies in the dinghy both day and night on permanent guard duty; and you can get rid of this guard only by killing him or throwing him violently overboard. The two of you must ask yourselves if you have the courage to attempt this. As far as my going with you, I do not shirk any danger which offers some hope of safety. For I suppose that not even you wish to squander your lives without any reason, as if they were worthless. See whether you approve of this plan: I will throw each of you into leather bales, tie them up with straps, and put them among my clothes as luggage, leaving the ends open a bit, to be sure, so that you can breathe and get food. Then I will shout out that my slaves have jumped overboard into the sea during the night out of fear of harsher punishment, and when we have arrived at the port, I will carry you out like baggage without arousing any suspicion." I said: "Is that so? You will tie us up as though we are solid objects, whose bowels never give them trouble? Or do you suggest that we are people who do not sneeze or snore, or just because this kind of trick was successful once?[128] So suppose that for one day we can endure being tied up: but what if a calm or contrary wind detains us at sea? What are we to do

---

[128] According to Plutarch (*Vit. Caes.* 49), Cleopatra had herself wrapped up in a carpet and delivered to Julius Caesar.

12 turi sumus? | $^{\phi L}$vestes quoque diutius vinctas ruga consu-
mit, et chartae alligatae mutant figuram. ^{L}iuvenes adhuc
laboris expertes statuarum ritu patiemur pannos et vin-
13 cula? | adhuc aliquod iter salutis quaerendum est. inspicite
quod ego inveni: Eumolpus tamquam litterarum studiosus
utique atramentum habet. hoc ergo remedio mutemus
colores a capillis usque ad ungues. ita tamquam servi
Aethiopes et praesto tibi erimus sine tormentorum iniuria
hilares et permutato colore imponemus inimicis." |
14 "quidni?" inquit Giton "etiam circumcide nos, ut Iudaei
videamur, et pertunde aures, ut imitemur Arabes, et in-
creta facies, ut suos Gallia cives putet: tamquam hic solus
color figuram possit pervertere et non multa una oporteat[549] consentiant, ut omni ratione[550] mendacium constet.
15 | puta infectam medicamine faciem diutius durare posse;
finge nec aquae asperginem imposituram aliquam corpori
maculam nec vestem atramento adhaesuram, quod frequenter etiam non accersito ferrumine infigitur: age,
numquid et labra possumus tumore taeterrimo implere?
numquid et crines calamistro convertere? numquid et
frontes cicatricibus scindere? numquid et crura in orbem
pandere? numquid et talos ad terram deducere? numquid
barbam peregrina ratione figurare? $^{\phi L}$color arte composi-
16 tus inquinat corpus, non mutat. | ^{L}audite quid timenti suc-
currerit: praeligemus vestibus capita et nos in profundum
mergamus." 103. "nec istud dii hominesque patiantur"
Eumolpus exclamat "ut vos tam turpi exitu vitam finiatis.
immo potius facite quod iubeo. mercennarius quidem[551]

---

549 oporteat *Heinsius*: oportet
550 ut omni ratione *Crusius*: et non natione
551 quidem *Schmeling*: inquit

then? Even clothes that are folded too long get creased and worn, and if papyrus sheets are tied up they lose their shape. We are still young men and not used to suffering, and will we endure being packaged in rags and ropes like statues? We must keep searching for some route to safety. Consider this plan I just thought of: Eumolpus as literary man is sure to have some ink. With this means let us change our color from head to foot. And so like Ethiopian slaves we will also be at your service, cheerful without the severity of tortures, and by changing the color of our bodies we will trick our enemies." "Why not?" said Giton. "And while you are at it, circumcise us so that we look like Jews, pierce our ears so we imitate Arabs, and chalk our faces so Gaul thinks we are her citizens. As if this new color alone could undo our shape, and it were unnecessary that many things be consistent to make a successful deception from every angle. Suppose that the stain of dye applied to our faces can last for some time; imagine that a sprinkling of water will not leave any spot on our body, and that our clothes will not stick to the ink, which happens often even when glue is not applied: but tell me, can we fill out our lips for that hideously swollen look? Can we change our hair with curling-tongs? Can we cut up our foreheads to leave scars? Can we make ourselves bow-legged? Can we bend our ankles on to the ground? Or trim our beards to a foreign cut? Artificial colors stain the body without changing the shape. Listen to the solution of a scared person: let us tie our heads in our clothes and drown ourselves in the deep ocean." 103. Eumolpus shouted: "May gods and men not allow you to end your lives in such a disgraceful way. Instead, do what I tell you. My servant is a barber, as you found out from his razor: let

meus, ut ex novacula comperistis, tonsor est: hic continuo
radat utriusque non solum capita sed etiam supercilia. |
2 sequar ego frontes notans inscriptione sollerti, ut videa-
mini stigmate esse puniti. ita eaedem litterae et suspi-
cionem declinabunt quaerentium et vultus umbra suppli-
3 cii tegent." | non est dilata fallacia, sed ad latus navigii
furtim processimus capitaque cum superciliis denudanda
4 tonsori praebimus. | implevit Eumolpus frontes utriusque
ingentibus litteris et notum fugitivorum epigramma per
5 totam faciem liberali manu duxit. | unus forte ex vectori-
bus, qui acclinatus lateri navis exonerabat stomachum
nausea gravem, notavit sibi ad lunam tonsorem intempes-
tivo inhaerentem ministerio, execratusque omen, quod
imitaretur naufragorum ultimum votum, in cubile reiectus
6 est. | nos[552] dissimulata nauseantis devotione ad ordinem
tristitiae redimus, silentioque compositi[553] reliquas noctis
horas male soporati consumpsimus.

〈 * * * 〉

104. {*Lichas*}[554] "videbatur mihi secundum quietem
Priapus dicere: 'Encolpion quod quaeris, scito a me in
2 navem tuam esse perductum.'" | exhorruit Tryphaena et
"putes" inquit "una nos dormiisse; nam et mihi simu-
lacrum Neptuni, quod Bais 〈in〉 tetrastylo[555] notaveram,
3 videbatur dicere: 'in nave Lichae Gitona invenies.'" | "hinc
scies" inquit Eumolpus "Epicurum hominem esse divinum, qui eiusmodi ludibria facetissima ratione condem-
4 nat." 〈. . .〉 | ceterum Lichas ut Tryphaenae somnium

---

[552] nos *Dousa*: non
[553] compositi *Burman*: composito
[554] *See n. 527.*
[555] Bais 〈in〉 tetrastylo *Bücheler*: Baistor asylo

him at once shave the heads and eyebrows of both of you.
I will follow his work and mark your foreheads with a skill-
ful inscription to make you appear slaves punished by
branding. The same letters will both divert the suspicions
of the inquisitive and at the same time conceal your faces
under the shadow of punishment." We did not put off
implementing this trick of misrepresentation, but proceeded stealthily to the side of the ship and presented our
heads and eyebrows to the barber for him to strip bare.
Eumolpus filled both of our foreheads with large letters,
and with a generous hand scrawled the notorious inscription for runaway slaves over the whole of our faces. One
of the passengers happened to be extremely seasick, and
leaning over the side of the ship to vomit, observed in the
moonlight the barber engrossed in his inauspicious duties.
The man cursed this for an evil omen, because it looked
like the final offering of shipwrecked sailors, and then
threw himself back into his bunk. Pretending not to hear
the curse of the seasick man, we went back to our melan-
choly procedure, and after settling ourselves in silence,
spent the remaining hours of the night in fitful sleep. . . .

104. [Lichas said:] "I thought I heard in my sleep Priapus say: 'In regard to Encolpius whom you are looking for,
I want you to appreciate that he has been brought by me
on to your ship.'" Tryphaena shuttered and said: "You
would think we had slept together; for I also had a dream
in which the statue of Neptune, which I had noticed in the
tetrastyle shrine in Baiae, seemed to say: 'You will find
Giton on board Lichas' ship.'" To which Eumolpus said:
"This will show you what a godlike man Epicurus was, for
he condemns such nonsense in the most witty fashion."
. . . But as Lichas prayed for a favorable result from Try-

expiavit, "quis" inquit "prohibet navigium scrutari, ne vi-
5 deamur divinae mentis opera damnare?" ⟨. . .⟩ | is qui
nocte miserorum furtum deprehenderat, Hesus no-
mine,[556] subito proclamat: "ergo illi {qui}[557] sunt, qui nocte
ad lunam radebantur pessimo medius fidius exemplo? audio enim non licere cuiquam mortalium in nave neque
ungues neque capillos deponere nisi cum pelago ventus
irascitur." 105. excanduit Lichas hoc sermone turbatus et
"itane" inquit "capillos aliquis in nave praecidit, et hoc
nocte intempesta? attrahite ocius nocentes in medium, ut
2 sciam quorum capitibus debeat navigium lustrari." | "ego"
inquit Eumolpus "hoc iussi. nec in[558] eodem futurus navigio auspicium mihi feci, sed quia {nocentes}[559] horridos
longosque habebant capillos, ne viderer de nave carcerem
facere, iussi squalorem damnatis auferri; simul ut notae
quoque litterarum non obumbratae[560] comarum praesidio
3 totae ad oculos legentium acciderent.[561] | inter cetera
apud communem amicam consumpserunt pecuniam
meam, a qua illos proxima nocte extraxi mero unguen-
tisque perfusos. ad summam, adhuc patrimonii mei reli-
quias olent." ⟨. . .⟩ |
4   itaque ut tutela navis expiaretur, placuit quadragenas
utrisque plagas imponi. nulla ergo fit mora: aggrediuntur
nos furentes nautae cum funibus temptantque vilissimo
5 sanguine tutelam placare. | et ego quidem tres plagas
Spartana nobilitate concoxi. ceterum Giton semel ictus
tam valde exclamavit, ut Tryphaenae aures notissima voce

---

[556] Hesus nomine L: laeso omine t[mg]
[557] deleted Segebade   [558] in Bücheler: non
[559] deleted Fraenkel   [560] obumbratae Bücheler: adum-
bratae   [561] acciderent Heinsius: accederent

phaena's dream, he said: "There is no objection to searching the ship, for we would not wish to seem to censure the workings of the divine mind." . . . Hesus, the one who had caught us at our wretched deception in the dark, suddenly shouted: "Then those were the ones who were being shaved in the dark by moonlight. That is a very bad example, I swear, for I am told that no mortal on a ship is permitted to cut his nails or hair, except when the wind and sea are raging." 105. Lichas was alarmed by the statement and his anger flared: "What's all this? Has someone been cutting hair on board my ship, and at the dead of night too? Quick, bring the guilty men out here, so I can see whose heads have to roll to purify the ship." "I ordered this," said Eumolpus. "Since I was about to sail on the same ship, I did not prescribe an evil omen for myself, but because they had dirty and long hair, I ordered the filth to be removed from these criminals, so that I did not seem to turn the ship into a prison. Another reason was to have all the branded letters strike the eyes of the readers and not be screened by the protection of hair. Among other things they squandered my money on a whore they shared. Last night when I dragged them away from her, they were reeking of wine and perfume. To sum it up, they still stink of the last of my money." . . .

And so to appease the tutelary deity of the ship, it was decided that forty lashes should be laid on each of us. There was no delay: some angry sailors carrying ropes' ends attacked us and tried to placate the guardian spirit with our really worthless blood. I myself stomached three lashes with Spartan pride, but Giton after being struck once screamed so loudly that his all too familiar voice rang clearly in the ears of Tryphaena. She was not the only one

293

6 repleret. | non sola[562] {ergo}[563] turbata est, sed ancillae
etiam omnes familiari sono inductae ad vapulantem de-
7 currunt. | iam Giton mirabili forma exarmaverat nautas
coeperatque etiam sine voce saevientes rogare, cum ancillae pariter proclamant: "Giton est, Giton, inhibete crude-
8 lissimas manus; Giton est, domina, succurre." | deflectit
aures Tryphaena iam sua sponte credentes raptimque ad
9 puerum devolat. | Lichas, qui me optime noverat, tam-
quam et ipse vocem audisset, accurrit et nec manus nec
faciem meam consideravit, sed continuo ad inguina mea
luminibus deflexis movit officiosam manum et "salve" in-
10 quit "Encolpi." | miretur nunc aliquis Ulixis nutricem post
vicesimum annum cicatricem invenisse originis indicem,
cum homo prudentissimus confusis omnibus corporis in-
diciorumque lineamentis ad unicum fugitivi argumentum
11 tam docte pervenerit. | Tryphaena lacrimas effudit de-
cepta supplicio—vera enim stigmata credebat captivorum
frontibus impressa—sciscitarique submissius coepit, quod
ergastulum intercepisset errantes, aut cuius tam crudeles
manus in hoc supplicium durassent. meruisse quidem
contumeliam aliquam fugitivos, quibus in odium bona sua
venissent. 106. concitatus iracundia prosiliit Lichas et "o
te" inquit "feminam simplicem, tamquam vulnera ferro
praeparata litteras biberint. utinam quidem hac se inscriptione frontis maculassent: haberemus nos extremum sola-

---

[562] sola *Boschius*: solum ergo
[563] *deleted Schmeling*

---

[129] In Homer (*Od.* 19.467–75), Eurycleia, the nurse of Odysseus, recognized him after twenty years by a scar on his leg.

in total confusion, but all her maids were drawn to the sound of the well-known voice, and came running to Giton, as he was being flogged. The beauty of Giton's body had already disarmed the sailors, and without speaking a word he had begun to appeal to his tormentors. Then the maids all together shouted: "It's Giton, Giton, stop hitting him with your vicious hands. Mistress, it's Giton, come, help him." On her own Tryphaena had already turned her eager ears toward them and hastily flew down to the boy. Lichas, who knew me intimately, raced forward, as if he himself had heard my voice. He did not waste a look at my hands or face, but at once with his eyes trained on my private parts applied a solicitous hand to them, and said: "Greetings, Encolpius." Would anyone now be surprised that Ulysses' nurse recognized his scar as the indication of his of identity after twenty years,[129] when this most wise Lichas hit so cleverly upon the sole proof of a runaway slave, despite the total blurring of the features and general appearance of my body? Tryphaena shed copious tears, for she was fooled by the marks of our punishment—she believed that the tattoos on our foreheads were authentic brandings put on prisoners—and she began in a subdued way to inquire what prison had cut short our wanderings, and whose ruthless hands had been so hardened as to inflict such punishment. But she conceded that runaway slaves like us, who turned in hatred against good things they had enjoyed, deserved some punishment. 106. Hot with rage, Lichas leaped forward and said: "You are such a gullible woman, to think that these wounds were made by branding irons and had absorbed the inky letters. I only wish that they had disfigured themselves with such inscriptions on their foreheads, for then we would have had

cium. nunc mimicis[564] artibus petiti sumus et adumbrata
2 inscriptione derisi." | volebat Tryphaena misereri, quia
non totam voluptatem perdiderat, sed Lichas memor adhuc uxoris corruptae iniuriarumque,[565] quas in Herculis
portu[566] acceperat, turbato vehementius vultu proclamat:
3 | "deos immortales rerum humanarum agere curam, puto,
intellexisti, o Tryphaena. nam imprudentes noxios in nostrum induxere navigium, et quid fecissent admonuerunt
pari somniorum consensu. ita vide ut possit[567] illis ignosci,
quos ad poenam deus ipse[568] deduxit. quod ad me attinet,
non sum crudelis, sed vereor ne quod remisero patiar." |
4 tam superstitiosa oratione Tryphaena mutata negat se in-
terpellare supplicium, immo accedere etiam iustissimae
ultioni, nec se minus grandi vexatam iniuria quam Licham,
cuius pudoris dignitas in contione proscripta sit.

⟨ * * * * ⟩

107. {*Eumolpus*}[569] "me, ut puto, hominem non igno-
tum, elegerunt ad hoc officium petieruntque ut se re-
2 conciliarem aliquando amicissimis. | nisi forte putatis iu-
venes casu in has plagas incidisse, cum omnis vector nihil
3 prius quaerat quam cuius se diligentiae credat. | flectite
ergo mentes satisfactione lenitas, et patimini liberos ho-
4 mines ire sine iniuria quo destinant. | saevi quoque im-
placabilesque domini crudelitatem suam impediunt, si

564 mimicis $t^{mg}p$: inimici
565 iniuriamque p^{1v}, rp^2: contumeliarumque
566 portu *Walsh*[1]: porticu
567 possit p^{2v}: prosit
568 deus ipse *Müller*: ipse deus
569 *See n. 527.*

some consolation. As it is, we have been tricked by clever devices from stage farces, and mocked by letters they themselves sketched." Tryphaena wanted him to show pity, because she had not lost all her memory of pleasure with Giton, but Lichas was still mindful of the seduction of his wife and the insults he had suffered in the port of Hercules, and so with his face distorted by even more anger, he shouted: "Tryphaena, I think you realize that the immortal gods take some interest in the affairs of men, for they have led these criminals unaware on board my ship, and they warned us in two almost matching dreams about their actions. So, consider how it is possible to pardon people whom god himself had delivered for punishment. As for myself, I am not a cruel man, but I fear that any of their offenses I exculpate, I will pay for myself." Such words about superstition had an impact on Tryphaena, who said that she would not interfere with the punishment, and actually she even approved of vengeance, when it was properly called for; after all she had been insulted no less injuriously than Lichas, when her moral decency was publicly disputed. . . .

107. "I am a man of some reputation, as I think," said Eumolpus, "and my friends have chosen me for this function, in which they ask me to restore harmony between themselves and those who had once been their best friends. Surely you cannot suppose that the young men fell unsuspectingly into a snare, when it is well known that every voyager's first concern is to learn into whose care he is entrusting himself. Therefore alter your harsh opinion of them, which has already been softened by the amends they made, and let them go without harm to their destination. Even harsh and unforgiving masters rein in their

quando paenitentia fugitivos reduxit, et dediticiis hostibus
5 parcimus. quid ultra petitis aut quid vultis? | in conspectu
vestro supplices iacent iuvenes, ingenui, honesti, et quod
utroque potentius est, familiaritate vobis aliquando con-
6 iuncti. | si mehercules intervertissent pecuniam vestram,
si fidem proditione laesissent, satiari tamen potuissetis hac
poena quam videtis. servitia ecce in frontibus cernitis et
vultus ingenuos voluntaria poenarum lege proscriptos." |
7 interpellavit deprecationem Lichas et "noli" inquit "cau-
8 sam confundere, sed impone singulis modum. | ac primum
omnium, si ultro venerunt, cur nudavere crinibus capita?
vultum enim qui permutat, fraudem parat, non satisfac-
9 tionem. | deinde, si gratiam a legato moliebantur, quid ita
omnia fecisti, ut quos tuebaris absconderes? ex quo apparet casu incidisse noxios in plagas et te artem quaesisse,
10 qua nostrae animadversionis impetum eluderes. | nam
quod invidiam facis nobis ingenuos honestosque cla-
mando, vide ne deteriorem facias confidentia causam.
quid debent laesi facere, ubi rei ad poenam confugiunt? |
11 at enim amici fuerunt nostri: eo maiora meruerunt suppli-
cia; nam qui ignotos laedit, latro appellatur, qui amicos,
12 paulo minus quam parricida." | resolvit Eumolpus tam
iniquam declamationem et "intellego" inquit "nihil magis

cruel punishment, when runaway slaves say they are sorry and return home; after all, we spare even enemies who surrender. What more do you seek or what do you want? The youths who lie before your eyes begging for mercy are free and respectable, and what is more to the point than either of these two conditions, they were once bound to you in friendship. I swear that if they had embezzled your money or if they had betrayed your trust, you could, nevertheless, feel satisfied by the punishment which you see inflicted. Look now, you perceive the tattoos of slavery on their foreheads, on the faces of freeborn men outlawed by a self-imposed penalty." Lichas interrupted this plea for mercy and said: "Do not confuse the issue, put a beginning and end to one point at a time. And first of all, if they came on board on their own initiative, why did they shave their heads? The man who disguises his appearance is preparing to deceive, not to make amends. Next, if they were devising a way to gain favor through a mediator, why did you do everything to protect and hide them? From this it seems clear that the criminals fell into the trap by accident, and that you have been searching for some device to ward off the impact of our punishment. By calling them freeborn and respectable men, the point being that you are shifting the ill will to us, see to it that you do not make your case worse by overconfidence. What should the injured parties do when the guilty have recourse to their own punishment? But you say that they were our friends, surely they were, and so they deserve even harsher punishments: the one who attacks strangers is called a robber, but the one who attacks his friends is virtually a family murderer." Eumolpus rebutted this totally unfair harangue by saying: "I understand that the strongest accusa-

obesse iuvenibus miseris quam quod nocte deposuerunt capillos: hoc argumento incidisse videntur in navem, non
13 venisse. | quod velim tam candide ad aures vestras perveniat quam simpliciter gestum est. voluerunt enim antequam conscenderent exonerare capita molesto et supervacuo pondere, sed celerior ventus distulit curationis
14 propositum. | nec tamen putaverunt ad rem pertinere, ubi inciperent quod placuerat ut fieret, quia nec omen nec
15 legem navigantium noverant." | "quid" inquit Lichas "attinuit supplices radere? nisi forte miserabiliores calvi solent esse. quamquam quid attinet veritatem per interpretem quaerere? quid dicis tu, latro? quae {sola}[570] salamandra supercilia tua excussit?[571] cui deo crinem vovisti? pharmace, responde."

108. obstupueram ego supplicii metu pavidus, nec quid in re manifestissima dicerem inveniebam. turbatus et deformis <. . .> praeter spoliati capitis dedecus superciliorum etiam aequalis cum fronte calvities, ut nihil nec facere
2 deceret nec dicere. | ut vero spongia uda facies plorantis detersa est et liquefactum per totum os atramentum omnia scilicet lineamenta fuliginea nube confudit, in odium
3 se ira convertit. | negat Eumolpus passurum se, ut quisquam ingenuos contra fas legemque contaminet, interpellatque saevientium minas non solum voce sed etiam
4 manibus. | aderat interpellanti mercennarius comes et

[570] *deleted Pithoeus in Notis*
[571] excussit *L*: exussit *Dousa, editors*

tion against these wretched young men is that they shaved off their hair in the night, and from this it seems to be proved that they boarded the ship by chance and not deliberately. Now I should like the plain truth of what took place to come to your ears just as plainly as it happened. They wanted to remove the annoying and useless weight of hair from their heads before they embarked, but the wind came up too fast and forced them to postpone this treatment. They did not think it made any difference where they began what they had decided upon, because they were ignorant of sailors' omens and the code of the sea." Lichas said: "But why should it be important for suppliants to shave their heads? Unless perhaps bald men are naturally more pitiable. But what is the use of trying to get to the truth through a negotiator? What do you have to say for yourself, you criminal? Did some salamander make your eyebrows fall off? To which deity did you dedicate your locks? Answer me, you scapegoat."

108. I was absolutely astonished and intimidated by fear of punishment, and I could not find anything to say, for the case was only too clear. I was such a confused and ugly person . . . for besides the disgrace of my head stripped of hair, my eyebrows were as bald as my forehead, it did not seem right to do or say anything. But when a wet sponge was wiped over my doleful countenance, and the ink running over my whole face obscured all my features in a smutty cloud, their anger turned to hatred. Eumolpus said that he would not allow anyone to disfigure free men in defiance of what was custom and law, and he mediated between us and those threatening and raging against us not merely with words but also with force. His servant stood by him as he intervened, and one or two of the most

unus alterque infirmissimus vector, solacia magis litis
5 quam virium auxilia. | nec quicquam pro me deprecabar,
sed intentans in oculos Tryphaenae manus usurum me
viribus meis clara liberaque voce clamavi, ni abstineret a
Gitone iniuriam mulier damnata et in toto navigio sola
6 verberanda. | accenditur audacia mea iratior Lichas, in-
dignaturque quod ego relicta mea causa tantum pro alio
7 clamo. | nec minus Tryphaena contumelia saevit accensa
8 totiusque navigii turbam diducit in partes. | hinc mercen-
narius tonsor[572] ferramenta sua nobis et ipse armatus dis-
tribuit, illinc Tryphaenae familia nudas expedit manus, ac
ne ancillarum quidem clamor aciem destituit, uno tantum
gubernatore relicturum se navis ministerium denuntiante,
9 si non desinat rabies libidine perditorum collecta. | nihilo
minus tamen perseverat dimicantium furor, illis pro ultione, nobis pro vita pugnantibus. multi ergo utrimque
sine morte labuntur, plures cruenti vulneribus referunt
veluti ex proelio pedem, nec tamen cuiusquam ira laxatur.
10 | tunc fortissimus Giton ad virilia sua admovit novaculam
infestam,[573] minatus se abscisurum causam tot miseriarum, inhibuitque Tryphaena tam grande facinus non dis-
11 simulata missione. | saepius ego cultrum tonsorium super
iugulum meum posui, non magis me occisurus quam
Giton quod minabatur facturus. audacius tamen ille tragoediam implebat, quia sciebat se illam habere novacu-
12 lam, qua iam sibi cervicem praeciderat. | ᴼᴸstante ergo

[572] tonsor *deleted Burman*
[573] infestam *Pithoeus in Notis*: infertam *or* insertam

feeble passengers who in the dispute added moral support rather than physical. I interceded in no way for myself. I shook my fists in Tryphaena's face, and in a clear and firm voice shouted that I would resort to physical violence, if that convicted woman, and the only person on the ship who deserved flogging, did not refrain from mistreating Giton. Because of my brazenness Lichas' rage grew even hotter, and he was also angry at me for deserting my own defense and shouting so loudly for another's. Equally incensed at the insult, Tryphaena was in a rage and caused the whole ship's company to divide into factions. On our side Eumolpus' servant, the barber, distributed his blades to us and kept one for himself, while on the other side the household slaves of Tryphaena readied their bare fists for action, and not even the shouting maids abandoned the front line. The helmsman alone stood apart and gave notice that he would leave the rudder unattended, if this uncontrolled madness, stirred up by the passions of the degenerate, did not cease. Nonetheless, the fury of the combatants persisted, for them a matter of vengeance, for us a matter of life and death. Many fell on both sides without fatal results, even more retreated, blood dripping down from wounds, just like a real battle, but still no one's anger abated. Then Giton in a very brave act turned the menacing razor to his genitals, and threatened to cut off the cause of so many troubles, but Tryphaena averted such a serious action by an unconditional pardon. Again and again I put the barber's knife to my throat, but I was no more going to kill myself than Giton meant to do what he threatened. Still he filled the tragic role more boldly, because he knew he had the razor with which he had earlier cut his throat. The battle lines were drawn on both sides,

303

utraque acie, cum appareret futurum non tralaticium bellum, aegre expugnavit gubernator, ut caduceatoris more
13 Tryphaena indutias faceret. | data ergo acceptaque ex
more patrio fide praetendit[574] ramum oleae a tutela navigi
raptum, atque in colloquium venire ausa |

14   "quis furor" exclamat "pacem convertit in arma?
        quid nostrae meruere manus? non Troius heros
        hac in classe vehit decepti pignus Atridae,
        nec Medea furens fraterno sanguine pugnat.
   5   sed contemptus amor vires habet. ei[575] mihi, fata
        hos inter fluctus quis raptis evocat armis?
        cui non est mors una satis? ne vincite pontum
        gurgitibusque feris alios immittite fluctus."

109. haec ut turbato clamore mulier effudit, haesit paulisper acies, revocataeque ad pacem manus intermisere
bellum. utitur paenitentiae occasione dux Eumolpus et
castigato ante vehementissime Licha tabulas foederis
2 signat, quis haec formula erat: | "ex tui animi sententia, ut
tu, Tryphaena, neque iniuriam tibi factam a Gitone quereris,[576] neque si quid ante hunc diem factum est obicies
vindicabisve aut ullo alio genere persequendum curabis;
ut tu nihil imperabis puero repugnanti, non amplexum,
non osculum, non coitum venere constrictum, nisi pro qua
3 re praesentes numeraveris denarios centum. | item, Licha,

[574] praetendit *Muretus*: protendit
[575] ei *Bücheler*: et
[576] quereris *l*[mg]: quaeraris

---

[130] This verb of saying is embedded in the poem.

and when it was clear that this would be no ordinary war, the helmsman with some difficulty prevailed on Tryphaena to accept the role of herald and conclude a treaty. Once the age-old customary guarantees had been given and accepted, Tryphaena extended an olive branch taken from the ship's figurehead, and venturing to enter into a dialogue with us, "declaimed:[130] What madness makes us turn peace into war? What actions of our hands deserved this? No Trojan hero carries off the wife of the cuckolded son of Atreus in this fleet, no Medea raving mad uses her brother's blood for a weapon.[131] Rejected love leads on to violence. Woe is me: who takes up arms among these waves, thus calling for death? For whom is one death not enough? Do not try to get the better of the sea and graft new waves of blood onto the savage floods."

109. As the woman poured out these words in a distressed tone, the battle lines came to a standstill for a moment; and with our hands summoned again to peace, we allowed the war to lapse. Our leader Eumolpus seized the opportunity of their show of mercy, and after first dressing down Lichas most warmly, sealed the articles of the treaty, the terms of which were: "You, Tryphaena, do hereby swear in all honesty not to complain about any insult hurled at you by Giton. If any wrong has been done to you before this date, you will not hold it against him, nor punish him, nor will you take steps to proceed against him in any other way. You will not impose any service on the boy against his will, no hugs, no kisses, no activity tied up in sex, unless you pay one hundred *denarii* in cash for

[131] Paris abducted Helen, Menelaus' wife, and Medea killed her own brother, Apsyrtus.

ex tui animi sententia, ut tu Encolpion nec verbo contumelioso insequeris nec vultu, neque quaeres ubi nocte dormiat, aut si quaesieris pro singulis iniuriis numerabis
4 praesentes denarios ducenos."[577] | in haec verba foederibus compositis arma deponimus, [L]et ne residua in animis etiam post iusiurandum ira remaneret, praeterita aboleri
5 osculis placet. | exhortantibus universis odia detumescunt, epulaeque ad certamen prolatae conciliant hilaritate con-
6 vivium.[578] | [OL]exsonat ergo cantibus totum navigium, et quia repentina tranquillitas intermiserat cursum, alius exultantes quaerebat fuscina pisces, alius hamis blandien-
7 tibus convellebat praedam repugnantem. | ecce etiam per antemnam pelagiae consederant volucres, quas textis harundinibus peritus artifex tetigit; illae viscatis illigatae viminibus deferebantur ad manus. tollebat plumas aura volitantes, pinnasque per maria inanis spuma torquebat. |
8 iam Lichas redire mecum in gratiam coeperat, iam Tryphaena Gitona extrema parte potionis spargebat, cum Eumolpus et ipse vino solutus dicta voluit in calvos stigmososque iaculari, donec consumpta frigidissima urbanitate rediit ad carmina sua coepitque capillorum elegidarion dicere: |

9   [OφL]"quod solum formae decus est, cecidere capilli,
         vernantesque comas tristis abegit hiemps.
      nunc umbra nudata sua iam tempora maerent,
         areaque attritis ridet adusta pilis.

[577] ducenos p^{2v}: ducentos
[578] convivium t^{mg}: concilium

this service. Likewise you, Lichas, do hereby swear in all honesty that you will not persecute Encolpius with insulting words or looks, that you will not try to find out where he sleeps, or if you do make such inquiries, you will pay two hundred *denarii* in cash for each injurious act." On these terms the treaty was ratified, and we laid down our arms, but fearful that some vestige of anger might linger in our hearts even after swearing the oath, we resolved to wipe out the past with kisses. With everyone encouraging peace, our hatred subsided, and the feast that had been deferred because of the battle promoted goodwill all round. So while the whole ship rang with our singing, and because a sudden calm interrupted our forward motion, one man went after leaping fish with a spear, and another tried with baited and inviting hooks to bring in resisting prey. But to our surprise, even seabirds settled on the yardarm, which an experienced fowler touched with interwoven limed twigs; the birds became attached to the sticky and flexible branches and were brought down to our hands. A slight breeze caught their plumage flitting down, and the thin sea spray whirled their feathers over the surface of the water. By then Lichas had begun to be reconciled to me, and Tryphaena was already sprinkling the dregs of her drink over Giton, when Eumolpus, himself well into his cups, proposed a few words of satire against those who were bald and branded. But when his dull wit had been exhausted, he went back to composing poetry and began to recite a little poem about hair: "The hair which is the glory of the body has now fallen out, and the bleak winter has driven away the spring's foliage. Now the bare temples of the head mourn the loss of their shade, and with the hair worn away a sun-browned spot smiles on

307

5 o fallax natura deum: quae prima dedisti
     aetati nostrae gaudia, prima rapis." |

⟨ * * * ⟩

10   *OL*"infelix, modo crinibus nitebas
     Phoebo pulchrior et sorore Phoebi.
     at nunc levior aere vel rotundo
     horti tubere, quod creavit imber,[579]
5 ridentes fugis et times puellas.
     ut mortem citius venire credas,
     scito iam capitis perisse partem."

110. plura volebat proferre, credo, et ineptiora prae-
teritis, cum ancilla Tryphaenae Gitona in partem navis
inferiorem ducit corymbioque dominae pueri adornat
2 caput. | immo supercilia etiam profert de pyxide sciteque
iacturae lineamenta secuta totam illi formam suam reddi-
3 dit. | agnovit Tryphaena verum Gitona, lacrimisque tur-
4 bata tunc primum bona fide puero basium dedit. | *L*ego
etiam si repositum in pristinum decorem puerum gaude-
bam, abscondebam tamen frequentius vultum intellege-
bamque me non tralaticia deformitate esse insignitum,
5 quem alloquio dignum ne Lichas quidem crederet. | sed
huic tristitiae eadem illa succurrit ancilla, sevocatumque[580] me non minus decoro exornavit capillamento;
immo commendatior vultus enituit, quia flavum[581] corym-
bion erat. |

⟨ * * * ⟩

6 *OL*ceterum Eumolpus, et periclitantium advocatus et praesentis concordiae auctor, ne sileret sine fabulis hilaritas,
7 multa in muliebrem levitatem coepit iactare: | quam facile
adamarent, quam cito etiam filiorum obliviscerentur, nul-

all. Oh you gods of insincere essence: the first joys you
awarded to our youthful heads are the first joys you snatch
back from us. . . . You unhappy man, a moment ago your
hair was sleek, more beautiful than Phoebus and the sister
of Phoebus. But now you are smoother than bronze or the
round garden mushroom cap that is born in rain, and you
flee in fear from the scoffing girls. To make you believe
how quickly death can come, you have to recognize that
already part of your individuality has been lost."

110. I believe that he wanted to produce additional
lines of poetry even more silly than the last, when a maid
of Tryphaena took Giton below deck and decorated the
boy's head with one of her mistress' wigs. In fact, she even
brought out some eyebrows from a box, and expertly following the lines of lost hair completely restored his former
beauty. Tryphaena recognized her own Giton and, moved
to tears, gave the boy for the first time a kiss of real affection. Even as I was happy to see the boy restored to his
former beauty, I kept hiding my face, for I realized that I
was conspicuous with an uncommon ugliness, since not
even Lichas considered me worth talking to. But the same
maid, coming to my rescue, addressed my sadness, for she
called me away and dressed my head with just as beautiful
a set of curls; actually my face shone to better advantage
because the wig was golden. . . . Then Eumolpus who was
both our spokesman when we were in peril and the author
of our present harmony, fearing that our merriment might
subside without some good stories, began to hurl many
taunts at the fickleness of women: how easily they fall in

---

579 imber *Jahn*: unda   580 sevocatumque *Goldast*: evoca-
tumque   581 flavum t^{mg}: flaucorum

lamque esse feminam tam pudicam, quae non peregrina
8 libidine usque ad furorem averteretur. | nec se tragoedias
veteres curare aut nomina saeculis nota, sed rem sua memoria factam, quam expositurum se esse, si vellemus au-
dire. conversis igitur omnium in se vultibus auribusque sic
orsus est:

$^{O\phi L}$111. "matrona quaedam Ephesi tam notae erat pudicitiae, ut vicinarum quoque gentium feminas ad specta-
2 culum sui evocaret. | haec ergo cum virum extulisset, non
contenta vulgari more funus passis prosequi crinibus aut
nudatum pectus in conspectu frequentiae plangere, in
conditorium etiam prosecuta est defunctum, positumque
in hypogaeo Graeco more corpus custodire ac flere totis
3 noctibus diebusque coepit. | sic afflictantem se ac mortem
inedia persequentem non parentes potuerunt abducere,
non propinqui; magistratus ultimo repulsi abierunt, com-
plorataque singularis exempli femina ab omnibus quintum
4 iam diem sine alimento trahebat. | assidebat aegrae fidis-
sima ancilla, simulque et lacrimas commodabat[582] lugenti
et quotienscumque[583] defecerat positum in monumento
5 lumen renovabat. | una igitur in tota civitate fabula erat,
solum illud affulsisse verum pudicitiae amorisque exemplum omnis ordinis homines confitebantur, cum interim
imperator provinciae latrones iussit crucibus affigi secun-

[582] commodabat *Rittershusius*: commendabat
[583] quotienscumque *R*: quotiensque *B*: quotiens

love, how quickly they forget to think about even their own children, how no woman is so chaste that she cannot be driven to mad distraction by lust for a foreigner. He was not thinking about those old ancient tragedies or names notorious in earlier ages, but an affair that happened in his own lifetime, which he would set out for us, if we wished to hear it. So we all turned our eyes and ears to him, and he began.

111. "A certain married woman of Ephesus had such a reputation for chastity that she drew women even from the surrounding communities just to gaze at her. At the funeral ritual when she buried her husband, she was not satisfied with just escorting the body to the grave, as is the general custom, with hair untied and blowing round freely, or with just beating her naked breast for all the crowds to see, but she followed the dead man even into his tomb, and when the body was laid in an underground vault after the Greek fashion, she began to watch and to weep over it both night and day. Thus torturing herself and courting death by starvation, she could not be led away from the tomb by her parents or relatives; finally the magistrates left her, after they had been rebuffed. Everyone showed deep sorrow for her as a woman of unique character, who was now spending her fifth day without food. The most trusted maid sat by the sorrowful woman, and at the same time lent tears to the mourning widow, and refilled the lamp placed in the tomb whenever it went short of oil. There was only one subject of conversation in the whole city: people of every class acknowledged that this alone was the true example of chastity and love. At about this same time the governor of the province ordered that some thieves be crucified near the small building in which the

311

dum illam casulam, in qua recens cadaver matrona defle-
6 bat. | proxima ergo nocte cum miles, qui cruces asservabat
ne quis ad sepulturam corpus detraheret, notasset sibi
{et}[584] lumen inter monumenta clarius fulgens et gemitum
lugentis audisset, vitio gentis humanae concupiit scire quis
7 aut quid faceret. | descendit igitur in conditorium, visaque
pulcherrima muliere primo quasi quodam monstro infer-
8 nisque imaginibus turbatus substitit. | deinde ut et corpus
iacentis conspexit et lacrimas consideravit faciemque unguibus sectam, ratus scilicet id quod erat, desiderium extincti non posse feminam pati, attulit in monumentum
cenulam suam coepitque hortari lugentem ne persevera-
ret in dolore supervacuo ac nihil profuturo gemitu pectus
diduceret: omnium eundem esse exitum {sed} et idem[585]
domicilium, et cetera quibus exulceratae mentes ad sani-
9 tatem revocantur. | at illa ignota consolatione percussa
laceravit vehementius pectus ruptosque crines super cor-
10 pus[586] iacentis imposuit. | non recessit tamen miles, sed
eadem exhortatione temptavit dare mulierculae cibum,
donec ancilla vini odore corrupta primum ipsa porrexit ad
humanitatem invitantis victam manum, deinde refecta
potione et cibo expugnare dominae pertinaciam coepit
11 et | 'quid proderit' inquit 'hoc tibi, si soluta inedia fueris,
si te vivam sepelieris, si antequam fata poscant, indemna-
12 tum spiritum effuderis? | "id cinerem aut manes credis
sentire sepultos?" vis tu reviviscere? vis discusso muliebri

---

584 *deleted Bücheler*
585 sed *(omitted A)* et idem *R, L:* sedeidem *B*
586 corpus *Nisbet:* pectus

---

132 Verg. *Aen.* 4.34.

woman was weeping over her late husband's body. So on the next night, when a soldier, guarding the crosses to prevent anyone taking down a body for burial, observed a light shining brightly among the tombs and heard the groans of a grieving woman, a very human weakness made him desirous to know who it was or what she was doing. Accordingly he went down into the tomb, and on seeing this beautiful woman, at first stood still in total confusion as though he had seen some portent or ghosts from the underworld. But when he noticed the body of the dead man and had taken into account the tears and the face scratched by her nails, he came to the correct conclusion that the woman could not bear the loss of the dead one. He therefore brought his bit of supper into the tomb and proceeded to urge the grieving woman not to persist in her hopeless sorrow and break her heart with useless lamentations: he said that the same end, the same resting place awaited us all, and added all those other things which restore wounded minds to sanity. But she was not moved by the rhetoric of consolation, tore at her breast more violently, pulled out her hair, and laid it on the body of the dead man. Still the soldier did not withdraw, but with the same encouragement tried to press some food on her servant, until the maid was seduced by the fragrance of the wine. She first extended her own hand, overcome by the kindness of the invitation, and once she was refreshed by the drink and food, began to lay siege to her mistress' obstinacy, and said: 'What will this benefit you, if you faint from hunger, if you bury yourself alive, if you breathe out your innocent life before the Fates summon it? "Do you believe that the ashes or shades of the buried dead have sensibilities?"[132] Do you wish to come to life again? Hav-

errore, quam diu licuerit, lucis commodis frui? ipsum te
13 iacentis corpus admonere[587] debet ut vivas.' | nemo invitus
audit, cum cogitur aut cibum sumere aut vivere. itaque
mulier aliquot dierum abstinentia sicca passa est frangi
pertinaciam suam, nec minus avide replevit se cibo quam
ancilla quae prior victa est. 112. ceterum scitis quid ple-
rumque soleat temptare humanam satietatem. quibus
blanditiis impetraverat miles ut matrona vellet vivere, is-
2 dem etiam pudicitiam eius aggressus est. | nec deformis
aut infacundus iuvenis castae videbatur, conciliante gratiam ancilla ac subinde dicente: 'placitone etiam pugnabis
amori? {nec venit in mentem, quorum consederis arvis?}'
quid diutius moror? ne hanc quidem partem corporis
mulier abstinuit, victorque miles utrumque persuasit. |
3 iacuerunt ergo una non tantum illa nocte qua nuptias fecerunt, sed postero etiam ac tertio die, praeclusis videlicet
conditorii foribus, ut quisquis ex notis ignotisque ad monumentum venisset, putaret[588] expirasse super corpus viri
4 pudicissimam uxorem. | ceterum delectatus miles et forma
mulieris et secreto, quicquid boni per facultates poterat
coemebat et prima statim nocte in monumentum ferebat.
5 | itaque unius cruciarii parentes ut viderunt laxatam cus-
todiam, detraxere nocte pendentem supremoque manda-
6 verunt officio. | at miles circumscriptus dum desidet, ut
postero die vidit unam sine cadavere crucem, veritus sup-

---

587 admonere *p*: ammonere *or* commonere
588 putaret *Bücheler*: putasset

---

133 Verg. *Aen.* 4.38–39.

ing shaken off this womanly failing, do you wish to enjoy the comforts of life, while you can? The very corpse of your husband lying there should encourage you to want to live.' No one is averse to listen when urged to take food or stay alive. And so the woman being thirsty after several days of abstinence allowed her resolution to be broken, and filled herself with food no less greedily than the maid who had earlier been won over. 112. And you know which temptation generally assails a person on a full stomach. The same inducements the soldier had used to persuade the woman to live, were now employed to conduct an assault on her chastity. In the eyes of the chaste woman the young man appeared neither unattractive nor ill-spoken, and the maid meanwhile promoted indulgence and repeatedly said: 'Will you fight against even a pleasing passion?' {Does it not come into your mind in whose fields you are sitting?}[133] Why do I still delay getting to the point? The woman did not hold back even this gratification of the flesh, and the conquering hero talked her into both. So they slept together not only on their wedding night, but on the next night and on the third. The doors of the vault were of course closed, so that any acquaintance or stranger who came to the tomb would assume that the most chaste wife had breathed her last over her husband's body. The soldier, delighted both by the woman's beauty and their trysting place, would buy whatever delicacies he could afford and as soon as it got dark, he would bring them to the tomb. So when the parents of one of the crucified men noticed that the watch was lax, they took down the hanging corpse of their son and administered the last rites. The soldier was tricked while he neglected his duties, and on the next day when he saw that one cross had no corpse, he

315

plicium, mulieri quid accidisset exponit: nec se expectatu-
rum iudicis sententiam, sed gladio ius dicturum ignaviae
suae. commodaret modo illa perituro locum et fatale
7 conditorium familiari ac viro sacraret.[589] | mulier non
minus misericors quam pudica 'nec istud' inquit 'dii si-
nant, ut eodem tempore duorum mihi carissimorum hominum duo funera spectem. malo mortuum impendere
8 quam vivum occidere.' | secundum hanc orationem iubet
ex arca[590] corpus mariti sui tolli atque illi quae vacabat
cruci affigi. usus est miles ingenio prudentissimae feminae, posteroque die populus miratus est qua ratione mortuus isset in crucem."

[OL]113. risu excepere fabulam nautae, erubescente non
mediocriter Tryphaena vultumque suum super cervicem
2 Gitonis amabiliter ponente. | at non Lichas risit, sed ira-
tum commovens caput "si iustus" inquit "imperator fuisset, debuit patris familiae corpus in monumentum referre,
3 mulierem affigere cruci." | non dubie redierat in animum
Hedyle[591] expilatumque libidinosa migratione navigium. |
4 sed nec foederis verba permittebant meminisse, nec hila-
ritas quae occupaverat mentes, dabat iracundiae locum. |
5 ceterum Tryphaena in gremio Gitonis posita modo implebat osculis pectus, interdum concinnabat spoliatum crini-
6 bus vultum. | [L]ego maestus et impatiens foederis novi non
cibum, non potionem capiebam, sed obliquis trucibusque
7 oculis utrumque spectabam. | omnia me oscula vul-
nerabant, omnes blanditiae, quascumque mulier libidi-

---

589 sacraret *Vannini*[2]: faceret
590 arca *l*[mg], *tp*: area
591 Hedyle *Bücheler*: hedile

was in fear of his own execution and explained to the
woman what had happened. He declared that he would
not await the verdict of the judge, but would use his sword
to impose sentence on himself for neglect of duty. He
wanted her only to adapt a place for a man to die in and
consecrate the vault which was ordained by fate, both to
her lover and her husband. The woman, who was no less
sympathetic than she was chaste, remarked: 'Heaven forbid that I should see simultaneously the two corpses of the
men dearest to me. I prefer to sacrifice a dead man than
kill a living one.' After this short speech she ordered that
her husband's body be removed from the coffin and fastened to the vacant cross. The soldier availed himself of
the wise woman's stroke of genius, and the next day the
people wondered how the dead man had managed to get
on the cross."

113. The sailors greeted this story with laughter, while
Tryphaena blushed deeply and laid her face lovingly on
Giton's neck. But Lichas was not amused, shook his head
angrily and said: "If the governor had been a just man, he
would have put the husband's body back in the tomb and
attached the woman to the cross." No doubt Hedyle had
come back to his mind as well as his ship plundered during
her lascivious escapade. But the terms of the treaty did not
allow him to resurrect past grudges, and the general
cheerfulness which put us in a good mood left no room for
bad temper. Tryphaena was now settled in Giton's lap and
smothering his breast with kisses and occasionally trying
to enhance his shaven appearance. I was depressed and
uneasy about this new agreement, and took no food or
drink, but watched both of them with oblique and savage
glances. Every kiss, every act of endearment that the

317

nosa fingebat. nec tamen adhuc sciebam utrum magis
puero irascerer, quod amicam mihi auferret, an amicae,
quod puerum corrumperet: utraque inimicissima oculis
8 meis et captivitate praeterita tristiora. | accedebat huc
quod neque Tryphaena me alloquebatur tamquam fami-
liarem et aliquando gratum sibi amatorem, nec Giton me
aut tralaticia propinatione dignum iudicabat aut, quod
minimum est, sermone communi{vo}cabat,[592] credo, veritus ne inter initia coeuntis gratiae recentem cicatricem
9 rescinderet. | inundavere pectus lacrimae dolore paratae,
gemitusque suspirio tectus animam paene submovit. |

〈 * * * 〉

10 in partem voluptatis temptabat admitti, nec domini super-
cilium induebat, sed amici quaerebat obsequium. |

〈 * * * 〉

11 {*Ancilla Tryphaenae ad Encolpium*}[593] "si quid ingenui
sanguinis habes, non pluris illum[594] facies quam scor-
tum.[595] si vir fueris, non ibis ad spintriam."[596] |

〈 * * * 〉

12 me nihil magis pudebat quam ne Eumolpus sensisset,
quicquid illud fuerat, et homo dicacissimus carminibus
vindicaret. |

〈 * * * 〉

13 iurat Eumolpus verbis conceptissimis.

〈 * * * 〉

114. dum haec taliaque iactamus, inhorruit mare nu-
besque undique adductae obruere tenebris diem. discur-
runt nautae ad officia trepidantes velaque tempestati sub-
2 ducunt. | sed nec certus[597] fluctus ventus impulerat, nec

---

[592] *deleted Vannini*[2]   [593] *See n. 527.*
[594] illum *Courtney*[1]: illam

randy woman conjured up, wounded me. I did not yet
know whether I was angrier with the boy for taking away
my mistress, or with my mistress for seducing the boy:
both were most offensive to my eyes and more depressing
than my past internment. What added to my state was that
Tryphaena was not speaking to me as a close friend and
once favorite lover, and Giton did not judge me worth the
effort to drink to my health even casually, or at least to
include me in the general conversation. I suppose he was
afraid of reopening a recent scar just at the initial stages
of reconciliation. Tears arising from resentment over-
flowed my breast, and groans hidden under sighs almost
made me faint. . . . He tried to get invited to share their
pleasure, not wearing the haughtiness of a master, but
asking for the indulgence of a friend. . . . "If you have a
drop of noble blood, you will regard him as nothing more
than a prostitute. If you are going to be a real man, you
will not go to a whore." . . . Nothing embarrassed me more
than the fear that Eumolpus was conscious of what had
gone on, and that the man in control of all the repartees
might take revenge on me in verse. . . . Eumolpus swore
an oath in the most solemn terms. . . .

114. While we discussed these and other things, the sea
grew rough and clouds gathered from every quarter, over-
whelming the daylight in darkness. The sailors ran nervously to their duties and furled the sails against the storm.
The wind was not driving the waves out of just one direc-

---

595 scortum *Putschius*: spurcam *or* sportam
596 spinthriam *t*[mg]: spintam
597 certus *Jungermann*: certos

3 quo destinaret cursum gubernator sciebat. | Sicilia modo
ventos dabat,[598] saepissime Italici litoris aquilo possessor
convertebat huc illuc obnoxiam ratem,[599] et quod omnibus
procellis periculosius erat, tam spissae repente tenebrae
lucem suppresserant, ut ne proram quidem totam guber-
4 nator videret. | itaque {hercules}[600] postquam <maris
ira>[601] infesta convaluit, Lichas trepidans ad me supinas
5 porrigit manus et | "tu" inquit "Encolpi, succurre pericli-
tantibus, id est vestem illam divinam sistrumque redde
navigio. per fidem, miserere, quemadmodum quidem
6 soles." | et illum quidem vociferantem in mare ventus
excussit, repetitumque infesto gurgite procella circumegit
7 atque hausit. | Tryphaenam autem prope iam <peremp-
tam>[602] fidelissimi rapuerunt servi, scaphaeque impositam
cum maxima sarcinarum parte abduxere certissimae
8 morti. <. . .> | applicitus cum clamore flevi et "hoc" inquam
"a diis meruimus, ut nos sola morte coniungeret. sed non
9 crudelis fortuna concedit. | ecce iam ratem fluctus evertet,
ecce iam amplexus amantium iratum dividet mare. igitur,
si vere Encolpion dilexisti, da[603] oscula, dum licet: ulti-
10 mum hoc gaudium fatis properantibus rape." | haec ut ego
dixi, Giton vestem deposuit, meaque tunica contectus ex-
eruit ad osculum caput. et ne sic cohaerentes malignior
fluctus distraheret,[604] utrumque zona circumvenienti
11 praecinxit et | "si nihil aliud, certe diutius" inquit "iuncta

[598] Sicilia modo ventos dabat *Humphreys–Sullivan*: Siciliam
modo ventus dabat   [599] ratem *Goldast*: partem
   [600] *deleted Müller*
   [601] <maris ira> infesta *Bücheler*: manifesta
   [602] *added Vannini*[2]: exanimatam *added Bücheler*
   [603] da *Jungermann*: ad*L*   [604] distraheret *t*[mg]: detraheret

tion, and the helmsman did not know which way he should steer the ship. At one moment Sicily sent the winds, but most often the north wind, dominating the Italian coastline, turned the submissive ship this way and that, and what was more dangerous than all the squalls was the very thick darkness that suddenly blotted out the lights, so that the helmsman could not see even to the end of the prow. And so after the dangerous anger of the storm reached its height, Lichas, who was trembling, stretched out his pleading hands to me and said: "Encolpius, help us in our peril, I mean to tell you, return that sacred robe and rattle to the ship. In heaven's name, pity us, just as you used to do." But even as he shouted out, the wind swept him into the sea, where he was attacked again and again by a hostile squall, until the storm whirled him round and sucked him under. Tryphaena, now almost half-dead, was grabbed by her always faithful slaves, placed in the dinghy with most of her luggage, and rescued from almost certain death. . . . I clung to Giton, wept out loud and said: "Our just deserts from the gods is their judgment to unite us only in death. But cruel Fortune does not bestow on us even that. You can see that the waves will capsize the ship, that the angry sea will separate the lovers even as they embrace. So if you ever really loved Encolpius, kiss him while you can, and snatch the last joy from the onrushing Fates." As I spoke, Giton laid his clothes aside, I covered him with my tunic, and he lifted his head for a kiss. So that no spiteful wave could tear us apart as we clung to each other, Giton fastened his belt round us and tied us together, and said: "If nothing else, once death has united us, it will carry us

nos mors feret, vel si voluerit ⟨mare⟩[605] misericors ad
idem litus expellere, aut praeteriens aliquis tralaticia humanitate lapidabit, aut quod ultimum est iratis etiam fluc-
12 tibus, imprudens harena componet." | patior ego vinculum
extremum, et veluti lecto funebri aptatus expecto mortem
13 iam non molestam. | peragit interim tempestas mandata
fatorum omnesque reliquias navis expugnat. non arbor
erat relicta, non gubernacula, non funis aut remus, sed
quasi rudis atque infecta materies ibat cum fluctibus. |

⟨ * * * ⟩

14 procurrere piscatores parvulis expediti navigiis ad praedam rapiendam. deinde ut aliquos viderunt qui suas opes
defenderent, mutaverunt cupiditatem[606] in auxilium.

⟨ * * * ⟩

115. audimus murmur insolitum et sub diaeta magistri
2 quasi cupientis exire beluae gemitum. | persecuti igitur
sonum invenimus Eumolpum sedentem membranaeque
3 ingenti versus ingerentem. | mirati ergo quod illi vacaret
in vicinia mortis poema facere, extrahimus clamantem
4 iubemusque bonam habere mentem. | at ille interpellatus
excanduit et "sinite me" inquit "sententiam explere; labo-
5 rat carmen in fine." | inicio ego phrenetico manum iubeo-
que Gitona accedere et in terram trahere poetam[607] mu-
gientem. |

⟨ * * * ⟩

6 hoc opere tandem elaborato casam piscatoriam subimus
maerentes, cibisque naufragio corruptis utcumque curati
7 tristissimam exegimus noctem. | postero die cum ponere-
mus consilium cui nos regioni crederemus, repente video

---

[605] voluerit ⟨mare⟩ *added Müller*   [606] cupiditatem *Jacobs*:
crudelitatem   [607] poetam *l*[c]: porcam

322

together surely a longer time. Or if the sea has mercy and wishes to cast us up on the same shore, either someone passing by will cover us with stones out of common humanity, or even the angry waves as a last rite will cause the sand, unconscious of its pious act, to cover us." I submitted to our final bond, and like a man arranged on his funeral bed, awaited death that no longer was a worry. Meanwhile the storm, so ordered by the Fates, lived out its life of violence and reduced the ship to pieces. No mast, no steering oars, no rope or oar remained, but like a rough and shapeless piece of timber she drifted on the waves. . . . Some fishermen equipped with small boats put out to sea to seize the booty, but when they saw that there were some survivors ready to protect their possessions, they changed their plans from greed to rescue. . . .

115. We heard a strange low noise, like the groaning of a wild beast wanting to escape, coming from under the master's cabin. When we chased down the sound, we found Eumolpus sitting there heaping up verses on a large sheet of parchment. We were surprised at his having time to write poetry when death was so near, and we dragged him out protesting and implored him to be sensible. But he was furious at being disturbed and said: "Allow me to complete my thought; the poem suffers from some difficulties at the close." I grabbed hold of this lunatic and told Giton to come and help me drag the bellowing poet ashore. . . . When this task was at last completed, we advanced in a sad mood to the fishermen's cottages, and having somewhat refreshed ourselves with food spoiled in the shipwreck, we passed a very miserable night. Next day as we were discussing into which region we should ven-

corpus humanum circumactum levi vertice ad litus de-
8 ferri. | substiti ergo tristis coepique umentibus[608] oculis
9 maris fidem inspicere et | "hunc forsitan" proclamo "in
aliqua parte terrarum secura expectat uxor, forsitan igna-
rus tempestatis filius aut pater;[609] utique reliquit aliquem,
10 cui proficiscens osculum dedit. | haec sunt consilia morta-
lium, haec vota {magnarum cogitationum}.[610] en homo
11 quemadmodum natat." | adhuc tamquam ignotum defle-
bam, cum inviolatum os fluctus convertit in terram, agno-
vique terribilem paulo ante et implacabilem Licham pedi-
12 bus meis paene subiectum. | non tenui igitur diutius
lacrimas, immo percussi semel iterumque manu[611] pectus
et "ubi nunc est" inquam "iracundia tua, ubi impotentia
13 tua? | nempe piscibus beluisque expositus es, et qui paulo
ante iactabas vires imperii tui, de tam magna nave ne tabu-
14 lam quidem naufragus habes. | ite nunc mortales, et
magnis cogitationibus pectora implete. ite cauti, et opes
15 fraudibus captas per mille annos disponite. | nempe hic
proxima luce patrimonii sui rationes inspexit, nempe diem
etiam, quo venturus esset in patriam, animo suo fixit.[612]
16 dii deaeque, quam longe a destinatione sua iacet. | sed
non sola mortalibus maria hanc fidem praestant. [φL]illum
bellantem arma decipiunt, illum diis vota reddentem
penatium[613] suorum ruina sepelit. ille vehiculo lapsus pro-
perantem spiritum excussit, cibus avidum strangulavit,
17 abstinentem frugalitas. | si bene calculum ponas, ubique

608 humentibus t^{mg}: viventibus
609 pater *Bücheler*: patrem
610 *deleted Fraenkel*   611 manu *L*: manibus *l*
612 fixit *Oevering*: finxit
613 penatium φ: penatum *L*

ture, I suddenly noticed a human body caught in a swirling but gentle eddy and carried ashore. So I stopped still and sad, and with moist eyes began to reflect on the treachery of the sea. "Perhaps," I cried, "somewhere in the world a cheerful wife awaits this man, perhaps a son or father who knows nothing of the storm; he surely left someone behind whom he kissed when he set out. So much for human schemes and desires. Look how the man floats." I was still weeping over him as if he were a perfect stranger, when a wave turned his unmarked face toward land, and I recognized Lichas, who a little while earlier had been fierce and relentless, now cast up almost at my feet. I could no longer keep back my tears, beat my breast again and again, and said: "Where are your bad temper and ungovernable rages now? Instead, you are at the mercy of fish and beasts. A little while ago you were boasting about the strength of your command, but now you are shipwrecked and do not have even a plank from that very great ship. Go now, mortal men, and fill your breasts with great schemes. Go, you safe and secure people, and make arrangements for the riches you gained by fraud and thought would last a thousand years. Surely it was only yesterday when he checked the accounts of his estates, and surely he had settled in his own mind even the day when he would come home. My gods and goddesses, how far away he lies from his destination. But it is not only the seas that keep faith in such fashion with mortals. The weapons of the warrior fail him in battle, and a man in the act of paying his vows to the gods is buried in the collapse of his own house. A man slips from his carriage and immediately breathes his last; the glutton chokes on his food; the abstemious man dies from eating too little. If you reckon everything carefully, there

325

naufragium est. ^{L}at enim fluctibus obruto non contingit[614]
sepultura. tamquam intersit, $^{\phi L}$periturum corpus quae
ratio consumat, ignis an fluctus an mora. quicquid feceris,
18 omnia haec eodem ventura sunt. | ^{L}ferae tamen corpus
lacerabunt. tamquam melius ignis accipiat; immo hanc
poenam gravissimam credimus, ubi servis irascimur. |
19 quae ergo dementia est, omnia facere, ne quid e[615] nobis
relinquat sepultura?" |

⟨ * * * ⟩

20 et Licham quidem rogus inimicis collatus manibus adole-
bat. Eumolpus autem dum epigramma mortuo facit, oculos ad arcessendos sensus longius mittit.

⟨ * * * ⟩

116. hoc peracto libenter officio destinatum carpimus
iter ac monumento temporis in montem sudantes conscen-
dimus, ex quo haud procul impositum arce sublimi oppi-
2 dum cernimus. | nec quod[616] esset sciebamus errantes,
donec a vilico quodam Crotona esse cognovimus, urbem
3 antiquissiman et aliquando Italiae primam. | cum deinde
diligentius exploraremus qui homines inhabitarent nobile
solum quodve genus negotiationis praecipue probarent
4 post attritas bellis frequentibus opes, | "o m⟨e⟩i"[617] inquit
"hospites, si negotiatores estis, mutate propositum aliud-
5 que vitae praesidium quaerite. | sin autem urbanioris no-
tae homines sustinetis semper mentiri, recta ad lucrum

[614] contingit *Goldast*: contigit
[615] e *L*: de *Jacobs*
[616] quod *Bücheler*: quid
[617] *added Burma*n

are shipwrecks everywhere. But of course there is no burial for a man drowned in the waves. As if the method that destroys a perishable body makes a difference: fire or waves or the lapse of time. Whatever you do, everything ends up in the same way. Of course wild beasts will tear up a body. As if fire would give it a better welcome; when we are angry with our slaves, we believe that fire is the severest possible punishment. So what madness is this, that we do everything to see to it that there is nothing of us left behind for burial?" . . . So the pyre that cremated the body of Lichas was erected by his enemies' hands. While Eumolpus composed an epitaph for the dead man, he cast his eyes off into the distance in search of inspiration. . . .

116. After we had gladly performed this duty and decided which way to go, we took to the road and in no time at all began to sweat as we climbed a mountain, from which we saw in the near distance a city set on a lofty height. Since we were lost, we did not know what city it was, until we learned from some estate manager that it was Croton,[134] a very old city and once the foremost in Italy. When we then inquired more to the point about what kind of men lived in this famous place and what kind of business interests in particular they followed, since their wealth had been diminished by so many wars, the man said: "My dear sirs, if you are businessmen, change your plans and look for some other kind of livelihood. If, however, you are of a more cosmopolitan bent and can lie incessantly, you are running straight on the road to riches.

[134] Croton on the south coast of Italy in the province of Bruttium was virtually uninhabited by the first century AD.

6 curritis. | in hac enim urbe non litterarum studia celebran-
   tur, non eloquentia locum habet, non frugalitas sanctique
   mores laudibus ad fructum perveniunt, sed quoscumque
   homines in hac urbe videritis, scitote in duas partes esse
7 divisos. | nam aut captantur aut captant. in hac urbe nemo
   liberos tollit, quia quisquis suos heredes habet, non ad
   cenas,[618] non ad spectacula admittitur, sed omnibus pro-
8 hibetur commodis, inter ignominiosos latitat. | qui vero
   nec uxores[619] umquam duxerunt nec proximas necessitu-
   dines habent, ad summos honores perveniunt, id est soli
   militares, soli fortissimi atque etiam innocentes habentur.
9 | adibitis" inquit "oppidum tamquam in pestilentia cam-
   pos, in quibus nihil aliud est nisi cadavera quae lacerantur
   aut corvi qui lacerant."

⟨ * * * ⟩

117. prudentior Eumolpus convertit ad novitatem rei
   mentem genusque divitationis[620] sibi non displicere con-
2 fessus est. | iocari ego senem poetica levitate credebam,
   cum ille "utinam quidem sufficeret largior scaena, id est
   vestis humanior, instrumentum lautius[621] quod praeberet
   mendacio fidem: non mehercules praedam[622] istam differ-
3 rem, sed continuo vos ad magnas opes ducerem. | atquin
   promitto" ⟨. . .⟩ quicquid exigeret, dummodo placeret
   vestis, rapinae comes, et quicquid Lycurgi villa grassanti-
   bus praebuisset. nam nummos in praesentem usum deum
4 matrem pro fide sua reddituram. ⟨. . .⟩ | "quid ergo?" in-

618 cenas *Bongars*: scenas
619 uxores *L*: uxorem *Bücheler*
620 divitationis *Gruterus*: divinationis
621 lautius *Gulielmius*: latius
622 praedam *Müller*: peram *or* poenam

For in this city literary studies have no prominence, eloquence no place, sober habits and decent morals do not lead to any rewards. Just know that whatever men you will see in this city are divided into two classes: those who are hunted for their fortunes and the legacy hunters themselves. In this city no one raises children, because whoever has his own heirs is not invited to dinners or admitted to public performances, but he is deprived of all advantages and is hidden away among the people who live in disgrace. But those who have never taken wives and have no close relatives reach the highest positions: they alone are regarded as men having the qualities of soldiers, they alone are courageous and even blameless. You will enter a town that is like a plague-stricken countryside, in which there is nothing other than corpses being torn to pieces and crows doing the tearing." . . .

117. Eumolpus had a clearer picture of the future and directed his attention to this novel situation and declared that such a method of getting rich appealed to him. I thought that the old man was joking and speaking in poetic frivolity, but then he said: "I wish that we had more elaborate stage properties, I mean more civilized costumes, and more splendid stage machinery to lend plausibility to our deception: I swear I would not put off plundering, but would straight away lead you to great riches. Even so I promise" . . . whatever he should demand, as long as the clothes I had worn for the burglary were satisfactory, and whatever Lycurgus' villa had yielded to us when we robbed it.[135] I knew that the mother of the gods would provide the money for our present needs according to her promise. . . .

[135] A lost episode.

quit Eumolpus "cessamus mimum[623] componere? facite
5 ergo me dominum, si negotiatio placet." | nemo ausus est
artem damnare nihil auferentem. itaque ut duraret inter
omnes tutum mendacium, in verba Eumolpi sacramen-
tum iuravimus: uri, vinciri, verberari ferroque necari, et
quicquid aliud Eumolpus iussisset. tamquam legitimi gla-
diatores domino corpora animasque religiosissime addici-
6 mus. | post peractum sacramentum serviliter ficti domi-
num consalutamus, elatumque ab Eumolpo filium pariter
condiscimus,[624] iuvenem ingentis eloquentiae et spei,
ideoque de civitate sua miserrimum senem exisse, ne aut
clientes sodalesque filii sui aut sepulcrum quotidie causam
7 lacrimarum cerneret. | accessisse huic tristitiae proximum
naufragium, quo amplius vicies sestertium amiserit; nec
illum iactura moveri, sed destitutum ministerio non
8 agnoscere dignitatem suam. | praeterea habere in Africa
trecenties sestertium fundis nominibusque depositum;
nam familiam quidem tam magnam per agros Numidiae
9 esse sparsam, ut possit vel Carthaginem capere. | secun-
dum hanc formulam imperamus Eumolpo ut plurimum
tussiat, ut sit ⟨modo astrictioris⟩[625] modo solutioris stomachi cibosque omnes palam damnet; loquatur aurum et
argentum fundosque mendaces et perpetuam terrarum
10 sterilitatem; | sedeat praeterea quotidie ad rationes tabu-
lasque testamenti omnibus ⟨astantibus⟩[626] renovet. et ne
quid scaenae deesset, quotienscumque aliquem nostrum

[623] mimum p^2: in unum
[624] condiscimus *Gulielmius*: condicimus
[625] *added Wehle*
[626] *added Rose*[3]

"Why then," said Eumolpus, "do we delay staging our farce? Make me the director, if you like the business." No one dared condemn a scheme that cost nothing. And so to make sure that the imposture stayed safe among us all, we swore an oath dictated by Eumolpus, that we would accept being burned, fettered, flogged, put to the sword, or whatever else Eumolpus had ordered. Just as if we were real gladiators, we most solemnly pledged our bodies and souls to our master. After we had sworn this oath we posed as slaves and saluted our master and at the same time learned by heart the plot of his farce: Eumolpus had buried a son, a youth of great eloquence and promise, and because of this the wretched old man had left his own country so that he would escape the daily cause of his tears, when he saw his son's dependents and friends, or his tomb. A recent shipwreck, in which he had lost more than two million sesterces, had added to his sorrows. He was not worried by the financial loss, but as he was thus deprived of his retinue of slaves to wait on him, he could not see the signs of his high social position. Another twist to the farce: in Africa he had thirty million sesterces invested in farms and loans, and had such a large number of slaves spread among his fields in Numidia that they could capture Carthage at least. Following Eumolpus' own story pattern, we told him to cough a lot, to suffer from constipation at one time, and the next time diarrhea, and to complain openly about all his food. He was to talk about gold and silver, about farms which had not met expectations, and about the continued unproductivity of the soil. Moreover, every day he was to sit and work at his accounts, and revise the terms of his will in front of everyone. To make the scene on the stage complete, he was to call us by the wrong names, whenever

vocare temptasset, alium pro alio vocaret, ut facile appareret dominum etiam eorum meminisse qui praesentes
11 non essent. | his ita ordinatis, "quod bene feliciterque eve-
niret" precati deos viam ingredimur. sed neque Giton sub
insolito fasce durabat, et mercennarius Corax, detractator[627] ministerii, posita frequentius sarcina male dicebat
properantibus affirmabatque se aut proiecturum sarcinas
12 aut cum onere fugiturum. | "quid? vos" inquit "iumentum
me putatis esse aut lapidariam navem? hominis operas
locavi, non caballi. nec minus liber sum quam vos, etiam
si pauperem pater me reliquit." nec contentus maledictis
tollebat subinde altius pedem et strepitu obsceno simul
13 atque odore viam implebat. | ridebat contumaciam Giton
et singulos strepitus eius pari clamore prosequebatur.

⟨ * * * * ⟩

^{OφL}118. "multos," inquit Eumolpus "o iuvenes, carmen
decepit. nam ut quisque versum pedibus instruxit sen-
sumque teneriore[628] verborum ambitu intexit, putavit se
2 continuo in Helicona[629] venisse. | ^{OL}sic forensibus minis-
teriis exercitati frequenter ad carminis tranquillitatem
tamquam ad portum feliciorem[630] refugerunt, credentes
facilius poema extrui posse quam controversiam senten-
3 tiolis vibrantibus pictam. | ceterum neque generosior spi-
ritus vanitatem[631] amat, neque concipere aut edere par-
tum mens potest nisi ingenti flumine litterarum inundata.
4 | refugiendum[632] est ab omni verborum, ut ita dicam, vili-

---

[627] detractator p^2: detractor   [628] teneriore B: teneriorem
[629] Helicona *Müller*: Heliconem
[630] feliciorem EI: faciliorem
[631] vanitatem p^2: sanitatem
[632] refugiendum *Bücheler*: effugiendum

he tried to summon any one of us, to make it abundantly clear that our master was also thinking of slaves who were absent. Once these things were all arranged, and we had prayed to the gods that it would all turn out successfully and happily, we set off on our way. But Giton was not holding up under his unaccustomed burden, and Corax, the hired man who always shirked his duties, kept putting down his bundle and cursing us for walking too fast, and said that either he would throw away the baggage or run off with his load. "What's going on?" he asked. "Do you think that I am a pack animal or a ship for hauling rocks? I hired myself out to do a man's work, not a horse's. I'm just as free a person as you are, even if my father did leave me a poor man." But he could not be satisfied with curses, and he often lifted his leg high and filled the road with disgusting noises and also smells. Giton kept laughing at his defiance and followed the sound of each fart with a matching noise. . . .

118. "Poetry, my young friends," said Eumolpus, "has deceived many into believing that each has scaled Mount Helicon,[136] as soon as he has shaped his lines into feet, and has woven into it a more subtle meaning with a circumlocution of words. Thus men who have been trained for forensic oratory often take refuge in the tranquility of poetry as in some safer haven, in the belief that a poem is easier to construct than a declamation adorned with flashy epigrams. But the nobler spirit hates empty words, and the mind cannot conceive or give birth unless it is first steeped in the vast flood of literature. We must avoid all cheap vulgarity of language, so to speak, and take up words re-

[136] Located in Boeotia and sacred to the Muses.

tate et sumendae voces a plebe semotae,[633] ut fiat 'odi
5 profanum vulgus et arceo.' | praeterea curandum est ne
sententiae emineant extra corpus orationis expressae, sed
‹ut›[634] intexto vestibus colore niteant. Homerus testis et
lyrici Romanusque Vergilius et Horatii curiosa felicitas.
ceteri enim aut non viderunt viam qua iretur ad carmen,
6 aut visam[635] timuerunt calcare. | ecce belli civilis ingens
opus quisquis attigerit nisi plenus litteris, sub onere labe-
tur. non enim res gestae versibus comprehendendae sunt,
quod longe melius historici faciunt, sed per ambages deorumque ministeria et fabulosum sententiarum tormentum
praecipitandus est liber spiritus, ut potius furentis animi
vaticinatio appareat quam religiosae orationis sub testibus
fides: tamquam, si placet, hic impetus, etiam si nondum
recepit ultimam manum."

‹ * * * ›

119. orbem iam totum victor Romanus habebat,
qua mare, qua terrae, qua sidus currit utrumque.
nec satiatus erat. gravidis freta pulsa carinis
iam peragebantur; si quis sinus abditus ultra,
5 si qua foret tellus, fulvum quae mitteret aurum,
hostis erat, ratibusque[636] in tristia bella paratis
quaerebantur opes. non vulgo nota placebant
gaudia, non usu plebeio trita voluptas.
aes Ephyrae captum[637] laudabat miles; in ima[638]

---

633 semotae *Pius*[1]: summotae
634 *added Boschius*
635 visam *LeFèvre*: versum
636 ratibusque *Harrison*[3]: fatisque
637 aes Ephyrae captum *Magnelli*: aesepyre cum *B, p*[1]
638 ima *Gifanius*: unda

mote from popular use, so that this pronouncement is recognized: 'I hate the common crowd and avoid it.'[137] Moreover, we must take care that terse and pointed observations do not stand out from the body of the work, but that their color and brilliance are woven into the texture of the material. Homer, the lyric poets, Roman Virgil, and the painstaking artistry of Horace all prove this. But others have either not seen the path that leads to poetry, or if they have seen it, were afraid to walk in it. For example, whoever undertakes the great theme of the Civil War, unless he is well versed in literature, will sink under the burden. Historical achievements should not be dealt with in verse, for historians do this far better. Rather it should be the free spirit of genius that plunges headlong through dark metaphors, divine interventions, and the anguish of meaning in legends, so that it gives the impression of prophetic frenzy rather than the trustworthy accuracy of a solemn account read before witnesses. As an example, if you like, here is my bold attempt at such, though it has not received my final touches." . . .

119. The triumphant Roman was now in control of the whole world, the seas and lands and wherever the sun and moon shone, yet he was still hungry. Now the heavily loaded ships drove the sea-lanes before them and assailed the waves, in search of some hidden remote bay, or some land that could yield yellow gold, all such places being the enemy. With such ships prepared for war, the pursuit for wealth went on and on. Familiar everyday joys and pleasures, cheapened by their use among the lower classes, were no longer seen as good enough to give satisfaction. Common soldiers became connoisseurs of Corinthian

[137] Hor. *Carm.* 3.1.1.

10   quaesitus tellure nitor certaverat ostro;
    hinc Numidae crustas,[639] illinc nova vellera Seres,
    atque Arabum populus sua despoliaverat arva.
    ecce aliae clades et laesae vulnera pacis.
    quaeritur in silvis circo[640] fera, et ultimus Hammon
15   Afrorum excutitur, ne desit belua dente
    ad mortes pretiosa; fremens[641] premit advena classes
    tigris et aurata gradiens vectatur in aula,
    ut bibat humanum populo plaudente cruorem.
    heu, pudet effari perversaque[642] prodere facta:[643]
20   Persarum ritu male pubescentibus annis
    surripuere viros exsectaque viscera ferro
    in venerem fregere, atque ut fuga nobilis aevi
    circumscripta mora properantes differat annos.
    *OφL*quaerit se natura nec invenit. omnibus ergo
25   scorta placent fractique enervi corpore gressus
    et laxi crines et tot nova nomina vestis,
    *OL*quaeque virum quaerunt. ecce Afris eruta terris
    citrea mensa greges servorum ostrumque renidens
    ponitur ac maculis imitatur vilius[644] aurum,
30   quae censum[645] trahat. hoc sterile ac male nobile
            lignum
    turba sepulta mero circum venit, omniaque orbis
    praemia correptis miles vagus esurit armis.
    *OφL*ingeniosa gula est. Siculo scarus aequore mersus

---

[639] crustas *l*^mg*ct*: accusatius *or* accusant
[640] circo *Junius*: auro
[641] fremens *Bouhier*: fames
[642] perversaque *Müller*: peritturaque
[643] facta *Burman*: fata
[644] vilius *Gronovius*: vilibus
[645] censum *P^c*, *Stubbe*: sensum

bronze; (10) bright shiny things acquired from deep mines rivaled the traditional purple; from here Numidians sent inlaid marbles, from there Chinese offered raw silks, and Arabs went so far as to strip their fields bare. Add to this all the other disasters and the scars from broken peace agreements. Wild animals are hunted down in their forests as game for the Circus, and near Jupiter's shrine in far-off Africa the lion is pursued and captured to ensure that this beast with its precious and deadly saber teeth is available at all times. Strange ravening creatures weigh down our boats, like the prowling tiger shipped in a golden cage to drink the blood of men to the applause of the crowd. I shrink in shame from even talking about and exposing our destiny and ruin. (20) Boys who had hardly reached puberty are stripped of their manhood in Persian rituals, and with their genitals cut off by knives are turned into sexual objects, so that the swift passing of the peak age of the male might be encompassed in some delay and the speeding years retarded. Nature seeks the natural and does not find it. So all take their pleasures in catamites, in their soft mincing steps and flowing hair, in so many kinds of novel clothes, and in everything where manhood is sought in vain. Citrus trees are dug up in African soil and used to make tables, whose polished finish reflects hordes of slaves and purple garments, and in their mottled surfaces the tables imitate gold, a cheaper substance than citrus wood, (30) and attract the viewer's eye. Around this wood, whose tree bears no fruit and is unworthy of fame, reclines a mob dead drunk on wine, and there is a soldier of fortune in all his armor hungering after all the best the world has to offer. Gluttony is a vice[138] clever enough to bring the

[138] Mart. 13.62.2.

ad mensam vivus perducitur, atque Lucrinis
35 eruta litoribus vendunt conchylia cenas,
ut renovent per damna famem. iam Phasidos unda
orbata est avibus, mutoque in litore tantum
solae desertis adspirant frondibus aurae.
^{OL}nec minor in campo furor est, emptique Quirites
40   $^{O\phi L}$ad praedam strepitumque lucri suffragia vertunt.
venalis populus, venalis curia patrum,
est favor in pretio. senibus quoque libera virtus
exciderat, sparsisque opibus conversa potestas,
ipsaque maiestas auro corrupta iacebat.
45   ^{OL}pellitur a populo victus Cato; tristior ille est,
qui vicit, fascesque pudet rapuisse Catoni.
{namque hoc dedecoris populo morumque ruina}[646]
non homo pulsus erat, sed in uno victa potestas
Romanumque decus. quare iam[647] perdita Roma
50 ipsa sui merces erat et sine vindice praeda.
praeterea gemino deprensam gurgite plebem[648]
faenoris ingluvies[649] ususque exederat aeris.
nulla est certa domus, nullum sine pignore corpus,
sed veluti tabes tacitis concepta medullis
55 intra membra furens curis latrantibus errat.
$^{O\phi L}$arma placent miseris, detritaque commoda luxu

---

[646] *Verse 47 deleted Broukhusius*   [647] iam *t*: tam
[648] plebem *Burman*: praedam
[649] ingluvies *Palmerius*: illuvies

---

[139] Near Baiae in the region of the Bay of Naples.

[140] River flowing into the eastern end of the Black Sea, famous for pheasants.   [141] Cato the Younger committed suicide in North Africa rather than surrender to Caesar in 46.

wrasse alive in a tank of Sicilian water to the table, and to see to it that oysters which are dug up from beds in the Lucrine lake[139] bring in paying customers for dinners, by renewing appetites through exorbitant costs. And now the stream of the Phasis[140] is bereft of all pheasants, and on its silent banks breezes blow through uninhabited trees. The madness in our politics continues to grow, and the good old Romans are bought (40) who then change their votes in favor of plunder to accompany the politicians' rhetoric promising wealth. The votes of the mob are for sale, as are those of the corrupt Senate, whose support has a price. These old men had abandoned moral excellence, their power was influenced by those passing out money, and their very majesty was corrupted by gold and lay humiliated. Cato[141] was voted out of office by the mob; Caesar, the unhappy victor, felt the sting of shame for having seized power from him. {For the shame of the people and the downfall of character lay in this,} It was not the rejection of a man, but in the fall of this one person the power and glory of the great people of Rome were dealt a death-blow. (50) So now Rome itself was in disgrace, setting the price for her own sale, ripe for plunder, and without hope of a champion to rescue it. Moreover greed in borrowed capital and usury attendant to ready money caught the common people in a twin whirlpool and virtually ate them up. No home or person is safe and unmortgaged. This usury is like a wasting disease that starts silently in the bones, as a madness, spreading through the limbs of the people, raging as with cares barking at their heels. Those now suffering take up arms, and all the fortunes wiped out

vulneribus reparantur. inops audacia tuta est.
^{OL}hoc mersam caeno Romam somnoque iacentem
quae poterant artes sana ratione movere,
60 ni furor et bellum ferroque excita^{650} libido?
        ^{OΦL}120. tres tulerat Fortuna duces, quos obruit
            omnes
armorum strue diversa feralis Enyo.
Crassum Parthus habet, Libyco iacet aequore
        Magnus,
Iulius ingratam perfudit sanguine Romam,
65 et quasi non posset tellus tot ferre sepulcra,
divisit cineres. hos gloria reddit honores.
        ^{OL}est locus exciso penitus demersus hiatu
Parthenopen inter magnaeque Dicarchidos arva,
Cocyti^{651} perfusus aqua; nam spiritus, extra
70 qui furit effusus, funesto spargitur aestu.
non haec autumno tellus viret aut alit herbas
caespite laetus ager, non verno persona cantu
mollia discordi strepitu virgulta loquuntur,
sed chaos et nigro squalentia pumice saxa
75 gaudent ferali circum tumulata cupressu.
has inter sedes Ditis pater extulit ora
bustorum flammis et cana sparsa favilla,
ac tali volucrem Fortunam voce lacessit:
        ^{OΦL}'rerum humanarum divinarumque potestas,
80 Fors, cui nulla placet nimium secura potestas,

---

^{650} excita *Junius*: excissa
^{651} Cocyti s^{mg}, *l*: Cocytia

by debauchery are recovered for them by murder. Boldness caused by poverty can safely risk everything. What methods of healthy reasoning could stir Rome from the filth in which it was submerged or the lethargy in which it lay, (60) none but rage and war and lust encouraged by the sword?

120. Fortune produced three generals, and Enyo, deadly goddess of war, buried them all under different piles of arms.[142] The Parthians have stuffed Crassus, Pompey the Great lies dead near the Libyan shore, and Julius stained ungrateful Rome with his blood. As though the earth could not bear up under the weight of so many graves, she divided their ashes. Fame pays honors such as she wishes. Between Parthenope's Naples and the fields of Dicarchus' Puteoli there lies a spot deep in a cloven chasm, awash with the water of Cocytus;[143] and the wind that rushes (70) furiously outside is laced with its deadly spray. The earth here is never green in autumn, no field is luxuriant with pleasant turf or nurtures herbs, the soft thickets are not filled with springtime songs, and no short quick notes of rival birds resound. Instead there is total chaos, and filthy rocks of black pumice stone are pleased to be buried round about by funereal cypress trees. In such an abode Dis,[144] lord of Hell, raised his head which was flecked with the white ashes from the flames of funerals, and challenged winged Fortune with these words: 'Magistrate of all human and divine affairs, (80) Mistress Chance, who never approves of any power too firmly es-

142 Crassus in 55, Pompey in 48, and Caesar in 44.
143 One of the rivers of the underworld.
144 The Greek god Pluto, lord of the underworld.

341

quae nova semper amas et mox possessa relinquis,
^{OL}ecquid Romano sentis te pondere victam,
nec posse ulterius perituram extollere molem?
ipsa suas vires odit Romana iuventus
85 et quas struxit opes, male sustinet. aspice late
luxuriam spoliorum et censum in damna furentem.
$^{O\phi L}$aedificant auro sedesque ad sidera mittunt,
expelluntur aquae saxis, mare nascitur arvis,
et permutata rerum statione rebellant.
90 en etiam mea regna petunt. perfossa dehiscit
molibus insanis tellus, iam montibus haustis
antra gemunt, et dum vanos[652] lapis invenit usus,
inferni manes caelum sperare fatentur.
^{OL}quare age, Fors, muta pacatum in proelia vultum
95 Romanosque cie ac nostris da funera regnis.
iam pridem nullo perfundimus ora cruore,
nec mea Tisiphone sitientes perluit artus,
ex quo Sullanus bibit ensis et horrida tellus
extulit in lucem nutritas sanguine fruges.'
100 121. haec ubi dicta dedit, dextrae coniungere
dextram
conatus rupto tellurem solvit hiatu.
tunc Fortuna levi defudit pectore voces:
'o genitor, cui Cocyti penetralia parent,
si modo vera mihi fas est impune profari,
105 vota tibi cedent; nec enim minor ira rebellat
pectore in hoc leviorque exurit flamma medullas.

[652] vanos ϕ, r^{mg}: vanus *or* varios

tablished, who is always eager for something new and quickly forsakes her conquests, do you not feel that you are crushed under the dead weight of Rome, and that you cannot raise higher that massive city that is doomed to fall? The Roman youth hates its own strength, and can barely sustain the wealth it has piled up. Look about at the plundered riches of wars, extravagance raging to its own ruin. They build with gold and raise their homes to the stars, the sea waters are dammed up by stone piers, new seas grow in the middle of fields, and in rebellion they turn nature's arrangement of all things upside down. (90) And now they trespass even on my kingdom. The earth is dug way down to allow for madmen's foundations and yawns wide open; the mountains are hollowed out and the caves within groan, and while marble is put to frivolous uses, the shades in hell declare their hope of reaching the upper air. Therefore, Chance, act now and change your face of peace to one of war, stir up the Romans and deliver their corpses to our kingdom. It is a long time since I drenched my face with blood, and my Tisiphone, the Fury, has not bathed her thirsty limbs since Sulla's[145] sword drank deep, and the rugged earth brought forth produce fertilized with blood.'

121. (100) After he said this, he strained to take her hand and thus broke up the earth in a yawning chasm. Fortune then poured out these words from her fickle heart: 'Father, whom the inmost depths of Cocytus obey, your prayers will be answered, if I may foretell the truth and remain unharmed, for the anger that breaks out in my heart is no less than yours, nor is the flame that burns in

---

[145] Dictator of Rome who massacred the followers of Marius in 82, in the so-called Social Wars.

omnia, quae tribui Romanis arcibus, odi
muneribusque meis irascor. destruet istas
idem, qui posuit, moles deus. et mihi cordi
110   quippe cremare viros et sanguine pascere luxum.
cerno equidem gemina iam stratos morte Philippos
112   Thessaliaeque rogos et funera gentis Hiberae[653]
114   et Libyae; cerno tua, Nile, gementia claustra
115   Actiacosque sinus et Apollinis arma timentes.
113   iam fragor armorum trepidantes personat aures.
116   pande, age, terrarum sitientia regna tuarum
atque animas accerse novas. vix navita Porthmeus
sufficiet simulacra virum traducere cumba;
classe opus est. tuque ingenti satiare ruina,
120   pallida Tisiphone, concisaque vulnera mande:
ad Stygios manes laceratus ducitur orbis.'
      122. vixdum finierat, cum fulgure rupta corusco
intremuit nubes elisosque abscidit ignes.
subsedit pater umbrarum, gremioque reducto
125   telluris pavitans fraternos palluit ictus.
continuo clades hominum venturaque damna
auspiciis patuere deum. namque ore cruento
deformis Titan vultum caligine texit:
civiles acies iam tum spectare[654] putares.

---

[653] *Arrangement of lines 112–114–115–113–116 proposed by Suringar.*   [654] spectare *Crusius*: spirare

---

[146] Brutus and Cassius were defeated by Antony and Octavian in 42 at Philippi in Macedonia; Pharsalus in Thessaly was where Caesar defeated Pompey in 48.

[147] Munda in Spain was where Caesar defeated the followers of Pompey in 45.   [148] Libya is a reference to Caesar's victory in 46 over the followers of Pompey.

my marrow less fierce. All the gifts I bestowed on the heights of Rome I now hate, and I resent having given so many. The same god, Mars, who raised up those massive structures, will also bring them down. It will please me (110) to burn up those men and then feed their debauchery with their own blood. Already I see the fields of Philippi strewn with the corpses of twin battles, and the blazing pyres of Thessaly[146] and the dead of Spain[147] and Libya;[148] and, River Nile,[149] I see your barriers groan, and soldiers at the Gulf of Actium[150] terrified by Apollo's weapons. The crash of arms sets off alarms in my trembling ears. Come, open the thirsty kingdoms of your territories and summon fresh souls. The old ferryman Charon will hardly have the strength to transport the ghosts of the men in his boat; a whole fleet is necessary for the work. (120) Bloodless Tisiphone, gorge yourself on the widespread carnage, and devour the dismembered body parts: the world is torn to pieces and led down to the Stygian shades.'

122. She had barely finished, when a cloud was shaken and torn by shimmering lightning and emitted a burst of fire. Dis, the father of the shades sank down, and having closed the chasm in the earth's bosom, grew pale in fear of the lightning bolts of Jupiter, his brother. At once the slaughter of men and the disasters to come were made plain by the omens sent by the gods. For Titan, the sun, disgusting with his bloodstained mouth, veiled his face in darkness: you would have thought that even then he was

---

[149] Nile refers to the place of Pompey's murder in 48, after he fled from Pharsalus.

[150] Octavian defeated Antony at Actium in 31.

130 parte alia plenos extinxit Cynthia vultus
  et lucem sceleri subduxit. rupta tonabant
  verticibus lapsis[655] montis iuga, nec vaga passim
  flumina per notas ibant morientia ripas.
  armorum strepitu caelum furit et tuba Martem
135 sideribus tremefacta ciet, iamque Aetna voratur
  ignibus insolitis et in aethera fulmina mittit.
  ecce inter tumulos atque ossa carentia bustis
  umbrarum facies diro stridore minantur.[656]
  fax stellis comitata novis incendia ducit,
140 sanguineoque recens descendit Iuppiter imbre.
  haec ostenta brevi solvit deus. exuit omnes
  quippe moras Caesar, vindictaeque actus amore
  Gallica proiecit, civilia sustulit arma.
   Alpibus aeriis, ubi Graio numine[657] pulsae
145 descendunt rupes et se patiuntur adiri,
  est locus Herculeis aris sacer. hunc nive dura
  claudit hiemps canoque ad sidera vertice tollit:
  caelum illinc cecidisse putes. non solis adulti
  mansuescit radiis, non verni temporis aura,
150 sed glacie concreta rigent[658] hiemisque pruinis:
  totum ferre potest umeris minitantibus orbem.
  haec ubi calcavit Caesar iuga milite laeto
  optavitque[659] locum, summo de vertice montis
  Hesperiae campos late prospexit et ambas
155 intentans cum voce manus ad sidera dixit:
  'Iuppiter omnipotens, et tu, Saturnia tellus,
  armis laeta meis olimque onerata triumphis,

---

[655] lapsis *δW*: lassis   [656] minantur *Goldast*: minatur
  [657] numine *Burman*: nomine   [658] rigent *Lipsius*: riget
or rigens   [659] optavitque *s*mg, *l*mg*ct*: oravitque

witnessing civil strife. (130) In another quarter Cynthia, the moon, had darkened her full face and withdrawn her light from the crimes. The mountaintops slipped down and the broken ridges thundered into fragments. Wandering streams were dying and no longer flowed along familiar banks. The heavens raged with the clash of arms, a tremulous trumpet rouses Mars down from the sky, and now Aetna is devoured by unusual flames and erupts, sending fiery rocks into the air. Among the tombs and unburied bones the faces of the shades menace with an ominous hissing. A bright meteor in the company of comets brings conflagration, (140) and Jupiter comes down in fresh showers of blood. Quickly the god made these portents plain, for Caesar shrugged off all obstacles of delay, and driven by a passion for vengeance, laid aside his arms in a foreign war in Gaul and took them up in a civil war. High in the Alps, where the cliffs slope down, thus allowing themselves to be approached, there is a spot trodden by a Greek god, a place of altars sacred to Hercules; the frozen snow of winter surrounds it and heaves it up to the stars with a white peak. You would think that from there the sky had fallen away. The rays of the full sun and the breezes of springtime do not soften it, (150) but everything lies hardened by the ice and frost of winter. It can carry the whole world on its threatening shoulders. When Caesar with his exultant army trod these heights, he chose the highest mountaintop to look out over the wide fields of Italy, and lifting his voice and both hands toward heaven, said: 'Almighty Jupiter, and you, Land of Saturn, once proud of my victories and loaded with my triumphs, I call

testor, ad has acies invitum accersere Martem,
invitas me ferre manus. sed vulnere cogor,
160 pulsus ab urbe mea, dum Rhenum sanguine tingo,[660]
dum Gallos iterum Capitolia nostra petentes
Alpibus excludo, vincendo certior exul.
sanguine Germano sexagintaque triumphis
esse nocens coepi. quamquam quos Gloria terret,
165 aut qui sunt qui bella vetent?[661] mercedibus emptae
ac viles operae, quorum est mea Roma noverca.
at[662] reor, haud impune, nec hanc sine vindice
     dextram
vinciet ignavus. victores ite furentes,[663]
ite mei comites, et causam dicite ferro.
170 namque omnes unum crimen vocat, omnibus una
impendet clades. reddenda est gratia vobis,
non solus vici. quare, quia poena tropaeis
imminet et sordes meruit victoria nostra,
iudice Fortuna cadat alea. sumite bellum
175 et temptate manus. certe mea causa peracta est:
inter tot fortes armatus nescio vinci.'
    haec ubi personuit, de caelo Delphicus ales
omina[664] laeta dedit pepulitque meatibus auras.
nec non horrendi nemoris de parte sinistra
180 insolitae voces flamma sonuere sequenti.
ipse nitor Phoebi vulgato latior[665] orbe
crevit et aurato praecinxit fulgure vultus.

---

[660] tingo *M₁V₂ Dr*: vinco
[661] vetent *Mössler*: vident
[662] at *P*: ut
[663] furentes *A*: ferentes

upon you to witness that I do not willingly summon Mars to these battles, and that I do not willingly raise my hands for war. But I am forced by my grievances, (160) banished from my own city, even as I stained the Rhine with blood and closed off the Alpine routes to the Gauls seeking to sack the Capitol again. These victories make my exile doubly sure. My shedding German blood and my countless triumphs rendered me guilty. Yet who is terrified by fame, and who are they who forbid me to make war? Who else but base hirelings bought at a high price, no real sons of my mother Rome. But I think that no coward will safely tie up my strong hand without my avenging it. My comrades, fierce in victory, gather round and plead our cause with the sword. (170) We are all indicted on one charge, the same doom hangs over us. My thanks must be given to you, for I was not alone when I was victorious. Therefore because punishment threatens our trophies, and our victories merit nothing but disgrace, let the die be cast and Fortune decide. Commence the war and prove your strength. My case is surely already won, and armed among so many brave men I cannot conceive of defeat.' As he spoke these words aloud, the Delphic raven flew from the sky, presenting a happy omen, and beat the air with its advance. And from the left quarter of the gloomy grove (180) strange voices resounded, followed by flames. Phoebus the sun shone brighter than his wont, and his face was set in a halo of golden splendor.

---

664 omina *As*, *lct*: omnia
665 latior δ*s*, *lct*: laetior

123. fortior ominibus movit Mavortia signa
Caesar et insolitos[666] gressu prior occupat ausus.
185   prima quidem glacies et cana vincta pruina
non pugnavit humus mitique horrore quievit.
sed postquam turmae nimbos fregere ligatos
et pavidus quadrupes undarum vincula rupit,
incaluere nives. mox flumina montibus altis
190   undabant modo nata, sed haec quoque—iussa
        putares—
stabant, et vincta fluctus stupuere ruina,[667]
et paulo ante fluens[668] iam concidenda iacebat.
tum vero male fida prius vestigia lusit
decepitque pedes; pariter turmaeque virique
195   armaque congesta strue deplorata iacebant.
ecce etiam rigido concussae flamine nubes
exonerabantur, nec rupti turbine venti
derant aut tumida confractum grandine caelum.
ipsae iam nubes ruptae super arma cadebant,
200   et concreta gelu ponti velut unda ruebat.
victa erat ingenti tellus nive victaque caeli
sidera, victa suis haerentia flumina ripis;
nondum Caesar erat, sed magnam nixus in hastam
horrida securis frangebat gressibus arva,
205   qualis Caucasea decurrens arduus arce
Amphitryoniades, aut torvo Iuppiter ore,
cum se verticibus magni demisit Olympi
et periturorum disiecit[669] tela Gigantum.
  dum Caesar tumidas iratus deprimit arces,

---

[666] insolitos M_1Dr, s^{mg}: insolito   [667] ruina *Reiske*: pruina
[668] fluens *Colladonius*: lues
[669] disiecit *Gulielmius*, p^2: deiecit

123. Heartened by these omens, Caesar deployed the standards of war, and first on the march took up untried ventures. At the beginning the ice and ground, frozen by white frost, offered the troops no opposition but lay quiet in a soft shivering. But once the cavalry had broken up the ice fields, and the hooves of the terrified horses had shattered the frozen bonds of water, then the snows melted. Quickly thereafter the rivers (190) took on new life and poured down from the mountain heights, but—you would have thought that someone had ordered it—these now were standing still. The waves froze, the destruction stopped, and the water that just before was a torrent, now was hard enough to cut. The ground that was treacherous earlier now led them to misstep and tricked them as they attempted to get footholds. Cavalry and infantry and weapons alike all fell in a heap and in despair. The clouds were buffeted by freezing winds and released their burden; whirlwinds appeared, and the sky was broken by swollen hail. Now the clouds themselves burst and fell on the armed men, (200) and masses of ice like sea waves showered down. The earth was conquered by deep snow, the stars of heaven were obliterated, and the rivers clung to their banks frozen. Caesar was still not yet conquered, but leaning on his tall spear, crushed the rough ground in his fearless stride. Just so did the son of Amphitryon[151] hasten down the steep summit of Caucasus; just so did scowling Jupiter descend from the heights of great Olympus and scatter the arms of the doomed Giants. While angry Caesar trod the swollen peaks underfoot,

[151] Hercules.

210   interea volucer motis conterrita pinnis
      Fama volat summique petit iuga celsa Palati
      atque hoc Romanos[670] tonitru ferit omnia fingens:[671]
      iam classes fluitare mari totasque per Alpes
      fervere Germano perfusas sanguine turmas.
215   arma, cruor, caedes, incendia totaque bella
      ante oculos volitant. ergo pulsata tumultu
      pectora perque duas scinduntur territa causas.
      huic fuga per terras, illi magis unda probatur
      et patria pontus iam tutior; est magis arma
220   qui temptare velit fatisque iubentibus uti.[672]
233   ac velut ex alto cum magnus inhorruit auster
234   et pulsas evertit aquas, non arma ministris,
235   non regimen prodest, ligat alter pondera pinus,
236   alter tuta sinus[673] tranquillaque litora quaerit:
237   hic dat vela fugae Fortunaeque omnia credit.
221   quantum quisque timet, tantum fugit.[674] ocior ipse
      hos inter motus populus, miserabile visu,
      quo mens icta iubet, deserta ducitur urbe.
      gaudet Roma fuga, debellatique Quirites
225   rumoris sonitu maerentia tecta relinquunt.
      ille manu pavida natos tenet, ille penates
      occultat gremio deploratumque relinquit
      limen et absentem votis interficit hostem.
      sunt qui coniugibus maerentia pectora iungant,
230a   grandaevosque patres <*** [675]
230b   ***> onerisque ignara iuventus
      id pro quo metuit, tantum trahit. omnia secum

[670] Romanos *Bouhier*: Romano   [671] fingens *Watts*: sigma
[672] *verses 233–37 placed after 220 Ehlers*
[673] sinus *Bursian*: sinu

(210) swift Rumor was frightened, beat her wings, and in flight sought out the tall hill of the Palatine. She strikes the Romans with this thunder, inventing every kind of shock: already Caesar's ships have put to sea, and his cavalry, drenched in German blood, is raging through all the Alps. Before the eyes of the masses flit arms and blood and slaughter, fire and all the images of war. Their hearts are shaken in confusion and in fear are divided between two courses of action. One man chooses to flee by land, another puts more trust in the sea, a safer opportunity than his own country. (220) Others prefer to take to arms and to follow the dictates of Fate. They act like the fierce south wind when from the sea it rages and turns over the driven waves: riggings do no good for the crew, the rudder is useless, one ties together the heavy planks of pine, another seeks the safety of inlets and calm shores, and a third man sets sail for flight and trusts all things to Chance. Each one flees in proportion to his fear. In this turmoil the people of Rome themselves can flee faster (a terrible sight) because they need but follow their stricken minds, and the city is abandoned. Rome is glad to flee, and its old families subdued by the sound of rumors leave their homes in sorrow. One holds tight to his children in his trembling arms, another hides the household gods in his lap, and mourning over his threshold, leaves the house and calls down death on his unseen enemy. Some clasp their wives to their sorrowful breasts, (230) and young men unaccustomed to burdens carry their aged fathers, and take with them only

---

674 fugit. *Bücheler punctuates*
675 *lacuna indicated Müller*

353

232 hic vehit imprudens praedamque in proelia ducit.
238 quid tam parva queror? gemino cum consule
        Magnus,
  ille tremor Ponti saevique repertor Hydaspis
240 et piratarum scopulus, modo quem ter ovantem
  Iuppiter horruerat, quem fracto gurgite Pontus
  et veneratus erat submissa Bosphoros unda,
  pro pudor, imperii deserto nomine fugit,
  ut Fortuna levis Magni quoque terga videret.
245   124. ergo tanta lues divum quoque numina
        vicit,[676]

  consensitque fugae caeli timor. ecce per orbem
  mitis turba deum terras exosa furentes
  deserit atque hominum damnatum avertitur agmen.
  Pax prima ante alias niveos pulsata lacertos
250 abscondit galea victum caput atque relicto
  orbe fugax Ditis petit implacabile regnum.
  huic comes it submissa Fides et crine soluto
  Iustitia ac maerens lacera Concordia palla.
  at contra, sedes Erebi qua rupta dehiscit,
255 emergit late Ditis chorus, horrida Erinys
  et Bellona minax facibusque armata Megaera
  Letumque Insidaeque et lurida Mortis imago.
  quas inter Furor, abruptis ceu liber habenis,

---

[676] vicit *Jacobs*: vidit

---

[152] River in northern India, never visited by Pompey.
[153] Pompey cleared much of the eastern Mediterranean of pirates in 67.
[154] In 81, 71, 61.

what they fear to lose. Only the fool drags all his goods with him, thus taking added booty into battle. But why complain about such petty ills? Pompey the Great, the same one who made Pontus tremble and discovered the fierce Hydaspes,[152] (240) the same one who broke up the pirate bands[153] and lately celebrated three triumphs,[154] enough to arouse the awe of Jupiter, the same one to whom the conquered Black Sea and the Bosporus[155] in submission bowed down in worship, this same man accompanied by the two consuls fled Rome in shame and gave up his claim to the imperial title. So it happened that fickle Fortune witnessed also the back of Great Pompey turned in flight.

124. Such a great calamity broke the power even of the gods, and the fear in heaven added to the rout. All round the earth the gentler deities abandoned in loathing the mad world, and turned their faces away from the doomed army of mankind. Peace leads the way before all others, her snow-white arms showing bruises, (250) her vanquished head hidden beneath her helmet, and leaving the world behind, turns in flight to the inexorable realm of Dis. She is joined in departure by humble Faith, by Justice with her unbound hair, and by Concord in tears and in a rent cloak. In the opposite direction where the hall of Erebus[156] is opened and gapes wide, the whole company of Dis is disgorged, a grim Erinys, the threatening Bellona goddess of war, Megaera ringed with torches, Destruction, Ambush, and the pallid face of Death. Among them all rushes Madness, like a steed with a broken rein, and

[155] Pompey passed here in 65 in the war against Mithridates.
[156] God of darkness, another name for Hades.

sanguineum late tollit caput oraque mille
260 vulneribus confossa cruenta casside velat;
haeret detritus laevae Mavortius umbo
innumerabilibus telis gravis, atque flagranti
stipite dextra minax terris incendia portat.
 sentit terra deos mutataque sidera pondus
265 quaesivere suum; namque omnis regia caeli
in partes diducta ruit. primumque Dione
Caesaris arma[677] sui ducit, comes additur illi
Pallas et ingentem quatiens Mavortius hastam.
Magnum[678] cum Phoebo soror et Cyllenia proles
270 excipit ac totis similis Tirynthius actis.
intremuere tubae ac scisso Discordia crine
extulit ad superos Stygium caput. huius in ore
concretus sanguis, contusaque lumina flebant,
stabant arrosi[679] scabra rubigine dentes,
275 tabo lingua fluens, obsessa draconibus ora,
atque inter torto laceratam pectore vestem
sanguinea tremulam[680] quatiebat lampada dextra.
haec ut Cocyti tenebras et Tartara liquit,
alta petit gradiens iuga nobilis Appennini,
280 unde omnes terras atque omnia litora posset
aspicere ac toto fluitantes orbe catervas,
atque has erumpit furibundo pectore voces:
'sumite nunc, gentes, accensis mentibus arma,
sumite et in medias immittite lampadas urbes.
285 vincetur, quicumque latet; non femina cesset,
non puer aut aevo iam desolata senectus;

---

[677] arma *Passerat*: acta [678] Magnum *Gevaerts*: magnaque
[679] arrosi *Harrison*[3]: aerati *or* irati
[680] sanguinea tremulam *s*[mg]: sanguineam tremula

tosses up his head and (260) covers his face, already
scarred by a thousand wounds, in a gory helmet. In his left
hand he grips the well-worn shield of Mars, weighed down
with countless spear points, and in his right he waves a
blazing brand and carries fire to threaten the whole world.
Earth felt the action of the gods, the stars were moved but
sought their former poise, and the whole palace of the sky
was split and collapsed. Dione[157] was the first to champion
the side of her own Caesar, then Pallas[158] joined her, and
then Mars brandishing his massive spear. Phoebus and his
sister[159] sided with Pompey, as did Cyllene's son Mercury,
(270) and so too Tirynthian Hercules, much like him in all
his deeds. The trumpets blasted in quavering tones, and
Discord with disheveled hair raised her Stygian head up
toward the gods of heaven. On her face blood had clotted,
tears ran from her bruised eyes, her teeth covered in rusty
scales were eaten away, her tongue was dripping with de-
caying matter, her face beset with snakes, beneath her torn
clothes her breasts writhed, and in her bloody hand she
waved a quivering torch. Leaving behind the darkness of
Cocytus and Tartarus,[160] she went forward in search of the
high ridges of the proud Apennine, (280) from where she
could see all the lands and coasts, and the armies stream-
ing over the whole world. She spewed forth these words
from her maddened breast: 'All nations, take up arms now
and fill your hearts with fire, take up arms, and hurl torches
into the hearts of cities. Whoever hides from the fray will
be lost; let no woman delay, no child, no man wasted by

157 Venus.   158 Minerva.
159 Apollo and Diana.
160 Rivers in Hades.

ipsa tremat tellus lacerataque tecta rebellent.
tu legem, Marcelle, tene. tu concute plebem,
Curio. tu fortem ne supprime, Lentule, Martem.
290 quid porro tu, dive, tuis cunctaris in armis,
non frangis portas, non muris oppida solvis
thesaurosque rapis? nescis tu, Magne, tueri
Romanas arces?[681] Epidamni moenia quaere
Thessalicosque sinus humano sanguine tingue.'
295 factum est in terris, quicquid Discordia iussit." |

2   cum haec Eumolpus ingenti volubilitate verborum ef-
fudisset, tandem Crotona intravimus. ubi quidem parvo
deversorio refecti, postero die amplioris fortunae domum
quaerentes incidimus in turbam heredipetarum sciscitan-
3   tium quod genus hominum aut unde veniremus. | ex
praescripto ergo consilii communis exaggerata verborum
volubilitate, unde aut qui essemus, haud dubie credenti-
bus indicavimus. ᴸqui statim opes suas summo cum certa-
4   mine in Eumolpum congesserunt. ⟨. . .⟩ | certatim omnes
heredipetae[682] muneribus gratiam Eumolpi sollicitant.

⟨ * * * ⟩

125. dum haec magno tempore Crotone aguntur ⟨. . .⟩
et Eumolpus felicitate plenus prioris fortunae esset oblitus {statum}[683] adeo, ut {suis}[684] iactaret neminem gratiae
suae ibi posse resistere impuneque suos, si quid deli-

---

[681] arces *Passerat*: acies   [682] heredipetae *lt*ᵐᵍ: *omitted rtp*
[683] *deleted George*   [684] *deleted Müller, but note the po-*
lyptoton, suis . . . suae . . . suos

---

[161] Consul in 49, partisan of Pompey.
[162] C. Scribonius Curio, supporter of Caesar.

old age; let the earth itself quake and the shattered houses join the fight. You, Marcellus,[161] uphold the law. You, Curio,[162] stir up the rabble crowds. You, Lentulus,[163] do not slow down the god of war. (290) You, divine Caesar, why are you a laggard in your arms, why do you not break down the gates, why do you not strip the towns of their walls, and seize their treasures? You, Pompey the Great, do you not know how to defend Rome's citadels? So, seek out the alien walls of Epidamnus,[164] and stain red the bays of Thessaly with human blood.' All was done on earth, just as Discord ordered it."

After Eumolpus had poured out these lines in a monstrous flow of verbiage, we finally entered Croton, where we were refreshed in a small inn. The next day we looked for a more impressive house, and fell in with crowd of legacy hunters who wanted to know what sort of people we were and where we came from. So, following the terms of our joint policy, we informed the gullible questioners of our origin and identity by deluging them with a torrent of words. At once they competed feverishly to put their financial resources into Eumolpus' hands. . . . All the legacy hunters vied to win Eumolpus' favor by offering him gifts. . . .

125. This sort of thing went on for a long time in Croton. . . . Eumolpus was flushed with success, and so far forgot his former precarious condition as to boast that no one there could resist his charm, and that through the kindness of his friends his dependents could act with im-

[163] Consul in 51, partisan of Pompey.
[164] Dyrrachium, Illyrian coastal town where Pompey set up an advanced base.

2 quissent in ea urbe, beneficio amicorum laturos. | ceterum ego, etsi quotidie magis magisque superfluentibus bonis saginatum corpus impleveram putabamque a custodia mei removisse vultum Fortunam, tamen saepius tam consue-
3 tudinem meam cogitabam quam causam, et | "quid" aiebam "si callidus captator exploratorem in Africam miserit mendaciumque deprehenderit nostrum? quid, si mercennarius Eumolpi[685] praesenti felicitate lassus indicium ad amicos detulerit totamque fallaciam invidiosa proditione
4 detexerit? | nempe rursus fugiendum erit et tandem expugnata paupertas nova mendicitate revocanda. dii deaeque, $^{\phi L}$quam male est extra legem viventibus: quicquid meruerunt, semper expectant."

⟨ * * * ⟩

^{L}126. {*Chrysis ancilla Circes ad Polyaenum*}[686] "quia nosti venerem tuam, superbiam captas vendisque am-
2 plexus, non commodas.[687] | quo enim spectant flexae pectine comae, quo facies medicamine attrita et oculorum quoque mollis petulantia, quo incessus arte[688] compositus et ne vestigia quidem pedum extra mensuram aberrantia,
3 nisi quod formam prostituis ut vendas? | vides me: nec auguria novi nec mathematicorum caelum curare soleo, ex vultibus tamen hominum mores colligo, et cum spatiantem
4 vidi, quid cogitet[689] scio. | sive ergo nobis vendis quod peto, mercator paratus est, sive, quod humanius est, com-
5 modas, effice ut beneficium debeamus.[690] | nam quod servum te et humilem fateris, accendis desiderium aestuan-

---

[685] Eumolpi *l*: *omitted others*   [686] *See n. 527.*
[687] commodas *Lipsius*, p^2: commodos
[688] arte *Dousa*: tute   [689] cogitet *Burman*: cogites
[690] debeamus *Anton*: debeam

punity, if they committed any wrongdoings in the city. But though I had daily filled my already stuffed body with more and more abundance of good things, and I was beginning to feel that Fortune had turned her malevolent gaze away from me, nevertheless I kept thinking just as often about my usual misfortunes as about the cause of them all. And so I said to myself: "What if some cunning legacy hunter sends an investigator to Africa and finds out about our lies? Or suppose that servant of Eumolpus grows weary of our present good luck and hints to these friends, and in hateful treachery exposes our whole fraudulent scheme? Of course we will have to flee, and the poverty that we had finally beaten back, we will have to return to, and start begging again. By the gods and goddesses, how nasty it is for outlaws, always waiting to get what they deserve." . . .

126. "Because you appreciate the power of your sexual appeal, you affect arrogance and sell your embraces rather than make them readily available. Otherwise, what's the point of your combed and wavy hair, your face plastered with makeup, the melting wantonness of your eyes, and your artfully composed manner of walking, so that not even a footstep is out of place, all of it meaning of course that you prostitute your good looks for money? Look at me: I know nothing about fortune-telling, and I'm not accustomed to interpret the heavens of the astrologers, but I can draw conclusions about men's character from their faces, and when I watch a man walk, I know what's on his mind. Therefore if you're selling what I want, I know of a waiting buyer, or if you do the gracious thing and make it easily available, let me be in your debt for a favor. For since you admit that you're a slave and low-class,

tis. quaedam enim feminae sordibus calent, nec libidinem
concitant, nisi aut servos viderint aut statores altius cinc-
6 tos. | harena aliquas accendit aut perfusus pulvere mulio
7 aut histrio scaenae ostentatione traductus. | ex hac nota
domina est mea: usque ab orchestra quattordecim transilit
et in extrema plebe quaerit quod diligat." |

8   itaque oratione blandissima plenus "rogo" inquam
"numquid illa, quae me amat, tu es?" multum risit ancilla
post tam frigidum schema et "nolo" inquit "tibi tam valde
9 placeas. | ego adhuc servo numquam succubui, nec hoc dii
10 sinant, ut amplexus meos in crucem mittam. | viderint
matronae, quae flagellorum vestigia osculantur; ego etiam
si ancilla sum, numquam tamen nisi in equestribus sedeo."
11 | mirari equidem tam discordem libidinem coepi atque
inter monstra numerare, quod ancilla haberet matronae
superbiam et matrona ancillae humilitatem. |

12   *OL*procedentibus deinde longius iocis rogavi {ancil-
lam}[691] ut in platanona perduceret dominam. placuit puellae consilium. itaque collegit altius tunicam flexitque se in
13 eum daphnona qui ambulationi haerebat. | nec diu morata
dominam producit e latebris laterique meo applicat, mu-
14 lierem omnibus simulacris emendatiorem. | nulla vox est
quae formam eius possit comprehendere, nam quicquid
15 dixero, minus erit. | crines ingenio suo flexi per totos se
umeros effuderant, frons minima et quae radices capillo-
rum retro flexerat, supercilia usque ad malarum scriptu-

[691] *omitted* L: ancillam O

---

[165] The first fourteen rows in the theater immediately behind
the orchestra, which was reserved for senators, was set aside for
the *equites*.

you're in fact arousing the desire of a woman in heat. For some women are stimulated sexually by the dregs of male company, and they cannot rouse any desire unless they can stare at slaves or public servants who have their tunics hitched up. The arena inflames some women, or a grimy muleteer, or an actor disgraced by exhibiting himself on stage. My mistress is one of this type: she leaps over the first fourteen rows from the orchestra,[165] and seeks out something to love among the lowest of the low."

And so at my most charming best I said: "Are you that one then who loves me?" The maid laughed out loud at my clumsy maneuver and said: "Don't be so conceited. I've never yet gone to bed with a slave. May the gods forbid that I should ever witness a lover of mine on a cross. Let the married women see to that, since they're the ones who kiss the scars left by whips. I might be only a maid, but the only laps I climb on belong to knights." I began to marvel at this paradox of sexual preferences and to count them as portents of things to come, because the maid had the pride of a respectable married woman, and the respectable woman the low tastes of a maid.

After our bantering had gone on for some time, I asked her to bring her mistress into a clearing surrounded by plane trees, a suggestion that pleased the girl. And so she hitched her tunic up higher and turned into the laurel grove that bordered the path. After a few moments she escorted her mistress out of the shadows and settled her next to me, a woman more perfect than any statue. No words could do justice to her beauty, for whatever I say will fall short of reality. Her hair cascaded in natural waves and flowed all over her shoulders; her forehead was narrow and from it her hair went back in curls; her eyebrows

ram currentia et rursus confinio luminum paene permixta,
16 | oculi clariores stellis extra lunam fulgentibus, nares pau-
lulum inflexae et osculum quale Praxiteles habere Dio-
17 nen[692] credidit. | iam mentum, iam cervix, iam manus, iam
18 pedum candor intra auri gracile vinculum positus: | Pa-
rium marmor extinxerat. itaque tunc primum Dorida vetus amator contempsi.

⟨ * * * * ⟩

quid factum est, quod tu proiectis, Iuppiter, armis
   inter caelicolas fabula muta iaces?[693]
nunc erat a torva submittere cornua fronte,
   nunc pluma canos dissimulare tuos.
5 haec vera est Danae. tempta modo tangere corpus,
   iam tua flammifero membra calore fluent.

⟨ * * * * ⟩

127. delectata illa risit tam blandum, ut videretur mihi
plenum os extra nubem luna proferre. mox digitis guber-
nantibus vocem "si non fastidis" inquit "feminam ornatam
et hoc primum anno virum expertam, concilio tibi, o iuve-
2 nis, sororem. | habes tu quidem et fratrem, neque enim
me piguit inquirere, sed quid prohibet et sororem adop-
tare? eodem gradu venio. tu tantum dignare et meum
3 osculum, cum libuerit, agnoscere." | "immo" inquam ego
"per formam tuam te rogo ne fastidias hominem peregri-
num inter cultores admittere. invenies religiosum, si te

692 Dionen *Jahn*: Dianam
693 iaces *Fraenkel*: taces

166 Sculptor of the fourth century, famous among other things
for the Cnidian Aphrodite.

ran down to the contours of her cheeks, and almost met again near her eyes which were brighter than the stars that sparkle outside the light of the moon; her nose was slightly aquiline; her mouth was like the one that Praxiteles[166] attributed to Diana. How to describe her chin, her neck, her hands, and her gleaming feet held under a delicate band of gold. Parian marble paled by comparison. So now for the first time I looked down on my old affair with Doris. . . . "What happened, Jupiter,[167] to make you throw away your arms and cause you to lie among the gods with your reputation muted? By now you ought to have sprouted horns from your lowering head; by now you ought to have hidden your white hair under a swan's feathers. This is the genuine Danaë. Dare only to touch her body, and your limbs will melt in heated passion." . . .

127. She was charmed with this and smiled so enticingly that it seemed to me that the moon was showing her full face from beyond a cloud. With her fingers seeming to guide her words she said: "If you do not disdain a elegant woman who this year for the first time in her life had a man, I offer you a sister, young man. It is true that you already have a boy-partner, for I do not regret having made inquiries, but what is there to keep you from choosing a sister? I come to you on the same terms. When it is your pleasure, kindly think me worthy and allow my kiss." I replied: "Rather it is I who should implore you by your beauty not to look down on this foreigner, but to admit him as one of your worshippers. You will find him a devout adherent, if you allow him to worship you. So that you do

[167] Jupiter adopted the form of a bull to seduce Europa, a swan for Leda, and a shower of gold for Danaë.

adorari permiseris. ac ne me iudices ad hoc templum
{Amoris}[694] gratis accedere, dono tibi fratrem meum." |

4 "quid? tu"[695] inquit illa "donas mihi eum sine quo non
potes vivere, ex cuius osculo pendes, quem sic tu amas,

5 quemadmodum ego te volo?" | haec ipsa cum diceret,
tanta gratia conciliabat vocem loquentis, tam dulcis sonus
pertemptatum mulcebat aëra, ut putares inter auras ca-
nere Sirenum concordiam. itaque <toto> miranti {et toto}
mihi caelo[696] clarius nescioquid relucente libuit deae no-

6 men quaerere. | "ita" inquit "non dixit tibi ancilla mea me
Circen vocari? non sum quidem Solis progenies, nec mea
mater, dum placet, labentis mundi cursum detinuit;
habebo tamen quod caelo imputem, si nos fata con-
iunxerint. immo iam nescioquid tacitis cogitationibus deus

7 agit. | nec sine causa Polyaenon Circe amat: semper inter
haec nomina magna fax surgit. sume ergo amplexum, si
placet. neque est quod curiosum aliquem extimescas:

8 longe ab hoc loco frater est." | dixit haec Circe, implici-
tumque me bracchiis mollioribus pluma deduxit in terram
vario gramine indutam. |

9   Idaeo qualis[697] fudit de vertice flores
    terra parens, cum se concesso[698] iunxit amori
    Iuppiter et toto concepit pectore flammas:

---

[694] *omitted L*: amoris O   [695] tu p^2: ni   [696] toto miranti
mihi caelo *Rose*^{2}: miranti et toto mihi caelo *O, L*
    [697] qualis *Hadrianides*: quales   [698] concesso s^{mg}: confesso

---

[168] Circe, daughter of Helios and Perse, is a sorceress in Homer (*Od.* 10.230–574), where she changes the bodies of Odysseus' companions into pigs. She detained Odysseus for one year,
while Calypso delayed him for seven.

.

not think that I came to the temple without any offering,
I give you my boy-partner as a gift." She replied: "What
are saying? Are you giving me the one who is your whole
life, the one whose kisses you hang on, the one you love in
the way that I want you to love me?" Even as she spoke
these words, there was so much charm in her voice and
such a sweet sound pervaded and caressed the air that you
would have conjured up images of the Sirens' songs trans-
mitted harmoniously on the breezes. So in my state of awe,
and while the whole sky acquired for me an unspeakably
bright light, I was pleased to ask the goddess' name. "So,"
she said, "my maid did not tell you that my name is
Circe?[168] Not that I am the child of the Sun, or that my
mother, at her pleasure, ever stayed the course of the
smoothly gliding world. But I shall consider myself to be
in heaven's debt, if the Fates bring the two of us together.
Surely now with silent design god has a plan in mind. Not
without cause does Circe love Polyaenus,[169] for between
these names a large torch of passion stands up. So come
to my arms, if that is what you want. There is no reason
why you should fear prying eyes, for your boy-partner is
far away from here." Circe said this, enfolded me in arms
softer than down, and drew me to the ground covered with
flowers of various colors. These flowers were such as
mother Earth spread on the summit of Ida, when Jupiter
united with the submissive Juno,[170] and he took to himself

---

[169] Polyaenus = much praised, the assumed name of Encolpius in Croton, and an epithet of Odysseus.

[170] Refers to the scene in Homer (*Il.* 14.211–360) where Hera
distracts Zeus from the fighting around Troy by inviting him to a
dalliance on Mount Ida.

emicuere rosae violaeque et molle cyperon,
5   albaque de viridi riserunt lilia prato:
talis humus Venerem molles clamavit in herbas,
candidiorque dies secreto favit amori. |

10 in hoc gramine pariter compositi mille osculis lusimus,
quaerentes voluptatem robustam.

〈 * * * 〉

*L*128. {Circe ad Polyaenum}[699] "quid est?" inquit
"numquid te osculum meum offendit? numquid spiritus
ieiunio marcens?[700] numquid alarum neglegens sudor?
si, ut credo, haec[701] non sunt, numquid Gitona times?" |
2 perfusus ego rubore manifesto etiam si quid habueram
virium perdidi, totoque corpore velut laxato "quaeso" inquam "regina, noli suggillare miserias. veneficio contactus
sum." |

〈 * * * 〉

3 {Circe}[702] "dic, Chrysis, sed verum: numquid indecens
sum? numquid incompta? numquid ab aliquo naturali
vitio formam meam excaeco? noli decipere dominam
4 tuam. nescioquid peccavimus." | rapuit deinde tacenti spe-
culum, et postquam omnes vultus temptavit, quos solet
inter amantes usus[703] fingere,[704] excussit vexatam solo ves-
5 tem raptimque aedem Veneris intravit. | ego contra dam-
natus et quasi quodam visu in horrorem perductus interrogare animum meum coepi, an vera voluptate fraudatus
essem: |

6   *OφL*nocte soporifera veluti cum somnia ludunt
errantes oculos effossaque protulit aurum

---

[699] *See n. 527.*
[700] marcens *Bücheler*: macer
[701] si, ut credo, haec *Schmeling*[5]: puto si haec *L*

all the flames of love: roses, violets, and soft galingale, and white lilies laughed in the green meadows. Such a surface summoned acts of love to the soft grass, and the brighter day intensified our covert lovemaking. We lay together on the grass and kissed a thousand times in our game of love, seeking to achieve mature pleasure. . . .

128. "What is the problem?" she said. "Do my kisses offend you? Has my enthusiasm become feeble from not eating? Is there unwashed sweat in my armpits? If, as I believe, it is none of these, are you afraid of Giton?" My whole face was flushed crimson, and even if I had had some strength, I lost it, and with my whole body limp, I said: "Please, my queen, do not add insult to my misery. I have been bewitched by a poison." . . . "Chrysis, tell me honestly," said Circe, "am I unattractive? Is my hair a mess? Does some natural blemish ruin my beauty? Please do not delude your mistress; somehow I have done something wrong." Then she snatched a mirror from the maid, who had not replied, and after she tried all the facial expressions which practice is wont to sketch among lovers, she shook out the cloak that was rumpled from lying on the ground, and immediately entered the shrine of Venus. On the other hand, I acted like a condemned person, someone who was horror-stricken, as if he had seen a ghost, and I began to ask myself, whether I had been cheated out of a real pleasure: "It was like in a heavy slumber at night, when dreams beguile our errant eyes,

---

702 *See n. 527.*

703 usus *Bücheler*: risus

704 fingere *Cuperus*: frangere

in lucem tellus: versat manus improba furtum
thesaurosque rapit; sudor quoque perluit ora
5   et mentem timor altus habet, ne forte gravatam
excutiat gremium secreti conscius auri:
mox ubi fugerunt elusam gaudia mentem
veraque forma redit, animus quod perdidit optat
atque in praeterita se totus imagine versat. |

⟨ * * * ⟩

7   ^{L}{Giton ad Encolpion}[705] "itaque hoc nomine tibi gratias
ago, quod me Socratica fide diligis. non tam intactus Alcibiades in praeceptoris sui lectulo iacuit."

⟨ * * * ⟩

129. {Encolpius ad Gitonem}[706] "crede mihi, frater,
non intellego me virum esse, non sentio. funerata est illa
pars corporis, qua quondam Achilles eram." |

⟨ * * * ⟩

2   veritus puer, ne in secreto deprehensus daret sermonibus
locum, proripuit se et in partem interiorem aedium[707]
fugit. |

⟨ * * * ⟩

3   ^{OL}cubiculum autem meum Chrysis intravit codicillosque
mihi dominae suae reddidit, in quibus haec erant scripta:
4   "Circe Polyaeno salutem.[708] | si libidinosa essem, quererer
decepta; nunc etiam languori tuo gratias ago. in umbra
5   voluptatis diutius lusi. | quid tamen agas, quaero, et an tuis
pedibus perveneris domum; negant enim medici sine ner-
6   vis homines ambulare posse. | narrabo tibi, adulescens,
paralysin cave. numquam ego aegrum tam magno periculo

[705] See n. 527.
[706] See n. 527.

and the dug-up earth exposes gold to the light of day; our greedy hands finger the stolen goods and snatch the treasures; sweat bathes our faces, and a great fear holds our minds that perhaps someone aware of the hidden gold will shake it out of our laden breast. But soon when these deceptive joys have fled from our minds, and the reality of the true shape of things returns, our mind aspires to the treasure it has lost and concerns itself totally in the shadow of the past." . . . [Giton] "So on this account I thank you for loving me as ethically as Socrates. Alcibiades never lay so untouched on his master's couch." . . .

129. "My boy-partner, you must believe me when I say I do not see myself as a man, I do not feel like one. That part of my body for which I was known as Achilles is dead and buried." . . . The boy was afraid that if he were caught alone with me, it would provide a platform for scandal, and so he tore himself away and fled into the inner part of the house. . . . Chrysis then came into my room and handed me a letter from her mistress Circe, which read as follows: "Circe greets Polyaenus. If I were a lustful woman, I would complain that I had been deceived. Instead I am thankful even for your impotence. I spent too much time in foreplay of love. I am asking you now how you are, and whether you got home safely on your own two feet. For doctors say that a man without sexual strength cannot walk around. I will tell you what, young man: you should be afraid of becoming a paralytic. I have never seen a sick person in such grave danger. Your genital area has already

---

707 interiorem aedium *l*: aedium interiorem
708 Circe Polyaeno sal. *BR*: *omitted others*

7   vidi: medius {fidius}[709] iam peristi. | quod si idem frigus
genua manusque temptaverit tuas, licet ad tubicines mit-

8   tas. | quid ergo est? etiam si gravem iniuriam accepi, ho-
mini tamen misero non invideo medicinam. si vis sanus
esse, Gitona[710] relega.[711] recipies, inquam, nervos tuos, si

9   triduo sine fratre dormieris. | nam quod ad me attinet, non
timeo ne quis inveniatur cui minus placeam. nec speculum

10 mihi nec fama mentitur. vale, si potes." | ut intellexit
Chrysis perlegisse me totum convicium, "solent" inquit
"haec fieri, et praecipue in hac civitate, in qua mulieres

11 etiam lunam deducunt. | itaque huius quoque rei cura
agetur. rescribe modo blandius dominae animumque eius
candida humanitate restitue. verum enim fatendum est:

12 ex qua hora iniuriam accepit, apud se non est." | libenter
quidem parui ancillae verbaque codicillis talia imposui:
130. "Polyaenos Circae salutem. fateor me, domina, saepe
pecasse; nam et homo sum et adhuc iuvenis. numquam

2   tamen ante hunc diem usque ad mortem deliqui. | habes
confitentem reum: quicquid iusseris, merui. proditionem
feci, hominem occidi, templum violavi: in haec facinora

3   quaere supplicium. | sive occidere placet, ⟨cum⟩[712] ferro
meo venio, sive verberibus contenta es, curro nudus ad

4   dominam. | illud unum memento, non me sed instrumenta

5   peccasse. paratus miles arma non habui. | quis hoc turba-
verit nescio. forsitan animus antecessit corporis moram,

[709] *deleted Thomas*
[710] Gitona *Müller*: Gitonem
[711] relega *Delz*: roga
[712] *added Bücheler*

died. If the same chill attacks your knees and hands, you can send for the funeral musicians. So what is to be done for me? Even if I have been terribly insulted by you, I do not begrudge such a wretched creature as you a cure. If you want to get better, send Giton away. I think that you will recover your potency, if you sleep for three nights without your boy-partner. So far as I am concerned, I have no fear of finding someone who will consider me less attractive than you do. In the end my mirror and my reputation do not lie. Get well soon, if you can." When Chrysis realized that I had read through the whole invective, she said: "These things will happen, especially in this town, where women can draw even the moon down from the sky. And so a remedy will be found for this thing too. Merely write back with some flattering words to my mistress and restore her vitality by stating openly your kindness toward her. I must tell you the truth: since the time you insulted her, she has not been herself." I gladly obeyed the maid, and wrote the following words on a tablet: 130. "Polyaenus to Circe, greetings: I confess, dear lady, that I have often made mistakes, for after all I am only human and still in my youth. But before this day I have never committed an act that resulted in death. You see the culprit confessing before you, and I deserve whatever punishment you order. I have been a traitor, I murdered a man, I profaned a temple: find a punishment for these crimes. If your verdict is execution, I will come with my sword; or if you let me off with a whipping, I will run unclothed to you, my mistress. Remember only this one thing, not I but my equipment was at fault. I was a soldier ready for battle, but I had no arms. Who is responsible for this catastrophe, I do not know. Perhaps my eagerness ran ahead of my lagging

forsitan dum omnia concupisco, voluptatem tempore
6 consumpsi. | non invenio quod feci. paralysin tamen ca-
vere iubes: tamquam ea[713] maior fieri possit quae abstulit
mihi per quod etiam te habere potui. summa tamen excu-
sationis meae haec est: placebo tibi, si me culpam emen-
dare permiseris." |

⟨ * * * ⟩

7 *L*dimissa cum eiusmodi pollicitatione Chryside curavi
dilgentius noxiosissimum corpus, balneoque praeterito
modica unctione usus, mox cibis validioribus pastus, id
est bulbis cochlearumque sine iure cervicibus, hausi par-
8 cius merum. | hinc ante somnum levissima ambulatione
compositus sine Gitone cubiculum intravi. tanta erat pla-
candi cura, ut timerem ne latus meum frater convelleret.
131. postero die, cum sine offensa corporis animique
consurrexissem, in eundem[714] platanona descendi, etiam
si locum inauspicatum timebam, coepique inter arbores
2 ducem itineris expectare Chrysidem. | nec diu spatiatus
consederam, ubi hesterno die fueram, cum illa intervenit
3 comitem aniculam trahens. | atque ut me consalutavit,
"quid est" inquit "fastose? ecquid bonam mentem habere
coepisti?" |
4 in⟨terea anicu⟩la[715] de sinu licium protulit varii coloris
filis intortum cervicemque vinxit meam. mox turbatum
sputo pulverem medio sustulit digito frontemque re-
5 pugnantis signavit. | hoc peracto carmine ter me iussit
expuere terque lapillos conicere in sinum, quos ipsa prae-

713 ea *Bücheler*: iam
714 eundem *t*: idem
715 *added Bücheler*

body; perhaps in my desire to enjoy everything, I exhausted all pleasure in dallying. I cannot account for what I did. Then you tell me to beware of paralysis, as if the disease that deprived me of the chance to possess you could get any worse. My apology, however, really amounts to this: I will give you satisfaction, if you allow me to atone for my guilt." . . . After I had sent Chrysis off with such promises, I took extra care of my most offensive body. I thought it best to forgo the bath, rubbed myself down with just a small amount of perfumed oil, next I dined on really healthy foods, like onions and snails' heads without sauce, and finished this off by drinking very sparingly. I then settled myself for sleep with the gentlest of walks, and without Giton I went to my room, for I was so anxious to appease her that I was afraid that my boy-partner might sap my strength. 131. Next day when I rose sound in body and mind, I went down to the same grove of plane trees, in spite of my fear that the place was unlucky, and I waited there among the trees for Chrysis to lead the way. After I had walked about for just a short time and sat down in the same place I had been yesterday, Chrysis came on the scene, dragging an old woman with her. When she had greeted me she said: "How's it going, you haughty lover? Have you begun to come to your senses?"

In the meantime the old woman took from her pocket a twisted ball of various colored threads, and tied it round my neck. Next she mixed some dust with her own saliva, took it up with her middle finger, and ignoring my attempt to ward her off, marked my forehead with it. Once her chant was finished, she ordered me to spit three times and then toss some pebbles into my underwear three times, after she had uttered a spell over them and had wrapped

cantatos purpura involverat, admotisque manibus temp-
6 tare coepit inguinum vires. | dicto citius nervi paruerunt
7 imperio manusque aniculae ingenti motu repleverunt. | at
illa gaudio exultans "vides" inquit "Chrysis mea? vides,
quod aliis leporem excitavi?"[716] |

⟨ * * * ⟩

8   *OL*mobilis[717] aestivas platanus diffuderat umbras
        et bacis redimita Daphne tremulaeque cupressus
        et circum tonsae trepidanti vertice pinus.
        has inter ludebat aquis errantibus amnis
    5   spumeus et querulo vexabat rore lapillos.
        dignus amore locus: testis silvestris aedon[718]
        atque urbana Procne, quae circum gramina fusae
        et molles violas cantu sua rura colebant. |

9   premebat illa resoluta marmoreis cervicibus aureum
torum myrtoque florenti quietum ⟨aera⟩[719] verberabat. |
10 itaque ut me vidit, paululum erubuit, hesternae scilicet
iniuriae memor; deinde ut remotis omnibus secundum
invitantem consedi, ramum super oculos meos posuit, et
11 quasi pariete interiecto audacior facta | "quid est" inquit
"paralytice? ecquid hodie totus venisti?" "rogas" inquam
ego "potius quam temptas?" totoque corpore in amplexum
eius immissus non praecantatis[720] usque ad satietatem
osculis fruor.

⟨ * * * ⟩

[716] aliis leporem excitavi, *cf. Ovid AA 3.662*
[717] mobilis *P*: nobilis
[718] silvestris aedon *c*: silvesterisdon *B*: *others*
[719] *added Ernout*
[720] praecantatis *B*: precantis

them in purple material. She then placed her hands on my member and began to test its powers. Before anyone could utter a word, the muscle tissue in my penis responded to her command, and with a mighty throbbing filled the old woman's hands. She was overjoyed and said: "My dear Chrysis, do you see the hare that I've started for others to enjoy?" . . . "The waving plane tree spread its summer shade: Daphne the laurel wreathed with berries, the cypresses quivering, and on all sides the swaying tops of shorn pines. Among all these a foaming creek played with straying waters and shook pebbles loose with its plaintive flow. The place was best fit for love. The woodland nightingale Philomela was a witness, and the urban swallow Procne, both hovered over the grass and the tender violets, and extolled their rural haunts in song."

Circe lay resting, relaxed with her marble-white neck on a golden couch, and she fanned the still air with a spray of flowering myrtle. So when she saw me, the memory of the previous day's affront clearly caused her to blush a little. When all the escorts had been dismissed, I sat next to her at her invitation. She placed the flowering myrtle over my eyes, and considering this a kind of wall between us, she grew bolder and said: "How is everything, my paralytic? Have you come here today a complete man in every way?" I replied: "You ask me, rather than feeling for yourself." I threw my whole body into her arms, and enjoyed her kisses until I could kiss no more, there being no need of magic spells. . . .

*L*132. {Encolpius de Endymione puero}[721] ipsa corporis
pulchritudine me ad se vocante trahebat ad venerem. iam
pluribus osculis collisa labra crepitabant, iam implicitae
manus omne genus amoris invenerant, iam alligata mutuo
ambitu corpora animarum quoque mixturam fecerant. |

⟨ * * * ⟩

2   manifestis matrona contumeliis verberata tandem ad ul-
tionem decurrit vocatque cubicularios et me iubet catomi-
3   zari.[722] | nec contenta mulier tam gravi iniuria mea convo-
cat omnes quasillarias familiaeque sordidissimam partem
4   ac me conspui iubet. | oppono ego manus oculis meis,
nullisque precibus effusis, quia sciebam quid meruissem,
5   verberibus sputisque extra ianuam eiectus sum. | eicitur
et Proselenos, Chrysis vapulat, totaque familia tristis inter
se mussat quaeritque quis dominae hilaritatem confude-
6   rit. ⟨. . .⟩ | itaque pensatis vicibus animosior verberum
notas arte contexi, ne aut Eumolpus contumelia mea hila-
7   rior fieret aut tristior Giton. | *OL*quod solum igitur salvo
pudore poteram, contingere languorem simulavi, condi-
tusque lectulo totum ignem furoris in eam converti, quae
mihi omnium malorum causa fuerat: |

8   ter corripui terribilem manu bipennem,
        ter languidior coliculi repente thyrso
        ferrum tremuit,[723] quod trepido male dabat usum.
        nec iam poteram, quod modo conficere libebat;
   5   namque illa metu frigidior rigente bruma
        confugerat in viscera mille operta rugis.
        ita non potui supplicio caput aperire,

---

[721] *See n. 527.*   [722] catomizari *Salmasius*: catorogare
[723] tremuit *l*ᵐᵍ: timui

132. The physical beauty of her body called out to me, and she drew me down to make love to her. Now from our lips came a gentle smacking sound, as we kissed again and again; now our intertwined hands had explored the great diversity in love; now our bodies wrapped in mutual embrace created also a union of souls. . . . The lady was stung by the conspicuous insults arising from my impotence, and then resorted to revenge: she called her personal attendants and ordered me to be hoisted and flogged. Not satisfied with such a severe punishment of me, she called up all her seamstresses and the lowest class of her slaves, and ordered them to spit on me. I put my hands to my eyes for cover, never appealing with prayers for pardon, because I knew I deserved it all, then I was whipped, spat upon, and thrown out of her presence. Proselenus was also thrown out, Chrysis was flogged, and the whole household gloomily muttered among themselves, asking who had upset their mistress' high spirits. . . . And so after weighing my options I became more constructive, and carefully hid the marks left by the whipping, so that Eumolpus would not be amused by my ill-treatment nor Giton depressed. The only thing I could do to hide my shame was to claim fatigue, and so having buried myself in bed, I turned all the fire of my anger on the cause of all of my troubles: "Three times my hand seized the dreaded two-edged knife, three times my member suddenly became softer than a cabbage stalk out of fear for the steel, which was of no use for a trembling hand. So what I would just now have liked to do, I could not do. For my penis, colder from fear than the stiff ice of winter, had fled into my groin and was hidden in a thousand wrinkles. I was unable to expose its head for

379

sed furciferae mortifero timore lusus
ad verba, magis quae poterant nocere, fugi. |

9   erectus igitur in cubitum hac fere oratione contuma-
cem vexavi: "quid dicis" inquam "omnium hominum deorumque pudor? nam ne nominare quidem te inter res
10 serias fas est. | hoc de te merui, ut me in caelo positum ad
inferos traheres? ^Lut traduceres annos primo florentes
vigore senectaeque ultimae mihi lassitudinem imponeres?
rogo te, mihi apodixin ‹non›⁷²⁴ defunctoriam redde." |
11 haec ut iratus effudi,

> ^{OL}illa solo fixos oculos aversa tenebat,
> nec magis incepto vultum sermone movetur
> quam lentae salices lassove papavera collo. |

12 nec minus ego tam foeda obiurgatione finita paenitentiam
agere sermonis mei coepi secretoque rubore perfundi,
quod oblitus verecundiae meae cum ea parte corporis
verba contulerim, quam ne ad cognitionem quidem ad-
13 mittere severioris notae homines solerent. | mox perfricata
diutius fronte "quid autem ego" inquam "mali feci, si dolorem meum naturali convicio exoneravi? aut quid est
quod in corpore humano ventri male dicere solemus aut
gulae capitique etiam, cum saepius dolet? quid? non et

---

⁷²⁴ *added Müller*

---

¹⁷¹ The first two lines are exact quotations from Virgil (*Aen.*
6.469–70), and the third adapts two Virgilian half-lines (*Ecl.* 5.16,
Aen. 9.436). Though this is a pastiche of Virgil, Encolpius tries to
elevate the tone of his tirade by comparing his drooping penis

decapitation, but frustrated by the mortal fear shown by this rogue member, I fled for refuge to words, which could hurt it more seriously."

So I raised myself on my elbow and reproached my impotent member with words something like these: "What do you have to say for yourself, you embarrassment to men and gods? For it is improper even to mention your name in a serious conversation. Did I deserve this from you, that when you had placed me in heaven, you should then drag me down to hell? That you should make an exhibition of my prime years of vigor and then saddle me with the weakness of extreme old age? I ask you now, give me serious proof of your power." As I poured out these words in anger, "She turned away and kept her eyes fixed on the ground, her face was not more moved by these opening words than pliant willows or poppies with their drooping necks."[171] After I had finished this disgraceful reproach, I began to feel regret at what I had said, and a secret blush came all over me, because I had forgotten my modesty and actually argued with that part of my body which more dignified men are accustomed not even to acknowledge. Then after scratching my forehead for some time, I said: "But what harm have I done in relieving my indignation with some abuse? And then, what about the fact that we regularly curse parts of our human anatomy, like our belly, or throat, and even our head, when at times it aches? And

with the downcast eyes of Dido in the underworld. Had Encolpius continued with the the third line in Virgil's description of the Carthaginian queen (*Aen.* 6.471), he would have likened his limp member to flint and marble, an unfortunate comparison.

Ulixes cum corde litigat suo, ^Let quidam tragici oculos suos
14 tamquam audientes castigant? | podagrici pedibus suis
male dicunt, chiragrici manibus, lippi oculis, et qui offen-
derunt saepe digitos, quicquid doloris habent in pedes
deferunt: |

15   ^{OL}quid me constricta spectatis fronte Catones
                damnatisque novae simplicitatis opus?
            sermonis puri non tristis gratia ridet,
                quodque facit populus, candida lingua refert.
      5   nam quis concubitus, Veneris quis gaudia nescit?
                quis vetat[725] in tepido membra calere toro?
            ipse pater veri doctos[726] Epicurus amare[727]
                iussit et hoc vitam dixit habere τέλος." |

                    ⟨ * * * ⟩

16 ^L"nihil est hominum inepta persuasione falsius nec ficta
severitate ineptius."

                    ⟨ * * * ⟩

      ^{OL}133. hac declamatione finita Gitona voco et "narra
mihi" inquam "frater, sed tua fide: ea nocte, qua te mihi
Ascyltos subduxit, usque in iniuriam vigilavit an contentus
2   fuit vidua pudicaque nocte?" | tetigit puer oculos suos
conceptissimisque iuravit verbis sibi ab Ascylto nullam
vim factam.

                    ⟨ * * * ⟩

positoque in limine genu sic deprecatus sum numen aver-
sum:[728] |

3   "Nympharum Bacchique comes, quem pulchra
                Dione

      [725] vetat *Dousa*: petat

what about Ulysses?[172] Did he not argue with his own heart, and were there not some tragic figures who cursed their eyes, as if they could hear? Men suffering from gout damn their feet, those with arthritis their hands, those half-blind their eyes, and those who regularly stub their toes blame all pains on their feet. Why do you followers of Cato look at me with wrinkled foreheads and condemn my verbal tirade with its new-style candor? A lighthearted charm smiles through refined language, and my faithful depiction recounts what men actually do. Who is ignorant of mating rituals or the pleasures of love? Who opposes two bodies in hot passion warming a bed? Epicurus himself, the father of truth, advised wise men to love, and said that love is life's true goal." . . . "There is nothing more misleading than silly prejudice of men, or more silly than hypocritical moralizing." . . .

133. With my declamation finished, I called to Giton and said: "Tell me, my boy-partner, but speak on your honor. That night when Ascyltos took you away from me, did he keep awake until he raped you, or was he satisfied with a lonely and chaste night?" The boy touched his eyes and swore in the most solemn words that Ascyltos had used no force on him. . . . I knelt down on the threshold and in these words entreated the hostile deity: "Comrade[173] of the Nymphs and Bacchus, whom beautiful

172 Hom. *Od.* 20.18.   173 Priapus.

---

726 doctos *Canterus*: doctus

727 amare *Canterus*: in arte *or* in arce

728 numen aversum *anonymous in Burman*: numina versu

divitibus silvis numen dedit, inclita paret
cui Lesbos viridisque Thasos, quem Lydus adorat
vestifluus[729] templumque tuis imponit Hypaepis:
5   huc ades, o[730] Bacchi tutor Dryadumque voluptas,
et timidas admitte preces. non sanguine tristi
perfusus venio, non templis impius hostis
admovi dextram, sed inops et rebus egenis
attritus facinus non toto corpore feci.
10   *OφL*quisquis peccat inops, minor est reus. *OL*hac
     prece quaeso,
exonera mentem culpaeque ignosce minori,
et quandoque mihi fortunae arriserit hora,
non sine honore tuum patiar decus. ibit ad aras,
*Bp*sancte, tuas hircus, pecoris pater, ibit ad aras
15   *OL*corniger et querulae fetus[731] suis, hostia lactens.
spumabit pateris hornus liquor, et ter ovantem
circa delubrum gressum feret ebria pubes." |

⟨ * * * ⟩

4   dum haec ago curaque sollerti deposito meo caveo, intravit delubrum anus lacertis crinibus nigraque veste deformis, extraque vestibulum me iniecta manu duxit.

⟨ * * * ⟩

*L*134. {Proselenos anus ad Encolpium}[732] "quae striges
comederunt nervos tuos, aut quod purgamentum {in}[733]
2   nocte calcasti in trivio aut cadaver? | ne[734] a puero quidem
te vindicasti, sed mollis, debilis, lassus tamquam caballus

---

729 vestifluus *Turnebus*: septifluus *or* semper flavius
730 o *c*: et   731 fetus *Junius, s, l*mg: festus
732 *See n. 527.*   733 *deleted Gold*ast
734 ne *Bücheler*: nec

384

Dione[174] assigned as god over the rich forests, whom famous Lesbos and green Thasos obey, whom the loose-
robed Lydian worships and built a temple in your own city
of Hypaepa:[175] come here, o guardian of Bacchus and the
delight of the Dryads, hearken to my humble prayers. I
am not stained with dark blood as I come to you, I am not
a wicked enemy who has profaned temples, but when I
was poor, destitute, and worn out, I did commit a crime,
not, however, with my whole body. (10) He bears less guilt,
who in poverty transgresses. This is my prayer: relieve my
mind and pardon the lesser offense, and whenever in due
season Fortune smiles on me, I will not allow your glory
to remain without honor. Holy one, a horned goat and the
father of the flock will go to your altars, and the young of
a grunting sow, a suckling sacrifice. The new wine of the
year will foam in the bowls, and the young men drunk on
wine will circle three times round your shrine in joyous
steps." . . . As I was reciting these lines and watching
carefully over my offering, the old woman[176] entered the
shrine; she was ugly, with disheveled hair and wearing
black clothes; she laid hands on me and led me out of the
porch. . . .

134. "Were they witches who ate away your potency, or
is it that you stepped in some shit or on a corpse at the
crossroads in the dark? You've not avenged yourself even
with the boy, but you're effeminate, feeble, tired like a nag

174 Venus.
175 A small town in Lydia at the base of Mount Tmolus.
176 Probably Proselenus.

in clivo, et operam et sudorem perdidisti. nec contentus
ipse peccare, mihi deos iratos excitasti."[735] |

⟨ * * * ⟩

3   ^{OL}ac me iterum in cellam sacerdotis nihil recusantem perduxit impulitque super lectum et harundinem ab ostio
4   rapuit nihilque respondentem mulcavit. | ac nisi primo
ictu harundo quassata impetum verberantis minuisset,
5   forsitan etiam bracchia mea caputque fregisset. | ingemui
ego utique propter mascarpionem, lacrimisque ubertim
manantibus obscuratum dextra caput super pulvinum in-
6   clinavi. | nec minus illa fletu confusa altera parte lectuli
sedit aetatisque longae moram tremulis vocibus coepit
7   accusare, donec intervenit sacerdos. ⟨. . .⟩ | "quid? vos"
inquit "in cellam meam tamquam ante recens bustum
venistis? ^{Op}utique die feriarum, quo etiam lugentes
8   rident." ⟨. . .⟩ | ^{L}{Proselenos ad Oenotheam sacerdotem
Priapi de Encolpio}[736] ^{OL}"o" inquit "Oenothea, hunc adu-
lescentem quem vides, malo astro natus est; nam neque
9   puero neque puellae bona sua vendere potest. | ^{L}num-
quam tu hominem tam infelicem vidisti: lorum in aqua,
10   non inguina habet. | ^{OL}ad summam, qualem putas esse qui
de Circes toro sine voluptate surrexit?" ^{L}his auditis Oenothea inter utrumque consedit motoque diutius capite
"istum" inquit "morbum sola sum quae emendare scio. |
11   et ne putetis perplexe agere, rogo ut adulescentulus mecum nocte dormiat. ⟨. . .⟩ nisi illud tam rigidum reddidero
quam cornu: |

12   ^{OL}quicquid in orbe vides, paret mihi. florida tellus,
cum volo, siccatis arescit languida sucis,

---

[735] excitasti *Wouweren*: extricasti   [736] *See n.* 527.

on a hill, and you wasted all your efforts and sweat. Not satisfied with your own transgression, you had to go and stir up the gods' anger against me." . . . And again she led me completely unresisting into the room of the priestess, pushed me onto the bed, grabbed a cane from the door, and beat me; again I did not resist. And if the cane had not shattered at the first stroke and lessened the force of her blow, it is possible that she might have broken even my arms and head. Because of the flogging I groaned a good deal, and weeping tears by the bucket I covered my head with my right arm, and bent over the pillow. She was similarly upset, covered with tears, and sat down on another part of the bed. With a quivering voice she began to curse her old age for dragging out her life so long, when the arrival of the priestess disrupted her. . . . "What's all this?" she said, "and why have you come into my room as if you're mourners at the grave of someone who just died? And especially on a holiday when even mourners are allowed to smile." . . . "Ah, Oenothea," she said, "this youth you see before you was born under an malevolent star, since he cannot sell his goods to boys or girls. You've never seen such an unlucky creature: he's got a piece of wet leather, his thing is impotent. To tell you how bad it is, what sort of man do you think could get out of bed with Circe and not have had sex?" After hearing this, Oenothea sat down between us, shook her head for some time, and said: "I'm the only woman who knows how to cure this disease. Don't think that I'll do anything elaborate; I want the young man to sleep the night with me. . . . ‹May I suffer the gods' anger,› if I don't turn that thing into an erection as stiff as a horn: Everything you see in the world obeys me. When I will it, the flowering earth grows barren, the juices of the

387

cum volo, fundit opes, scopulique atque horrida
  saxa
Niliacas iaculantur aquas. mihi pontus inertes
5 submittit fluctus, zephyrique tacentia ponunt
ante meos sua flabra pedes. mihi flumina parent
Hyrcanaeque tigres et iussi stare dracones.
quid leviora loquor? lunae descendit imago
carminibus deducta meis, trepidusque furentes
10 flectere Phoebus equos revoluto cogitur orbe.
tantum dicta valent. taurorum flamma quiescit
virgineis extincta sacris, Phoebeia Circe
carminibus magicis socios mutavit Ulixis,
Proteus esse solet quicquid libet. his ego callens
15 artibus Idaeos frutices in gurgite sistam
et rursus fluvios in summo vertice ponam."

135. inhorrui ego tam fabulosa pollicitatione conterri-
2 tus, anumque inspicere diligentius coepi. ⟨. . .⟩ | "ergo"
exclamat Oenothea "imperio parete." ⟨. . .⟩ detersisque
curiose manibus inclinavit se in lectulum ac me semel ite-
3 rumque basiavit. ⟨. . .⟩ | ^{L}Oenothea mensam veterem
posuit in medio altari⟨aque⟩ {quam}[737] vivis implevit car-
bonibus, et camellam etiam vetustate ruptam pice tempe-
4 rata refecit. | tum clavum, qui detrahentem secutus cum
camella lignea fuerat, fumoso parieti reddidit. ^{OL}mox in-
cincta quadrato pallio cucumam ingentem foco apposuit,
simulque pannum[738] de carnario detulit furca, in quo faba
erat ad usum reposita ^{L}et sincipitis vetustissima particula

[737] *added and deleted* Stöcker
[738] panarium l^{mg}

plants dry up; when I will it, the earth pours out it riches, while crags and rough rocks spurt waters like the Nile. For me the sea makes its waves stand calm, and at my feet the winds lay their blasts in silence. Rivers obey me, and Hyrcanian[177] tigers and snakes, so ordered by me, stand quiet. But why speak of trivial things? The orb of the moon, drawn down by my spells, descends toward earth, and Phoebus in fear (10) is forced to turn round his fiery steeds and reverse his course. So great is the power of words. The flaming urges of bulls are calmed and quenched by sacrificing virgins; Circe, child of Phoebus, transformed Ulysses' crew by magic spells, and Proteus assumes new shapes, as it pleases him. I am skilled in all these arts and will plant the bushes growing on Mount Ida in the sea, and will set in turn the rivers on its lofty peak."

135. I shuddered in horror at her promises, the kind that were celebrated in legend, and was terrified by their implications, and then I began to look more closely at the old woman. . . . "Now do as I tell you," shouted Oenothea. . . . She wiped her hands carefully, leaned over the bed, and kissed me several times. . . . Oenothea set up an old table in the middle of the room and filled its altar with live coals, on which she warmed up some pitch and so repaired a cup that had cracked with age. When she took down the wooden cup, the nail on which it hung had also come away, and so she replaced it in the wall blackened with grime. Then she put on a square-shaped cloak and set an enormous kettle on the hearth. At the same time she used a fork to lift from the larder a bag containing beans stored there for cooking, and then an ancient piece

---

[177] The area around the southern part of the Caspian Sea.

5 mille plagis dolata. | ᴼᴸut solvit ergo licio pannum, partem
leguminis super mensam effudit iussitque me diligenter
purgare. servio ego imperio granaque sordidissimis puta-
6 minibus vestita curiosa manu segrego. | at illa inertiam
meam accusans ipsa fabas[739] tollit, dentibusque folliculos
pariter spoliat atque in terram veluti muscarum imagines
despuit. |

⟨ * * * ⟩

7 mirabar equidem paupertatis ingenium singularumque
rerum quasdam artes: |

8   non Indum fulgebat ebur, quod inhaeserat auro,
    nec iam calcato radiabat marmore terra
    muneribus delusa suis, sed crate saligna
    impositum Cereris vacuae nemus et nova terrae
5   pocula, quae facili vilis rota finxerat actu.
    hinc mollis[740] tiliae[741] calices {et}[742] de caudice lento
    vimineae lances maculataque testa Lyaeo.
    at paries circa palea satiatus inani
    fortuitoque luto clavos[743] numerabat agrestes,
10   et viridi iunco gracilis pendebat harundo.
    praeterea quae fumoso suspensa tigillo
    conservabat opes humilis casa, mitia sorba
14   et thymbrae veteres et passis uva racemis
13   inter odoratas pendebant texta coronas[744] ⟨. . .⟩
15   qualis in Actaea quondam fuit hospita terra

[739] ipsa fabas *Bücheler*: improba
[740] mollis *s, t*: molli
[741] tiliae t^mg: sillae *or* stilla
[742] calices {et} *Harrison*[3]: latus
[743] clavos *s*: clavus
[744] *verses 13 and 14 transposed Bücheler*

of hog's cheek hacked by a thousand blows. After she loosened the string of the bag, she poured out some of the beans on the table and told me to shell them carefully. I followed her orders and with my fingers meticulously separated the kernels from the really dirty covering of shells. But she reproved me for being slow and herself snatched up the beans, and in a moment tore off the shells with her teeth and spat them out on the ground, where they lay scattered like carcasses of flies. . . . I admired the resources of poverty and certain examples of artistry displayed in individual objects: "No Indian ivory set in gold shone here, the earth did not gleam with marble beneath our feet, nor was it mocked for its own gifts, but there was a thicket bed of husked straw set on a willow frame, and new cups made of clay and fashioned by a wheel turned with easy motion, then drinking bowls of soft lime wood, wicker plates of pliant wood, wine jars stained red. The walls all about were stuffed with light straw and randomly applied mud, and sported rustic nails, (10) from which hung a slim broom tied together with green rushes. Besides this, the lowly cottage kept a wealth of goods suspended from smoke-darkened beams: ripe service berries, dried Cretan thyme, and bunches of raisins, all hung woven into fragrant wreaths . . . Such was the hostess Hecale[178] who once upon a time lived on Attic soil and was

[178] She was a poor woman who warmly welcomed Theseus. Callimachus, who wrote about Hecale, came from Cyrene, a city said to have been founded by Battus.

391

digna sacris Hecale,[745] quam Musa loquentibus
　　annis
Battiadae veteris[746] mirando tradidit ore.[747]

　　　　⟨ * * * ⟩

136. dum illa carnis etiam paululum delibat et dum
coaequale natalium suorum sinciput in carnarium furca
reponit, fracta est putris sella, quae staturae altitudinem
adiecerat, anumque pondere suo deiectam super foculum
2　mittit. | frangitur ergo cervix cucumulae ignemque modo
convalescentem restinguit. [L]vexat cubitum ipsa stipite
ardenti [OL]faciemque totam excitato cinere perfundit.[748] |
3　consurrexi equidem turbatus anumque non sine risu erexi.
[L]statimque, ne res aliqua sacrificium moraretur, ad refi-
4　ciendum ignem in viciniam[749] cucurrit.[750] | [OL]itaque ad
casae ostiolum processi, cum ecce tres anseres sacri[751]
[L]qui, ut puto, medio die solebant ab anu diaria exigere,
[OL]impetum in me faciunt foedoque ac veluti rabioso stridore circumsistunt trepidantem. atque alius tunicam
meam lacerat, alius vincula calceamentorum resolvit ac
trahit; unus etiam, dux ac magister saevitiae, non dubitavit
5　crus meum serrato vexare morsu. | oblitus itaque nugarum
pedem mensulae extorsi coepique pugnacissimum animal
armata elidere manu. nec satiatus defunctorio ictu, morte
me anseris vindicavi: |

6　　　tales Herculea Stymphalidas arte coactas

745 Hecale *Pius*², *s*, *ct*: Hecates
746 Battidae veteris *Pius*², *s*, *ct*: Bacchineas veteres
747 ore *Courtney*¹: aevo　　　　748 perfundit *l*ᵃᶜ: perfudit
749 viciniam *l*ᵐᵍ: vicinia　　　750 cucurrit *Schoppius*: cucurri
751 sacri *deleted Müller*

392

worthy of annual rites. The Muse of the old poet who lived in Battus' town in the years of eloquence described her with admiring voice."

136. While she was still tasting a small bit of the meat, and at the same time replacing in the larder the hog's cheek, which was as old as she was, the rotten chair on which she stood to increase her height broke apart, and sent her on to the hearth, hurled there by her own weight. In all this commotion the neck of the pot broke and extinguished the fire, which had just now got a good start. Her elbow was injured by a burning brand, and her whole face was covered with the ash sent flying as she fell. In some alarm I got to my feet and chuckling to myself raised the woman upright. She immediately ran off to the neighbors to have them rekindle the fire, so that there would be no delay in beginning the ceremony. So I made my way to the small door of the cottage, when all of a sudden three sacred geese attacked me. I suppose they were accustomed at midday to demand their daily food portion from the old woman. I was trembling while they emitted a hideous and also furious hissing and surrounded me. One of them tore my tunic, the second pulled the laces of my sandals loose and dragged them away, while the third, the leader and master of the savagery, did not hesitate to attack my leg with its jagged bill. And so, no longer taking the situation as a joke, I wrenched a leg off the little table and began to hammer at the aggressive animal with the weapon in my hand. Not content with a superficial blow, I took my revenge by beating the goose to death: "In just the same way, I suppose, the Stymphalian birds fled into the sky, when

ad caelum fugisse reor pavideque[752] ruentes[753]
Harpyias, cum Phineo maduere veneno
fallaces epulae. tremuit perterritus aether
5 planctibus insolitis, confusaque regia caeli. |

⟨ * * * ⟩

7 [L]iam reliqui evolutam[754] passimque per totum effusam
pavimentum collegerant fabam, orbatique, ut existimo,
duce redierant in templum, cum ego praeda simul {at-
que}[755] ac vindicta gaudens post lectum occisum anserem
8 mitto vulnusque cruris haud altum aceto diluo. | deinde
convicium verens abeundi formavi consilium, collectoque
9 cultu meo ire extra casam coepi. | necdum liberaveram[756]
cellulae limen, cum animadverto Oenotheam cum testo
10 ignis pleno venientem. | reduxi igitur gradum proiectaque
veste, tamquam expectarem morantem, in aditu steti. |
11 collocavit illa ignem quassis[757] harundinibus collectum,
ingestisque super pluribus lignis excusare coepit moram,
quod amica se non dimisisset nisi tribus[758] potionibus e
lege siccatis. "quid porro tu" inquit "me absente fecisti, aut
12 ubi est faba?" | ego qui putaveram me rem laude etiam
dignam fecisse, ordine illi totum proelium exposui, et ne
diutius tristis esset, iacturae pensionem anserem obtuli. |

752 pavideque *Harrison*[3]: penesque
753 ruentes *Harrison*[3]: fluentes
754 evolutam *Müller*: revolutam
755 *deleted Thielmann*
756 liberaveram *l*: libaveram
757 quassis *l*: cassis
758 nisi tribus *Bücheler*: tribus nisi

they were compelled to do so by the skill of Hercules,[179] and just so in panic the Harpies hurried away, once the deceptive feast had been drenched in the poison meant for Phineus.[180] The upper air trembled and shook with unaccustomed lamentations, and the palace of heaven was thrown into disorder." . . . The two remaining geese had by now gathered up the beans that were spilled and scattered all over the floor, and I think that because they were bereft of their leader, they returned to the shrine. I was pleased both with my booty and with the revenge I had taken, and I threw the dead goose behind the bed and bathed the superficial wound in my leg with vinegar. Since I was afraid of being reprimanded, I made plans to withdraw, and so I gathered up all my belongings and started to leave the house. I had not yet crossed the threshold of the little room, when I saw Oenothea approaching with a pot full of live coals. So I retraced my steps, threw my cloak down, and stood at the entrance as though I were just waiting for her belated return. She arranged the coals in a pile, added some broken reeds, heaped up more sticks for fuel, and then began to apologize for returning late, saying that her woman friend would not let her go, until the customary three glasses of wine had been drained. "What in turn did you do while I was away?" she asked, "and where're the beans?" I thought I had done something praiseworthy, so I described to her the entire battle just as it happened. And so that she would not continue to be depressed, I produced the goose as compensation for the

[179] The birds were exterminated by Hercules as one of his twelve labors.   [180] Phineus was harassed by the Harpies, who befouled his food.

13 quem ^{OL}anus ut vidit, tam magnum acremque[759] clamo-
rem sustulit, ut putares iterum anseres limen intrasse. |

14 confusus itaque et novitate facinoris attonitus quaerebam
quid excanduisset aut quare anseris potius quam mei mi-
sereretur. 137. at illa complosis manibus "scelerate" inquit

2 "etiam[760] loqueris? | nescis quam magnum flagitium admi-
seris? occidisti Priapi delicias, anserem omnibus matronis
acceptissimum. itaque ne te putes nihil egisse, si ma-

3 gistratus hoc scierint, ibis in crucem. | polluisti sanguine
domicilium meum ante hunc diem inviolatum, fecistique
ut me quisquis voluerit inimicus sacerdotio pellat." |

⟨ * * * ⟩

4 ^L"rogo" inquam "noli clamare: ego tibi pro ansere strutho-
camelum reddam." |

⟨ * * * ⟩

5 dum haec me stupente in lectulo sedet anserisque fatum
complorat, interim Proselenus cum impensa sacrificii venit, visoque ansere occiso sciscitata causam tristitiae et
ipsa flere vehementius coepit meique misereri tamquam

6 patrem meum, non publicum anserem, occidissem. | ita-
que taedio fatigatus "rogo" inquam "expiare manus pretio
liceat.[761] ⟨. . .⟩ si vos provocassem, etiam si homicidium
fecissem. ecce duos aureos pono, unde possitis et deos et

7 anseres emere." | quos ut vidit Oenothea, "ignosce" inquit

8 "adulescens, sollicita sum tua causa. | amoris est hoc argu-

759 acremque *Cornelissen*: aeque
760 etiam *Dousa*: et
761 liceat *Dousa*: licet

loss of the beans. When the old woman saw it, she raised such a violent and great uproar you would have thought the geese had entered the room again. I was dismayed and astonished that my actions were characterized as a new kind of crime, and asked her why she had flared up and why she was more sorry for the goose than for me. 137. She clapped her hands and said: "You villain, do you have the impudence even to ask? Don't you realize what a terrible offense you've committed? You've killed the favorite of Priapus, the goose which is the most acceptable and pleasing to married women. Don't imagine that your deed was a mere nothing: if the magistrates should learn of this, you'll go to the cross. Until today my little house had never been polluted, but now you've defiled it with blood, and the result of what you've done is to give any enemy of mine who wants it the power to expel me from my priesthood." . . . "Please do not make such a commotion," I said: "I will give you an ostrich to replace the goose." . . . While I stood there amazed at these things, she sat on the bed and wept over the death of the goose. Proselenus in the meantime came in with the purchases for the sacrifice, and when she saw that the goose had been killed, asked the reason for all the grief. Then she also began to weep even more loudly and said that she was very sorry for me, as if I had killed my own father and not a municipal goose. I grew disgusted and tired and said: "Please let me cleanse my hands by paying for the bird. . . . It would be another thing if I had insulted you, or even if I had murdered someone. Look, I am laying down two *aurei* here, with which you can buy both gods and geese." After Oenothea saw the gold coins, she said: "Now, young man, please forgive me. I've been upset on your behalf,

mentum, non malignitatis. itaque dabimus operam ne quis
hoc sciat. tu modo deos roga ut illi facto tuo ignoscant." |

9   ^{OφL}quisquis habet nummos, secura navigat[762] aura
       fortunamque suo temperat[763] arbitrio.
       uxorem ducat Danaen ipsumque licebit
       Acrisium iubeat credere quod Danae.[764]
  5   carmina componat, declamet, concrepet omnes
       et peragat causas sitque Catone prior.
       iurisconsultus "parret, non parret"[765] habeto
       atque esto quicquid Servius et Labeo.
       multa loquor: quod vis nummis praesentibus opta,
 10   et veniet. clausum possidet arca Iovem.[766] |

            ⟨ * * * ⟩

10 ^Linfra manus meas camellam vini posuit, et cum digitos
pariter extensos porris apioque lustrasset, avellanas nuces
cum precatione mersit in vinum. et sive in summum redierant sive subsederant, ex hoc coniecturam ducebat.[767]
nec me fallebat inanes scilicet ac sine medulla ventosas
nuces in summo umore consistere, graves autem et plenas
integro fructu ad ima deferri. |

            ⟨ * * * ⟩

11 recluso pectore extraxit fartissimum[768] iecur et inde mihi
12 futura praedixit. | immo, ne quod vestigium sceleris super-
esset, totum anserem laceratum verubus confixit epu-

---

[762] navigat *Vincentius*: naviget   [763] temperat *B*, *Vincentius*: temperet   [764] Danae *Courtney*²: Danaen
[765] parret non parret *B*: paret non paret
[766] Iovem *last word in the O*δ *family of manuscripts*
[767] hoc coniecturam ducebat *Dousa*: hac coniectura dicebat
[768] fartissimum *Heinsius*: fortissimum

and this is proof of affection and not of ill will. And so we'll do our best to ensure that no one hears about this. For your part, you must merely pray to the gods to pardon what you've done." "Whoever has money sails with a fair breeze, and governs his fortune as he wishes. Such a one can marry Danaë and persuade Acrisius to believe what he got Danaë to believe.[181] Let him write poetry, make speeches, snap his fingers at everyone, win his cases, and outdo Cato. As a jurist let him have his 'it is proven' or 'it is not proven,' and be all that Servius and Labeo[182] were. I have spoken more than enough: with ready cash just pray for what you want, and it will come. Your money box holds Jupiter locked up." . . . She placed a bowl of wine below my hands, and when she had spread my fingers out equally, she cleansed them with leeks and celery, and then dropped hazelnuts into the wine, while adding a prayer. Accordingly as the nuts returned to the surface or sank, she made deductions from this, but I did not fail to notice that the empty nuts, the ones without a kernel and filled with air, stayed on the surface, while the heavy ones, ripe and full, were carried to the bottom. . . . She opened up the breast of the goose and drew out a very fat liver, and from that foretold my future. Moreover, to make certain that no trace of my crime was left behind, she tore up the whole goose and pierced the pieces with spits. She prepared quite an elegant meal for me, though she had said just

---

[181] Jupiter changed himself into a shower of gold and impregnated Danaë, daughter of Acrisius.

[182] Two famous Roman jurists.

lasque etiam lautas paulo ante, ut ipsa dicebat, perituro
13 paravit. ‹. . .› | volabant inter haec potiones meracae.

‹ * * * ›

138. profert Oenothea scorteum fascinum, quod ut
oleo et minuto pipere atque urticae trito circumdedit
2 semine, paulatim coepit insere ano meo. ‹. . .› | hoc cru-
delissima anus spargit subinde umore femina mea.

‹ * * * ›

nasturcii sucum cum habrotono miscet perfusisque ingui-
nibus meis viridis urticae fascem comprehendit omniaque
infra umbilicum coepit lenta manu caedere. |

‹ * * * ›

3 aniculae quamvis solutae mero ac libidine essent, eandem
viam temptant et per aliquot vicos secutae fugientem
4 "prende furem" clamant. | evasi tamen omnibus digitis
inter praecipitem decursum cruentatis. |

‹ * * * ›

5 "Chrysis, quae priorem fortunam tuam oderat, hanc vel
cum periculo capitis persequi destinat." |

‹ * * * ›

6 "quid huic formae aut Ariadne habuit aut Leda simile?
quid contra hanc Helene, quid Venus posset? ipse Paris,
dearum litigantium[769] iudex, si hanc in comparatione vidisset tam petulantibus oculis, et Helenen huic donasset
7 et deas. | saltem si permitteretur osculum capere, si illud
caeleste ac divinum pectus amplecti, forsitan rediret hoc
corpus ad vires et revivscerent[770] partes veneficio, credo,

---

[769] litigantium *Dousa*: libidinantium
[770] revivscerent *anonymous in Burman*: resipiscerent

---

[183] Ariadne rescued Theseus from the labyrinth; see Bodel[3].

moments before that I was at death's door. . . . Along with the courses of the meal, cups of neat wine made the rounds rapidly. . . .

138. Oenothea brought out a leather dildo, covered it with oil, ground pepper, and crushed nettle seeds, and proceeded by degrees to insert it up my rectum. . . . the vicious old woman immediately afterward sprinkled my thighs with this liquid. . . . She mixed nasturtium juice with southernwood and soaked my private parts with it. Then she took a bunch of green nettles and began to whip gently all the area below my navel. . . . Although the poor old creatures were besotted with wine and sexual desires, they made an attempt at the same route, pursued me as I fled through several streets, and shouted: "Grab the thief." But I escaped, though all my toes were bleeding from my headlong flight. . . . "Chrysis detested your earlier career, but intends to follow you in your new occupation even at the peril of her life." . . . "What had the beauty of Ariadne[183] and Leda[184] in common with hers? How could Helen or Venus stand before her? If Paris[185] himself, who played the role of judge among the competing goddesses, had once cast his wanton glances at her and compared her with them, he would have sacrificed both Helen and the goddesses to her. If only I were allowed to seize a kiss and embrace this heavenly and divine breast, perhaps my body would regain its strength, and those parts of me drugged, I believe, with poison, would come back to life. All the insults she piled on me have not discouraged me: the fact

[184] Leda was the mother of Helen by Zeus.
[185] Paris was the judge in a beauty contest between Hera, Aphrodite, and Athena, and he awarded first prize to Aphrodite.

8   sopitae. | nec me contumeliae lassant: quod verberatus
     sum, nescio; quod eiectus sum, lusum puto. modo redire
     in gratiam liceat."

                        ⟨ * * * ⟩

     139. torum frequenti tractatione vexavi, amoris mei
     quasi quandam imaginem |

                        ⟨ * * * ⟩

2   "non solum me numen et implacabile fatum
         persequitur. prius Inachia Tirynthius ora
         exagitatus onus caeli tulit, ante profanus[771]
     5   Laomedon gemini satiavit numinis iram,[772]
     4   Iunonem Pelias sensit, tulit inscius arma
         Telephus et regnum Neptuni pavit[773] Ulixes.
         me quoque per terras, per cani Nereos aequor
         Hellespontiaci sequitur gravis ira Priapi." |

                        ⟨ * * * ⟩

3   quaerere a Gitone meo coepi num aliquis me quaesisset.
     "nemo" inquit "hodie. sed hesterno die mulier quaedam
     haud inculta ianuam intravit, cumque diu mecum esset
     locuta et me accersito sermone lassasset, ultimo coepit
     dicere te noxam meruisse daturumque serviles poenas, si
     laesus in querela perseverasset." |

                        ⟨ * * * ⟩

4   nondum {querelam}[774] finieram, cum Chrysis intervenit
     amplexuque effusissimo me invasit et "teneo te" inquit
     "qualem speraveram: tu desiderium meum, tu voluptas
     mea, numquam finies hunc ignem, nisi sanguine extinx-
     eris." |

                        ⟨ * * * ⟩

5   unus ex noviciis servulis subito accurrit et mihi dominum

that I was flogged, I have forgotten; that I was thrown out of her presence, I now consider as sport. My only wish is that I can return to her service." . . .

139. I tormented the bed with my constant tossing and turning, as if I sought to cuddle some sort of ghost of my loved one . . . "Divine will and inexorable Fate pursue others besides me. Before me the son of Tiryns[186] was driven from the shore of Argus and bore the weight of heaven; before me Laomedon[187] committed sacrilege and appeased the anger of the twin gods; Pelias felt the power of Juno; Telephus ignorant of his real enemy took up arms; and Ulysses was in awe of Neptune's domain. I too, over land and over the sea of hoary Nereus, am hunted down by the heavy wrath of Hellespontine Priapus." . . . I proceeded to inquire of my Giton whether anyone had asked about me. He said: "Not today, but yesterday a rather elegant woman came in the door, and when she had spoken to me for a long enough time to tire me out with searching questions, finally said that you deserved punishment and that you would suffer the tortures reserved for slaves, if the person you offended persisted in the complaint." . . . I had not yet finished, when Chrysis interrupted and hugged me most warmly, and said: "I hold you in my arms, just the kind of man I'd always hoped for: you're my desire, my pleasure, and you'll never put out this flame, unless you quench it with my blood." . . . One of the new

---

[186] Hercules.   [187] He angered Apollo and Poseidon.

---

771 profanus $l^{mg}ct^{mg}$: profanam
772 *verse 5 before 4 transposed Bücheler*
773 pavit *Dousa*, p^2: cavit   774 *deleted Fraenkel*

iratissimum esse affirmabit, quod biduo iam officio defuis-
sem. recte ergo me facturum, si excusationem aliquam
idoneam praeparassem. vix enim posse fieri, ut rabies iras-
centis sine verbere consideret.

〈 * * * 〉

140. matrona inter primas honesta, Philomela nomine, quae multas saepe hereditates officio aetatis extor-
serat, tum anus et floris extincti, filium filiamque ingerebat
orbis senibus, et per hanc successionem artem suam per-
2 severabat extendere. | ea ergo ad Eumolpum venit et com-
mendare liberos suos eius prudentiae bonitatique ‹coepit:
neque enim nosse se quemquam alium cui mallet›[775] credere spes[776] et vota sua. illum esse solum in toto orbe
terrarum, qui praeceptis etiam salubribus instruere iu-
3 venes quotidie posset. | ad summam, relinquere se pueros
in domo Eumolpi, ut illum loquentem audirent ‹. . .› quae
4 sola posset hereditas iuvenibus dari. | nec aliter fecit ac
dixerat, filiamque speciosissimam cum fratre ephebo in
cubiculo reliquit simulavitque se in templum ire ad vota
5 nuncupanda. | Eumolpus, qui tam frugi erat ut illi etiam
ego puer viderer, non distulit puellam invitare ad pyge-
6 siaca[777] sacra. | sed et podagricum se esse lumborumque
solutorum omnibus dixerat, et si non servasset integram
simulationem, periclitabatur totam paene tragoediam
7 evertere. | itaque ut constaret mendacio fides, puellam
quidem exoravit ut sederet supra commendatam bonita-

[775] *added Müller*
[776] spes *Heinsius*: se
[777] pygesiaca *l*[mg]: pigiciaca *L*: Aphrodisiaca *Bücheler*

servants suddenly rushed up and swore that my master was absolutely furious with me for having neglected my duties for the last two days; I would be well advised to come up with some believable excuse, for it did not seem at all possible that the rage of this furious man would be allayed without my being flogged. . . .

140. There was a very respectable married woman by the name of Philomela, who by exploiting the advantages of her youthful sexual allure had often managed to wring out a great many legacies. But now that the bloom was off the rose and had withered, she imposed her son and daughter on childless old men, and by this use of the next generation continued to practice her trade. Accordingly she approached Eumolpus, and began to claim that she wanted to entrust her children to his wise counsel and upright nature: she did not know anyone else to whom she preferred to entrust the hopes she placed in her children. He was the only person in the whole world who could daily instruct the young with wholesome principles. In short, she would leave her children in Eumolpus' house to attend his discourses . . . Such was the only legacy that could be given to the young. She was as good as her word, deposited in his room an exceedingly beautiful daughter with her youthful brother, and departed under the pretense of going to the temple to offer vows in public. Eumolpus, who was so chaste that even I seemed a likely boy-partner to him, did not hesitate to invite the girl to sacral sodomy. But because he had told everyone that he suffered from gout and enervated loins, he ran the risk of destroying the whole staged performance, if he did not preserve the sham in its entirety. So to support the credibility of his deception, he begged the girl sit on top of his upright nature,

tem, Coraci autem inperavit ut lectum, in quo iacebat,
subiret positisque in pavimento manibus dominum lumbis
8 suis commoveret. | ille lente[778] parebat imperio puel-
9 laque[779] artificium pari motu remunerabat. | cum ergo res
ad effectum spectaret, clara Eumolpus voce exhortabatur
Coraca ut spissaret officium. sic inter mercennarium ami-
10 camque positus senex veluti oscillatione ludebat. | hoc
semel iterumque ingenti risu, etiam suo, Eumolpus fece-
11 rat. | itaque ego quoque, ne desidia consuetudinem per-
derem, dum frater sororis suae automata per clostellum
miratur, accessi temptaturus an pateretur iniuriam. nec
se reiciebat a blanditiis doctissimus puer, sed me numen
inimicum ibi quoque invenit. |

⟨ * * * ⟩

12 "dii maiores sunt qui me restituerunt in integrum. Mercurius enim, qui animas ducere et reducere solet, suis
beneficiis reddidit mihi quod manus irata praeciderat, ut
scias me gratiosiorem esse quam Protesilaum aut quem-
13 quam alium antiquorum." | haec locutus sustuli tunicam
Eumolpoque me totum approbavi. at ille primo exhorruit,
deinde ut plurimum crederet, utraque manu deorum
beneficia tractat. |

⟨ * * * ⟩

14 "Socrates, deorum hominumque ⟨iudicio sapientissi-
mus⟩,[780] gloriari solebat, quod numquam neque in taber-

778 lente *Schoppius*: lento
779 puellaque *Cuperus*: puellaeque
780 *added Ruterius*

188 He was the first Greek to die in the Trojan War, and his
wife Laodamia persuaded Mercury to allow her husband to re-

and at the same time ordered Corax to go under the bed on which he was lying, and with his hands braced on the floor and his back against the mattress, to move his master up and down with his own loins. The slave obeyed slowly, and the girl replied to the technique with matching movements. So when the affair seemed to be approaching a climax, Eumolpus in a loud voice encouraged Corax to redouble his duties. Thus interposed between the servant and the prostituted girl the man played at a game called, as it were, Swing. Eumolpus repeated the performance several times amid great laughter including his own. I also wanted to join in the action so that I did not get out of practice, and while the girl's brother was watching her mechanical sex act through the keyhole, I approached him to see if he would accept my advances. The boy like his sister was an expert in these things, and did not scorn my caresses, but here also the hostile deity found me out. . . . "There are greater gods who have restored me to full strength. For Mercury, who is accustomed to convey souls to and from the underworld, has by his kindnesses restored to me what an angry hand had taken away. Thus you can understand that I am luckier than Protesilaus[188] or any other of the ancients." With these words I lifted up my tunic and commended my whole body to Eumolpus. At first he seemed terrified, but then to convince himself fully, he fondled in both hands the gift of the gods. . . . "Socrates, the wisest of all in the estimation of gods and men, used to boast that he had never looked inside a tav-

turn once to earth for three hours to see her. By invoking this myth for comparison does Encolpius foretell that he will be potent for only three hours?

nam conspexerat nec ullius turbae frequentioris concilio
oculos suos crediderat. adeo nihil est commodius quam
15 semper cum sapientia loqui." ⟨. . .⟩ | "omnia" inquam "ista
vera sunt; nec ulli enim celerius homines incidere debent
in malam fortunam, quam qui alienum concupiscunt.
unde plani autem, unde levatores viverent, nisi aut locellos
aut sonantes aere sacellos pro hamis in turbam mitterent?
sicut muta animalia cibo inescantur, sicut homines non
caperentur, nisi spei[781] aliquid morderent."

⟨ * * * ⟩

141. "ex Africa navis, ut promiseras, cum pecunia tua
et familia non venit. captatores iam exhausti liberalitatem
imminuerunt. itaque aut fallor aut fortuna communis coe-
pit redire ad paenitentiam suam." |

⟨ * * * ⟩

2 "omnes qui in testamento meo legata habent praeter libertos meos hac condicione percipient quae dedi, si corpus
meum in partes conciderint et astante populo comede-
rint." |

⟨ * * * ⟩

3 "apud quasdam gentes scimus adhuc legem servari, ut a
propinquis suis consumantur defuncti, adeo quidem ut
obiurgentur aegri frequenter, quod carnem suam faciant
4 peiorem. | his admoneo amicos meos ne recusent quae
iubeo, sed quibus animis devoverint spiritum meum, eis-
5 dem etiam corpus consumant." ⟨. . .⟩ | excaecabat pecu-
niae ingens fama oculos animosque miserorum. ⟨. . .⟩
Gorgias paratus erat exsequi. |

⟨ * * * ⟩

6 "de stomachi tui recusatione non habeo quod timeam.
sequetur imperium, si promiseris illi pro unius horae

ern, or trusted his eyes over any gathering of a large crowd. The lesson is that nothing is more profitable than a continuous dialogue with wisdom." . . . "All these things," I said, "are very true, and no group of men deserves to fall more quickly into trouble than the covetous. But how could hustlers and pickpockets live, if they did not throw out small boxes or little purses jingling with coins into the crowd, like fishermen baiting hooks? Just as dumb animals are enticed by bait, so too men would not be caught unless they nibbled on some hope." . . .

141. "The ship from Africa that you had promised was bringing your money and slaves has not arrived. The legacy hunters are already drained dry and have curtailed their generosity. So unless I am mistaken our usual shared luck is about to make us regret what we have been doing." . . . "All those who have legacies in my will, with the exception of my freedmen, will take possession of what I have left them only on this condition, that they cut my body in pieces and eat it in the sight of the people as witnesses." . . . "We know that in some countries a custom is still observed that the bodies of dead people are eaten by their relatives. A result of this is that sick people are often blamed for spoiling their own flesh. Because of this, I warn my friends not to refuse to follow my instructions, but to consume my body with the same enthusiasm, with which they have damned my soul." . . . The rumor of his great wealth blinded the eyes and minds of these fools. Gorgias was ready to carry out the stipulations. . . . "I have no fear that your stomach will reject me. It will obey you, if you

---

781 nisi spei *Bücheler*: nisi spe *or* spe nisi

7 fastidio multorum bonorum pensationem. | operi modo
oculos et finge te non humana viscera sed centies sester-
8 tium comesse. | accedit[782] huc quod aliqua inveniemus
blandimenta, quibus saporem mutemus. neque enim ulla
caro per se placet, sed arte quadam corrumpitur et stoma-
9 cho concilatur averso. | quod si exemplis quoque vis[783]
probari consilium, Saguntini obsessi[784] ab Hannibale hu-
10 manas edere carnes nec hereditatem expectabant. | Pete-
lini[785] idem fecerunt in ultima fame, nec quicquam aliud
in hac epulatione captabant nisi tantum ne esurirent. |
11 cum esset Numantia a Scipione capta, inventae sunt
matres quae liberorum suorum tenerent semesa in sinu
corpora."

⟨ * * * ⟩

[782] accedit *Bücheler*: accedet
[783] quoque vis *Bücheler*: vis quoque
[784] obsessi *Rittershusius*: oppressi
[785] Petelini *Puteanus*, t^{mg}: Petavi

promise it a compensation of many good things in return for the disgusting action of one hour. Just cover your eyes and imagine that you have not eaten a human corpse but ten million sesterces. Besides, we will come up with some seasoned sauces that will change the taste. For no flesh tastes good by itself, but has to be disguised artfully and made acceptable to our reluctant stomach. But if you wish my plan to be supported by historical precedents, the people of Saguntum when besieged by Hannibal ate human flesh and they were not expecting any legacy.[189] The people of Petelia[190] acted the same way in the depths of famine, and they were not hoping for any profit out of this feast but only to avoid dying by starvation. When Numanita was captured by Scipio,[191] some mothers were discovered holding the half-eaten bodies of their children to their bosoms." . . .

[189] In 219 BC.
[190] In Bruttium in southern Italy.
[191] Captured in 133.

FRAGMENTA

Numeri fragmentorum 1–25 sunt Bücheleri. omisit Müller fragmenta 17 et 18 ad Petronium falso relata. fragmenta deinceps sequentia 26–51 novis numeris signavit Müller[5-6] post Courtney[2], quos ego teneo. *Anth. Lat.* = Anthologia Latina; R. = Riese (Lipsiae, 1894–1906); SB. = Shackleton Bailey (Stuttgardiae, 1982); B. = Bücheler (Berolini, 1862); de fragmentis 19, 20, 21, 25–51 cf. Courtney[2] (46–73).

1 Serv. ad Verg. *Aen.* 3.57

auri sacra fames] sacra id est execrabilis. tractus est autem sermo ex more Gallorum. nam Massilienses quotiens pestilentia laborabant, unus se ex pauperibus offerebat alendus anno integro publicis ‹sumptibus›[1] et purioribus cibis. hic postea ornatus verbenis et vestibus sacris circumducebatur per totam civitatem cum execrationibus, ut in ipsum reciderent mala totius civitatis, et sic proiciebatur.[2] hoc autem in Petronio lectum est.

---

[1] *added Bücheler*   [2] proiciebatur *Bücheler*: praecipitabatur

FRAGMENTS

The numbering of Fragments 1–25 was made by Bücheler. Müller omitted Fragments 17 and 18, which were falsely attributed to Petronius. Müller (1995 and later) followed Courtney[2] and adopted the sequence of Fragments that I follow below. *Anth. Lat.* = *Anthologia Latina*; R. = Riese (Leipzig, 1894–1906); SB. = Shackleton Bailey (Stuttgart, 1982); B. = Bücheler (Berlin, 1862). On Fragments 19, 20, 21, 25–51, see Courtney[2] (46–73).

1 Servius, *Commentary on Virgil*

"sacred hunger for gold." "Sacred" here means "accursed." The language is taken from Gallic custom. For whenever the people of Massilia were troubled by a plague, one of the poor people would volunteer to be fed for an entire year at public expense on food of special purity. He would then be decked out in sacred boughs and robes, and led round the whole city while the inhabitants cursed him, so that the ills of the whole city might fall on him. He was then cast out. This account is read in Petronius.[1]

[1] Some scholars speculate that Encolpius served as a scapegoat in Massilia, and that the *Satyrica* began in that city.

2 Serv. ad Verg. *Aen.* 12.159

si autem a verbo non venerint, communia sunt. nam simi-
liter <et>[1] masculina et feminina in *tor* exeunt, ut hic et
haec senator, hic et haec balneator, licet Petronius usur-
paverit "balneatricem" dicens.

[1] *added Bücheler*

3 Ps.-Acro ad Hor. *Epod.* 5.48

Canidia rodens pollicem] habitum et motum[1] Canidiae
expressit furentis. Petronius ut monstraret furentem, "pollice" ait "usque ad periculum roso."

[1] motum *Bücheler*: motus

4 Sid. Apoll. *Carm.* 23

145   quid vos eloquii canam Latini,
       Arpinas, Patavine, Mantuane, . . .
155   et te Massiliensium per hortos
       sacri stipitis, Arbiter, colonum
       Hellespontiaco parem Priapo?

5a Prisc. *Inst*. 8.16 (*GL* II, p. 381), 11.29 (*GL* II, p. 567)

[inter exempla quibus deponentium verborum participia
praeteriti temporis passivam significationem habere de-
clarat] Petronius "animam nostro amplexam pectore."

2 Servius, *Commentary on Virgil*

but if they (i.e., nouns of the feminine gender ending in –*tor*) are not derived from a verb, they are common in gender, both masculine and feminine ending alike in –*tor*. For example, *senator* is both male and female senator, *balneator* is both male and female bath attendant, though Petronius employs the term *balneatrix* ("bath woman") in his writings.

3 Pseudo-Acro, *Commentary on Horace*

"Canidia biting her thumb." He has described the appearance and feelings of Canidia in a rage. Petronius in wishing to portray a person in a rage speaks of him "biting his thumb to the quick."

4 Sidonius Apollinaris

"Why should I extol you in verse as the best of Latin eloquence, sons of Arpinum, Padua, and Mantua?[1] . . . Also you, the Arbiter, amid the gardens of Massilia, describing the hallowed tree trunk, the match for Priapus of the Hellespont?

[1] The respective hometowns of Cicero, Livy, and Virgil. Petronius (Arbiter) is next mistakenly identified with Encolpius.

5a Priscian, *Institutes of Grammar*

[quoting examples by which he shows that the past participles of deponent verbs have a passive meaning] Petronius, "the soul embraced in our breast."

5b Boeth. *In. Isagog. Porphyr. comm.*[1] 2.32 (*CSEL* 48.132.2–5 Brandt)

et ego: "faciam" inquam "libentissime. sed quoniam iam matutinus, ut ait Petronius, sol tectis arrisit, surgamus, et si quid illud est, diligentiore postea consideratione tractabitur."

6 Fulg. *Myth.* 1 (pp. 12–13 Helm)

nescis . . . quantum Satyram matronae formident. licet mulierum verbialibus undis et causidici cedant nec grammatici muttiant, rhetor taceat et clamorem praeco compescat, sola est quae modum imponit furentibus, licet Petroniana subet[1] Albucia.

[1] subet *Bücheler*: subit

7 Fulg. *Myth.* 3.8 (p. 73 Helm)

[de suco myrrhae valde fervido] unde et Petronius Arbiter ad libidinis concitamentum myrrhinum se poculum bibisse refert {in libro XIIII. ubi Quartilla interposita Ascilto et Encolpio propinato iterum illa parte Ascilti tribuit ad potandum. unde ait Quartilla "quicquid satirei fuit, Encolpius ebibit?"}[1]

[1] *deleted Bursian as interpolated from 20.7*

5b Boethius, *Commentary on Porphyry*, Isagoge (Victorinus' translation)

and I said, "I shall be very glad to do it. But since the morning sun, in Petronius' words, has now smiled on the house roofs, let us rise, and if there is any other point, it will be treated later with more careful attention."

6 Fulgentius, *Mythologies*

you do not realize . . . how much married women are terrified of satire. Before the flood of women's words lawyers might retreat, schoolmasters stop mumbling, the rhetorician stand silent, and the herald suppress his cry. Satire alone can put an end to their madness, though it be Petronius' character Albucia[1] who is in heat.

[1] This character does not appear in the extant *Satyrica*.

7 Fulgentius, *Mythologies*

[commenting on the strength of myrrh extract] so Petronius too recounts that he drank a cup of myrrh to excite his sexual desire. {This is in Book 14, where Quartilla, who is standing between Ascyltos and Encolpius, gives Encolpius a second toast to drink, originally intended for Ascyltos. After which Quartilla says: "Has Encolpius drunk all the satyrion there was?"}

8 Fulg. *Cont.* 156–57 (pp. 98–99 Helm)

Tricerberi enim fabulam iam superius exposuimus in modum iurgii forensisque litigii positam. unde et Petronius in Euscion ait "Cerberus forensis erat causidicus."

9 Fulg. *Serm* 42 (p. 122 Helm)

FERCULUM dicitur missum[1] carnium. unde et Petronius Arbiter ait "postquam ferculum allatum est."

> [1] missum *Bücheler*: missus

10 Fulg. *Serm.* 46 (p. 123 Helm)

VALGIA vero sunt labellorum obtortiones in supinatione factae. sicut et Petronius ait "obtorto valgiter labello."

11 Fulg. *Serm.* 52 (p. 124 Helm)

ALUCINARE dicitur vana somniari, tractum ab alucitis, quos nos conopes dicimus. sicut Petronius Arbiter ait "nam contubernalem[1] alucitae molestabant."

> [1] contubernalem *Bücheler*: contum vernali me

12 Fulg. *Serm.* 60 (p. 126 Helm)

MANUBIES dicuntur ornamenta regum. unde et Petronius Arbiter ait "tot regum manubies penes fugitivum repertae."

8 Fulgentius, *Explanation of the Content of Virgil*

now we earlier explained about the relevancy of the fable of the three-headed Cerberus to a quarrel and litigation in court. So too Petronius remarks against Euscion,[1] "the advocate was a Cerberus in court."

[1] This character does not appear in the extant *Satyrica*.

9 Fulgentius, *Explanation of Archaic Words*

a course of meats is said to be a *ferculum*. So too Petronius says, "after the course of meats was brought in."

10 Fulgentius, *Explanation of Archaic Words*

valgia really means the twisting of lips which happens in vomiting. So also Petronius says, "with lips twisted in vomiting."

11 Fulgentius, *Explanation of Archaic Words*

alucinare means to dream about useless things, and is derived from *alucitae*, which we call *conopes* (mosquitoes). As Petronius says, "For the mosquitoes were bothering my bed companion."

12 Fulgentius, *Explanation of Archaic Words*

manubies mean the ornaments of kings. Hence Petronius Arbiter says, "So many ornaments of kings found in the possession of a runaway."

419

13 Fulg. *Serm.* 61 (p. 126 Helm)

AUMATIUM dicitur locum secretum publicum sicut in theatris aut in circo. unde et Petronius Arbiter ait "in aumatium memet ipsum conieci."

14 Isid. *Orig.* 5.26.7

dolus est mentis calliditas, ab eo quod deludat: aliud enim agit, et aliud simulat. Petronius aliter existimat dicens "quid est, iudices, dolus? nimirum ubi aliquid factum est quod legi dolet. habetis dolum, accipe nunc malum."

15 *Glossarium S. Dionysii*

petaurum genus ludi. Petronius "petauroque iubente modo superior <modo inferior>."[1] DANIEL

[1] *added Housman*

16 *Glossarium S. Dionysii*

Petronius "satis constaret eos nisi inclinatos non solere transire cryptam Neapolitanam" *ex Glossario S. Dionysii*. DANIEL

[Fragmenta 17–18 spuria sunt]

{**17** In alio glossario

supples suppumpis, hoc est supinis pedibus. Petron. Tullia, media vel regis. Petronius. PITHOEUS

13 Fulgentius, *Explanation of Archaic Words*

aumatium is the term for public latrine such as in theaters or the circus. Hence Petronius says, "I hurled myself into the latrine."

14 Isidore, *Origins*

dolus is mental cunning because it deludes: for it does one thing and pretends to do another. Petronius thinks otherwise when he says, "Gentlemen of the jury, what does *dolus* mean? Surely when something is done which ridicules the court. You have the word *dolus*, now let me tell you about *malum* (evil)."

15 *Glossary of St. Dionysius*

petaurus (springboard or seesaw) is a kind of game: Petronius, "Now lifted higher, now lower, in the control of the springboard."

16 *Glossary of St. Dionysius*

Petronius: "There was much agreement that they did not usually pass through the tunnel at Naples[1] without bending low."

[1] The *crypta Neapolitana* survive under the rocky ridge of Cape Posilippo.

Fragments 17–18 are spurious

{**17** In Another Glossary

suppes suppumpis, that is with feet bent backward. *Tullia, media vel regia*, Tullia, middle or royal.

421

18 Nicolaus Perottus, *Cornu copiae* (p. 200.26 editionis Aldinae anni MDXIII)

Cosmus etiam excellens unguentarius fuit, a quo unguenta dicta sunt Cosmiana. idem [*Iuvenalis 8.86*] "et Cosmi toto mergatur aheno." Petronius "affer nobis, inquit, alabastum Cosmiani."}

19 Terent. Maur. *Metr.* 2486–96 (*GL* VI, p. 399)

> Horatium videmus
> versus tenoris huius
> nusquam locasse iuges,
> at Arbiter disertus
2490 > libris suis frequentat.
> agnoscere haec potestis,
> cantare quae solemus:
> "Memphitides puellae
> sacris deum paratae."
2495 > "tinctus colore noctis
> manu puer loquaci"

Aelius Festus Asmonius 3.17 (*GL* VI, p. 138)

huius tenoris ac formae quosdam versus poetas lyricos carminibus suis indidisse cognovimus, ut et apud Arbitrum invenimus, cuius exemplum

> "Memphitides puellae
> sacris deum paratae."
> "tinctus colore noctis,"
> "Aegyptias choreas."

18 Nicolaus Perottus, *Cornucopiae*

Cosmos was a superb manufacturer of perfumes, and Cosmian perfumes are named after him. The same writer [Juvenal] says, "and though he be plunged in a whole jug from Cosmos." Petronius: "bring us, he said, an alabaster box of Cosmian."}

19 Terentianus Maurus, *On Meters*

We see that Horace nowhere used verses of this rhythm continuously, but the learned Petronius employs it often in his works. You can recognize them in lines we used to sing: "Maidens of Memphis,[1] fitted out for the rites of the gods." "The boy colored with the black of night while his hands express."

[1] Memphis is a city in Egypt and was the center of the worship of Isis in antiquity.

Aelius Festus Asmonius[1]

we know that the lyric poets inserted some lines with this rhythm and form in their works, as we find also in the Arbiter, for example, "Maidens of Memphis, fitted out for the rites of the gods." Again, "The boy colored with the black of night," "depicts Egyptian dances."

[1] Also known as Aelius Festus Apthonius, a form of the name now believed to be a corruption.

20 Terent. Maur. *Metr*. 2849–65 (*GL* VI, p. 409)

	nunc divisio, quam loquemur, edet
2850	metrum, quo memorant Anacreonta
	dulces composuisse cantilenas.
	hoc Petronius invenitur usus,
	Musis cum lyricum refert eundem
	consonantia verba cantitasse,
2855	et plures alii. sed iste versus
	quali compositus tome sit edam.
	"iuverunt segetes meum laborem."
2858	"iuverunt" caput est id hexametri . . .
2861	quod restat "segetes meum laborem,"
	tale est ceu "triplici vides ut ortu
	Triviae rotetur ignis
	volucrique Phoebus axe
2865	rapidum pererret orbem."

Aelius Festus Asmonius 4.1 (*GL* VI, p. 153)

. . . metrum erit anacreontion, siquidem ⟨Anacreon⟩ eo frequentissime usus sit, sed et apud nos plerique, inter quos Arbiter Satyricon ita: "triplici . . . orbem."

20 Terentianus Maurus, *On Meters*

now the arrangement, of which we will speak, will give us the meter in which they say that Anacreon[1] wrote his sweet old songs. Petronius is found to have used this meter, when he relates that the same lyric poet sang often in words harmonious to the Muses; likewise did several others. But I will explain with what kind of caesura this verse is composed. In the line *iuverunt segetes meum laborem* ("The harvest helped my labor"), the word *iuverunt* is the beginning of a hexameter; what is left, *segetes meum laborem*, is like:

> *triplici vides ut ortu*
> *Triviae rotetur ignis*
> *volucrique Phoebus axe*
> *rapidum pererret orbem.*

("You see how the fire of Trivia[2] revolves in her triple[3] rising, and how Phoebus in his winged chariot traverses the swift globe.")

[1] Sixth-century Greek poet. [2] Diana. [3] Selene in the sky, Artemis on earth, Hecate in the underworld.

Aelius Festus Asmonius

. . . the meter will be Anacreontic, inasmuch as Anacreon used it so often, but many poets used it in our literature, among them the Arbiter in his *Satyricon* has this, *triplici . . . orbem*. (See translation above.)

21 Diom. *Ars. gram.* 3 (*GL* I, p. 518)

et illud hinc est comma quod Arbiter fecit tale

> "anus recocta vino
> trementibus labellis."

22 Serv. *In art. Don.* (*GL* IV, p. 432.22)

item Quirites dicit numero tantum plurali. sed legimus apud Horatium hunc Quiritem, ut sit nominativus hic Quiris. item idem Horatius "quis te Quiritem?" cuius nominativus erit hic Quirites, ut dicit Petronius.

Pomp. *Comm. in art. Don.* (*GL* V, p. 167.9)

nemo dicit "hic Quirites" sed "hi Quirites," licet legerimus hoc. legite in Petronio, et invenietis de nominativo singulari hoc factum, et ait Petronius "hic Quirites."

23 Auctor de dubiis nominibus (*GL* V, p. 578.23)

fretum generis neutri et pluraliter freta, ut Petronius "freta Nereidum."

21 Diomedes, *The Art of Grammar*

from this also comes that caesura employed thus by the Arbiter:

> *anus recocta vino*
> *trementibus labellis.*

("An old woman, soaked in wine, her lips trembling.")

22 Servius, *On the Grammar of Donatus*

again he uses *Quirites* ("citizens") only in the plural. But in Horace we read *hunc Quiritem* ('this citizen"), making the nominative *hic Quiris*. The same Horace also writes *Quis te Quiritem?* ("Who has restored you as citizen?"). Here the nominative will be *hic Quirites*, a form used by Petronius.

Pompeius, *Commentary on the Grammar of Donatus*

no one says *hic Quirites* ("this citizen"), but *hi Quirites* ("these citizens"), though we have read the former. Read Petronius, and you will find this usage of the nominative singular, for Petronius says *hic Quirites* ("this citizen").

23 Anonymous grammarian

fretum ("strait") is neuter, and its plural is *freta* ("straits"), as Petronius writes *freta Nereidum* ("straits of the Nereids"[1]).

[1] Sea nymphs.

24 Hieron. *Ep. ad Demetr*. 130.19 (*CSEL* 56, p. 199.16 Hilberg)

cincinnatulos pueros et calamistratos et peregrini muris olentes pelliculas, de quibus illud Arbitri est

"non bene olet qui bene semper olet,"

quasi quasdam pestes et venena pudicitiae virgo devitet.

25 Fulg. *Myth*. 2.6 (pp. 45–46 Helm)

[de Prometheo] quamvis Nicagorus . . . primum illum formasse idolum referat et, quod vulturi iecur praebeat, livoris quasi pingat imaginem. unde et Petronius Arbiter ait

"qui[1] vultur iecur intimum pererrat
pectusque eruit[2] intimasque fibras,
non est quem lepidi[3] vocant poetae,
sed cordis <mala>,[4] livor atque luxus."

[1] qui *Fulgentius*: cui   [2] pectusque eruit *Nisbet*: et querit pectus   [3] lepidi p^2: tepidi   [4] *added med*.

CARMINA IN CODICE LEIDENSI VOSSIANO
LAT. Q. 86 (= Z) SERVATA

26 inveniat[1] quod quisque velit.[2] non omnibus unum est quod placet. hic spinas colligit, ille rosas.

[1] inveniat *Scaliger*: inveniet   [2] velit Z^c: velet

Anth. Lat. 464 R. = 462 SB. = fr. 35 B.

24 Jerome, *Letters*

a virgin should avoid boys with curled and wavy hair, and whose skin smells like foreign mice, for they are like certain plagues and poisons to chastity. The Arbiter is speaking about them when he says, "The man who smells good always does not smell good."[1]

[1] Mart. 2.12.4. Jerome could be thinking of similar sentiments expressed at Petron. *Sat.* 2.1 or 119.33.

25 Fulgenius, *Mythologies*

[on Prometheus] although Nicagoras . . . records that Prometheus was the first to have embodied the image, and that he exposes his liver to a vulture, as if it portrays a metaphor for envy. From this Petronius also says: "The vulture that probes our inmost liver and tears out our heart and inmost entrails, is not a bird, as our witty poets claim, but the evils of our heart, envy and lust."

POEMS PRESERVED IN ONE MANUSCRIPT

26 Let each man find what suits his taste. There is no one thing that pleases all. This one gathers thorns, that one roses.

27 iam nunc ardentes autumnus fregerat[1] horas[2]
atque hiemem tepidis spectabat Phoebus habenis,
iam platanus iactare comas, iam coeperat uvas
adnumerare suas defecto[3] palmite vitis.
5   ante oculos stabat quidquid promiserat annus.

[1] fregerat *Scaliger*: regerat   [2] horas *Housman*: umbras
[3] defecto p^2: desecto

Anth. Lat. 465 R. = 463 SB. = fr. 38 B.

28 primus in orbe deos fecit timor,[1] ardua caelo
fulmina cum caderent discussaque Maenala[2] flammis
atque ictus flagraret Athos, mox Phoebus ad ortus
lustrata devectus[3] humo lunaeque senectus
5   et reparatus honos, hinc signa effusa per orbem
et permutatis distinctus[4] mensibus annus.
profecit[5] vitium iamque[6] error iussit inanis
agricolas primos Cereri dare messis[7] honores,
palmitibus plenis Bacchum vincire, Palemque
10   pastorum gaudere manu. natat arbiter omnis
Neptunus demersus aquae,[8] Pallasque[9] tabernas
vindicat. et voti reus et qui vendidit urbem,[10]
iam sibi quis‹que›[11] deos avido certamine fingit.

[1] *Cf. Stat.* Theb. *3.661, Fulg. Myth. 1.1*   [2] Maenala *Peerlkamp*: moenia   [3] devectus *Heinsius*: deiectus   [4] distinctus *Riese*: disiunctis   [5] profecit *anon.*: proiecit   [6] iamque
Bücheler: atque   [7] messis p^2: mensis   [8] natat arbiter
omnis Neptunus demersus aquae *Courtney*[2]: natat obru[P]tus
omnis Neptunus demersus aqua   [9] Pallasque *Scaliger*: palli-
dasque   [10] urbem p^2: orbem   [11] *added Scaliger*

Anth. Lat. 466 R. = 464 SB. = fr. 27 B.

430

27 Now already autumn had broken the scorching hours, and Phoebus[1] looked to winter with cooler reins, now the plane tree had begun to shed her leaves, now the vine with its pruned shoots had begun to count out its grapes. Whatever the year had promised was standing before our eyes.

[1] The sun.

28 It was fear first created the gods in the world, when lightning bolts fell from high heaven, and Arcadian mountains were dashed to pieces in flames, and Athos was struck and set ablaze; soon Phoebus was carried below the earth, which had been traversed, and rose again; the moon grew old and waned and then recovered its glory, next the starry signs were scattered through the world and the year divided into changing months. The falsehood spread, and soon the vain superstition compelled the farmers to offer to Ceres[1] the harvest's first fruits, to garland Bacchus with loaded vine shoots, and to delight Pales[2] with the shepherds' handiwork. Submerged Neptune swims, lord of all the sea, and Pallas claims for herself the workshops. Both the man obliged to fill a vow and the one who sold the whole world for a price, now each one in greedy competition invents gods for his own use.

[1] Goddess of agriculture.   [2] Goddess of shepherds.

29 nolo ego semper idem capiti suffundere costum
   nec noto[1] stomachum conciliare mero.
taurus amat gramen mutata carpere valle
   et fera mutatis sustinet ora cibis.
5 ipsa dies ideo nos grato perluit haustu,
   quod permutatis umbra[2] recurrit equis.

---

[1] noto *Palmerius*: toto   [2] umbra *Baehrens*: ora

Anth. Lat. 467 R. = 465 SB. = fr. 33 B.

30 uxor legitimus[1] debet quasi census amari,
   nec censum vellem semper amare meum.

---

[1] legitimus *Scaliger*: legis inus

Anth. Lat. 468 R. = 466 SB = fr. 34 B.

31 linque tuas sedes alienaque litora quaere,
   ⟨o⟩[1] iuvenis; maior rerum tibi nascitur ordo.[2]
ne succumbe malis; te noverit ultimus Hister,
te Boreas gelidus securaque regna Canopi
5 quique renascentem Phoebum cernuntque
         cadentem.[3]
maior in externas Ithacus[4] descendat harenas.

---

[1] *added Scaliger*   [2] maior . . . ordo, *cf. Verg. Aen.*
7.44   [3] cadentem *Dousa fil.*: iacentem   [4] Ithacus
Palmerius: itacui

Anth. Lat. 469 R. = 467 SB = fr. 37 B.

29 I do not wish to suffuse my hair always with the same perfume, nor win over my stomach with familiar wine. The bull loves to graze on grass by changing the valley pasture, and wild beasts sustain their appetite by filling their mouths with a change of food. For this reason the day itself bathes us with a pleasant draft, only because the night returns after having changed its steeds.

30 A wife ought to be loved like wealth obtained legally, but I would not wish to love even my wealth forever.

31 O youth, leave your home and seek foreign shores; a greater series of events is created for you. Do not give in to misfortunes; the Danube, the furthest boundary, the icy North and the untroubled kingdoms of Egypt, and the men who discern Phoebus rising and then setting, all will learn of you. Let a greater Odysseus disembark on distant sands.[1]

---

[1] This is said by some sort of oracle.

32 nam nihil est quod non mortalibus adferat usum.
    rebus in adversis, quae iacuere, iuvant.
    sic rate demersa fulvum deponderat aurum,
      remorum levitas naufraga membra vehit.
5   cum sonuere tubae, iugulo stat divite ferrum;
      barbara contemptu[1] proelia pannus habet.

[1] contemptu *Dousa*: contempnit

Anth. Lat. 470 R. = 468 SB. = fr. 36 B.

33 parvula securo tegitur mihi culmine sedes
    uvaque plena mero fecunda[1] pendet ab ulmo.
    dant rami cerasos, dant mala rubentia silvae
    Palladiumque nemus pingui se vertice frangit.
5   iam qua deductos[2] potat brevis[3] area fontes,
    Corycium mihi surgit olus malvaeque supinae
    et non sollicitos missura papavera somnos.
    praeterea[4] sive alitibus contexere fraudem
    seu magis imbelles libuit circumdare cervos
10   aut tereti lino pavidum subducere piscem,
    hos tantum novere dolos me sordida rura.
    i nunc et vitae fugientis tempora vende
    divitibus cenis! me si manet exitus idem,
    hic precor inveniat consumptaque tempora poscat.

[1] fecunda *Scaliger*: facunda   [2] deductos *vulgo*: diduc-
tos   [3] brevis *Bailey*[1]: levis   [4] praeterea *Oudendorp*
placed here: after contexere

Anth. Lat. 471 R. = 469 SB. = fr. 50 B.

32 For there is nothing that does not serve the needs of mortals. In adversity things that were despised are found to be of use. So when a ship sinks, yellow gold weighs it down, while the lightness of the oars bears up the shipwrecked crew. When the trumpets sound, the sword is at the rich man's throat; the barbarians' arms hold the rags of the poor man in contempt.

33 My little house is covered by a good solid roof, and the wine-laden grapes hang from the fruitful elm. The boughs yield cherries, the orchards produce ruddy apples, and the branches of the olive grove, sacred to Pallas,[1] break under their rich heads. And now where the small garden drinks the channeled spring water, Corycian saffron[2] rises up for me, as do the floppy mallows and poppies about to send untroubled sleep. Moreover, whether it is my pleasure to weave snares for birds, or rather to entrap timid deer, or to pull up fish with a slender line, these are the only tricks my poor farm has known. Go, then, and barter the hours of a fleeting life for rich dinners. If the same death waits for me, I pray that it would find me here and call me to account for the times I have spent.

[1] Athena gave the olive tree to Athens and became goddess of the city.　　[2] Corycus in Asia Minor was famous for saffron.

34 non satis est quod nos mergit[1] furiosa iuventus
    transversosque rapit fama sepulta probris.
    en etiam famuli cognata e faece recentes[2]
    inter tam crassas[3] luxuriantur[4] opes.
5   vilis servus habet regni bona, cellaque capti
    deridet Vestam[5] Romuleamque casam.
    idcirco virtus medio iacet obruta caeno,
    nequitiae classes candida vela ferunt.

[1] mergit *Bücheler*: mergis   [2] cognata e faece recentes *Müller*: cognataque faece sepulti   [3] inter tam crassas *Petschenig*: intesta merassas   [4] luxuriantur *Scaliger*: luxantur   [5] Vestam *Barthius*: festam

Anth. Lat. 472 R. = 470 SB. = fr. 32 B.

35 sic et membra solent auras includere ventris,[1]
    quae penitus mersae cum rursus abire laborant,
4   verberibus rimantur iter. nec desinit ante
3   frigidus adstrictis[2] qui regnat in ossibus horror
5   quam tepidus laxo manavit corpore sudor.

[1] ventris *Riese*: ventis   [2] frigidus adstrictis *Reiske*: et frigidus strictis

Anth. Lat. 473 R. = 471 SB. = fr. 39 B.

34 It is not enough that maddened youth engulfs us, and our good name, buried in disgrace, sweeps us off course. Behold, slaves buried in the dregs of the wine to which they are related[1] run riot among our coarsest wealth. Cheap slaves have the estates of kings, and prison cells laugh at Vesta[2] and the hut of Romulus. So virtue lies sunk in deep mud, and prosperous sails bear up the fleets of the depraved.

[1] As *faex Romuli*, the dregs of society.   [2] Goddess of the hearth.

35 So, too, the body shuts in the belly's winds, which when they again work hard to emerge from the depths, search with sharp blows for a way out. And the cold shiver that rules over the constricted bones will not end until a warm sweat breaks out on the loosened structure of the body.[1]

[1] The poem compares flatulence to a volcanic eruption.

36 o litus vita mihi dulcius![1] o mare felix
    cui licet ad terras ire subinde meas!
o formosa dies! hoc quondam rure solebam
    Iliados rabidas[2] sollicitare manus.
5   hic fons, hic lacus[3] est, illic sinus egerit algas;
    haec statio est tacitis fida[4] cupidinibus.
pervixi, neque enim fortuna malignior umquam
    eripiet nobis quod prior hora[5] dedit.

[1] dulcius *Scaliger*: dulcior   [2] Iliados rabidas *Courtney*[2]:
Iliadas armatas   [3] hic fons hic lacus *Heinsius*: hic fontis
locus   [4] fida *Pithoeus*: victa   [5] prior hora *Scaliger*:
priora

Anth. Lat. 474 R. = 472 SB. = fr. 51.1–6 et 17–18 B.

37 haec ait et tremulo deduxit vertice canos
    consecuitque genas; oculis nec defuit[1] imber,
sed qualis rapitur per vallis improbus amnis,
    cum gelidae periere nives et languidus Auster
5   non patitur glaciem resoluta vivere terra,
gurgite sic pleno facies manavit et alto
    insonuit gemitu turbatum[2] murmure pectus.

[1] defuit *Scaliger*: debuit   [2] turbatum Scaliger: turbato

Anth. Lat. 475 R. = 473 SB. = fr. 40 B.

36 O seashore sweeter to me than life! O lucky sea, to which it is given to come often to my lands! O lovely day! In these fields long ago I used to rouse the impetuous hands of Ilias.[1] Here is the spring, here the pool, there the bay carries out the seaweed; this is a haven safe for silent longings. I have lived through it all, and never will spiteful Fortune wrench away from me what times past have given.

[1] A woman's name.

37 This said, he tore the white hair from his trembling head and slashed his cheeks; in his eyes a rain of tears, like an unruly river that sweeps through the valleys after the frozen snows have melted, and the soft south wind does not allow ice to live on land now thawed, just so his face ran with tears in full flood, and his heart troubled with low crying resounded in deepest pain.

38 nam citius flammas mortales ore[1] tenebunt
quam secreta tegant. quicquid demittis in aurem,[2]
effluit et subitis rumoribus oppida pulsat.
nec satis est vulgasse fidem: cumulatius exit
5   proditionis opus famamque onerare laborat.
sic commissa verens[3] avidus reserare[4] minister
fodit humum regisque latentes prodidit aures;
concepit nam terra sonos calamique loquentes
incinuere[5] Midam qualem narraverat index.

[1] ore *Scaliger*: ora   [2] demittis in aurem *Francius*: dimittis in aula   [3] verens *Fulgentius*: ferens   [4] reserare *Fulgentius*: servare   [5] incinuere *Palmerius*: invenere

Anth. Lat. 476 R. = 474 SB. = fr. 28 B.

39 illic alternis depugnat pontus et aer,
    hic rivo tenui pervia ridet humus.
illic demersas[1] complorat navita puppis,
    hic pastor miti perluit amne pecus.
5   illic immanes mors obvia[2] solvit hiatus,
    hic gaudet curva falce recisa Ceres.
illic inter aquas urit sitis arida fauces,
    hic †da periuro basia multa viro†.
naviget et fluctus lasset mendicus Ulixes:
10   in terris vivet candida Penelope.

[1] demersas *Baehrens*: divisas   [2] obvia *Heinsius*: oblita

Anth. Lat. 477 R. = 475 SB. = fr. 51.7–16 B.

38 Far sooner will people hold fire in their mouths than keep secrets. Whatever you let fall into an ear gets known and batters the cities in hasty hearsay. It is not enough to have made common knowledge of promised secrecy: the words of betrayal, now greatly elaborated on, go forth and pains are taken to improve the report. So the greedy slave fearing that he might disclose secrets dug a hole and betrayed into it that the king was hiding long ass' ears. For the hole in the earth absorbed his words, and the reeds began to speak and sang how Midas[1] was such a one as the informer had told about.

[1] Apollo punished Midas by giving him the ears of an ass.

39 There the sea and sky fight it out by turns, here the ground, with a shallow stream running through it, smiles. There the sailor mourns his sunken ship, here the shepherd washes his flock in the gentle river. There death meets and destroys the monstrous gaping jaws of greed, here the harvest gladly bows to the curved sickle. There among the waters dry thirst burns[1] the throats, here kisses are lavished on faithless men. Let the beggar Ulysses sail on and weary the waves: the fair Penelope will live on land.

[1] Because of salinity.

40 qui non vult[1] properare[2] mori nec cogere fata
    mollia praecipiti rumpere fila manu,
hactenus iratum mare noverit. ecce refuso
    gurgite securos obluit unda pedes;
5   ecce inter virides iactatur mytilus algas
    et rauco trahitur lubrica concha sono;[3]
ecce recurrentes qua versat fluctus harenas
    discolor attrita calculus exit humo.
haec quisquis calcare potest, in litore tuto
10   ludat et hoc solum iudicet esse mare.

[1] non vult *Christ*: moluit   [2] properare *Lindenbrog*: pro
pare   [3] sono *Klotz*: sinu

Anth. Lat. 478 R. = 476 SB. = fr. 52 B.

41 non est forma satis, nec quae vult bella videri
    debet vulgari more placere sibi.
dicta, sales, lusus, sermonis gratia, risus
    vincunt naturae candidioris opus.
5   condit enim formam quicquid desumitur[1] artis,
    et nisi velle subest, gratia nuda perit.

[1] desumitur *Bailey*[1]: consumitur

Anth. Lat. 479 R. = 477 SB. = fr. 31 B.

CARMINA IN CODICE LEIDENSI VOSSIANO
LAT. F. III (= Y) SERVATA

42 fallunt nos oculi, vagique sensus
oppressa ratione mentiuntur.
nam turris, prope quae quadrata surgit,

40 The man who does not wish to be in haste to die, nor force the Fates to snap the tender threads with hasty hands, let him know just so much of the angry sea. Look where the wave washes his feet still safe, the ebbing waters flowing back; look where the mussel is tossed about among the green seaweed, and the slippery whorled shell with its hoarse resonance is rolled along; look where the wave turns the sand running back, there colored pebbles go out on rippled flats. Whoever is able to tread on these, let him play here, safe on the shore, and let him judge that just this alone is the sea.

41 Outward beauty is not enough, and the woman who wishes to be fair must not be conceited, as is the custom among the common people. Words, wit, play, sweet talk, laughter, all aid in changing the product of an overly innocent character. For whatever is spent on artfulness seasons beauty, and unless there is an underlying willingness to please, unadorned loveliness is wasted.

POEMS PRESERVED IN ANOTHER MANUSCRIPT

42 Our eyes deceive us, and our erring senses, once reason is overwhelmed, transmit falsehoods.[1] That nearby tower which rises foursquare, at a distance seems round

---

[1] This poem may be compared with Lucretius, *DRN* 4.

detritis procul angulis rotatur.
5   Hyblaeum refugit satur liquorem,
et naris[1] casiam frequenter odit.
hoc illo magis aut minus placere
non posset,[2] nisi lite destinata
pugnarent dubio tenore sensus.

[1] naris p^2: maris   [2] posset p: poss^{n}t

Anth. Lat. 650 R. = *fr.* 29 B. *praecedunt duo Petronii carmina quae leguntur 14.2 et 83.10*

43 somnia, quae mentes ludunt volitantibus umbris,
non delubra deum nec ab aethere numina mittunt,
sed sibi quisque facit. nam cum prostrata sopore
urguet membra quies et mens sine pondere ludit,
5   quidquid luce fuit, tenebris agit. oppida bello
qui quatit et flammis miserandas eruit urbes,
tela videt versasque acies et funera regum
atque exundantes profuso[1] sanguine campos.
qui causas orare solent, legesque forumque
10   et pavidi cernunt inclusum chorte[2] tribunal.
condit avarus opes defossumque invenit aurum.
venator saltus canibus quatit. eripit undis
aut premit eversam periturus navita puppem.
scribit amatori meretrix, dat adultera munus.
15   et canis in somnis leporis vestigia latrat;
in noctis spatium miserorum vulnera durant.

[1] profuso *Scaliger*: perfuso   [2] chorte *Mommsen*: corde

Anth. Lat. 651 R. = *fr.* 30 B. *Cf. Courtney*[2] 64–65, *Deufert*

like a wheel and its angles worn away. Taste buds after too much rich food shrink from the honey of Hybla, and our nostrils hate the scent of cinnamon. One thing could not please us more or less than another, if our senses were not at war in a fixed dispute on an indecisive course.

43 Dreams that mock our minds with flitting shadows do not issue from the shrines of the gods, nor are they sent by divinities from heaven, but each person creates his own dreams. For when quiet weighs down our limbs overcome in sleep, and our mind plays unchecked, it reenacts in the night whatever was thought during the day. The man who causes towns to shake in war and in flames destroys cities deserving our pity, sees weapons in his dreams and routed battle lines and the deaths of kings and the plains overflowing and running with blood. Those who often plead cases, envisage in dreams both laws and courts and are terrified to see their platform surrounded by a mob. The miser dreams of hiding his wealth and finding gold dug out of the earth. The hunter dreams of flushing out animals from the woods with his dogs. The sailor dreams of rescuing his ship from the waves, or as he is about to die hugs the overturned vessel. The mistress writes to her lover, the adulteress gives hers a gift. And the dog in his sleep barks, scenting tracks of the hare. The pangs of the wretched continue into the watches of the night.[1]

[1] On dreams, see again Lucretius, *DRN* 4; the idea of wish-fulfillment in dreams was known in antiquity.

CARMINA EX CODICE BELLOVACENSI
(= X) EDITA

44 sic contra[1] rerum naturae munera nota
     corvus maturis frugibus ova refert.
  sic format lingua fetum cum protulit ursa,
     et piscis nullo iunctus amore parit.
5   sic Phoebea chelys studio[2] resoluta parentis
     Lucinae tepidis naribus ova fovet.
  sic sine concubitu textis apis excita ceris
     fervet et audaci milite castra replet.
  non uno contenta valet natura tenore,
10   sed permutatas gaudet habere vices.

[1] sic contra *Fulgentius*: sicut sunt   [2] studio *Courtney*[2]:
victo

Anth. Lat. 690 R. = fr. 26 B.

45 Indica purpureo genuit me litore tellus,
     candidus accenso qua redit orbe dies.
  hic ego divinos inter generatus honores
     mutavi Latio barbara verba sono.
5   iam dimitte tuos, Paean o Delphice, cycnos:
     dignior haec vox est quae tua templa colat.

Anth. Lat. 691 R. = fr. 41 B.

46 naufragus eiecta nudus rate quaerit eodem
     percussum telo, cui sua fata fleat;[1]

[1] fleat *Jacobs*: legat

POEMS TAKEN FROM ANOTHER
MANUSCRIPT

44 So, contrary to the known duties of the nature of things, the raven lays eggs when the crops are ripe. So, the bear gives birth and then shapes her young with her tongue, and fish, never coupling in love, still give birth. So, the tortoise of Apollo,[1] relaxed in the affection of parenting Lucina,[2] cares for her eggs with warm nostrils. So, the bee, born without an act of sex and roused from its web of wax, bustles about and fills her camp with bold warriors. Nature's strength resides in not being content with one steady course, but she delights in all varieties and changes.

[1] The tortoise is connected to Apollo because the lyre is made out of a tortoise shell, and Apollo is the deity of music.　　[2] One of the goddesses of childbirth.

45 On its red shore the land of India bore me,[1] where the radiant day returns in an orb of fire. Here I was born among divine offerings and exchanged my barbaric speech for the Latin tongue. O Delphic healer,[2] dismiss your swans: mine is a voice more worthy to dwell in your temples.

[1] A poem on a parrot.　　[2] Apollo.

46 A sailor naked from a shipwreck seeks out the sympathetic ear of a man stunned by the same blow, to whom he

grandine qui segetes et totum perdidit annum
    in simili deflet tristia damna[2] sinu.
5   funera conciliant miseros, orbique[3] parentes
    coniungunt gemitus, et facit hora pares.
nos quoque confusis feriemus sidera verbis,
    et fama est iunctas[4] fortius ire preces.

[2] damna *Müller*: fata   [3] orbique *Binetus*[mg]: sortique
[4] iunctas *Binetus*[mg]: constans

Anth. Lat. 692 R. = fr. 42 B.

47 si Phoebi soror es, mando tibi, Delia, causam,
    scilicet ut fratri quae peto verba feras:
"marmore si quando[1] struxi tibi, Delphice, templum
    e levibus calamis candida verba dedi,
5   nunc si nos audis atque es divinus, Apollo,
    dic mihi, qui nummos non habet, unde petat."

[1] si quando *Bücheler*: Sicanio

Anth. Lat. 693 R. = fr. 44 B.

48 omnia quae miseras possunt finire querelas
    in promptu voluit candidus esse deus.
vile olus et duris haerentia mora rubetis
    pungentis[1] stomachi composuere famem.
5   flumine vicino stultus sitit, et riget[2] Euro,
    cum calidus tepido consonat igne rogus.

[1] pungentis *Dousa fil.*: pugnantis   [2] et riget *Binetus*[mg]:
effugit

can bemoan his fate. A farmer who has lost his wheat field to hail and a whole year's harvest weeps about his sad losses on a breast similarly afflicted. Deaths unite the wretched, and bereaved parents join together in their groaning, and the fated hour makes them equals. With joined voices we will hammer at the stars. The saying is that prayers united go up more forcefully.

47 If you are Phoebus' sister, Delia, I entrust my cause to you, to be sure that is, that you carry to your brother the words of my petition: "God of Delphi, if ever I built for you a temple of marble, and I have sung clear songs on slender reeds, now if you hear me and are indeed divine, tell me where a man who has no money might look for it."

48 All things that can end our wretched complaints, an honest god has set in readiness before us. Common vegetables and berries clinging to rough bramble allay the gnawing hunger of the belly. He is a fool who goes thirsty with a river nearby, and is stiff with cold facing the east wind, when a hot funeral pyre resounds with a warm blaze. The law sits armed around the savage threshold of a bride:

lex armata sedet circum fera limina nuptae:
  nil metuit licito fusa puella toro.
quod satiare potest, dives natura ministrat:
10   quod docet infrenis[3] gloria, fine caret.

[3] infrenis *Binetus*[mg]: inferius

Anth. Lat. 694 R. = *fr.* 45 B.

49 militis in galea nidum fecere columbae:
  apparet, Marti quam sit[1] amica Venus.

[1] sit *Binetus*[mg]: sic

Anth. Lat. 695 R. = *fr.* 46 B.

50 Iudaeus licet et porcinum numen[1] adoret
  et caeli summas advocet auriculas,[2]
ni tamen et ferro succiderit inguinis oram[3]
et nisi nodatum solverit arte caput,
5   exemptus populo patria[4] migrabit ab urbe
et non ieiuna sabbata lege premet.

[1] numen *Binetus*[mg]: nomen   [2] auriculas *Binetus*[mg]: agricolas   [3] oram *Binetus*[mg]: aram   [4] patria *Courtney*[2]: Graia

Anth. Lat. 696 R. = *fr.* 47 B.

51 una est nobilitas argumentumque coloris
  ingenui, timidas non habuisse manus.

Anth. Lat. 697 R. = *fr.* 47.7–8 B.

the girl spread out on a lawful bed incurs no penalty. Rich nature supplies everything needed to satisfy us: that which unbridled vanity teaches us to seek after has no bounds.

49 Doves made a nest in a soldier's helmet: it is obvious how much Venus loves Mars.

50 Though a Jew worships in fact a pig-god[1] and sends summons to the ears of high heaven, unless he also cuts around the edge of his prick, and unless he cleverly removes the knot around his dickhead, he will be banished from his people, will move from his home city, and break the sabbath by not observing abstinence.

[1] The logic seems to be that if you do not eat it (and the Romans did eat it), you worship it.

51 There is one illustriousness and proof of a noble cast of mind, that a man has brave hands.[1]

[1] Hands brave enough to commit suicide.

451

SENECA

APOCOLOCYNTOSIS

INTRODUCTION

DATE, AUTHOR, TITLE

The short satirical pamphlet of about fifteen pages of Latin on the death, apotheosis, and attempt to enter heaven by the Roman emperor Claudius (10 BC–AD 54; r. 41–54) is almost certainly entitled *Apocolocyntosis* (hereafter, *Apoc.*), and very likely the work of the amateur philosopher and super-rich landowner Lucius Annaeus Seneca, also known as Seneca the Younger, or just Seneca (4 BC–AD 65).

The opening words of the *Apoc.* run: *quid actum sit in caelo ante diem III idus* ("the proceedings in heaven on the thirteenth of October in the new year"). The official sounding language of government and business hits a snag right at the outset: "in heaven." The work before us is going to be pseudo-history, satirical, and humorous. October 13 is notable, if the date refers to the year 54, when the Roman emperor Claudius was murdered (less likely, died of natural causes).

Since the work is short, Seneca could have composed it in a brief period, perhaps in time for the *Saturnalia* in Rome, which began on December 17, a festival lasting a few days during which the Roman world was turned upside down. (Seneca's assessment of Claudius' entire reign?) He would have written it quickly after Claudius' death because the impact of such political and satirical tracts is short-lived. This comical satire of Claudius' deification surely amused, but also bewildered, those who had heard Claudius' panegyric, read out by the new emperor Nero but widely known to have been written by Seneca, the boy-emperor's tutor (Tac. *Ann.* 13.3). His panegyric was a public and civic document and had to conform to elements that promoted the continuity and safety of the state. In the *Apoc.*, however, which was a personal pamphlet, Seneca could resort to sarcasm and low humor.

Though a well-versed, if derivative, Stoic philosopher, Seneca showed little control over his animosity in savaging the dead emperor. In his defense, he had compelling reasons for his actions. Claudius had earlier exiled him to Corsica (41–49), probably on false charges of adultery with the royals, and while there he had bent over backward to flatter Claudius in his *Consolatio ad Polybium* (12.3–14.2), in the hopes that the emperor would commute his sentence. Claudius would not and left Seneca groveling on Corsica.

Agrippina the Younger (15–59), great-granddaughter of Augustus, after her marriage (her third) to Claudius (49), persuaded him to allow Seneca to return to Rome, where she made him tutor to her young son Nero (37–68; r. 54–68). Nero was the son of Agrippina and Cn. Domitius Ahenobarbus; Claudius did have a son of his own, Brittanicus (41–55), with his third wife (married in 38) Messalina (ca. 20–48). Though defended by some revisionist historians, Messalina probably did sneak out of the palace and Claudius' bed at night and function hard and long as an entertainer in a brothel, where she once is said to have pleased as many as twenty-five customers in a competition with a paid prostitute (surely a slight exaggeration by Pliny *NH* 10.83). Claudius had Messalina executed (48) and then married Agrippina, acts of equal valor. Somehow Agrippina persuaded Claudius to set aside his own son Brittanicus and adopt Nero as his heir. When Claudius conveniently died of poison in 54, Nero became emperor, and within a few months Brittanicus too was advantageously carried off by poison just short of his fourteenth birthday. Agrippina herself lived only until 59, when Nero had her beaten to death. The Julio-Claudian line was quickly dying out.

The audience of the *Apoc.* had heard Nero's panegyric of Claudius written by Seneca, and now heard Seneca's satire of Claudius and his powerful imperial freedmen, who had first exiled him, and after his return, had treated him with a high degree of insolence. With these enemies destroyed, Seneca dares to make fun of them. The immediate winner in this royal struggle in 54 was Agrippina, and Seneca surely understood her methods and aims: she would be co-regent of the Roman Empire, but with more power than her son. In his satire on the deification of Claudius, Seneca is careful to avoid any hint of implication of Agrippina in her husband's arrogant treatment of him or in his lawlessness in murdering many of his own citizens: after all, for five years she was his closest advisor. There is no direct criticism of her, but the structure of the situation on the Palatine is, to say the least, awkward. She poisoned Claudius and then had him deified; she was wife of the emperor and now wife of a deity (at least for public consumption). Her imperial control was increasing; she was more skilled in imperial matters than her seventeen-year-old son, and she easily could send Seneca back to Corsica, should he try to turn Nero against her. Simply by laying out the elements of the situation, Seneca got as close to criticizing her as he could. The fact that she was a domineering mother is clear from the actions of Nero, who had her beaten to death five years after Claudius' demise.

As tutor and advisor to the boy-emperor, Seneca hoped that his student would develop skills at ruling and thereby slowly push Agrippina aside, but Agrippina would not yield. The Julio-Claudian instincts for murder-as-a-convenient-solution were part of Nero's character. Even in the power politics of Rome, Seneca was vain enough to think that his cracker-barrel philosophy could alter and improve the character of Nero and have some beneficial influence on Agrippina. She was murdered in 59, Seneca in 65, Petronius in 66, Nero in 68, and numerous others along the way.

Most scholars now attribute the *Apoc.* to Seneca and list the title of the pamphlet as the *Apocolocyntosis of the Divine Claudius.* The term *divus Claudius* indicates that Claudius is dead, and, like many Roman emperors before and after him, has been deified by an accommodating Senate. It meant little more than a passive expression of patriotism, and maintenance of the cult of the emperor gave officials an opportunity to establish the positions of *seviri Augustales* to carry out cult duties. Wealthy freedmen around the empire were regularly made *sevir* (one of six) who would then pay large sums of money for the honor. Only the hopelessly religious and weak-minded would think that the emperor had actually become a deity. Most shared the opinion of the emperor Vespasian (Suet. *Vesp.*

INTRODUCTION

23.4), who on his deathbed supposedly uttered, *vae . . . puto deus fio* ("Alas . . . I suppose I am becoming a god.")

Inside the rare word *apocolocyntosis* is the Greek word κολοκύντη (gourd), with the common prefix ἀπο- and suffix -ωσις (cf. ἀπο-θέ-ωσις), with a meaning something like "becoming a gourd or pumpkin," and thus the title "The Divine Claudius' Metamorphosis into a Pumpkin, and the Elevation of that Pumpkin to a Place Among the Gods." We have here a play on the Greek terms *apathanatisis* or *apotheosis*, "deification." The Latin word for gourd is *cucurbita*, with the transferred meaning of "simpleton," "a gourd whose insides are dried out and is used to carry water," and thus "someone with water on the brain." The last definition is supported by Petronius *Satyrica* 39.12.

Both the name of the author, Seneca, and the title of the pamphlet, *Apoc.*, are supported by just one ancient source, Dio Cassius (ca. 155–235) in his Greek-language *Roman History* 60.35, and his attribution seems clear: "Seneca himself composed a work which he entitled *Apocolocyntosis*, as though it were some kind of deification." Only one medieval manuscript (Vaticanus Lat. 4498, 112v–118v) from the late fifteenth century in the L family gives the title as *Apoc.*, and this in an apparently later hand. The common title for the work in medieval manuscripts is *Ludus*. Just as it is obvious that the proof that Titus Petronius Niger, consul-suffect in 62, wrote the *Satyrica* would not stand up in a court of law where the verdict is rendered "without a doubt," so too the evidence concerning Seneca and the *Apoc.* Scholars have, however, assembled enough information to convince most others that the weight of evidence convinces them that Seneca wrote the *Apoc.* in 54, and Petronius wrote the *Satyrica* around 66. Because the biography of Petronius provided by Tacitus (*Ann.* 16.17–20) shows the character of a man who could have written the amusing, slightly risqué, *Satyrica*, scholars are willing to pair him with the *Satyrica*. The same sort of pairing is not so compatible for Seneca and the *Apoc.* From Tacitus' biography of Seneca (*Ann.* 15.60–64) and from Seneca's own writings, we see in him a dour, austere man, a pseudo-philosopher, and underneath it all a parody of an interesting human being. Tacitus does not mention that Seneca wrote the *Apoc.*, but then he overlooks the many dramas written by Seneca, as well. None of this contradicts the possibility that for once in his life Seneca displayed some wit and invention as he wrote the *Apoc.* The language of the *Apoc.* is highly literate and displays nothing that could not come from the pen of Seneca.

Just as Petronius probably read out his *Satyrica* first to a small coterie of intimate friends before it leaked out or was intentionally circulated more widely in Rome and then copied in quantity and distributed to various places in the empire, the *Apoc.* is likely to have been treated similarly, read out to Seneca's closest friends and Spanish relatives. If not among the very first to hear it, Nero surely knew of it soon after its composition, and though Claudius was his adoptive father, he must have enjoyed listening to the ridicule heaped on the dead emperor and the praise allotted him as the rising sun of a new era (4.1 vv. 25–32). Nero is the only living person mentioned in the *Apoc.*

Another person who would have heard the *Apoc.* at an early date was Agrippina, who had appointed Seneca tutor of the boy-emperor, after persuading Claudius to bring him back from exile on Corsica. This was not done to benefit Claudius, Seneca, or Nero, but to create an appearance of normalcy in the face of her grab for power. The personal relationship between Agrippina and Seneca must have been one of constantly rising tensions, as the mother of the emperor and the emperor jockeyed for the best positions, and Seneca acted as umpire.

GENRE

On first looking into the *Apoc.*, the reader immediately notes that the fifteen or so pages of Latin are a mixture of prose and original verse, a form often referred to as prosimetrum. Such a mixture is a hallmark of the so-called Menippean satire, named after Menippus of Gadara, who lived in the third century BC; the *Apoc.* is also a mixture of the serious and the comic. Though we have some six hundred fragments of Menippean satires by Varro (116–27), his themes do not seem to occur in the *Apoc.* Those that are prominent in the *Apoc.* (e.g., ascension into heaven, council of the gods, and descent into the underworld), are found in dialogues of Lucian (second century AD), who seems to have known well the works of Menippus, *Council of the Gods* and *Icaromenippus*, but there is no bite or sharp edge to the Menippean satires of Varro or Lucian, as is found in the *Apoc.*

The spirit and essence of the *Apoc.* seems to be closest to political lampoon pamphlets, written quickly after some event and against some person, circulated and then not thought worthy of recopying for personal collections. Such a pamphlet, which seems to have circulated under the radar of serious historians like Tacitus, was called a *libel-*

lus, and Suetonius (*Aug.* 55) informs us that Augustus issued an edict against publication of such anonymous and scurrilous *famosos libellos*, which were often directed against the emperor. It seems likely that the *Apoc.* is closer in intent and substance to such *libelli*, although in the hands of Seneca a thick literary texture was woven into the satire. The *Apoc.* has attracted so much attention because it is the only extant example of the genre, but it also seems certain that more than a few others were written.

MANUSCRIPTS

There are three families of manuscripts of the *Apoc.*, each of which is named after the most important manuscript in that family:

S Family

S   Sangallensis 569, Stiftbibliothek, St. Gallen,
     pp. 243–51, written near the end of the ninth or
     early tenth century on parchment, in Fulda,
     Germany. The famous manuscript is available
     for viewing at www.cesg.unifr.ch. There are at
     least fourteen other manuscripts that belong to
     this family, but all are probably derived from or
     influenced by S, or a lost copy of S. These four-
     teen manuscripts are of value only as supporting
     documents.

V Family

V   Valentianensis 411 (formerly 393), Bibliothèque
     Municipale, Valenciennes, fols. 90r–105r, writ-

ten in the late ninth century, on parchment, in France near Reims. This manuscript was apparently never copied.

L Family

L   Londiniensis Addit. 11983, British Library, London, fols. 21v–28v, written in the early twelfth century, on parchment, in France. There are at least twenty-nine other manuscripts that belong to this family, but all are probably derived from L or a lost copy of L, and all are of value only as supporting documents.

These three manuscripts prove the archetype (α) and show common errors and lacunae. S descends directly from α, while V and L have one intermediary step (β) away from α; L has also an intelligent corrector from the eleventh–twelfth centuries.

SECONDARY LITERATURE: SCHOLARLY WORK

All items listed here have discrete entries in the General Bibliography that follows this Introduction; unless otherwise stated, all items are arranged chronologically.

1. *Bibliographies*

Coffey[1], earliest systematic bibliography of the *Apoc.*, covering the years 1922 to 1958.

Eden[2] (156–60), short but highly selective, concise, appropriate.

Bringmann[2], systematic bibliography of the *Apoc.*, for the years 1959 to 1982.

Malaspina, bibliography beginning with 1900; it covers all the works of Seneca, with more than six thousand entries. The website www.seneca.it continues to add new items to Malaspina's 2005 work.

Bonandini[1] (341–79), bibliography for 1983 to 2006.

Vannini (xlvii–lxiv), analytical bibliography up to 2008.

Bonandini[2] (483–549), with an emphasis on the poetic sections.

Holzberg, bibliography is first alphabetical by author, then arranged by topic.

2. *Studies on the Manuscripts and Transmission of the Text*

Bücheler[1], editio maior of Petronius to which he attached the *Apoc.*; standard reference work for the text of the *Apoc.*; now supplemented by Roncali.

Bücheler[2], his collations of S and V laid the basis for the standard reference text of the *Apoc.*

Rossbach, discovered and collated L.

Heinze, detailed notes on the text.

Russo[1], early work on building the stemma.

Russo[2], in his five editions of the text he constructed the stemma still used today.

Eden[1], concise and understandable study of the manuscripts and the tradition.

Eden[2], using his earlier study, Eden arranges all manuscripts by family and identifies the problems with each manuscript.

Reynolds, a survey of the manuscripts and their tradition from a historical perspective.

Roncali (v–xxv), analysis in the preface to her Teubner edition.

Vannini (xxxiv–xlii), clear exposition of the manuscripts and the tradition.

3. *Latin Editions*

editio princeps, published in Rome in 1513 by Caius Sylvanus Germanicus, from a manuscript of the L family: *Lucii Annaei Senecae in morte Claudii Caesaris Ludus*. Cited for historical purposes only.

Bücheler[1], earliest of the modern critical editions of the *Apoc.*

Rossbach[2], this edition added much to the study of the text because he had discovered and collated L. The work, however, is marred by numerous errors in the apparatus.

Russo[2], produced five editions and is credited with building the stemma which Eden[1] proved. His apparatus is too brief to make his text useful.

Eden[2], text with apparatus, introduction, English translation, running commentary of great value.

Roncali, very conservative text, edited for the Teubner series. Fullest apparatus available.

Vannini, introduction, text without apparatus, Italian translation, bibliography, and valuable notes. In the most part the text is that of Roncali.

SENECA, APOCOLOCYNTOSIS

4. *Translations into English*

Athanassakis[2], earliest reliable translation into English.

Eden[2], English translation opposite the pages of Latin.

Sullivan[2] (207–42), Penguin translation set after translation of Petronius.

Roth, Bryn Mawr Commentary.

For the numerous translations into other languages, see those listed in Malaspina under Bibliographies above.

5. *Studies on the Author and Date*

Bickel[1], by the end of the work Seneca shows his hatred for Claudius because he had been exiled by him.

Bickel[2], evidence for dating to Seneca to 54.

Toynbee, suggests moving the date of the *Apoc.* to *Neronia* of 60.

Momiglino, refutes Toynbee and provides evidence for dating to 54.

Sullivan[1], gathers evidence for a literary feud between Seneca–Lucan and Petronius.

Bringmann[1], *Apoc.* belongs to the sharp political Roman satire of pamphlets.

Eden[2] (4–8), supports Seneca and a date of 54.

Bringmann[2], in his *Forschungsbericht* focuses on dating at pp. 885–89.

Sullivan[2] (204–18) in the Introduction to his translation, supports Seneca as author.

Kraft, Seneca at 10.3 has Augustus attack Claudius for his close connection to Marc Antony; Kraft misreads the text.

Bonandini[1], reviews the scholarship from 1983 to 2006, and supports Seneca as author and dating to 54.

Vannini (viii–xiv), makes a strong and tight case for the traditional authorship and dating.

6. *Studies on the Title*

Rossbach[1], posits a lost *Apoc.* that is different from the extant *Apotheosis*.

Athanassakis[1], Claudius is headless, penisless, and in the form of a pumpkin is passed around as in a ball game.

Eisenberg, meaning and purpose of the *Apoc.*

Reeve, the title, *Divi Claudii Apotheosis per saturam*, is not a satirical apotheosis but an apotheosis done in a mixture of prose and verse.

Eden[2] (1–4), review of the literature and evidence for *Apocolocyntosis*.

Stagni, analysis of the evidence from Dio Cassius and his Byzantine redactor.

Vannini (xiv–xix), discusses the literature and defends the title of *Apocolocyntosis*.

7. *Studies on the Genre*

Martin, holds that in an unguarded moment the philosopher became a satirist.

Sullivan[1], sets the *Apoc.* as part of a literary feud among the writers around Nero.

Eden[2] (13–17), sees connections to Menippean satire as a combination of prose and verse.

Adamietz (356–82), lists the *Apoc.* as a type of satire.

Nauta, classifies the *Apoc.* as Saturnalian literature.

467

Riikonen, defines Menippean satire and includes the *Apoc.* in it.

Coffey[2] (165–77), comments on literary history rather than criticism and places the *Apoc.* in with Varro and Petronius as Menippean satire. Most of the space in this book is given to Horace and Juvenal.

O'Gorman (95–108), holds that the *Apoc.* is not quite in the tradition of Horace, Persius, or Juvenal, and fits better with Menippean satire, as a repository of quotations.

Heil, notes that Seneca makes much of Claudius' birth outside of Italy and that he does not descend from Troy like the Julians.

Bonandini[1] (358–62), reviews the literature on the *Apoc.*

Vannini (xx–xxxiv), discourses on the special place of the *Apoc.* in Menippean satire.

Bonandini[2], offers a commentary on the nature of Seneca's use of Menippean satire and a detailed analysis of the numerous citations of Greek and Latin writers and of the poetic passages.

Roncali[2] (673–86)

8. *Study of the Poetry in the* Apoc.

Bonandini[2], provides the best study of the poetry.

9. Apoc. *as a Carnival*

Nauta, holds that the *Apoc.* is a work of Saturnalian literature.

Robinson, Claudius is a monster fit for the Saturnalia.

Bonandini[1] (353–58).

Bonandini[2] (11–43).

10. *Studies of the Reception of the* Apoc.

Eden[2] (17–23).
Courtney
Roncali[2] (683–86).

SIGLA

S   Sangallensis 569, ninth century
V   Valentianensis 411 (formerly 393), ninth century
L   Londiniensis British Library Addit. 11983, twelfth
     century

Guideline for notes to the Latin text: as long as one of the three families supports the reading in the text as well as modern editors, I do not as a rule record variants in the notes. If a number of editors find problems with a reading in all three families, I make my own judgment. Fundmental variants are in the notes.

SYMBOLS AND ABBREVIATIONS USED IN THE LATIN TEXT

⟨ ⟩   letters enclosed in angle brackets must be
          added to the text
{ }   letters enclosed in braces must be deleted
⟨ * * * ⟩   lacuna in the text of unknown length

469

GENERAL BIBLIOGRAPHY

Adamietz, J. *Die römische Satire.* Darmstadt, 1986. (See esp. pp. 356–82.)

Athanassakis[1], A. "Some Evidence in Defence of the Title *Apocolocyntosis* for Seneca's Satire." *TAPA* 104 (1974): 11–21.

Athanassakis[2], A., trans. *Senecae Apocolocyntosis Divi Claudii.* Lawrence, KS, 1975. English translation.

Baehrens, E. Review of Otto Weinreich, *Senecas Apocolocyntosis, die Satire auf Tod* (Berlin, 1923). In *Göttingische gelehrte Anzeigen* 189 (1927): 449–63.

Bickel[1], E. "Der Schluss der *Apokolokyntosis.*" *Philologus* 77 (1921): 219–27.

Bickel[2], E. "Die Datierung der *Apokolokyntosis.*" *Philologische Wockenschrift* 44 (1924): 845–48.

Birt, Th. *De Senecae Apocolocyntosi et Apotheosi Lucubratio.* Marburg, 1888. Latin edition.

Bonandini[1], A. "Seneca, *Apocolocyntosis* 1983–2006." *Lexis* 25 (2007): 341–79.

Bonandini[2], A. *Il contrasto menippeo: Prosimetro, citazioni e commutazione di codice nell' Apocolocyntosis di Seneca. Con un commento alle parte poetiche.* Labirinti 130. Trento, 2010.

Bringmann[1], K. "Senecas *Apocolocyntosis* und die politische Satire in Rom." *A&A* 17 (1971): 56–70.

Bringmann[2], K. "Senecas *Apocolocyntosis*: ein Forschungsbericht 1959–1982." *ANRW* II 32.2 (1985): 885–914.

Bücheler[1], F. *Petronii Satirae et Liber Priapeorum. Adiectae sunt Varronis et Senecae Satirae similesque reliquiae.* Berlin, 1862. [1862[1], 1871[2], 1882[3], 1904[4], 1912[5], 1922[6]]. Latin critical edition.

Bücheler[2], F. "Eine Satire des Annaeus Seneca," *Symbola Philologorum Bonnensium in honorem Friderici Ritscheleii Collecta* (Leipzig, 1864–1867), 31–89 = *Kleine Schriften* I (Leipzig–Berlin, 1915), 439–507.

Camden (a scholar cited by J. Gruter). *L. Annaeus Seneca a M. Antonio Mureto correctus et notis illustratus. Acced. Animadversiones Iani Gruteri.* Heidelberg, 1593.

Coffey[1], M. "Seneca, *Apocolocyntosis* 1922–1958." *Lustrum* 6 (1961): 239–71.

Coffey[2], M. *Roman Satire.* London, 1989[2].

Courtney, E. "The Nachleben of the *Apocolocyntosis*." *RhM* 147 (2004): 426–28.

Curio, C. S. *L. Annaei Senecae Philosophi etc. Opera quae extant omnia Coeli Secundi Curionis vigilantissima cura castigata etc.* Basil, 1557. Latin edition [it contains the edition of Rhenanus and the notes of Iunius].

De Nonno, M. "Seneca, *Apocolocyntosis* 2, 1." *RFIC* 124 (1996): 77–80.

Eden[1], P. T. "The Manuscript Tradition of Seneca's *Apocolocyntosis*." *CQ* 29 (1979): 149–61.

Eden[2], P. T. Seneca: *Apocolocyntosis*. Cambridge, 1984. Latin critical edition with English translation and notes.

Eisenberg, H. "Bedeutung und Zweck des Titels von Senecas *Apocolocyntosis*." *HSCP* 82 (1978): 265–70.

Faber, N. *L. Annaei Senecae Philosophi et M. Annaei Sen-*

ecae Rhetoris Opera quae exstant. Paris, 1587. Latin edition.

Fromond, L. *L. Ann. Senecae Philosophi Opera a Justo Lipsio emendata*. Antwerp, 1632[3]. Latin edition.

Gronovius, J. F. *L. Annaei Senecae Philosophi Opera Omnia. Ex ultima J. Lipsii et J. F. Gronovii emendatatione et M. Annaei Senecae quae extant*. Leiden, 1649. Latin edition.

Haase, F. *L Annaei Senecae Opera quae supersunt recognovit . . . Frid. Haase*. Leipzig, 1852–1862). 3 vols. Latin edition.

Heil, A. "Die Herkunft des Claudius. Etymologische Wortspiele in Seneca, *Apocolocyntosis* 5–6." *MH* 63 (2006): 193–207.

Heinze, R. "Zu Senecas *Apocolocyntosis*." *Hermes* 61 (1926): 49–78.

Heraeus, W. Re-edited Bücheler[5-6]

Holzberg, N. Bibliography of Seneca *Apocolocyntosis*, privately circulated. Arranged first by author, then by subject (2015).

Iunius, H. His notes are included in the edition of Curio.

Kraft, K. "Der politische Hintergrund von Senecas *Apocolocyntosis*." *Historia* 15 (1996): 96–122.

Lipsius, J. *L. Annaei Senecae Philosophi Opera quae extant omnia*. Antwerp, 1605. [1605[1], 1615[2], 1632[3] with Fromond's notes, 1652[4]]. Latin edition.

Malaspina, E., ed. *Bibliografia Senecana del XX Secolo*. Bologna, 2005.

Martin, J. M. K. "Seneca the Satirist." *G&R* 14 (1945): 64–71.

Momigliano, A. "Literary Chronology of the Neronian Age." *CQ* 38 (1944): 96–100.

Muretus, M. A. *L. Annaei Senecae Opera*. Paris–Rome, 1585. Latin edition.

Nauta, R. R. "Seneca's *Apocolocyntosis* as Saturnalian Literature." *Mnemosyne* 40 (1987): 69–96.

O'Gorman, E. "Citation and Authority in Seneca's *Apocolocyntosis*." In *Cambridge Companion to Roman Satire*, edited by K. Freudenburg, 95–108. Cambridge, 2005.

Reeve, M. D. "*Apotheosis . . . per saturam*." *CP* 79 (1984): 305–7.

Reimar, H. S. *Cassii Dionis Cocceiani Historiae Romanae Quae Supersunt*. 2 vols. Hamburg, 1750–1752.

Reynolds, L. D. "The Younger Seneca *Apocolocyntosis*." In Reynolds, ed., *Texts and Transmission. A Survey of the Latin Classics*, 361–62. Oxford, 1984.

Rhenanus, B. *Ludus L. Annaei Senecae de morte Claudii Caesaris nuper in Germania repertus*. Basil, 1515.

Riikonen, H. *Menippean Satire as a Literary Genre with Special Reference to Seneca's Apocolocyntosis*. Helsinki, 1987.

Robinson, T. "In the Court of Time: Reckoning of a Monster in the *Apocolocyntosis* of Seneca." *Arethusa* 38 (2005): 223–57.

Roncali[1], R. *L. Annaei Senecae Ἀποκολοκύντωσις*. Leipzig–Stuttgart, 1990. Latin critical edition.

Roncali[2], R. "*Apocolocyntosis*." In *Brill's Companion to Seneca: Philosopher and Dramatist*, edited by G. Damschen and A Heil, 673–86. Leiden, 2014.

Rossbach[1], O. "Der Titel der Satire des jüngeren Seneca." *Philologische Wochenschrift* 44 (1924): 799–800.

Rossbach[2], O. *L. Annaei Senecae Divi Claudii Apotheosis*

per saturam quae Apocolocyntosis vulgo dicitur. Bonn, 1926. Critical Latin edition.

Roth, P. *Seneca Apocolocyntosis.* Bryn Mawr, 1988. English translation.

Russo[1], C. F. "Studi sulla *Divi Claudii* Ἀποκολοκύντωσις." *La Parola del Passato* 1 (1946): 241–59.

Russo[2], C. F. *L. Annaei Senecae Divi Claudii* ΑΠΟΚΟΛΟ-ΚΥΝΤΩΣΙΣ. Florence, 1948. [1948[1], 1955[2], 1961[3], 1964[4], 1965[5]]. Latin critical edition.

Sonntag, C. *L. Annaeus Seneca, Apokolokyntosis . . .* in *Zur Unterhaltung der Freunde der altern Literatur* 2. Heft 69. Riga, 1790.

Stagni, E. "*Apocolocyntosis*: Appunti sulla tradizione di Dione Cassio-Xifilino." *RFIC* 122 (1994): 298–339.

Sullivan[1], J. P. "Petronius, Seneca, and Lucan: A Neronian Literary Feud?" *TAPA* 99 (1968): 453–67.

Sullivan[2], J. P. *Petronius, the Satyricon. Seneca, the Apocolocyntosis.* Harmondsworth, 1986[5]. English translation, pp. 209–42.

Toynbee, J. M. C. "Nero Artifex: The *Apocolocyntosis* Reconsidered." CQ 36 (1942): 83–93.

Vahlen, J. *Ennianae Poesis Reliquiae.* Leipzig, 1903[2]. Latin critical edition.

Vannini, G. *Seneca Apokolokyntosis.* Milan, 2008. Latin text with Italian translation and notes.

L. ANNAEI SENECAE DIVI
CLAUDII ΑΠΟΚΟΛΟΚΥΝΤΟΣΙΣ

1. Quid actum sit in caelo ante diem III idus Octobris anno
novo, initio saeculi felicissimi, volo memoriae tradere.
nihil nec offensae nec gratiae dabitur. haec ita vera. si quis
quaesiverit unde sciam, primum, si noluero, non respon-
debo. quis coacturus est? ego scio me liberum factum, ex
quo suum diem obiit ille, qui verum proverbium fecerat,
2   aut regem aut fatuum nasci oportere. | si libuerit re-
spondere, dicam quod mihi in buccam venerit. quis umquam ab historico iuratores exegit? tamen si necesse fuerit auctorem producere, quaerito ab eo qui Drusillam
euntem in caelum vidit: idem Claudium vidisse se dicet
iter facientem "non passibus aequis." velit nolit, necesse
est illi omnia videre quae in caelo aguntur: Appiae viae
curator est, qua scis et divum Augustum et Tiberium Cae-
3   sarem ad deos isse. | hunc si interrogaveris, soli narrabit:

---

[1] First reference in the *Apoc.* to the Golden Age of Nero.

[2] Proverbs are common in the *Apoc.* and *Satyrica*.

[3] Julia Druscilla (17–38), sister of the emperor Caligula. Suetonius (*Calig.* 24.1) reports that there were sexual relations between sister and brother from childhood.

[4] Claudius was lame (Suet. *Claud.* 30). The quotation is from
Virgil (*Aen.* 2.724).

APOCOLOCYNTOSIS

1. I wish to give future generations a record of the proceedings in heaven on the thirteenth of October in the new year, which began an era of prosperity.[1] It will be done without malice or favor. This is the honest truth. If anyone should ask for the source of my information, in the first place, if I do not wish to, I will not answer. Who will force me to do so? I know that I have the choice to speak or not, ever since the death of the fellow who gave truth to the proverb[2] that one should be born a king or a fool. If it pleases me to reply, I will say the first thing that my tongue offers. Who ever required sworn witnesses from an historian? But if it is demanded to produce a source, ask the man who saw Druscilla[3] go up to heaven: the same one will say that he saw Claudius making his way there, though "with unequal steps."[4] Like it or not, he cannot but see everything that happens in heaven: he is the custodian of the Appian Way, by which route, as you know, both the deified Augustus and Tiberius Caesar traveled to join the gods.[5] If you question this man, he will tell the story to you

[5] Augustus and Tiberius both died in Campania, and their bodies were returned to Rome on the Via Appia. Augustus was deified, Tiberius vilified.

coram pluribus numquam verbum faciet. nam ex quo in
senatu iuravit se Drusillam vidisse caelum ascendentem
et illi pro tam bono nuntio nemo credidit quod[1] viderit,
verbis conceptis affirmavit se non indicaturum etiam si in
medio foro hominem occisum vidisset. ab hoc ego quae
tum audivi, certa clara affero, ita illum salvum et felicem
habeam.

> 2. Iam Phoebus breviore via contraxerat actum[2]
>   lucis et obscuri crescebant tempora Somni,
>   iamque suum victrix augebat Cynthia regnum,
>   et deformis Hiems gratos carpebat honores
>   divitis Autumni iussoque senescere Baccho
>   carpebat raras serus vindemitor uvas. |

2 puto magis intellegi si dixero: mensis erat October, dies
III idus Octobris. horam non possum certam tibi dicere |
(facilius inter philosophos quam inter horologia conve-
3 niet) tamen inter sextam et septimam erat. | "nimis rustice.
<adeo his>[3] adquiescunt omnes poetae, non contenti ortus
et occasus describere, ut etiam medium diem inquietent:
tu sic transibis horam tam bonam?" |

4   iam medium curru Phoebus diviserat orbem

[1] quod S: quid VL
[2] actum *De Nonno*: arcum *Eden*: ortum
[3] <adeo his> *added Russo*: <adeo non> *Roncali*

---

[6] In modern parlance, an "Oxford secret": a secret told to only
one person at a time.
[7] Reports of things heard are not reliable, while eyewitnesses
carry more weight. Cf. Plaut. *Truc.* 489: *pluris est oculatus testis*

alone: in front of many people he will never say a word.[6]
For ever since he swore in the senate that he had seen
Druscilla go up to heaven, and, for reporting such good
news, no one has believed what he says he saw, he has
solemnly sworn that he will never again reveal what he has
seen, even if he had seen a man murdered in the middle
of the Forum. What I then heard[7] from him I here report
plain and clear, as I hope for his health and happiness.

2. Phoebus had already made short the arc of his light
on a briefer path, and the periods of shady sleep were
growing, and victorious Cynthia[8] was already increasing
her kingdom, and grim Winter was grabbing for the pleasing splendors of rich Autumn, and with Bacchus ordered
to mature, the tardy vintner was plucking the scattered
grapes. I think that it will be understood better if I say: it
was the month of October, the day the thirteenth of October. I cannot tell you the exact hour—it will be easier to
get philosophers to agree than clocks. Anyway it was between twelve noon and one o'clock. "Far too crude!" you
say. "Not content to describe sunrises and sunsets, all poets find so much pleasure in these habits that they now
disturb even the midday siesta: will you pass over such a
good hour like this?"[9] Phoebus in his chariot had passed

unus quam aurati decem ("one witness with eyes is worth more
than ten with big ears.")

[8] The moon.

[9] Poets disturb people at all hours of the day. In the *Satyrica*
a poet is stoned by men in public places, such as baths (Petron.
Sat. 91.3, 92.6), theaters (90.5, 92.6), porticoes (90.1). Martial
claims he cannot get away from poets (Mart. 3.44.12) even when
he is sitting on the toilet.

et proprior Nocti fessas quatiebat habenas
obliquo flexam deducens tramite lucem:

Claudius animam agere coepit nec invenire exitum poterat.

3. Tum Mercurius, qui semper ingenio eius delectatus
esset, unam e tribus Parcis seducit et ait: "quid, femina
crudelissima, hominem miserum torqueri pateris? nec
umquam tam diu cruciatus <c>esset?[4] annus sexagesimus
et quartus est, ex quo cum anima luctatur. quid huic et
2 reipublicae invides? | patere mathematicos aliquando ve-
rum dicere, qui illum, ex quo princeps factus est, omnibus
annis omnibus mensibus efferunt. et tamen non est mirum
si errant et horam eius nemo novit: nemo enim umquam
illum natum putavit. fac quod faciendum est:

'dede neci, melior vacua sine regnet in aula.'" |

3 sed Clotho "ego mehercules" inquit "pusillum temporis
adicere illi volebam, dum hos pauculos qui supersunt civitate donaret—constituerat enim omnes Graecos, Gallos,
Hispanos, Britannos togatos videre—, sed quoniam placet
aliquos peregrinos in semen relinqui et tu ita iubes fieri,
4 fiat." | aperit tum capsulam et tres fusos profert: unus erat
Augurini, alter Babae,[5] tertius Claudii. "hos" inquit "tres

---

[4] <c>esset *added Iunius*
[5] Babae *Muretus, comparing Seneca Ep. 15.9:* bad(a)e

---

[10] The Fates are Clotho, Lachesis, and Atropos.
[11] Claudius suffered from many ailments (Suet. *Claud.* 21.6,
30).

midorbit, and nearer to Night, was shaking his tiring reins, leading away his redirected light on a sloping path. Claudius began to gasp his last breath, but he could not find the proper exit.

3. Then Mercury, who had always been charmed by Claudius' wit, took one of the three Fates[10] aside and said: "You cruel woman, why are you allowing that poor man to be tortured? After being tormented so long, is he never to find rest?[11] This is the sixty-fourth year since he began to fight for breath. Why do you regard with malice him and the state of Rome? Let the astrologers[12] for once tell the truth: ever since he became emperor they have been burying him off every year, every month. And yet it is not surprising if they are wrong and no one knows Claudius' last hour: for no one ever thought that he had been born. Do what has to be done. 'Give him over to death, let a better man rule in the vacated court.'"[13] But Clotho said: "By god, I was going to give him a bit more time until he could reward with citizenship those few left over—for he had determined to see all Greeks, Gauls, Spaniards. and Britons in a toga—but since it is your pleasure to leave some foreigners as seed to start the next crop, and you order that it be done that way, so be it." Then she opens her little box and brings out three spindles: one was that of Augurinus, the second of Baba, the third of Claudius.[14]

---

[12] Astrologers were believed to inquire into the length of the lives of the emperors with a view toward possible assassination.

[13] Verg. *G.* 4.90: only one bee, and that the strongest, can rule over the hive.

[14] A-B-C, perhaps a rhyme for children to learn the letters of the alphabet.

uno anno exiguis intervallis temporum divisos mori iu-
bebo, nec illum incomitatum dimittam. non oportet enim
eum, qui modo se tot milia hominum sequentia videbat,
tot praecedentia, tot circumfusa, subito solum destitui.
contentus erit his interim convictoribus."

4. Haec ait et turpi convolvens stamina fuso
   abrupit stolidae regalia tempora vitae.
   at Lachesis, redimita comas, ornata capillos,
   Pieria crinem lauro frontemque coronans,
5   candida de niveo subtemina vellere sumit
   felici moderanda manu, quae ducta colorem
   assumpsere novum. mirantur pensa sorores:
   mutatur vilis pretioso lana metallo,
   aurea formoso descendunt saecula filo.
10   nec modus est illis: felicia vellera ducunt
   et gaudent implere manus: sunt dulcia pensa.
   sponte sua festinat opus nulloque labore
   mollia contorto descendunt stamina fuso;
   vincunt Tithoni, vincunt et Nestoris annos.
15   Phoebus adest cantuque iuvat gaudetque futuris
   et laetus nunc plectra movet, nunc pensa ministrat:
   detinet intentas cantu fallitque laborem.
   dumque nimis citharam fraternaque carmina
     laudant,
   plus solito nevere manus humanaque fata

---

15 Pierian = Thessalian Muses and the god Apollo.

16 The three Fates in Latin are the *Parcae*.

17 Line 9 of the poem in Latin is of a type called a "golden line," abAB, two adjectives (ab) in the same order as the following

"These three" she said, "I will command to die within one year, separated by short intervals of time, and I will not send Claudius off unattended. For a man who often used to see so many thousands of men following him, so many thousands going before him, and so many thousands crowding round him, ought not to be abandoned suddenly on his own. He will be happy in the meantime with these close friends."

4. She said these things and twirling the thread on an ugly spool, she snapped off and ended the royal years of that doddering life. But Lachesis, her tresses tied and locks adorned, garlanding her hair and brow with Pierian[15] laurel, takes from the snowy fleece the bright white yarn to be shaped by a lucky touch, which when drawn out took on a new color. The sisters[16] marvel at the spinner's work: the cheap wool transformed to a precious metal, a Golden Age spun down on a lovely thread.[17] No limits are set: they tease out the favored fleeces and they rejoice in filling their hands: the spinner's work is lovely. Of its own accord the work moved quickly, and with no effort the soft threads turn on to the twirling spool. The allotted time surpasses the years of Tithonus and of Nestor.[18] Phoebus is present and helps with a song and is full of joy for the future, and now happily plucks the strings, and now helps with the wool. He keeps them at their work by singing and charms their toil away; and while they praise their brother's lyre and songs lavishly, their hands spun out more than usual,

two nouns (AB). It is thought that the line alludes to the Golden Age of Nero.

[18] Tithonus and Nestor are common examples of longevity.

483

20   laudatam transcendit opus. "ne demite, Parcae"
       Phoebus ait "vincat mortalis tempora vitae
       ille mihi similis vultu similisque decore
       nec cantu nec voce minor. felicia lassis
       saecula praestabit legumque silentia rumpet.
25   qualis discutiens fugientia Lucifer astra
       aut qualis surgit redeuntibus Hesperus astris,
       qualis, cum primum tenebris Aurora solutis
       induxit rubicunda diem, Sol aspicit orbem
       lucidus et primos a carcere concitat axes:
30   talis Caesar adest, talem iam Roma Neronem
       aspiciet. flagrat nitidus fulgore remisso
       vultus et adfuso cervix formosa capillo." |

2 haec Apollo. at Lachesis, quae et ipsa homini formosis-
simo faveret, fecit illud plena manu et Neroni multos annos de suo donat. Claudium autem iubent omnes

     χαίροντας, εὐφημοῦντας ἐκπέμπειν δόμων.

et ille quidem animam ebulliit, et ex eo desiit vivere videri.
expiravit autem dum comoedos audit, ut scias me non sine
3 causa illos timere. | ultima vox eius haec inter homines
audita est, cum maiorem sonitum emisisset illa parte, qua
facilius loquebatur: "vae me, puto, concacavi me." quod
an fecerit, nescio; omnia certe concacavit.

   5. Quae in terris postea sint acta supervacuum est re-

---

[19] Nero is compared favorably with Apollo in the arts, and
then with the sun and moon.
[20] A quotation from Euripides, *Cresphontes*, frag. 449 v. 4,
August Nauck, *Tragicorum Graecorum Fragmenta* (Leipzig,
1889²).

and the work he praised surpasses the lot of a man. "Fates, take nothing away" said Phoebus, "let that one, who resembles me in looks and beauty, and no less in song and voice, surpass the duration of human life. He will provide for the weary people years of prosperity, and will break the silence imposed on the laws. Like the Morning Star rising and scattering the stars in flight, or like the Evening Star which rises with the stars' return, like the bright Sun which looks at the world and spurs on his first chariots from the starting gates, as soon as rosy Dawn has got rid of the shadows and leads in the day: such a Caesar is present, such a Nero[19] Rome will now behold. His bright face blazes with gentle radiance, his neck graceful under the flowing hair." So spoke Apollo. But Lachesis who herself favored such a handsome fellow did her job with a generous hand, and bestows on Nero many years from her own supply. As for Claudius, however, they ordered them all "in joy and solemn awe to carry him out of the house."[20] And indeed he did gurgle out his last breath, and from that moment ceased even appearing to be alive. However, he died while he was listening to some comic actors, so you understand that I have good reasons to fear them. The following were the last words of his to be heard on earth, after he had emitted a louder noise from that end from which he spoke the easiest: "Oh my, I think I just shat myself." For all I know, he did. He certainly shat on everything else.[21]

5. It is gratuitous to recount the proceedings of what happened on earth after that, for you know them very well,

---

[21] This might be an allusion to Claudius' proposed edict on making farting legal at banquets (Suet. *Claud*. 32).

ferre. scitis enim optime, nec periculum est ne excidant
quae memoriae gaudium publicum impresserunt: nemo
felicitatis suae obliviscitur. in caelo quae acta sint audite:
2 fides penes auctorem erit. | nuntiatur Iovi venisse quen-
dam bonae staturae, bene canum; nescio quid illum mi-
nari, assidue enim caput movere; pedem dextrum trahere.
quaesisse se cuius nationis esset: respondisse nescio quid
perturbato sono et voce confusa; non intellegere se linguam eius: nec Graecum esse nec Romanum nec ullius
3 gentis notae. | tum Iuppiter Herculem, qui totum orbem
terrarum pererraverat et nosse videbatur omnes nationes,
iubet ire et[6] explorare quorum hominum esset. tum Hercules primo aspectu sane perturbatus est, ut qui etiam non
omnia monstra timuerit. ut vidit novi generis faciem, insolitum incessum, vocem nullius terrestris animalis sed qualis esse marinis beluis solet, raucam et implicatam, putavit
4 sibi tertium decimum laborem venisse. | diligentius in-
tuenti visus est quasi homo. acccessit itaque et quod facil-
limum fuit Graeculo, ait:

τίς πόθεν εἰς ἀνδρῶν, ποίη[7] πόλις ἠδὲ τοκῆες;

Claudius gaudet esse illic philologos homines: sperat futurum aliquem historiis suis locum. itaque et ipse Homerico
versu Caesarem se esse significans ait:

---

6 et *omit* VL
7 ποίη *Gertz*: ποι η *S*: πόθι τοι Homer *Od.* 1.170

---

22 Claudius had numerous physical problems (Suet. *Claud.*
21.6, 30).   23 Hercules was much traveled and slew many
monsters. The "Twelve Labors of Hercules" are so famous from
mythology that Seneca can drag in a thirteenth.

and there is no danger of people forgetting the impression that the public rejoicing made on their memory: no one forgets his own good luck. Listen to the proceedings that took place in heaven: my informant is responsible for the reliability of the account. It was announced to Jupiter that someone of good size and with very white hair had arrived; he was making some sort of threat, for he kept shaking his head; he was dragging his right foot.[22] The messenger said that he had asked about his nationality; he made some answer with a confused noise and indistinct voice; the messenger did not understand his language: he was neither Greek nor Roman nor of any known race. Jupiter then instructed Hercules, who had wandered the whole world over and seemed to know every nation, to go and find out his nationality. Then at first sight of him Hercules was badly shaken, as though he had not yet had the occasion to fear all monsters. When he saw the strange sort of appearance, the weird way of walking, and the voice of no land animal but the kind that belonged to denizens of the deep, hoarse and inarticulate, he thought his thirteenth labor had come.[23] Upon closer inspection, it appeared to be something like a human. So he went up to him and, what is really easy for a little Greek, said: "Who are you and from where? What kind are your city and parents?"[24] Claudius was delighted that there were scholars there; he had hoped that there would be some place for his historical works.[25] And so he too in Homeric verse indicated that

[24] Hom. *Od.* 1.170.
[25] Claudius wrote numerous historical works (Suet. *Claud.* 41–42).

Ἰλιόθεν με φέρων ἄνεμος Κικόνεσσι πέλασσεν.

—erat autem sequens versus verior, aeque Homericus:

ἔνθα δ' ἐγὼ πόλιν ἔπραθον, ὤλεσα δ' αὐτούς.

6. Et imposuerat Herculi minime vafro,[8] nisi fuisset illic Febris, quae fano suo relicto sola cum illo venerat: ceteros omnes deos Romae reliquerat. "iste" inquit "mera mendacia narrat. ego tibi dico, quae cum illo tot annis vixi: Luguduni natus est, Munati[9] municipem vides. quod tibi narro, ad sextum decimum lapidem natus est a Vienna, Gallus germanus. itaque quod Gallum facere oportebat, Romam cepit. hunc ego tibi recipio Luguduni natum, ubi Licinus[10] multis annis regnavit. tu autem, qui plura loca calcasti quam ullus mulio perpetuarius, {Lugudunenses}[11] scire debes multa milia inter Xanthum et Rhodanum interesse." | excandescit hoc loco Claudius et quanto potest murmure irascitur. quid diceret nemo intellegebat. ille autem Frebrim duci iubebat. illo gestu solutae manus, et

2

8 vafro *Iunius*: fabro *SV*: fabros *L*
9 Munati *Rhenanus*: Marci
10 Licinus *Bücheler*: licinius
11 {Lugudunenses} *deleted Bücheler*

---

26 Hom. *Od*. 9.39–40. Cicones were wild Thracians.
27 Fever (*Febris*) was a divine power with a shrine on the Palatine.
28 L. Munatius Plancus founded Lyons in 44–43 and celebrated a triumph in 43.
29 Vienne is in Gallia Narbonensis (southern France bordering on the Mediterranean), once capital of the Allobroges.

he was Caesar and said: "The wind bearing me from Ilium brought me to the Cicones" (but the next verse likewise Homeric was truer), "there I sacked the city and slew all the people."[26]

6. And he would certainly have fooled Heracles who was not very sharp, if the goddess Fever[27] had not been there, who, after abandoning her temple, was the only one who had come with Hercules; she had left all the other gods at Rome. "He," she said, "tells only absolute lies. I, who have lived with him for so many years, tell you: he was born at Lyons; you see in front of you a fellow townsman of Munatius.[28] I tell you, he was born at the sixteenth milestone from Vienne,[29] a true Gaul.[30] And so, as a Gaul should do, he captured Rome.[31] I guarantee that he was born at Lyons, where Licinus[32] was king for many years. But you, who have tramped[33] over more places than any long-haul mule driver, ought to know that there are many miles between the Xanthus and the Rhône."[34] At this point Claudius flared up and expressed his anger in the best muttering he could manage. No one tried to understand what he was saying. As a matter of fact, he kept ordering that Fever be taken away for punishment. With that gesture of his shaking hand, which was steady enough only on

[30] A pun on the Latin word *germanus*: "sibling," "genuine," or "German."

[31] The Gauls sacked Rome in 390 BC.

[32] Licinus was born in Gaul, served as a slave of Julius Caesar, then as a freedman, and was appointed (16–15 BC) procurator of Gallia Lugdunensis by Augustus.

[33] Hercules was patron of travelers.   [34] Xanthus is a river in the Troad, near the site of Ilium, i.e., Troy.

ad hoc unum satis firmae, quo decollare homines solebat, iusserat illi collum praecidi. putares omnes illius esse libertos: adeo illum nemo curabat.

7. Tum Hercules "audi me" inquit "tu desine fatuari. venisti huc, ubi mures ferrum rodunt. citius mihi verum, ne tibi alogias excutiam." et quo terribilior esset, tragicus fit et ait: |

2   "exprome[12] propere sede qua genitus[13] cluas,
        hoc ne peremptus stipite ad terram accidas:
        haec clava reges saepe mactavit feros.
        quid nunc profatu vocis incerto sonas?
5   quae patria, quae gens mobile eduxit caput?
        edissere. equidem regna tergemini petens
        longinqua regis, unde ab Hesperio mari
        Inachiam ad urbem nobile advexi pecus,
        vidi duobus imminens fluviis iugum,
10   quod Phoebus ortu semper obverso videt,
        ubi Rhodanus ingens amne praerapido fluit
        Ararque, dubitans quo suos cursus agat,

[12] exprome *Rhenanus*: exprime
[13] sede qua genitus *Rhenanus*: sed qua genitus

---

[35] If mice can gnaw iron, humans must be superhuman (Herod. 3.75–76). The proverb also paints a picture of a fairyland. Such mice, it seems, were found on the island of Gyarus in the Cyclades according to Pliny (*NH* 8.222). Gyarus became a prison (Tac. *Ann.* 40.30.2), and Hercules implies that Claudius has come to such a place as Gyarus and so is condemned to *deportatio in insulam*, a worse punishment than *relegatio in insulam*, to which Claudius had sentenced Seneca.

such occasions when he was accustomed to indicate that people should be decapitated, he had ordered that her neck be severed. You would think that all those around him were his freedmen, the way no one paid him any attention.

7. Then Hercules said: "Listen to me. You there, stop playing the fool. You have come here where mice gnaw iron.[35] Tell me the truth and do it quickly, or I will shake this nonsense out of you." And that he might be more terrifying, he put on the mask of tragedy and said: "Declare quickly where you claim to have been born, lest you fall to the ground killed by my club of a tree trunk: this club has often slaughtered savage kings. Why now make noises in unintelligible tones of your voice? What country, what race produced that shaking head? Expound. For my part, while seeking the distant kingdoms of the three-bodied king Geryon,[36] whence from the Western sea to the city of Inachus[37] I drove the noble cattle, I saw a mountain ridge[38] overlooking two rivers,[39] which Phoebus sees opposite him as he rises, where the mighty Rhône with rapid currents flows, and the Saône, hesitating in which direction to push its waters, in silence washes the banks with

[36] For his tenth labor Hercules got the red oxen of the three-bodied monster Geryon from the island of Erythrea and brought them back to Argos, perhaps earlier passing near Lyons.

[37] Inachus was the founder of Argos.

[38] The Colline de Fourvière, on which Lyons was built.

[39] The Rhône (*Rhodanus*) and the Saône (*Arar*).

tacitus quietis adluit ripas vadis.
estne illa tellus spiritus altrix tui?" |

3 haec satis animose et fortiter, nihilo minus mentis suae
non est et timet μωροῦ πληγήν. Claudius, ut vidit virum
valentem, oblitus nugarum, intellexit neminem Romae
sibi parem fuisse, illic non habere se idem gratiae: gallum
4 in suo sterquilino plurimum posse. | itaque quantum in-
tellegi potuit, haec visus est dicere: "ego te, fortissime
deorum Hercule, speravi mihi adfuturum apud alios, et si
qui a me notorem petisset, te fui nominaturus, qui me
optime nosti. nam, si memoria repetis, ego eram qui tibi[14]
ante templum tuum ius dicebam totis diebus mense Iulio
5 et Augusto. | tu scis quantum illic miseriarum ego contu-
lerim, cum causidicos audirem diem et noctem. in quod
si incidisses, valde fortis licet tibi videaris, maluisses cloa-
cas Augeae[15] purgare: multo plus ego stercoris exhausi.
sed quoniam volo ⟨***⟩"

8. "⟨***⟩ non mirum quod in curiam impetum fecisti:
nihil tibi clausi est. modo dic nobis qualem deum istum

---

[14] tibi *SVL*: Tiburi *Bücheler, comparing Suetonius Augustus
72.2, perhaps correctly*   [15] Augeae *Bücheler*: auge

---

[40] The usual expression in tragedy θεοῦ πληγή, "coup or blow
of the god" (Soph. *Aj*. 278–79) is parodied by μωροῦ πληγή,
"coup or blow of the fool." In this Gallic context, an analogous
play on the common French expression *coup de foudre* is irresist-
ible.   [41] Latin *gallus* is both "a Gaul" and "a cock."
[42] Claudius was especially fond of attending court cases (Suet.
Claud. 14).   [43] The sixth labor of Hercules was to clean out
the stables of the three thousand cattle of King Augeas. There is
probably an allusion here to the work Claudius did on the drains
of Rome, as he built new aqueducts into the city.

hushed shallows. Is that land the nurse of your breath of life?" He said this with spirit and courage; none the less he is not in his right mind and fears the *coup de fou*.[40] When Claudius looked at the powerfully built man, he cut out all the nonsense and realized that although no one was his equal at Rome, in this place he did not have the same influence: a cock holds power only on his own dunghill.[41] And so as far as he could be understood, he seemed to say this: "I hoped that you, Hercules, strongest of the gods, would be there for me before all others, and if anyone had asked for a person to vouch for me, I was going to name you, who know me so well. For if you search your memory, I was the one who used to sit in judgment in front of your temple for whole days at a time in the months of July and August. You know what a great number of complaints I went over, when I was listening to the lawyers day and night.[42] If you had fallen into that, though you think that you are mighty tough, you would have preferred to clean out the sewers of Augeas: I drained off a lot more bullshit.[43] But since I wish ⟨***⟩"[44]

8. "⟨***⟩ [Speaker is an unidentifiable deity, addressing Hercules and opposed to Claudius] it is not surprising that you have charged into the senate: nothing is barred to

---

[44] There is a lacuna here of about one folium, which was already missing in the archetype. Eden[2] (98–99) summarizes what must have been lost: the end of Claudius' speech in which he asks Hercules for support to enter heaven; Hercules' reply to Claudius, their forced entry into the heavenly senate house, and Hercules' request that Claudius be deified; the uproar in the senate and Jupiter's inability to bring it to order; the beginning of a speech that picks up at the end of the lacuna (the beginning of our ch. 8), made to Hercules by an unknown deity, hostile to Claudius.

fieri velis. Ἐπικούρειος θεὸς non potest esse: οὔτε αὐτὸς
πρᾶγμα ἔχει τι[16] οὔτε ἄλλοις παρέχει. Stoicus? quomodo
potest 'rotundus' esse, ut ait Varro, 'sine capite, sine prae-
putio?' est aliquid in illo Stoici dei, iam video: nec cor nec
2 caput habet. | si mehercules a Saturno petisset hoc bene-
ficium, cuius mensem toto anno celebravit Saturnalicius[17]
princeps, non tulisset. illum deum[18] <induci>[19] ab Iove,
quem,[20] quantum quidem in illo fuit, damnavit incesti?
Silanum enim generum suum occidit. 'oro, per <quid>?'[21]
quod sororem suam, festivissiman omnium puellarum,
quam omnes Venerem vocarent, maluit Iunonem vocare.
3 | 'quare' inquit, 'quaero enim, sororem suam?' stulte,
stude: Athenis dimidium licet, Alexandriae totum. quia
'Romae' inquis, 'mures molas lingunt,' hic nobis curva corriget?[22] quid in cubiculo suo faciat nesci{o}et:[23] iam 'caeli

---

[16] ἔχει τι *Haase*: εχιε του

[17] Saturnalicius *Bücheler*: saturnaliaeius

[18] illum deum *SVL*: illud, nedum *Gronovius*

[19] <induci> *added Eden*[2]   [20] quem *Fromond*: qui

[21] oro, per <quid>? *Russo*: oro per quod *SVL*: propter(ea)
quod *Bücheler*   [22] corriget *Sonntag*: corrigit

[23] nesci{o}et: iam *Eden*[2]: nescio et iam

---

[45] Epicureans imagined gods as having no trouble themselves
and causing none to others (Diog. Laert. 10.139).

[46] The Stoic god is round like the cosmos, and so the perfect
man is round (Hor. *Sat.* 2.7.86). This carried to a logical conclusion is nonsense.

[47] That is, neither intelligence (head) or individuality (foreskin).

[48] The Saturnalia began on December 17 and was later ex-

you. Just tell us what sort of god you want him to be. He cannot be an Epicurean god: such a one neither has any trouble himself nor gives any to others.[45] A Stoic god? How can he be 'globular,'[46] as Varro says, 'with no head, with no foreskin'?[47] There is something of a Stoic god in him, I see it now: he has neither heart nor head. I swear that if he had asked this favor from Saturn, whose month he celebrated all year long as Carnival Emperor,[48] he would not have got it. Is he to be presented as a god by Jupiter, whom, as much as it was in him, he condemned for incest[49] by killing his son-in-law Silanus? Why I ask you? Because of his sister, the most charming girl of all, whom all men called Venus, while he preferred to call her Juno. 'Why his own sister?' I asked. Read your books, stupid. At Athens you can go halfway, at Alexandria the whole way.[50] Because you say 'at Rome the mice lick the millstones,'[51] is he the one to set crooked things straight for us? He will not know what he does in his own bed-

tended by Claudius to last five days, but many celebrated it throughout December.

[49] L. Iunius Silanus, great-great-grandson of Augustus, was accused of incest with his sister, Iunia Calvina, and committed suicide in 49 on the day of Claudius' marriage to Agrippina. By condemning Silanus for incest because of his relationship with his sister, Claudius is also condemning Jupiter for his relationship with his sister, Juno.

[50] At Athens, marriage was allowed between brother and sister of the same father, but not of the same mother; at Alexandria, marriage between full-brother and full-sister was practiced by the Ptolemies.   [51] Perhaps the meaning is something like this: in a properly run household and city, mice lick the millstones because the granaries are well built.

scrutatur plagas.' deus fieri vult? parum est quod templum
in Britannia habet, quod hunc barbari colunt et ut deum
orant μωροῦ εὐιλάτου τυχεῖν?"

9. Tandem Iovi venit in mentem, privatis intra curiam
morantibus ‹senatoribus non licere›[24] sententiam dicere
nec disputare. "ego" inquit "p.c., interrogare vobis permi-
seram, vos mera mapalia fecistis. volo ut servetis discipli-
nam curiae. hic, qualiscumque est, quid de nobis existima-
2 vit?" | illo dimisso primus interrogatur sententiam Ianus
pater. is designatus erat in kal. Iulias postmeridianus consul, homo, quantum via sua fert, qui semper videt ἄμα
πρόσσω καὶ ὀπίσσω. is multa diserte, quod in foro
viv‹eb›at,[25] dixit, quae notarius persequi non potuit et
ideo non refero, ne aliis verbis ponam quae ab illo dicta
3 sunt. | multa dixit de magnitudine deorum: non debere

---

[24] ‹senatoribus non licere› *added Bücheler*
[25] viv‹eb›at *added Bücheler*

---

[52] Difficult meaning: perhaps Claudius will be confused about
what he is doing in his own bedroom, because Messalina has
admitted a new lover there. And he has moved his attention to
the zones of heaven.

[53] Quotation from Ennius, *Iphigenia*, frag. 244, J. Vahlen, *En-
nianiae Poesis Reliquiae* (Leipzig, 1903²).

[54] There was a temple to Claudius at Colchester (Camulodu-
num; Tac. *Ann.* 12.32.4).

[55] In the formulaic curse or prayer, the suppliant asks θεοῦ . . .
τύχειν, "to chance upon a god"; μωροῦ, "fool," is substituted for
θεοῦ. Cf. note 40 above.

[56] The Latin *p.c.* is the abbreviation of *patres conscripti*, "honorable members of the senate."

[57] In the Republic consuls normally served for one year (years

room:[52] already 'he is searching the regions in the sky.'[53] Is it not enough that he has a temple in Britain,[54] that savages now worship him and, as if he were a god, pray 'to find a well disposed fool?'"[55]

9. Finally it occurred to Jupiter that with members of the public lingering in the senate house, it was out of order for senators to offer a motion or debate. He said, "Honorable members,[56] I gave you permission to ask questions, but you have made it an absolute shambles. I ask that you observe the rules of order of the house. This man, whatever he is, what will he think of us?" After Claudius had been dismissed, the first to be asked his opinion was Father Janus. He had been made consul-elect for the afternoon of the first of July,[57] a man, at least in his own street, who had simultaneous foresight and hindsight.[58] Because he was living in the Forum,[59] he made a long and glib speech that the official secretary could not completely follow, and therefore I do not report it, so as not to put words in his mouth that he didn't say. He said a great deal about the majesty of the gods: the honor of being a god should

were named after the two consuls); in the Empire they served as long as the emperor wished, e.g. two to four months. Often the emperor appointed himself consul. In the case before us Janus is consul for only one day and then only for the afternoon of that day. Roman officials usually did no work in the afternoon and seldom returned to the office after lunch, much like Roman officials in the twenty-first century.

[58] Echoes of Homer (*Il.* 3.109). Janus was pictured as two-faced on the same head: the beginning and the end, the past and the future. Therefore he is asked to speak first.

[59] Janus had a statue over the double archway of the Ianus Geminus, which led to the Argiletum at the Forum.

hunc vulgo dari honorem. "olim" inquit "magna res erat
deum fieri: iam Fabam²⁶ mimum fecisti. itaque ne videar
in personam, non in rem dicere sententiam, censeo ne
quis post hunc diem deus fiat ex his, qui ἀρούρης καρπὸν
ἔδουσιν aut ex his, quos alit ζείδωρος ἄρουρα. qui contra
hoc senatus consultum deus factus dictus pictusve erit,
eum dedi larvis et proximo munere inter novos auctoratos
4 ferulis vapulare placet." | proximus interrogatur senten-
tiam Diespiter Vicae Potae filius, et ipse designatus consul, nummulariolus. hoc quaestu se sustinebat: vendere
civitatulas solebat. ad hunc belle accessit Hercules et auri-
5 culam illi tetigit. censet itaque in haec verba: | "cum divus
Claudius et divum Augustum sanguine contingat nec minus divam Augustam aviam suam, quam ipse deam esse
iussit, longeque omnes mortales sapientia antecellat sit-
que e re publica esse aliquem qui cum Romulo possit

---

²⁶ Fabam *Bücheler, comparing Cicero, Letters to Atticus
1.16.13:* famam

---

⁶⁰ "Bean Farce." It seems that *Faba* (bean) is the name of a
comedy/farce (Cic. *Att.* 1.16.13). Beans are present in the cult
rituals of the dead and also in popular stories about ghosts; see
larvis, "evil spirits," below.　　　⁶¹ Those who eat the fruits of
the earth or grain-giving soil are mortals (Hom. *Il.* 6.142, 8.486).
⁶² Legal expressions of the kind used in the Roman senate (cf.
Plaut. *Asin.* 174).　　　⁶³ A native god of daylight commonly
identified with Jupiter. Vica Pota is also a native deity, but little
or nothing is known about her.　　　⁶⁴ Touching the earlobe as
an outward sign that a witness is called to attention (Plin. *NH*
11.251).　　　⁶⁵ The mother of Claudius is Antonia Minor,
daughter of Octavia (Augustus' sister) and Marc Antony.
⁶⁶ Claudius' father, Nero Claudius Drusus, was the son of

not be given to ordinary people. "Once," he said, "it was a great thing to be made a god: now you have made it a 'Bean Farce.'[60] Therefore, so that I do not seem to speak against the person involved but against the principle of the thing, I move that after this day no one be made a god from those who 'eat the fruit of the soil' or from those whom 'the grain-giving soil' nourishes.[61] Anyone who is made, spoken of, or portrayed as a god in contravention of this decree of the senate,[62] I vote that he be given over to the evil spirits and at the next gladiatorial show should be beaten with rods among the raw recruits." The next to be asked his opinion was Diespiter,[63] son of Vica Pota. He was also consul-elect, a small-time moneylender. By this he made a living: he used to sell citizenships. Hercules daintily approached him and touched his earlobe.[64] Diespiter accordingly framed his motion in these words: "Since the deified Claudius is related by blood to both the deified Augustus[65] and no less to the deified Augusta,[66] his grandmother, whom he himself had ordered to be a goddess, and whereas he far surpasses all mortal men in wisdom, and whereas it is in the interest of the state that there should be someone who can 'devour steaming turnips' with Romulus,[67] I move that from this day the deified

Tiberius Claudius Nero and Livia. Tiberius Claudius Nero divorced Livia in 39 BC so that Octavian (Augustus) could marry her; she was renamed Julia Augusta in AD 14.

[67] Romulus was thought to live in heaven but to have remained rude and rough (Mart. 13.16.1–2). The Latin words *ferventia rapa vorare* are the end of a hexameter. Eden[2] adduces Lucilius, frag. 1357, Frederick Marx, *C. Lucilii Carminum Reliquiae* (Leipzig, 1904), and is certain that the beginning of the line reads *Romulus in caelo*.

'ferventia rapa vorare,' censeo uti divus Claudius ex hac
die deus sit ita uti ante eum quis optimo iure factus sit,
eamque rem ad Metamorphosis Ovidi adiciendam." |
6 variae erant sententiae, et videbatur Claudius {sentent}-
iam²⁷ vincere. Hercules enim, qui videret ferrum suum in
igne esse, modo huc modo illuc cursabat et aiebat: "noli
mihi invidere, mea res agitur; deinde tu si quid volueris,
in vicem faciam: manus manum lavat."

10. Tunc divus Augustus surrexit sententiae suae loco
dicendae et summa facundia disseruit: "ego" inquit "p.c.,
vos testes habeo, ex quo deus factus sum, nullum me verbum fecisse: semper meum negotium ago. et non possum
amplius dissimulare et dolorem, quem graviorem pudor
2 facit, continere. | in hoc terra marique pacem peperi? ideo
civilia bella compescui? ideo legibus urbem fundavi, ope-
ribus ornavi, ut—? quid dicam, p.c., non invenio: omnia
infra indignationem verba sunt. confugiendum est itaque
ad Messalae Corvini, disertissimi viri, illam sententiam
3 'pudet imperii.' | hic, p.c., qui vobis non posse videtur
muscam excitare, tam facile homines occidebat quam ca-

---

²⁷ {sentent}iam *deleted Vannini*

⁶⁸ Romulus' apotheosis is recorded in Ovid (*Met*. 14.805–28),
as is Julius Caesar's (*Met*. 15.745–831), and that of Augustus is
foretold (*Met*. 15.868–70).
⁶⁹ The speech of Augustus is the longest in the *Apoc*., and its
style, choice and arrangement of words, and word rhythms seem
reminiscent of the *Res Gestae Divi Augusti*, the monumental
inscription composed by the emperor (with copies set up all over
the Empire) to celebrate his own deeds.   ⁷⁰ Compare the
wording here with that of *Res Gestae Divi Augusti* 13.

Claudius be a god just like anyone before him who was made a god with the best justification, and that an account of the event be appended to Ovid's *Metamorphoses*."[68] There was a variety of proposals and Claudius seemed to be winning the decision. For Hercules, who could see that his own iron was in the fire, rushed here and there and said: "Do not begrudge me my request; my own interests are involved. Then later if you want a favor, I will return it: one hand washes the other."

10. Then the deified Augustus[69] rose to his feet at his turn for expressing his opinion, and spoke with the utmost eloquence: "I have you, gentlemen of the senate, as witnesses" he said, "that since I became a god, I have not uttered a word. I always mind my own business. And yet I cannot hide my feelings any longer or conceal the pain that my sense of shame makes all the greater. Was it for this that I brought peace to land and sea?[70] Was this why I checked the civil wars? Was this why I laid a foundation of laws for Rome, beautified the city with public works, so that—? what should I say, gentlemen of the senate, I cannot find anything. All words fall short of my indignation. So I must fall back on that statement of the most eloquent man Messalla Corvinus:[71] 'I am ashamed of my power.' Gentlemen of the senate, this man here who gives you the impression that he cannot startle a fly, used to kill people as effortlessly as a dog squats on its haunches. But why am

[71] Valerius Messalla Corvinus (64 BC–AD 8) was appointed by Augustus to be the first *praefectus urbi*, but he resigned after only a few days because he felt that his power would be too great and could be misused by a lesser man (Tac. *Ann.* 6.11.4).

nis adsidit. sed quid ego de tot ac talibus viris dicam? non
vacat deflere publicas clades intuenti domestica mala. itaque illa omittam, haec referam; nam etiam si σφυρὸν
meum[28] {Graece}[29] nescit, ego scio: ἔγγιον γόνυ κνήμης.

4 | iste quem videtis, per tot annos sub meo nomine latens,
hanc mihi gratiam retulit, ut duas Iulias proneptes meas
occideret, alteram ferro, alteram fame; unum abnepotem
L. Silanum: videris, Iuppiter, an in causa mala—certe in
tua, si aequos futurus es. dic mihi, dive Claudi: quare
quemquam ex his, quos quasque occidisti, antequam de
causa cognosceres, antequam audires, damnasti? hoc ubi
fieri solet? in caelo non fit.

11. Ecce Iuppiter, qui tot annos regnat, uni Volcano
crus fregit, quem

$$\dot{ρ}ῖψε\ ποδὸς\ τεταγὼν\ ἀπὸ\ βηλοῦ\ θεσπεσίοιο,$$

et iratus fuit uxori et suspendit illam: numquid occidit? tu
Messalinam, cuius aeque avunculus maior eram quam
tuus, occidisti. 'nescio' inquis? di tibi malefaciant: adeo

---

[28] σφυρὸν meum *Eden*[2]: sormea *or* soror mea
[29] {Graece} *deleted Sonntag*

---

[72] The proverb perhaps has the general meaning of something
like "charity begins at home," but here transferred to "murder
begins at home." There is a similar proverb in Theocritus (*Id.*
16.18). Augustus was notably fond of such expressions (Suet. *Aug.*
25.4, 87). [73] Like all Roman emperors, Claudius used the
name Caesar Augustus.

[74] The two great-granddaughters of Augustus: Julia Livilla,
daughter of Germanicus, starved to death; Julia, daughter of Drusus Caesar, murdered by sword.

I talking about so many men and men of quality? I have no time to shed tears over national calamities when I consider family misfortunes. And so I will pass over the former and recall the latter. For even if my anklebone does not know it, I know that the knee is nearer than the shin.[72] That man you see in front of you, after all those years of hiding under my name,[73] paid me such thanks that he killed the two Julias, my great-granddaughters, one by the sword, the other by starvation,[74] and one great-great grandson, L. Silanus:[75] you will judge, Jupiter, whether it was for an unjustified cause—it was certainly the same as yours, if you are going to be fair. Tell me, deified Claudius, why did you condemn any of these men and women whom you killed, before you could examine the case, before you could hear the facts? Where is this the customary practice?[76] It does not happen in heaven.

11. Look at Jupiter: all these years he has been king, and in Vulcan's case alone did he break his leg, whom 'taking hold of his foot he hurled from heaven's threshold.'[77] And he got angry at his wife and hung her up.[78] Did he ever kill? You killed Messalina,[79] whose great-great-uncle I was as well as yours. 'I don't know,' you say? May the gods

<hr />

[75] See note 49.   [76] Claudius is said to have behaved strangely at trials (Suet. *Claud*. 15).

[77] Hephaestus (Vulcan to the Romans) was hurled from heaven, landing on the island of Lemnos, and crippled for life (Hom. *Il*. 1.591).

[78] Hera (Hom. *Il*. 15.17–24).

[79] Valeria Messalina, the great-granddaughter of Augustus' sister Octavia, was murdered in 48 on orders from Narcissus, an imperial freedman of Claudius.

2 istuc turpius est quod nescisti quam quod occidisti. | C.
Caesarem non desiit mortuum persequi. occiderat ille
socerum: hic et generum. Gaius Crassi filium vetuit Magnum vocari: hic nomen illi reddidit, caput tulit. occidit in
una domo Crassum, Magnum, Scriboniam {tristionias},[30]
<non> Assar<aci nat>ionem,[31] nobiles tamen, Crassum
3 vero tam fatuum ut etiam regnare posset. | hunc nunc
deum facere vultis? videte corpus eius dis iratis natum. ad
4 summam, tria verba cito dicat et servum me ducat. | hunc
deum quis colet? quis credet? dum tales deos facitis, nemo
vos deos esse credet. summa rei, p.c., si honeste inter vos
gessi, si nulli clarius respondi, vindicate iniurias meas. ego
5 pro sententia mea hoc censeo." | atque ita ex tabella reci-
tavit: "quandoquidem divus Claudius occidit socerum
suum Appium Silanum, generos duos Magnum Pom-
peium et L. Silanum, socerum filiae suae Crassum Frugi,
hominem tam similem sibi quam ovo ovum, Scriboniam
socrum filiae suae, uxorem suam Messalinam et ceteros
quorum numerus iniri non potuit, placet mihi in eum severe animadverti nec illi rerum iudicandarum vacationem

---

[30] {tristionias} *deleted Birt*
[31] <non> Assar<aci nat>ionem *added Eden*[2]

---

[80] Caligula, emperor 37 to 41.

[81] M. Iunius Silanus committed suicide on orders of Caligula.

[82] The son-in-law might be L. Silanus, cited in ch. 8, but a
better identification might be Pompeius Magnus.

[83] Appius Silanus.

[84] Cn. Pompeius Magnus had married Claudius' daughter
Antonia and was the son of M. Licinius Crassus Frugi.

damn you: the fact that you did not know is far worse than
the fact that you killed. Claudius did not stop persecuting
Gaius Caesar[80] even after his death. Gaius killed his
father-in-law;[81] Claudius killed his son-in-law[82] as well as
father-in-law.[83] Gaius forbade Crassus' son to be called
'the Great.' Claudius returned his title but removed his
head.[84] In one household he killed Crassus, Magnus, and
Scribonia,[85] no blue-blooded clan of Assaracus,[86] but they
were aristocrats all the same; Crassus indeed such a fool
that he could even have been an emperor. Is this the man
you now want to make a god? Look at his body, it was born
into the world when the gods were angry. In short, should
he be able to say three words in quick succession, he could
have me for a slave. Who will worship this man as a god?
Who will believe in him? While you create such gods, no
one will believe that you are gods. This is the point of my
argument, gentlemen of the senate, if I have conducted
myself honorably while with you, if I replied too bluntly
to no one, avenge the wrongs he has done to me. I put this
motion to you." And then he read out as follows from his
notebook: "Whereas the deified Claudius murdered his
father-in-law Appius Silanus, his two sons-in-law Pompeius Magnus and Lucius Silanus, his daughter's father-in-
law Crassus Frugi, a man as like himself as one egg is to
another, Scribonia his daughter's mother-in-law, his wife
Messalina and others too numerous to go into, I move that
he be severely punished and not given immunity from

[85] Scribonia, perhaps a descendant of Cn. Pompeius Magnus,
the Triumvir (Tac. *Hist.* 1.14).

[86] Not of the lofty aristocrats like the Julians, who traced their
family back to Troy.

dari eumque quam primum exportari et caelo intra tri-
6 ginta dies excedere, Olympo intra diem tertium." | pedi-
bus in hanc sententiam itum est. nec mora, Cyllenius illum
collo obtorto trahit ad inferos a caelo

unde negant redire quemquam.

12. Dum descendunt per viam Sacram interrogat Mercurius quid sibi velit ille concursus hominum, num Claudii
funus esset. et erat omnium formosissimum et impensa
cura, plane ut scires deum efferri: tubicinum, cornicinum,
omnis generis aenatorum[32] tanta turba, tantus conventus,
2 et etiam Claudius audire posset. | omnes laeti, hilares:
populus Romanus ambulabat tamquam liber. Agatho et
pauci causidici plorabant, sed plane ex animo. iurascon-
sulti e tenebris procedebant, pallidi, graciles, vix animam
habentes, tamquam qui tum maxime reviviscerent. ex his
unus, cum vidisset capita conferentes et fortunas suas
deplorantes causidicos, accedit et ait: "dicebam vobis: non
3 semper Saturnalia erunt." | Claudius, ut vidit funus suum,
intellexit se mortuum esse. ingenti enim μεγάλωι χορικῶι
nenia cantabatur {anapaestis}:[33]

"fundite fletus, edite planctus,
resonet tristi clamore forum:
cecidit pulchre cordatus homo,
quo non alius fuit in toto
5 fortiter orbe.
ille citato vincere cursu
poterat celeris, ille rebelles

---

[32] aenatorum *Bücheler*: senatorum
[33] {anapestis} *deleted Heraeus*

trial, and that he be deported as soon as possible, leaving heaven within thirty days and Olympus within three." Members rose to support this motion. Without delay Mercury seized him, twisting his neck, and dragged him from heaven to the underworld "from where they say, no one returns."[87]

12. While they were going down by way of the Via Sacra, Mercury inquired about the meaning of the great crowd: was it Claudius' funeral? And it was the most gorgeous spectacle, with no expense spared, so that you clearly knew that a god was being buried. There was such a mob of trumpet players and horn players and every kind of brass instrumentalist that even Claudius could hear it. Everyone was happy and full of joy. The people of Rome were walking around as if they were free men. Agatho[88] and a few advocates were weeping,[89] but clearly with sincerity. Legal authorities were emerging from the shadows, pale, thin, and barely breathing, as if men just at the point of coming back to life. One of these, when he had seen the advocates putting their heads together and crying over their bad luck, went up and said: "I kept telling you that Carnival Time would not last forever." When Claudius saw his own funeral, he realized that he was dead. For with a great song and dance a dirge was being sung: "Pour out your tears, declare your sorrows, let the Forum resound in sad cries. A man with a fine wit has fallen, no one in the whole world was braver than he. He could prevail over the

---

[87] Cf. Cat. 3.11–12.

[88] This individual is unidentified, but it is a common name.

[89] They are weeping because legal fees would now be regulated.

fundere Parthos levibusque sequi
Persida telis, certaque manu
10 tendere nervum, qui praecipites
vulnere parvo figeret hostes
pictaque Medi terga fugacis,
ille Britannos ultra noti
litora ponti
15 et caeruleos scuta Brigantas
dare Romuleis colla catenis
iussit et ipsum nova Romanae
iura securis tremere Oceanum.
deflete virum, quo non alius
20 potuit citius discere causas,
una tantum parte audita
saepe neutra. quis nunc iudex
toto lites audiet anno?
tibi iam cedet sede relicta
25 qui dat populo iura silenti,
Cretaea tenens oppida centum.
caedite maestis pectora palmis
o causidici, venale genus,
vosque poetae lugete novi,
30 vosque in primis qui concusso
magna parastis lucra fritillo."

13. Delectabatur laudibus suis Claudius et cupiebat diutius spectare. inicit illi manum Talthybius deorum {nuntius}[34] et trahit capite obvoluto, ne quis eum possit

---

[34] {nuntius} *deleted Camden*

speedy at full gallop, he could scatter the revolting Parthians and pursue the Persians[90] with light spears, and stretch the bow with sure hand, he could pierce with small wounds the enemy fleeing headlong and the painted backs of the fleeing Mede; he commanded the Britons who live beyond the shores of the known sea and the Brigantes[91] with their dark blue shields to submit their necks to Romulus' chains, and Ocean himself to tremble at the new laws of the Roman ax. Weep for the man who could master the intricacies of lawsuits faster than anyone, after hearing only one side of the case and often neither side.[92] Who will now as judge hear matters in dispute the whole year? The one who dispenses justice to the people of silence, ruling over a hundred Cretan cities,[93] will now yield his place to you and leave his seat. Pound your breasts with your hands in sorrow, you advocates, a race of men for sale, and you, the new poets, mourn, and especially you who have piled up great profits by shaking the dice box."[94]

13. Claudius was delighted to hear his praises and wanted to watch longer. The Talthybius[95] of the gods grabbed him with his hand and hauled him away, with his

---

[90] By 54 the Parthians were in control in the East under their able leader King Vologeses (51–78) and his brother Tiridates.

[91] Claudius invaded Britain in 43 (Cass. Dio 60.19–23).

[92] Claudius passed sentences quickly and gave verdicts based on no real reasons (Suet. *Claud*. 15.2).   [93] Minos had been king of Crete and then became a judge in the underworld, whose inhabitants are the "people of silence" (Verg. *Aen*. 6.432–33).

[94] Claudius was fond of playing dice (Suet. *Claud*. 5, 33.2).

[95] He was Agamemnon's herald (Hom. *Il*. 1.320). The Talthybius of the gods was Mercury.

agnoscere, per campum Martium, et inter Tiberim et viam
2 Tectam descendit ad inferos. | antecesserat iam compendiaria Narcissus libertus ad patronum excipiendum, et venienti nitidus, ut erat a balineo, occurrit et ait: "quid di ad homines?" "celerius" inquit Mercurius "et venire nos
3 nuntia." | dicto citius Narcissus evolat. omnia proclivia sunt, facile descenditur. itaque quamvis podagricus esset, momento temporis pervenit ad ianuam Ditis, ubi iacebat Cerberus vel, ut ait Horatius, "belua centiceps." pusillum perturbatur | (subalbam canem in deliciis habere adsueverat) ut illum vidit canem nigrum, villosum, sane non quem velis tibi in tenebris occurrere, et magna voce
4 "Claudius" inquit "veniet." | cum plausu procedunt cantantes εὑρήκαμεν συγχαίρωμεν. hic erat C. Silius[35] consul designatus, Iunctus[36] praetorius, Sex. Traulus,[37] M. Helvius, Trogus, Cotta, Vettius[38] Valens, Fabius, equ‹it›es[39] R., quos Narcissus duci iusserat. medius erat

---

[35] C. Silius *Muretus*: consilius   [36] Iunctus *Sonntag*: Iunius
[37] Traulus *Lipsius*: trallus   [38] Vettius *Bücheler*: tettius
[39] equites *editors*: eques

---

[96] Narcissus was Claudius' private secretary, powerful and wealthy. Agrippina forced him to commit suicide immediately after Claudius was murdered. He was given no ceremonial burial and could thus get to the underworld by a shortcut (a sewer?) before Claudius arrived.

[97] Dis, or Pluto, god of the underworld. On the ease of the descent to his gate, cf. Verg. *Aen.* 6.126–27.

[98] Hor. *Carm.* 2.13.33–35.

[99] In the cult of Isis and Osiris this is the ritual cry of inspired rejoicing at the incarnation of Osiris.

[100] C. Silius was the junior partner in an infamous marriage to

head wrapped up so that no one could recognize him, through the Campus Martius, and between the Tiber and the Via Tecta he descended into the underworld. Claudius' freedman Narcissus[96] had already gone on ahead by a short cut to welcome his master, and gleaming fresh because he has just come from the bath, he ran to meet him upon his entrance, and said: "What brings the gods to men?" But Mercury interrupted and said to him: "Go quickly now and announce our arrival." Faster than words Narcissus flies off. Everything slopes downward, the descent is easy. And so, despite his being gouty, he arrived in an instant at the gate of Dis,[97] where Cerberus lay, or as Horace says, "the hundred-headed monster."[98] He had been accustomed to keep a whitish bitch as a pet, and was a bit frightened, when he saw that black, shaggy dog, not at all the sort of thing you would like to meet in the dark, and in a loud voice he said: "Claudius is coming." Amid applause people came forward, singing, "We have found him, let us rejoice."[99] Here was Gaius Silius[100] consul designate, Iunctus the ex-praetor, Sextus Traulus, Marcus Helvius, Trogus, Cotta, Vettius Valens, Fabius,[101] Roman knights whom Narcissus had ordered executed. In the

Messalina, wife of Claudius, and was said to plot to topple Claudius. He and Messalina were executed in 48 (Tac. *Ann.* 11.26–28; Suet. *Claud.* 26.2, 29.3, 36).

[101] The seven persons mentioned after Silius are: Iunctus (Tac. *Ann.* 11.35–37), implicated in the Messalina plot and executed; Sextus Traulus (Tac. *Ann.* 11.36.4), lover of Messalina; M. Helvius, unknown; Trogus, executed, perhaps the man in Tac. *Ann.* 11.35.6; Cotta, unknown; Vettius Valens (Tac. *Ann.* 11.31.6), a physician, executed; Fabius, unknown.

in hac cantantium turba Mnester pantomimus, quem
Claudius decoris causa minorem fecerat ad Messaliam. |
5 cito rumor percrebuit Claudium venisse. convolant primi
omnium liberti Polybius, Myron, Arpocras,[40] Ampheus,
Pheronaotus,[41] quos Claudius omnes, necubi imparatus
esset, praemiserat. deinde praefecti duo Iustus Catonius
et Rufrius Pollio.[42] deinde amici Saturninus Lusius et
Pedo Pompeius et Lupus et Celer Asinius consulares.
novissime fratris filia, sororis filia, generi, soceri, socrus,
omnes plane consanguinei. et agmine facto Claudio occur-
6 runt. | quos cum vidisset Claudius, exclamat "πάντα
φίλων πλήρη. quomodo huc venistis vos?" tum Pedo
Pompeius "quid dicis, homo crudelissime? quaeris quomodo? quis enim nos alius huc misit quam tu, omnium
amicorum interfector? in ius eamus: ego tibi hic sellas[43]
ostendam."

---

[40] Arpocras *Bücheler*: arporas   [41] Pheronaotus | (= Φηρῶν
ἄωτος) *Eden²*: pherona otus   [42] Rufrius Pollio *Reimar
restored name, comparing Dio Cassius 60.23.2*: rufius pomfilius
[43] sellas *Vat. Lat. 4498* | (*L Family*): stellas

---

[102] Mnester, actor and dancer, lover of Caligula (Suet. *Calig.*
55.1, 36.1), partner of Messalina in bed, beheaded by Claudius.

[103] Polybius, freedman of Claudius and his secretary for peti-
tions, perhaps also for patronage, executed in 49.

[104] None of these freedmen are otherwise attested. It is possible that Arpocras was responsible for staging public events
(Suet. *Claud.* 26).   [105] Catonius, murdered in 43 after an
accusation from Messalina.   [106] Pollio, appointed Prefect of
the Praetorian Guard in 41, honored by Claudius in 44.

[107] Saturnius Lusius was a consul in 37, and later implicated

midst of this chanting company was the mime Mnester,[102] whom Claudius had cut shorter by a head for appearance's sake to suit Messalina. The rumor spread quickly that Claudius had arrived. Up rushed first of all the freedmen Polybius,[103] Myron, Arpocras, Ampheus, and Pheronaotus,[104] all of whom Claudius had dispatched on ahead so that he would not be unattended anywhere. Then came the two Prefects of the Praetorian Guard, Justus Catonius[105] and Rufrius Pollio.[106] Then his inner council members, the ex-consuls Saturninus Lusius,[107] Pedo Pompeius,[108] and Lupus[109] and Celer Asinius.[110] Finally the daughter of his bother,[111] the daughter of his sister,[112] his sons-in-law,[113] his fathers-in-law,[114] his mothers-in-law,[115] all obviously close kin. And forming into a line they came to meet Claudius. When Claudius had seen them he exclaimed: "Friends everywhere. How did you come here?" Then Pedo Pompeius said: "What are you talking about, you savage? You ask how? Who else sent us here but you, you murderer of all your friends? Let us go to court: I will show you the magistrates' benches here."

in the plotting of P. Suillius who was banished under Nero (Tac. *Ann.* 13.43.3).   [108] Pedo Pompeius, unknown.

[109] Cornelius Lupus, proconsul under Tiberius, consul in 42, implicated in the intrigues of P. Suillius.   [110] Servius Asinius Celer, consul in 38.   [111] Julia, daughter of Germanicus; see ch. 10.   [112] Julia, daughter of Livia and Drusus; see ch. 10.

[113] L. Silanus and Pompeius Magnus; see chs. 8, 10, 11.

[114] Appius Silanus and Crassus Frugi; see ch. 11.

[115] Domitia Lepida, Messalina's mother, murdered in 53; Scribonia, see ch. 11. If it seems that Claudius killed many of his relatives, Nero did even better, and Constantine the Christian was the best at it.

SENECA

14. Ducit illum ad tribunal Aeaci: is lege Cornelia,
quae de sicariis lata est, quaerebat. postulat, nomen eius
recipiat; edit subscriptionem: occisos senatores XXX‹V›,[44]
equites R. CC‹C›XXI,[45] ceteros ὅσα ψάμαθός τε κόνις
2 τε. | advocatum non invenit. tandem procedit P. Petronius,
vetus convictor eius, homo Claudiana lingua disertus, et
postulat advocationem. non datur. accusat Pedo Pompeius
magnis clamoribus. incipit patronus velle respondere.
Aeacus, homo iustissimus, vetat et illum, altera tantum
parte audita, condemnat et ait: αἴκε πάθοις τὰ ἔρεξας
3 δίκη εὐθεῖα γένοιτο. ingens silentium factum est. | stupe-
bant omnes novitate rei attoniti, negabant hoc umquam
factum. Claudio magis iniquum videbatur quam novum.
de genere poenae diu disputatum est, quid illum pati
oporteret. erant qui dicerent, Si‹syph›um diu laturam
fecisse{nt},[46] Tantulum siti periturum nisi illi succurrere-
4 tur, aliquando Ixionis miseri rotam sufflaminandam. | non
placuit ulli ex veteribus missionem dari, ne vel Claudius
umquam simile speraret. placuit novam poenam constitui

[44] XXX‹V› *added Bücheler, comparing Suetonius Claudius
29.2* [45] equites R. CC‹C›XXI *Baehrens, comparing Suetonius Claudius 29.2*: equites R. U [46] Si‹syph›um diu laturam fecisse{nt} *added and deleted Bücheler*

[116] Aeacus was a judge in the underworld with Minos and
Rhadamanthus. [117] Law enacted under Sulla in 81 BC, gov-
erning murder, attempted murder by sword, poison, and magic.
[118] Hom. *Il.* 9.385. [119] Consul in 19, proconsul 29–35,
legate under Caligula, advisor to Claudius.
[120] Hesiod Μεγάλα Ἔργα, frag. 286, R. Merkelbach, M. L.
West, *Fragmenta Hesiodea* (Oxford, 1967).

14. Pedo leads him to the tribunal of Aeacus;[116] he was holding court under the Lex Cornelia of Sulla about murderers.[117] Pedo requests of Aeacus that Claudius be charged by name and lays out the indictment: "Killed: senators, thirty-five; Roman knights, three hundred and twenty-one; others, 'as many as the grains of sand and specks of dust.'"[118] Claudius finds no advocate. At last Publius Petronius,[119] an old crony of his, a fellow of Claudian-style eloquence, steps forward and demands an adjournment. It is not granted. Pedo Pompeius begins the prosecution amid loud applause. The counsel for the defense wants to reply. Aeacus, a most impartial man, denies the request, and with only one side of the case heard, finds Claudius guilty and says: "Should you suffer for what you have done, justice would be immediate."[120] There was a profound silence. Everyone was struck dumb, astonished by the unprecedented ruling, and said that this had never been done before. It seemed to Claudius more unjust than unprecedented. There was a long discussion about the type of punishment he ought to suffer. There were some who said that Sisyphus had done his job of porterage for a long time, that Tantulus would die of thirst if aid were not given to him, that sooner or later the brake had to be put on Ixion's wheel.[121] It was resolved that none of the old-timers should be pardoned, so that not even Claudius could hope for something similar. It was decided that a

[121] The most often referenced group of ancient sinners and their punishments are the triad of Sisyphus (punished by having to roll a stone up a hill only to have it roll down), Tantulus (punished by not being able to reach nearby fruit and water), and Ixion (tied to a turning wheel).

debere, excogitandum illi laborem irritum et alicuius cupi-
ditatis spem sine effectu. tum Aeacus iubet illum alea lu-
dere pertuso fritillo. et iam coeperat fugientes semper
tesseras quaerere et nihil proficere:

15. Nam quotiens missurus erat resonante fritillo
utraque subducto fugiebat tessera fundo;
cumque recollectos auderet mittere talos,
lusuro similis semper semperque petenti,
5 decepere fidem: refugit digitosque per ipsos
fallax adsiduo dilabitur alea furto.
sic cum iam summi tanguntur culmina montis,
inrita Sisyphio volvuntur pondera collo. |

2 apparuit subito C. Caesar et petere illum in servitutem
coepit. producit testes, qui illum viderant ab illo flagris,
ferulis, colaphis vapulantem. adiudicatur. C. Caesari illum
Aeacus donat. is Menandro liberto suo tradidit, ut a cog-
nitionibus esset.

novel punishment ought to be instituted, some useless labor must be thought up, a hope of gratifying some desire without result. Then Aeacus ordered him to play dice using a dice box with a hole in it.[122] And already Claudius had begun to chase the dice that were ever slipping away, and he was getting nowhere.

15. As often as he was about to throw the dice from the rattling box, each of the two dice kept vanishing through the bottomless base; and when he dared to throw the recovered dice, always like someone about to play and always about to pick them up, they fooled him: the cunning die recoiled, and it slipped through his fingers in a continual trick. In the same way when the crests of the highest mountain are already touched, the great stone rolls down from Sisyphus' neck in futility. Suddenly Gaius Caesar turned up and began to ask for Claudius to be his slave. He produces witnesses who had seen Claudius being beaten by him with whips, canes, and fists. The judgment is made. Aeacus hands him over to Gaius Caesar. He in turn awards him to his freedman Menander to be his secretary for judicial matters.

[122] I would like to adduce a modern form of the sentence placed on Claudius. It comes from Gilbert and Sullivan, *Mikado*, Act 2, No. 6, *A More Humane Mikado* . . . [said of a billiard player] "And there he plays extravagant matches / in fitless finger stalls / on a cloth untrue / with a twisted cue / and elliptical billiard balls."

APPENDIX

SEATING CHART

SUMMUS

				Hermeros	Ascyltos or Agamemnon	Trimalchio (summus in summo)

MEDIUS

Habinnas	Ascyltos or Agamemnon	Encolpius (summus in medio)

Fortunata and Scintilla	Proculus	Diogenes (imus in imo)

IMUS

INDEX OF CHARACTERS IN
PETRONIUS

Agamemnon: teacher of rhetoric at Puteoli, with whom Encolpius is discussing education at the opening of the work, and who invites our triad of heroes to dinner at Trimalchio's. Named after Agamemnon, leader of the Greek expedition against Troy. 3.1, 6.1, 26.8, 28.6, 46.1, 48.4, 48.5, 48.7, 49.7, 50.2, 52.7, 65.5, 69.9, 78.8

Agatho: cosmetician. 74.15

Albucia: unknown woman. fr. 6

Ascyltos: Encolpius' companion along with Giton = triad of heroes. Name means "indefatigable" or "untroubled." 6.1, 6.2, 7.4, 9.6, 9.7, 10.4, 10.6, 11.2, 12.4, 12.6, 13.2, 14.1, 14.8, 15.7, 19.3, 19.5, 20.3, 20.5, 21.1, 22.1, 24.3, 24.4, 57.1, 58.1, 59.1, 72.5, 72.7, 79.9, 79.11, 80.5, 80.6, 80.8, 92.2, 92.4, 94.3, 94.10, 93.7, 93.9, 93.10, 97.3, 98.3, 133.1, 133.2

Bargates: manager of a boarding house. The name is probably Semitic. 96.4, 97.1

Cario: slave of Trimalchio. 71.2

Carpus: slave of Trimalchio whose job is to carve meat. 36.5, 36.7, 36.8, 40.5

Cerdo: slave of Trimalchio who carries sacred objects. 60.8

Chrysanthus: recently dead friend of Seleucus and others in Trimalchio's circle. 42.3

Chrysis: Circe's haughty maid. Name means "golden girl." 128.3, 129.3, 129.10, 130.7, 131.1, 131.7, 132.5, 138.5, 139.4

Cinnamus: steward of Trimalchio. 30.2

Circe: would-be lover of Encolpius, named after the witch who captivates Odysseus in Homer's *Odyssey*. 127.6, 127.7, 127.8, 129.4, 130.1, 134.9

Corax: hired servant of Eumolpus. 117.11, 140.7, 140.9
Corinthus: metal-worker, slave of Trimalchio. 50.4
Croesus: boy-love of Trimalchio. 64.5, 64.9

Daedalus: ingenious cook of Trimalchio, named after the great
    mythical inventor. 70.2, 74.5
Dama: freedman friend of Trimalchio. 41.10
Diogenes (C. Pompeius Diogenes): freedman friend of Trimalchio.
    38.10
Dionysus: slave of Trimalchio. 41.7
Doris: apparently a former lover of Encolpius. 128.18

Echion: freedman friend of Trimalchio, a rag-collector. 45.1
Egyptian Slave: slave of Trimalchio. 35.6
Encolpius: narrator and chief actor of the novel. The name is Greek
    and means "in the bosom," or "in the crotch." 20.7, 91.8, 92.6, 94.2,
    94.10, 102.5, 104.1, 105.9, 109.3, 114.5, 114.9
Endymion: beautiful boy but mysterious character who seems to ap-
    pear in the novel. 132.1
Ethiopian slaves: slaves of Trimalchio. 34.4
Eumolpus: bisexual poet, critic, con-man, masterminds the affair at
    Croton. A Greek name meaning "sweet singer." 91.1, 91.3, 92.1,
    92.5, 92.12, 94.3, 94.5, 94.7, 94.8, 94.12, 94.15, 95.4, 95.5, 95.6,
    95.7, 95.8, 96.4, 96.5, 97.1, 98.2, 98.3, 98.5; 99.4, 99.5, 99.6, 100.5,
    101.2, 101.3, 101.6, 101.9, 102.2, 102.3, 102.13, 103.1, 103.4, 104.3,
    105.2, 107.12, 108.3, 109.1, 109.8, 110.6, 113.12, 113.13, 115.2,
    115.20, 117.1, 117.4, 117.5, 117.6, 117.9, 118.1, 124.2, 124.3, 124.4,
    125.1, 132.6, 140.2, 140.3, 140.5, 140.9, 140.10, 140.13
Euscios: vague character. fr. 8

Felicio: slave of Trimalchio who carries sacred objects. 60.8
Fortunata: wife of Trimalchio. 37.2, 47.5, 52.8, 52.10, 52.11, 54.2,
    67.1, 67.3, 67.6, 67.9, 67.12, 70.10, 71.3, 71.11, 72.1, 73.5, 74.5,
    74.9, 74.10, 74.12, 75.6, 76.7

Gaius. *See* Trimalchio
Ganymede: freedman friend of Trimalchio. In mythology Ganymede,
    a Trojan prince, became beloved of Zeus. 44.1
Gavilla: unknown woman. 61.6

INDEX OF CHARACTERS

Giton: boy-love of Encolpius. Greek name for "neighbor." 9.1, 10.7, 16.1, 19.5, 20.8, 24.5, 25.3, 26.2, 26.10, 58.1, 60.7, 72.7, 72.9, 73.2, 79.3, 79.11, 91.1, 91.3, 92.3, 92.7, 93.4, 94.4, 94.7, 94.8, 94.9, 94.14, 96.2, 97.2, 97.4, 97.5, 98.1, 98.4, 98.5, 98.7, 98.8, 99.6, 100.4, 101.1, 101.6, 101.8, 102.14, 104.2, 105.5, 105.7, 108.5, 108.10, 108.11, 109.2, 109.8, 110.1, 110.3, 113.1, 113.5, 113.8, 114.10, 115.5, 117.11, 117.13, 128.1, 129.8, 130.8, 132.6, 133.1, 139.3

Glyco: resident of Puteoli. 45.7, 45.8, 45.9

Gorgias: inheritance-hunter in Croton. 141.5

Habinnas: friend of Trimalchio, a stonemason, important person in Puteoli. The name is probably Semitic. 65.5, 65.6, 67.3, 67.5, 67.10, 67.12, 68.4, 68.6, 69.4, 69.5, 71.5, 72.1, 72.4, 74.17, 75.1, 75.3, 77.1

Hedyle: apparently the wife of Lichas, seduced (?) by Encolpius. 113.3

Hermeros: freedman guest of Trimalchio, who sits next to (above) Encolpius at the table. 59.1

Hermogenes: resident of Puteoli. 45.9

Hesus: superstitious passenger on board Lichas' ship. 104.5

Homeristae: 59.2, 59.3, 59.6

Julius Proculus. See Proculus

Laenas: resident of Puteoli. 29.9

Lichas: ship's captain from Tarentum, an old enemy of Encolpius. 100.7, 101.4, 101.10, 101.11, 104.2 104.4, 105.1, 105.9, 106.1, 106.2, 106.4, 107.7, 107.15, 108.6, 109.1, 109.3, 109.8, 110.4, 113.2, 114.4, 115.11, 115.20

Lucrio: slave of Trimalchio who carries sacred objects. 60.8

Lycurgus: mysterious figure from a missing portion of the novel. 83.6, 117.3

Maecenatianus. See Trimalchio

Mammea: local political candidate in Puteoli. 45.10

M. Mannicius: owner of a block of flats where Encolpius and Eumolpus are staying. 95.3

Margarita: name of a dog at Trimalchio's Cena. 64.9

Massa: favorite young slave of Habinnas. 69.5

Melissa: woman mentioned in the Cena. 61.6, 62.11

PETRONIUS

Menelaus: employee of Agamemnon at his school. 27.4, 27.5, 81.1
Menophila: mate of Philargyrus. 70.10
Mithridates: slave of Trimalchio. 53.3

Nasta: overseer on an estate of Trimalchio. 53.5
Niceros: freedman guest of Trimalchio. 61.1, 61.3, 63.1
Norbanus: local political candidate in Puteoli. 45.10, 46.8

Oenothea: dissolute priestess of Priapus at Croton. Her name means "wine goddess" or perhaps "she whose god is wine." 134.8, 134.10, 135.2, 135.3, 136.9, 137.7, 138.1

Pannychis: young slave girl belonging to Quartilla. Her name means "All-night girl." 25.1
Pansa: Trimalchio was a beneficiary in this man's will. 47.12
Pergamene Youth: handsome boy seduced by Eumolpus. 85–87
Philargyrus: slave of Trimalchio. 70.10, 71.2
Phileros: freedman guest of Trimalchio. 43.1, 44.1
Phileros: lawyer in the Puteoli area. 46.8 (*Phileronem*). Cf. 63.1 (*Niceronem*)
Philomela: woman in Croton who panders her children to receive legacies. 140.1
Plocamus: freedman guest of Trimalchio. 64.2
Polyaenus: Encolpius' pseudonym at Croton. A Homeric epithet of Odysseus, meaning "much praised." 127.7, 129.4, 130.1
C. Pompeius Diogenes. *See* Diogenes
C. Pompeius Trimalchio Maecenatianus. *See* Trimalchio
Priapus: god of fertility who hounds Encolpius. 17.8, 21.7, 60.4, 104.1, 137.2, 139.2 v. 8, fr. 4
Primigenius: name of Echion's *cicaro* or a term of endearment. 46.8
Proculus: freedman guest of Trimalchio. 38.16
Proselenus: old bawd adept at magic. Name means "older than the moon." 132.5, 137.5
Psyche: Quartilla's maid. 20.2, 21.1, 25.1, 26.1

Quartilla: priestess of Priapus. Name is a diminutive of Quarta, "fourth in a sequence." 16.3, 19.3, 19.5, 20.7, 21.2, 21.7, 23.1, 24.4, 24.5, 25.1, 25.4, 26.2, 26.4

INDEX OF CHARACTERS

Safinius: magistrate in Puteoli or nearby. 44.6

Scaurus: member of a noble Roman family. 77.5

Scintilla: wife of Habinnas. Name means "spark." 66.5, 67.5, 67.6, 67.9, 67.13, 69.1, 69.2, 70.10, 74.12, 75.2

Scissa: soft-hearted (soft-headed?) friend of Habinnas. 65.10

Scylax: Trimalchio's dog. 64.7, 64.9

Seleucus: freedman guest of Trimalchio. 42.1

Serapa: Trimalchio's astrologer. 76.10

Soldier: unnamed. Disarms Encolpius. 82.2

Soldier: unnamed. Lover of the Widow of Ephesus. 111–12

Stichus: slave of Trimalchio in charge of his funeral. 77.7, 78.1, 78.2

Terentius: name of an innkeeper cited in the *Cena*. 61.6

Titus: magistrate of Puteoli. 45.5

Trimalchio (C. Pompeius Trimalchio Maecenatianus): great vulgarian freedman whose banquet occupies the middle one-third of the *Satyrica*. 26.9, 27.5, 28.2, 28.3, 28.4, 29.3, 30.2, 30.3, 31.8, 31.10, 32.1, 33.5, 34.1, 34.2, 34.7, 34.9, 35.7, 36.5, 36.7, 37.2, 37.4, 39.1, 40.7, 41.7, 41.8, 41.9, 47.1, 47.10, 48.1, 48.5, 48.6, 49.3, 49.5, 49.8, 50.1, 50.2, 52.4, 52.8, 53.2, 53.3, 53.6, 53.8, 53.9, 53.12, 54.1, 54.2, 54.5, 55.2, 55.4, 57.1, 59.1, 59.3, 59.6, 60.9, 61.1, 63.1, 64.2, 64.5, 64.7, 64.8, 64.11, 64.13, 65.2, 65.8, 66.1, 67.1, 67.2, 67.7, 68.1, 68.2, 68.3, 69.2, 69.8, 70.1, 70.5, 70.10, 71.1, 71.12, 72.1, 72.2, 72.4, 73.2, 73.5, 73.6, 74.1, 74.4, 74.6, 74.7, 74.8, 74.9, 74.10, 74.13, 75.2, 75.3, 78.5, 78.7, 79.6

Tryphaena: high-class prostitute traveling on Lichas' ship, whom Encolpius and Giton had known before. Name means "woman living a luxurious and dissolute life." 100.7, 101.5, 104.2, 104.4, 105.5, 105.8, 105.11, 106.2, 106.3, 106.4, 108.5, 108.7, 108.8, 108.10, 108.12, 109.2, 109.8, 110.1, 110.3 113.1, 113.5, 113.8, 114.7

Widow of Ephesus (*Matrona Ephesi*): very clever woman in the story told by Eumolpus. 111–12

INDEX OF OTHER NAMES IN
PETRONIUS

Achilles, 59.5, 129.1
Acrisius, 137.9 v. 4
Actaeus, 135.8 v. 15
Actium, 121 v. 115
Aeneas, 68.4
Aetna, 122 v. 135
Africa/African, 35.3, 48.3, 93.2
    v. 2, 117.8, 119 v. 15, 119
    v. 27, 125.3, 141.1
Agamemnon (son of Atreus),
    59.4
Ajax, 59.5, 59.7
Alcibiades, 128.7
Alexandria, 31.3, 68.3
Alps, 122–23 vv. 144, 162, 213
Amphitryoniades, 123 v. 206
Anacreon, fr. 20
Apelles (actor), 64.4
Apelles (painter), 83.2, 88.10
Apollo, 83.3, 83.5, 89 v. 4, 121
    v. 115. See also Phoebus
Appennines, 124 v. 279
Apulia, 77.3
Arabs, 102.14, 119 v. 12
Aratus, 40.1
Ariadne, 138.6
Asia, 2.7, 44.4, 75.10, 85.1

Atellan farce, 53.13, 68.5
Athena, 2.7, 38.3, 58.7
Athos, fr. 27 v. 3
Atrides, 108.14 v. 3
Attic, 38.3, 56.9
Augustalis (sevir), 30.2
Augustus, 60.7

Babylonia, 55.6 v. 3
Bacchus, 133.3 vv. 1, 5
Baiae, 53.10, 104.2
Battiades, 135.8 v. 17
Bellona, 124 v. 256
Bosphoros, 123 v. 242
Bromius, 41.6

Caesar (title of emperor), 51.2,
    51.3, 51.6, 76.2
Caesar, Julius, 38.10, 120–24
    vv. 64, 142, 152, 184, 203,
    209, 267
Calchas, 89 v. 3
Capitolium, 88.9, 122 v. 161
Cappadocia, 63.5, 69.2
Capua, 62.1
Carchedonius (Carthaginian),
    55.6 v. 13

527

Carthage, 117.8
Cassandra, 52.1, 74.14
Cato, 132.15 v. 1, 137.9 v. 6
Cato Uticensis, 119 vv. 45, 46
Caucasus, 123 v. 205
Cerberus, fr. 8
Ceres, 135.8 v. 4, fr. 27 v. 8
Chinese. *See* Seres
Chios, 63.3
Chrysippus, 88.4
Cicero, 3.2, 5 v. 20, 55.5
Circe (daughter of Helius),
    134.12 v. 12
Cocytus, 120–24 vv. 69, 103,
    278
Colchis, 93.2 v. 1
Concordia, 124 v. 253
Corinth, 31.9, 50.1, 50.2, 50.3,
    50.4, 50.5, 50.6
Crassus, 120 v. 63
Croton, 116.2, 124.2, 125.1
Cumae, 48.8, 53.2
Curio, 124 v. 289
Cyclops, 48.7, 98.5, 101.5,
    101.7
Cydonian, 69.7
Cyllenia, 124 v. 269
Cynic, 14.2 v. 3
Cynthia, 122 v. 130

Daedalus, 52.2
Danae, 126.18 v. 5, 137.9 vv. 3, 4
Danai, 89 vv. 10, 57
Daphne, 131.8 v. 2
Delos, 23.3 v. 4, 89 v. 4
Delphi, 122 v. 177
Democritus, 88.3
Demosthenes, 2.5, 5 v. 14

Diana, 59.4, 126.16
Dicarchis (Puteoli), 120 v. 68
Diomedes, 59.4
Dione, 124 v. 266, 133.3 v. 1
Dis (Pluto), 120–24 vv. 76, 251,
    255
Discord, 124 vv. 271, 295
Dryads, 133.3 v. 5

Egypt, 2.9, fr. 19
Enyo, 120 v. 62
Ephesus (actor), 70.13
Ephesus (city), 111.1
Epicurus, 104.3, 132.15 v. 7
Epidamnus, 124 v. 293
Erebus, 124 v. 254
Erinys, 124 v. 255
Ethiopian, 34.4, 102.13
Eudoxos, 88.4
Euhius, 41.6
Euripides, 2.3

Falernian wine, 21.6, 28.3, 34.6,
    55.3
Fama, 123 v. 211
Fates, 29.6
Felicio (Lucky Man), 67.9
Fides (Good Faith), 124 v. 252
Fors (Fortuna), 120 vv. 80, 94
Fortuna, 29.6, 43.7, 55.3, 101.1,
    120 v. 61, 120 v. 78, 121
    v. 102, 122 v. 174, 123 v. 237,
    123 v. 244, 125.2
Furor, 124 v. 258

Ganymede, 59.4, 83.3, 92.3
Gaul, 19.3, 102.14, 122 vv. 143,
    161

German, 122 v. 163, 123 v. 214
Giants (son of Ge), 123 v. 208
Greece/Greeks, 5 v. 15, 38.3, 46.5, 48.4, 59.3, 64.5, 76.10, 81.3, 83.2, 88.10, 111.2, 122 v. 144

Hammon (Ammon), 119 v. 14
Hannibal, 50.5, 101.4, 141.9
Harpys, 136.6 v. 3
Hecale, 135.8 v. 16
Helen, 59.4, 138.6
Helicon, 118.1
Hellespont, 139.2 v. 8, fr. 4
Hercules, 48.7, 83.5, 106.2, 122 v. 146, 136.6 v. 1
Hermeros (gladiator), 52.3
Hesperia, 122 v. 154
Hiberia, 121 v. 112
Hipparchus, 40.1
Hispania, 6.3
Homer, 2.4, 48.7, 59.4, 118.5
Horace, 118.5
Hybla, fr. 29 v. 5
Hydaspes, 123 v. 239
Hylas, 83.3, 83.5
Hypaepa, 133.3 v. 4
Hyperides, 2.8
Hyrcanian, 134.12 v. 7

Ida, 83.3, 89.5, 127.9 v. 1, 134.12 v. 15
Iliad, 29.9
Ilium, 50.5
Inachian, 139.2 v. 2
Incubo, 38.8
India, 38.4, 55.6 v. 9, 135.8 v. 1
Insidiae, 124 v. 257

Iphigenia, 59.5
Italy, 114.3, 116.2

Jews, 102.14
Juno, 25.4, 139.2 v. 4
Jupiter, 44.5, 44.17, 44.18, 47.4, 51.5, 56.6, 58.2, 58.5, 83.4, 88.9, 122 v. 140, 122 v. 156, 123 v. 206, 123 v. 241, 126.18 v. 1, 127.9 v. 3, 137.9 v. 10
Justice, 124 v. 253

Labeo, 137.9 v. 8
Lacedaemonian, 5 v. 10
Laconian, 40.2
Laocoon, 89 vv. 19, 43
Laomedon, 139.2 v. 5
Lares, 29.8, 60.8
Laserpiciarius, 35.6
Latin, 46.5, 48.4, 53.13, 59.3
Leda, 138.6
Lentulus, 124 v. 289
Lesbos, 133.3 v. 3
Letum, 124 v. 257
Liber, 41.8
Libya, 120–21 vv. 63, 114
Lucilius, 4.5
Lucina, fr. 26 v. 6
Lucretia, 9.5
Lucrinus, 119 v. 34
Lyaeus, 41.6, 135.8 v. 7
Lydian, 133.3 v. 3
Lyric (9) poets, 2.4, 118.5
Lysippus, 88.5

Macedonian, 86.4
(Pompeius) Magnus, 120–24 vv. 63, 238, 244, 269, 292

Manii, 45.7
Marcellus, 124 v. 288
Mars, 34.5, 55.6 v. 1, 122–24
    vv. 134, 158, 183, 261, 268,
    289
Marseilles (Massilia), fr. 1, fr. 4
Marsyas, 36.3
Masonian, 5 v. 12
Medea, 108.14 v. 4
Megaera, 124 v. 256
Memphis, fr. 19
Menecrates, 73.3
Mercury, 29.5, 67.7, 77.4,
    140.12
Midas, fr. 28 v. 9
Minerva, 29.3, 43.8
Mopsus, 55.4
Mors (Death), 124 v. 257
Muse, 68.7, 135.8 v. 6
Myron, 88.5

Nais, 83.3
Neapolitan, fr. 16
Neptune, 76.4, 89 v. 18, 104.2,
    139.2 v. 6, fr. 27 v. 11
Nereids, fr. 23
Nereus, 139.2 v. 7
Nile, 121 v. 114, 134.12 v. 4
Niobe, 52.2
Nocturnae (witches), 63.9, 64.1
Noric, 70.3
Numantia, 141.11
Numidia, 55.6 v. 4, 117.8, 119
    v. 11
Nymph, 83.5, 133.3 v. 1

Occupo, 58.11
Odyssey, 29.9

Olympus, 58.5, 123 v. 207
Opimius, 34.6, 34.7
Orcus, 34.10, 45.9, 46.7, 62.2

Palamedes, 66.7
Palatine, 123 v. 211
Pales, fr. 27 v. 9
Pallas, 124 v. 268, fr. 26 v. 11
Parcae (Fates), 29.6
Paris, 138.6
Paros, 126.17
Parthenope, 120 v. 68
Parthian, 120 v. 63
Pax, 124 v. 249
Pegasus, 36.2
Pelias, 139.2 v. 4
Pergamum, 85.1
Persians, 119 v. 20
Petelians, 141.10
Petraites (gladiator), 52.3, 71.6
Phasis, 93.2 v. 1, 119 v. 36
Phidias, 88.10
Philippi, 121 v. 111
Phineus, 136.6 v. 3
Phoebe, 89 v. 54
Phoebus, 109.10 v. 2, 122 v. 181,
    124 v. 269, 134.12 v. 10, fr. 20,
    fr. 27 v. 3. See also Apollo
Phrygians, 89 vv. 2, 42
Pieris, 5 v. 22
Pindar, 2.4
Plato, 2.5
Pompeii, 53.5, 53.6
Pompey the Great. See Magnus
Pontus, 123 vv. 239, 241
Porthmeus (Charon), 121 v. 117
Praxiteles, 126.16
Priam, 89 v. 56

INDEX OF OTHER NAMES

Procne, 131.8 v. 7
Protesilaus, 140.12
Proteus, 134.12 v. 14
Protogenes, 83.1
Publilius Syrus, 55.5
Punic, 31.11

Quirites, 21.1, 119 v. 39, 123
v. 224, fr. 22

Rhine, 122 v. 160
Rome, 5 v. 15, 29.3, 57.4, 69.9,
70.3, 71.12, 76.3, 92.10,
118.5, 119–24 vv. 1, 49, 58,
64, 82, 84, 95, 107, 166, 212,
224, 293

Saguntum, 141.9
Saturn, 122 v. 156
Saturnalia, 44.3, 58.2, 69.9
Scipio, 141.11
Seres (Chinese), 119 v. 11
Servius, 137.9 v. 8
Sibyl, 48.8
Sicily, 48.3, 114.3, 119 v. 33
Sinon, 89 v. 13
Sirens, 5 v. 11, 127.5
Socrates, 5 v. 13, 128.7, 140.14
Sol (Sun), 127.6
Sophocles, 2.3
Sparta, 105.5
Stygian, 121–24 vv. 121, 272
Stymphalian, 136.6 v. 1
Sulla, 120 v. 98
Syrian, 22.3, 22.5, 31.11
Syrtis, 93.2 v. 6
Syrus, 52.9

Tantalus, 82.5 v. 2
Tarentum, 38.2, 48.2, 59.4, 61.6,
100.7, 101.4
Tarquin, 9.5
Tarracina, 48.2
Tartarus, 124 v. 278
Telephus, 139.2 v. 6
Tenedos, 89 v. 29
Thasos, 133.3 v. 3
Thebes, 80.3
Thessaly, 89 v. 59, 121 v. 112,
124 v. 294
Thracian (ethnic), 55.4
Thracian (type of gladiator),
45.12, 75.4
Thucydides, 2.8
Tiryns, 124 v. 270, 139.2 v. 2
Tisiphone, 120 v. 97, 121 v. 120
Titan, 122 v. 128
Tritonis (Athena), 5 v. 9
Trivia (Diana), fr. 20
Troy, 52.2, 59.4, 89.1, 89 v. 27,
89 v. 53, 89 v. 65, 108.14 v. 2
Tyre, 30.11

Ulysses, 39.3, 48.7, 97.4, 97.5,
98.5, 105.10, 132.13, 134.12
v. 13, 139.2 v. 6

Venus, 29.8, 68.8, 85.5, 127.9
v. 6, 128.4, 132.15 v. 5, 138.6;
venus = sex, 109.2, 119 v. 22,
126.1, 132.1
Virgil, 68.5, 118.5

Zeuxis, 83.1

LUTHERAN THEOLOGICAL SOUTHERN SEMINARY

3 5898 00174 7159

LINEBERGER MEMORIAL LIBRARY
LUTHERAN THEOLOGICAL SOUTHERN SEMINARY
CENTER FOR GRADUATE STUDIES OF COLUMBIA
LENOIR-RHYNE UNIVERSITY
COLUMBIA SC 29203